A DEADLY INHERITANCE

ALSO BY KELLEY ARMSTRONG

THE DARKEST POWERS TRILOGY

The Summoning
The Awakening
The Reckoning

THE DARKNESS RISING TRILOGY

The Gathering
The Calling
The Rising

THE AGE OF LEGENDS TRILOGY

Sea of Shadows
Empire of Night
Forest of Ruin

The Masked Truth
Missing
Aftermath
Someone Is Always Watching

A DEADLY INHERITANCE

KELLEY ARMSTRONG

tundra

Text copyright © 2026 by K.L.A. Fricke Inc.
Cover images: (book cover) belterz / Getty Images; (blood) Yeti Studio; (blood splatter) sirawut; (smeared blood) TextureRealm; (scorpion) nuttapongg; (ribbon) PixieMe; (pendant) Taigi; (burnt paper) Ana Gram; (stained paper) Anja Kaiser; (grunge texture) panupong1982; (filigree) ilonitta; (grunge metal texture) anammarques / all Adobe Stock
Title page images: (smeared blood) TextureRealm; (scorpion) nuttapongg; (pendant) Taigi / all Adobe Stock

Tundra Books, an imprint of Tundra Book Group, a division of
Penguin Random House Canada Ltd., 320 Front Street West, Suite 1400,
Toronto, Ontario, M5V 3B6, Canada
penguinrandomhouse.ca

Published simultaneously in the United States of America by Tundra Books of Northern New York, an imprint of Tundra Book Group, a division of Penguin Random House Canada Ltd., P.O. Box 2040, Plattsburgh, NY 12901, USA

Tundra with colophon is a registered trademark of
Penguin Random House Canada Ltd.

All rights reserved. No part of this book may be reproduced, scanned, transmitted, or distributed in any form or by any electronic or mechanical means, including information storage and retrieval systems, without permission in writing from the publisher, except by a reviewer, who may quote brief passages in a review. No part of this book may be used or reproduced in any manner for the purpose of training artificial intelligence technologies or systems.

The authorized representative in the EU for product safety and compliance is Penguin Random House Ireland, Morrison Chambers, 32 Nassau Street, Dublin D02 YH68, Ireland, https://eu-contact.penguin.ie

Publisher's note: This book is a work of fiction. Names, characters, places and incidents either are the product of the author's imagination or are used fictitiously, and any resemblance to actual persons living or dead, events, or locales is entirely coincidental.

Library and Archives Canada Cataloguing in Publication

Title: A deadly inheritance / Kelley Armstrong.
Names: Armstrong, Kelley, author
Identifiers: Canadiana (print) 20250220954 | Canadiana (ebook) 20250220962 | ISBN 9781774888032 (softcover) | ISBN 9781774888049 (EPUB)
Subjects: LCGFT: Thrillers (Fiction) | LCGFT: Novels.
Classification: LCC PS8551.R7637 D42 2026 | DDC jC813/.6—dc23

Library of Congress Control Number: 2025940706

Edited by Lynne Missen
Cover designed by Zeena Baybayan
Production edited by Bharti Bedi
Typeset in Plantin MT Pro by Sean Tai

Printed in Canada

1 2 3 4 5   30 29 28 27 26

PROLOGUE
April 5, 2005

Texts to unknown number.

Rosalyn Chamberlain has fled Westdale Academy

As head of the Lilith Society, she kept a journal. Get it before the Liliths add it to the archives

Remove & destroy entries as needed

ONE
February 5, 2024

I'm pacing the tiny apartment I shared with my mother, as if another piece of furniture I can sell will magically appear. I started with the easy stuff. Like Mom's bed, which I sold five days after her death and then spent two days sobbing about it, torn between being glad not to see the reminder and wanting to curl up under the covers and let the fading scent of her shampoo lull me to sleep.

I just need to cover the rent until May. Four more months and then I'll be eighteen and no one can call Child Services. I've researched summer jobs that include boarding, and in September I'll be off to college with a full scholarship.

I'm not going to make it to May.

My mother died in November, and it's a miracle I've gotten through the past three months, working two part-time jobs while making sure my grades don't drop enough to lose the scholarship. I've scraped out the savings account Dad left when he died in a work accident four years ago. His modest life insurance payout was already long gone. Mom had kept planning to start her own policy, but there'd seemed no rush because, really, what were the chances of her dying just as young and as unexpectedly?

I look around again, but there's nothing left to sell. I'm already sleeping, eating, and studying on an air mattress. I wander into the kitchen and eye the appliances. Then I snort under my breath. They came with the apartment, and even if I could bring myself to steal them, someone was sure to notice the buyer wheeling it off down the hall.

When a knock comes at the door, I freeze and my heart races like a rabbit smelling a fox. That's my default mode these days, where every knock could be someone who's finally realized there's a seventeen-year-old living here alone.

"Miss Green?" a woman's voice says. "Liliana Green?"

Another knock, brisk and efficient. A government-official sort of knock. My heart's in full hammer as I peer through the peephole. On the other side is an older woman with a briefcase, her hair pulled back tight, dark circles under her eyes, worry lines permanently etched around her mouth. Beside her stands the landlord.

"I saw her go in there," the landlord says. "And like I told you, I haven't seen her mother in months. I'm worried about the kid."

No. He's worried about getting caught with an underage tenant. Or he found someone willing to pay more than the reduced rent Mom charmed him into.

Another knock, harder now. "Miss Green. I really need to speak to you about your living situation."

"Do you want me to unlock the door?" the landlord asks her.

My gaze flies to the chain, which is engaged. While they can't get in, that chain will tell them I'm here.

As the landlord jangles his keys, the woman gives a weary nod. Then her phone rings. She lifts a hand, telling the landlord to wait while she answers.

"Delores Hoffman, DCFS," she says.

DCFS. The Illinois Department of Child and Family Services. My stomach clenches.

I keep telling myself DCFS isn't the bogeyman. But I have plans and dreams, and they start with that college scholarship, which the upheaval of foster care would endanger.

Please, I just need a few months.

"Who gave you this number?" Ms. Hoffman says into her phone.

A pause.

"Yes, I'm trying to speak to her right now but—"

Another pause. "I don't know who this is—"

Pause. "Fine," Ms. Hoffman snaps. "But I will be following up with the director on that."

A moment later, I hear another woman's voice, distant, as if through a cellphone speaker.

"Liliana." Her Southern accent reminds me of Mom and makes my heart ache. "My name is Cecilia Robbins. I'm your grandparents' lawyer."

My breath catches. She must mean my mom's parents. My dad was raised by a single mom who died when I was little. My mother had been estranged from her family since before my birth, and I'd never even considered tracking them down after she died. If Mom cut off all contact, she had a reason.

Ms. Robbins continues, "I'm sorry I didn't get there before Ms. Hoffman arrived. I *am* on my way. Where are you now?"

"She's in the apartment," Ms. Hoffman says. "Refusing to answer the door."

A soft chuckle. "Good. You stay right there, Liliana."

Ms. Hoffman huffs. "I'm here to help her, not kidnap her."

"Are you familiar with Chamberlain Enterprises, Ms. Hoffman?" Ms. Robbins says. "You may not recognize the name, but please check your text messages and you'll see a link to the company's standing on the Fortune 500 list. It's number twenty-three."

"I don't—"

"Liliana's grandparents own Chamberlain Enterprises."

My head jerks up. I'm a business major. I know Chamberlain Enterprises—one of those massive multinational consumer corporations whose name the average person doesn't recognize . . . but they *will* recognize the brands the company owns.

"I don't see what that has to do with anything," Ms. Hoffman says.

A soft laugh. "Oh, yes, you do, Ms. Hoffman. You understand perfectly."

"I—"

"Liliana is the only child of their only child. Heiress to a billion-dollar fortune."

A *what*? My breath catches, and my brain reels, unable to process those words.

Ms. Robbins continues, "Liliana, just stay where you are. I'm entering the building now."

"It's controlled entry," the landlord says. "Someone will have to admit you."

"Someone already did. They even held the door for me. Amazing where Ben Franklin can take you."

I swear Ms. Hoffman grinds her teeth as the landlord blusters about security. Part of me thrills at the thought of this stranger coming to wrest me from the jaws of the DCFS. And another part screams that maybe I should just go with Ms. Hoffman, because I have no idea what would ever compel my mother to walk away from a family that owns a Fortune 500 company.

When heels click in the hall, I look into the peephole again as someone appears. She's a Black woman in her mid-thirties, with model-worthy cheekbones and a tapered cut with loose curls on top. Expertly applied makeup. A gold choker. And a suit that would cover six-months' rent in this place. Mom might never have worn anything that didn't come from a consignment shop, but she had an eye for fashion, and she could tell a Dior pantsuit from a knockoff in two seconds flat.

If Ms. Robbins is telling the truth, then I know exactly where my mother came by her fashion sense.

Ms. Robbins turns to the door. "Liliana?"

When I don't answer, she nods. "All right. This is a lot, and it absolutely isn't what I intended for our first meeting. You go sit down and try to relax. This is going to take a few minutes."

"A few minutes?" Ms. Hoffman says. "You cannot expect me to turn over a vulnerable child to you because you *claim* to work for her *alleged* grandparents."

"Liliana, hon?" Ms. Robbins says. "I'd like to email you a few things. I know Ms. Hoffman won't be the only one who will require significantly more proof. Do you have a phone?"

I pause. Then I say, "I sold it," and something almost like pain ripples across Ms. Robbins's composure.

Her voice softens. "All right. I'm going to pass a phone through the mail slot on your door. Just give me a minute to transfer some files."

When the phone appears, it's not some "burner phone" like I see in movies. It's a brand-new smartphone.

"It's unlocked," she says. "Just check the file folder. You can look at the documents I transferred while Ms. Hoffman and I sort this out."

"This is ridiculous," Ms. Hoffman says. "Tell the girl to come out—"

"She is a Chamberlain," Ms. Robbins replies, her voice lilting with amusement. "I don't tell her to do anything. And I'd suggest you don't either."

I'm sitting on the floor in my apartment, going through what Ms. Robbins sent me. It's mostly internet links, and I appreciate that she's letting me look it up on my own, but I also know websites can be faked. I take what I need from them and then confirm through secondary sources.

Chamberlain Enterprises is owned by the Chamberlain family. That seems obvious, but it's not always the case, and what throws me here is the thought that I never knew Mom's maiden name. I knew her full name was Rosalyn, but she'd always gone by Rose. Rose Green.

There's a DNA test report that supposedly proves Mom was the daughter of the Chamberlains. That could be faked, but one look at my grandparents tells me it's not. My grandmother has the tiny build and oversized eyes I share with Mom, and an old photo of my grandfather shows the platinum blond hair Mom and I must have inherited from him.

I also look up Ms. Robbins herself. Cecilia Robbins. Graduated from Stanford. Also from someplace called Westdale Academy, which must be a fancy private school if it's listed right beside Stanford. Immediately upon graduating, Ms. Robbins went to work for Chamberlain Enterprises, where her father is lead counsel. There's a photograph, and it's definitely the woman outside my door.

She also sent me another photo, one I can't stop looking at. A picture of two teenage girls with their arms around each other's shoulders. One is my mother and the other looks like Ms. Robbins.

I want to tell myself this is Photoshop or AI, and be furious at such a cheap shot, pretending she was friends with my mother, but there are other photos, too, of both of them, from toddlers to teens.

Not just friends.

Good friends.

The age works. Mom and Dad had me young—teenage pregnancy—and my research shows that Ms. Robbins is thirty-six, the same age as my mother.

One of the links she sent brings me to an old Savannah newspaper's society pages. The photo is of a girl dressed in fancy riding gear, hoisting a trophy beside a gray horse.

Rosalyn Chamberlain, 12, Takes Home Gold in Dressage

I stare at the photo. It's my mother, her smile unmistakable, with one corner of her mouth lifting higher than the other. It's also like looking at a photo of myself at that age . . . if I could ride a horse or knew what "dressage" even was.

This is my mother.

In a world I can't even imagine my mother inhabiting.

No, actually, I can totally picture her in that world. My funny, elegant mother, who charmed everyone she met. My mother fashioned a utopia in our home, and yet she never quite fit the world outside of it—the very average one of people struggling to make ends meet.

I can wonder what made her leave *her* world, but the answer comes when I turn to a photo sitting on the floor, the table that once held it long sold. A portrait of my parents—Rose and Will—beaming at each other, renewing their vows in a cheap Vegas chapel, like they did every five years. I have all those photos, and they're all like this, portraits of two people ridiculously in love.

A teenage pregnancy.

A Southern high-society family.

Did Mom leave?

Or was she pushed out?

And do I want to connect with grandparents who'd do that to their child? Their *only* child?

I think of Ms. Hoffman at the door, and I'm not sure I have a choice. But I'm about to find out.

By the time I let Ms. Hoffman and Ms. Robbins—"call me Cecilia"—into the apartment, my fate has been decided. Ms. Hoffman's superiors have already been contacted, all the appropriate proof given, and I'm in the custody of Cecilia Robbins. I don't think it normally happens at that speed, but it does for my grandparents.

Do I accept this at face value? Of course not. My father taught me to conduct research and check my facts and trust no one. I'd never thought that was strange. It's not like Dad was some weird conspiracist. He was laid-back and chill, always ready with a bad joke and an easy laugh. But when it came to protecting us, he was as cagey as anyone with a tinfoil hat.

And maybe now I know why.

Why Dad had been so careful. Why we'd moved around so much. Why we'd lived practically everywhere except the South.

Did the Chamberlains try to get Mom back? Had my parents decided they didn't want that—the bridge long burned—and kept two steps ahead of people who could afford to hire the best private detectives?

Well, there's a reason Cecilia Robbins showed up at my door, isn't there? It's not as if I reached out. Not as if she could have come across Mom's obituary, when I'd never written one or held a service.

I don't just trustingly toddle along after Ms. Robbins. I look up Ms. Hoffman on the DCFS website. I insist on speaking to her superior by video, and that might be very irregular, but again, it takes only a few words from my new lawyer to arrange it.

Ms. Hoffman showed up at my door at four-thirty this afternoon.

By eight, I'm on a flight to Savannah, with all my worldly possessions in a backpack.

TWO

We fly commercial. That's what Cecilia says, though it just means we fly on a normal plane—as opposed, apparently, to a private jet, because, as she explains, they're a bad look these days. Oh, Chamberlain Enterprises has one, of course, but they don't use it when anyone might be watching.

Flying commercial does not mean flying "coach," which seems to be the word for the section where most people sit. We're in first class, and the luxury of that is completely lost on me, as someone who's never even flown before.

When the meal arrives, Cecilia waves hers away, whispering to me, "It's terrible. I'll feed you properly later."

The flight attendant hovers, tray outreached toward me, and my stomach growls loud enough for Cecilia to hear it. With a look that might be a flush of embarrassment, she takes the tray with thanks and hands it to me.

"When did you last eat?" she asks softly.

"I had lunch." I won't mention that it was an apple from the box of "healthy snacks" my cafeteria puts out for free. When you're trying to keep a roof over your head, you calculate the exact amount of food you need to get through the day without fainting.

In my case, it's two bananas, one apple, and a packet of ramen mixed with canned tuna.

"How did my grandparents find me?"

Cecilia stiffens before catching herself. "Hmm?"

"How did my grandparents find me?" I repeat.

Silence stretches so long that I glance over.

Finally, she says, "Your mother sent me a photo every year at the holidays. When I didn't get one this year, I worried. I had . . . reason to believe she was last in Chicago. I hired investigators, but it took a while to find you."

"So it was you who found me. Not my grandparents." I focus on cutting into my chicken. "Are they meeting us at the airport?"

"Your grandparents are in Europe. Your grandmother isn't well."

"Ah."

That might explain why they sent their lawyer instead of coming to Chicago themselves. It doesn't explain why there's been no mention of even speaking to them. I'm pretty sure phones work in Europe.

"So what happens now?" I say. "Am I being whisked off to some grand estate to be raised as a proper heiress?"

"No, whisked off to Westdale Academy, to receive the best possible education, for admission to the best possible college."

I take a bite of chicken. "I've already been admitted to college. With a full scholarship."

"A state college."

"There's nothing wrong with that."

"You applied to three top-tier schools. Stanford. Harvard. Yale. I believe my alma mater was your first pick. Stanford for business, yes? An MBA?"

I say nothing, but my stomach flutters.

She continues, "You received early admission offers to all of them. *All*. But the top-tier ones didn't come with full scholarships, which you needed. So why did you apply to them?"

I cut a baby carrot in half. "Just dreaming."

"Well, you don't need to dream anymore. Stanford is yours. I can accept the offer on your behalf."

I stop, carrot halfway to my mouth. I'd only applied to those schools to see if I could get in. The thought of actually going to my top pick? And not having to worry about the cost?

I can't even process that. I'm not sure I dare. Maybe being the granddaughter of billionaires should have hit harder, but it's *too* big. When I was younger, I thought a billionaire had ten million dollars. Then I realized it was a *thousand* million, and my brain couldn't even conceive of that. How does anyone have that much money? *Why* does anyone have that much money?

I don't want to think about having billionaire grandparents. But going to Stanford? That's an actual dream, one that has just come true in the most casual way possible.

Well, you don't need to dream anymore. Stanford is yours.

Cecilia continues, "What you'll get at Westdale is more than a top-notch education. It's about making connections. Networking."

"Not my thing," I mumble as I quickly eat another carrot.

Her voice drops, softer. "It needs to start being your thing. You also need to spend time with kids like you. Kids who are accustomed to rubbing elbows with heiresses."

Rich kids, she means. I shiver as I think of the well-off students at some of my better schools. The popular, stuck-up ones who didn't even see people like me. Imagine a school *full* of them.

"I'm fine in a regular school," I say. "I'm already accepted at Stanford, so I don't need this Westdale place."

"You do," she says, her voice still soft. "I'm afraid that's non-negotiable. But trust me when I say it won't be as bad as you think."

"You went there," I say, remembering what I saw online.

"As did your mom. I actually went *because* of her. We grew up together—my dad is head counsel for Chamberlain Enterprises, and while I had the grades for Westdale, I didn't have the family connections. Your mom got me in, and I loved my time there. We both did. I know it sounds like some posh boarding school full of snobby brats, but Westdale is . . . unique."

"How?"

Her lips quirk. "Do you want the full story or just the parts that concern you?"

"Full story."

"Okay, then." She takes a deep breath. "Let's go back to the late 1800s. Higher education in the South is pretty much nonexistent. You won't even see a public high school until the 1900s. Southern families who want a good education for their kids send them north. But there's also a push for the New South. Industrialization, education, progressive thought, moving away from the . . ." She makes a face.

"The antebellum South."

"Yep, and the founders of Westdale saw an opportunity. Start a private boarding school at home. A prep school—preparing students for college. Headhunt top teaching talent. Focus on progressive politics. Build something to rival northern prep schools. Which they did. Initially, it was about fifty students over four years of high school, extremely exclusive, only the wealthiest Southern families. As Westdale's reputation grew, it stopped focusing on the

South and expanded to include three feeder schools—outside Atlanta, New York, and Los Angeles. Westdale itself became only for seniors and only for select students from those feeder schools."

I frown. "How does that work?"

"Prospective students attend one of the feeder schools, which are still *very* exclusive. The best of *those* are accepted to Westdale for their senior year, making it the most exclusive program in America. To get in, you need the money and connections to be accepted by one of those three feeder schools and *then* you need to apply to Westdale like you'd apply to college. Grades first, followed by service work and athletics. That leaves a maximum of forty kids, all seniors, all valedictorian-level students, like you."

"That's . . . daunting."

Her eyes sparkle. "But maybe a little exciting, too? Westdale doesn't have any silver-spoon kids coasting through life. No spoiled socialites who major in partying. These kids are driven. Ambitious. Top performers, every last one."

"Is the school business oriented? Are they all from corporate families?"

She shakes her head. "That was one of the early mandates of Westdale—that it would recognize excellence in all areas. The unity of commerce, science, and art." She catches my look and smiles. "You like that."

"It's interesting."

"That is definitely one word to describe Westdale."

I think it through, looking for more questions to ask. "So by now, being the start of second term, they've all applied to college."

"A formality really. Anyone who gets into Westdale is guaranteed to get into the college of their choice."

"Then why go to Westdale?"

"Prestige, but it's also a reward. Once they're in, they can relax and enjoy their final year, while making meaningful connections for their careers."

"Everyone just hangs out and enjoys a top-notch education they no longer need for college?"

"Why not? They've worked hard. Now they get to relax and do that very important networking."

I shake my head. "Students like that don't relax." Students like me, I mean, though I don't say it. "They competed to get in, which means they want something only Westdale can offer."

A flutter of her hand. "Some of them want to be named Optima, but that's not important—"

"What's Optima?"

A long pause. Then, as if reluctantly, she says, "Each year, one student joins an elite group composed of all former winners. It doesn't concern you."

"I'm disqualified because I'm enrolling late."

"No, but you don't need to run for Optima."

I bristle. "Because I'm a public school student and not on their level? I couldn't win, so I shouldn't run?"

"No, because you don't need it. You're a Chamberlain. There's nothing you'd get from making Optima that you don't already have. You can just relax and focus on making friends and getting used to your new life."

With that, she opens her phone. Conversation over. In other words, whatever this "Optima" thing is, she's not talking about it.

Which means I definitely want to know more.

After the flight, a driver conveys us to a hotel. I'm still unsettled—okay, maybe also a little grumpy—from the Optima conversation. Being introverted means I can be mistaken for non-competitive, when nothing could be further from the truth. It doesn't even matter whether I want the prize; I just like to win. If there's a competition at this school for the best of the best, then I will want to prove that I *could* be that student, that I'm at least a serious contender. I'll especially want to prove that I can do it without the privileges—boarding schools, tutors, job-free summers—the others have enjoyed.

My mood lifts when we reach the hotel, where I get a suite bigger than my entire apartment. The bathroom has a bidet, a toilet, a sunken tub, and a massive shower. There are four TVs—for the tub, the bed, the living room, and . . . the front hall. Under what circumstances is someone watching TV in the front hall?

After Cecilia leaves, I imagine Mom being here. I picture her rolling her eyes at the luxury but enjoying it, too. Enjoying it because it was a reminder of her old life.

She'd seemed so at home in our unending string of rented houses. She'd walk through each and say, "This is good, Will. I can make it work," and Dad would take her hand and say, "We can." Then they'd throw themselves into turning those run-down places into homes: Dad painting and fixing, Mom scouring thrift shops for curtains and artwork, and filling the house with the smell of baking.

I always figured this was how they grew up. Making do with what they had. I knew Dad did, with a single mom and zero support from his absent father. I presumed Mom's life had been the same and that when Dad brought home some little luxury for her—fancy chocolates or soaps—she loved them because they were something she'd never had. Except now I know she'd grown up in a world where people probably never ate corner-store chocolate or used drugstore soap.

Had she been faking contentment for Dad's sake? I honestly don't think so. I look back, and I don't remember ever glimpsing anything else.

Maybe, if you've had it all, you don't mind leading a simpler life. Your idea of what's important changes. And what was important to Mom had been Dad and me. Oh, she had her own interests—reading, shopping, volunteer work—but she'd always joked that she belonged in an earlier time, one where a woman could aspire to a career as a mom and wife and no one would bat an eye.

The new story seems to be that Mom was a young woman from a wealthy family, who left Westdale and was disowned for a teenage pregnancy, but she never regretted it because she was in love with my dad. She embraced her new life and didn't look back.

That's the happy answer. The easy answer.

But is it the truth?

When things got bad after Dad died, Mom still never went to her parents for help. For billionaires, a few thousand dollars to get back on her feet would have been like tossing pennies into a fountain. I can see her refusing to give them the chance to say "I told you so." But for my sake, she'd grovel. For me, she'd swallow her pride.

So why hadn't she done that? And does the fact she hadn't mean I really shouldn't be here?

For now, I think I need to trust her best friend and remember that I don't need to deal with my grandparents. When the dust settles, though, and no one's watching, I'll start digging, because I have a lot of questions to answer.

Investigating will wait until I have a laptop, which Cecilia has assured me will arrive tomorrow. For now, I use the temporary phone Cecilia gave me to send emails to anyone who'll miss me at school. Then I do something I haven't done since Dad died, and we gave up our rented houses for tiny apartments: I take a bath. I fill that tub to the brink and pour in lavender bath salts.

I stash the other two bottles—sage and lemon—in my backpack. When we took road trips, we'd sometimes stay in "nice" hotels. Mom always took whatever toiletries we didn't use, reasoning that we'd paid for them.

I spend way too long in that steaming, lavender-scented bath. Then I hop into the shower to wash my hair, because if they're giving me both options, I'm using them. Afterward, I pull on the thick cotton bathrobe and shuffle into my huge bedroom with its huge bed.

I've seen movies where fancy hotels like this put a chocolate on the pillow. I get an entire box from a local chocolatier. I pop one piece, and it's amazing.

I wash down a second chocolate with bottled water. I have five choices. *Five*. Of *water*. The one I pick is from the south of France. Drawn, I'm sure, from a mystical well, the whereabouts of which are known only to one monk, who guards the secret with his life.

I pull back the sheets and, again, I have to pause, this time to run my fingers over them. I've read about things like Egyptian cotton and gazillion-thread count, and I have no idea whether that's what this is, but I have never even *felt* sheets like this. Crisp and soft at the same time.

I shed the bathrobe, slide into those sheets, and smile like I haven't smiled in months. And that's before I feel an envelope on the other pillow. I pick it up to see "For expenses" written on the front. Inside are . . .

Hundred-dollar bills. A *sheaf* of hundreds, along with a few twenties for variety.

For expenses? Like what? The sudden need to buy a designer handbag? I shake my head and tuck the money under my pillow.

I should say something like "I could get used to this." But I'm not sure that's a good idea. At least not until I've answered my questions. Because if there's a reason Mom never went home again, then I'm only going to be living the life of an heiress until my eighteenth birthday, when I'm legally free. Until then, I'll enjoy what I can, while I can.

THREE

I sleep so soundly that when my alarm goes off at seven, I startle awake, looking around in confusion. Then I remember everything that's happened, and I lie there, taking time to mentally shift from panic to resolve.

Focus on the good. It's the first day in months that I've woken without worrying whether Child Services will knock on my door. The first day I've woken without immediately calculating how much money I have and how much I need to get through another month. Without wondering whether I can work more hours without my grades suffering.

Today I can eat a real breakfast, via room service. Mom always said room service is ridiculously overpriced. Dad would pick us up dinner instead, and we'd eat in bed while watching TV, which she said was the point of room service anyway.

I order coffee and a smoothie plus an egg sandwich *and* French toast. I tell them I'd also like either an apple or a banana. Neither is on the menu, and I may end up actually spending ten dollars for a banana, but it's not my money.

While I wait for breakfast, someone drops off five gold boxes with red ribbons, which makes me feel like a princess on Christmas morning.

Inside those boxes, I find clothing and a note reading "You need clothing, and I don't know your style, so here's a selection." There are five basic outfits, which amusingly fall into the category of "classic teen looks." There's jock, with an athleisure crop top and leggings. Prep, with a collared shirt and khakis. Popular crowd, with heels and a miniskirt. Goth girl, with a little black dress and Doc Martens. And vintage, with, yep, everything old that's new again.

I've never been a "type." I always just wanted to disappear.

Is that what I want now? To hide in the back and coast to graduation?

I'm not sure, but I feel like maybe it's time to try something new. To be my own person, like Mom was.

I try on all the looks. Back when I took dance classes, my teachers were devastated that I had no actual talent, because apparently, I'm built like a ballerina, even though I'm short—barely five two. After my involuntary semi-starvation, I'm paler and thinner than ever, my eyes huge in my face. So, yeah, prep doesn't really suit me any better than the crop top and leggings. As for the high heels and miniskirt, I'd need to drink a whole lotta shakes first.

Vintage suits me, so I definitely want more of that.

As for gothic, it *shouldn't* work. My look is the opposite of goth. And yet . . .

I turn in the mirror. I'm wearing the Docs and a gorgeous black minidress, with lace shoulders and a tiered skirt. Goth always made me think of hiding in black, but this is *not* hiding, and I really like it. Fun, flirty goth.

When breakfast arrives, I tip the delivery person twenty bucks. I'd give a hundred, but that might make them nervous, fearing

I've swiped it from Daddy's wallet and he'll demand it back. The breakfast included a hefty service charge, so I figure an extra twenty is fine.

By the time Cecilia knocks, I've eaten, dressed, and packed. I let her in, and she whistles at my outfit. "That is not what I would have picked, but damn, girl, it works. You want more of that?"

"Yes, please. I also took the vintage, but I want *actual* vintage. Not modern reproductions."

"Done and done."

She fires off a note on her phone. As for the outfits I didn't choose, she assures me they'll find good homes. A valet takes our luggage, and we follow at a leisurely pace, Cecilia asking how I slept and such. When we reach the elevator, the valet is already gone on ahead.

"You have your driver's license," she says as the doors close. Statement, not question. She's done her research.

"I got it because I took a job last summer that required one but didn't need me to actually drive. Mom and I used public transit."

"So you *can* drive but haven't?"

"Pretty much."

"All right then. I'll drive us out of the city, and then you can take over."

Before I can ask what she means, we're at the drop-off circle and walking to a Jeep that's fancier than any Jeep has a right to be.

"This is yours?" I ask.

She chuckles. "Not really my style. But I'm guessing it might be yours."

I glance over. "Did I mention I've never actually driven outside lessons?"

"Don't worry. It's the top-end model, which means it has the best safety features money can buy. An upcharge for side airbags? That's for normal people."

"Whose lives are worth far less?"

"Apparently."

We exchange a knowing eye roll, and I shake my head. When I move toward the Jeep, squinting against the sun, Cecilia clears her throat. I turn, and she's holding out a pair of sunglasses.

"I have others," she says, "but I think these will suit you."

I take them and glance at the name. Cartier. Another shake of my head, but I put them on, and they do help with the bright southern sunshine.

I open the passenger door and inhale the scent of leather.

"Fair warning," Cecilia calls from the driver's door. "You won't have much opportunity to use a vehicle at Westdale. Even on weekends, your time isn't really your own. But I thought you might like the *idea* of having one."

For escape. Knowing I *could* leave.

"I appreciate that," I say. "But I'm really not sure I should be driving anything this expensive."

"Pfft. It's fine. We have the best insurance money can buy."

I laugh and climb in the passenger side as the valet loads our bags.

Savannah had matched my image of the Deep South, with its mix of old and new. Once out of the city and on back roads, I drive, and I'm focused on the road, but when I glance up, I see live oaks, dripping kudzu, and endless orchards. Cecilia catches me eyeing roadside stands advertising peaches and pecans.

"I'm not sure Westdale would let you bring those in," she says. "They aren't organic."

At my look, she says, "Kidding. You're a Chamberlain. You could bring in a puppy and they'd only ask whether you need anyone to walk it for you."

I give a slow smile.

"No puppies," she says. "That was a joke. Well, not a joke, but not an invitation either." She pauses. "If you really want to check out a roadside stand, there's a good one in a couple of miles."

When I slow at the next stand, she says, "Keep going," and then directs me to one shortly after we turn onto a gravel road. The stand is small and doesn't look promising, but Cecilia hands me a twenty, and I get out. I walk over to a rickety wooden table with produce and a box with a slot and a sign that says "Pay here. Thieves will be shot."

I glance back at Cecilia, but she's looking down, probably at her phone. I peer along the driveway. The house is only about fifty feet away, and I'd really rather give my money to a human and not, you know, risk being *shot*, but there's no one around.

I select a bag of pecans and a quart of peaches. I presume I can get change out of the box, but I'm not opening it, in case someone watching from inside thinks I'm stealing. Then I realize I no longer *need* change, and I stuff the twenty in and turn back to the Jeep.

Before I can take another step, an engine roars. My head jerks up, hands clenching my pecans and peaches, expecting a car racing down that driveway to stop me. Instead, it's an old pickup coming along the road.

The truck is moving faster than I'd ever drive on gravel. It's so coated in dirt that I can't even tell the color, and the windows are tinted darker than can possibly be legal.

I turn and keep walking toward the Jeep.

"You!" a woman shouts, and I spin, just as something whizzes past my ear. Pain explodes, and I drop to the ground, peaches and pecans going everywhere.

"I paid!" I shout. "Check the box! I paid!"

Cecilia gets to me first, helping me up with a "What the hell?" Her hand touches my ear, and I feel the sting of it and the hot drip of blood. I realize the projectile only nicked my ear, that "explosion" of pain being mostly shock.

"What happened?" a voice says, footsteps coming with an uneven gait. I look up to see a portly woman with a steel-gray bun. My gaze flies to her hands, expecting to see a rifle. They're empty.

I swallow. "I paid. I put a twenty in the box."

The woman stops, breathing hard. Then her eyes widen. "Oh, you poor child. You thought I was calling you out for not paying? I was making sure you got change. I forgot to add it this morning."

"We don't need change," Cecilia says and then adds, "Thank you, though." Her finger touches my ear again. "What happened?"

"S-something hit me. I heard it whiz by. Like a . . . like a bullet. And I thought. . . . The sign says—" I swallow.

"Thieves will be shot," Cecilia mutters, proving she has indeed stopped here before.

"Oh, lord," the woman says. "I am so sorry. It's my husband's idea of a joke. Well, not really a joke. A warning, I guess. But we'd never actually shoot anyone."

I take deep breaths, trying to calm myself. "The truck. It must have spit up gravel and a stone clipped my ear and . . ." I laugh shakily as my face flames with embarrassment. "I'm sorry, ma'am."

"You said you heard a whizzing sound," Cecilia presses.

"The rock moving fast, I guess, like a bullet?" I look at the woman. "I'm really sorry."

"Let me get you a bandage for that ear."

"It's fine," Cecilia says, but the woman is already hobbling to the house.

Cecilia helps me to the truck and sits me on the passenger seat, sideways with my legs hanging out. She gives me a tissue for the blood and then tells me to wait as she paces around where I fell, squinting and bending and examining a nearby tree.

"Are you actually looking for a bullet?" I say.

"I'm being thorough."

"I made a mistake. The sign freaked me out. We definitely have guns in Chicago, but putting up a sign like that would be asking for trouble. I understand that it's different here in the countryside, and I overreacted."

She keeps scanning the ground.

"It was a stone," I say. "Thrown up by a pickup going way too fast on a gravel road."

The woman comes out with a bandage, and while Cecilia applies it, the woman brings a fresh bag of pecans and basket of peaches, and tries to give us our money back, but I'll only take the produce, with thanks and apologies for overreacting. She still fusses until Cecilia assures her it's fine and thanks her for her time.

"Would you drive, please?" I ask Cecilia when the woman finally leaves.

Cecilia nods, her face tight, and when she rounds the Jeep, she peers down the road. Then she shakes her head and gets into the driver's seat.

FOUR

We don't go much farther before Cecilia turns into a driveway. There's no signage, but it's obvious something lies past the stone walls and open wrought iron gate. As we turn in, I don't see any buildings, though. Just a long, winding road.

We pass forests and fields, then an orchard and greenhouses. Cecilia explains that the academy grows most of its own produce and has a chef from a Michelin-starred restaurant.

We reach a second gate, this one attached to a fence at least twelve feet high.

"Welcome to Westdale," Cecilia says.

I stare at those huge iron gates. "Do we need to buzz in or something? I don't see a call box."

"If anyone makes it this far, security has already been monitoring their progress. If you aren't expected, those gates will stay closed—"

The gates begin to mechanically open.

"I texted with your car model and license plate earlier," she says. "Like everything else here, security is state of the art. Don't let the exterior fool you."

I'm about to ask what she means, but then the academy appears.

"Holy shit," I whisper. "Well, I definitely chose the right outfit."

She laughs softly. "Not a lot of Gothic architecture out here, but the founders knew what they wanted."

Gothic is right. It's a massive dragon of a building, wings curling on either side. A gray stone structure, three stories tall, with arched windows, and spires.

As the Jeep creeps up the drive, I spot students out for their morning break. One guy is shooting hoops, and as we pass, I twist for a better look.

"You like that?" Cecilia says with a low chuckle. "Theo Dubois. His dad is Bernard Dubois."

"The movie director?"

"Yep, who himself also descended from Hollywood royalty. And Theo's mom is Trinity Nilsen, the actor."

"So that's why he looks like that."

She laughs under her breath. "It is."

Theo Dubois is tall, with golden curls and the sort of muscles that say he definitely fulfilled any athletics requirement. Watching him dunking so effortlessly, I kinda want to take up basketball myself. I'm not the only one, apparently. He's playing solo, but four girls and two guys sit on the lawn, watching.

"He has a fan club," I say.

"Theo Dubois has an *actual* fan club, hon. You've never heard of him?"

"Uh, no."

"Well, he's his own kind of famous. But that didn't get him into Westdale. Every school needs their golden boy, and you are looking at him: 4.0 GPA, MVP on his last school's winning basketball team. Directed a short film that debuted at Sundance. Helps little old ladies across the road every Sunday before church."

She looks at me. "I'm kidding about the last one. Mr. Theo's charity work is restricted to gracing Hollywood fundraisers with his presence. He has no time for anything that won't help him get ahead, and if you get in his way, he'll mow you down with a wink and a smile."

"I might not mind getting mowed down by him."

She bursts out laughing.

"Who are the others with him?" I ask as I discreetly remove the bandage from my ear.

"Nobodies."

My brows shoot up, and she shrugs. "Even at Westdale, there are nobodies, Liliana. Anyplace else, they'd be kings and queens. Here, they're rank and file."

"Okay. So besides Theo Dubois, who do I need—"

"Ah, there. That's who I want."

She stops the Jeep. All I see is a guy slouched on the front steps, reading what I think is his phone until I realize it's a paperback novel.

I can't tell much with that slouch, but he looks lean. Mostly what I see is dark hair hanging over his face as he reads. He's dressed in jeans, a plain black T-shirt, and motorcycle boots. He looks like he should have a vintage Harley beside him and a cigarette hanging from his lips.

When I climb from the Jeep, he glances up briefly, as if seeing movement. Then he stops. His gaze slides over me, and then quickly away, jaw setting as if he didn't mean to look. He goes back to his book, but I swear he's still watching me over the top of it.

"Mr. Maddox," Cecilia calls.

He closes the book with an audible sigh. "Ms. Cecilia."

"Whatcha reading, Maddox?"

He stuffs the book in his back pocket. Then he looks up, showing bronze skin and a face that's all angles. Strong jaw, carved cheekbones, sharp chin. Dark eyes meet mine with a studiously blank half-lidded stare.

"The new girl arrives," he says, in a deep voice with an accent I recognize from our year in Southern California.

"Liliana Chamberlain—" Cecilia begins.

"I know who she is."

"Then let me finish the introduction, Mads."

Chamberlain? I want to protest. My name is Liliana Green. But a coldly practical corner of my soul knows what Cecilia is doing. Here I will be Liliana Chamberlain, because the name proves I belong.

The guy rises, languidly, his gaze on me, eyes still shuttered.

"Maddox Moreno," Cecilia says. "Son of Marilyn Perez-Moreno, the tech wizard behind Chatbox and Snapshots and—"

"They're waiting for you inside, new girl," Maddox says.

"No, they're waiting for *me*," Cecilia says. "You are waiting for Liliana."

His dark brows rise. "Uh, no. I was—"

"You're going to show her around."

He snorts. "Do I look like the welcoming committee?"

"No, you look like a boy who owes me and is going to repay it by taking care of my girl here. Showing her around today. And looking out for her the rest of the term."

I open my mouth to protest, but Maddox beats me to it with "I'm not—"

"You owe me, unless you'd rather spend your last term in a prison school."

He looks at me. "Ignore Cecilia. She thinks she's funny."

"Oh come on, Mads. I'm giving you some bad-boy cred. Boost that thing you've got going on—James Dean by way of Holden Caulfield."

He rolls his eyes. "Showing your age, counselor. You gotta update your refs."

"Take Liliana around. Answer her questions. Look after her. That's an order."

"I don't really need—" I begin.

"An *order*, Maddox. Or I tell Mommy what you really did."

She walks past us into the house.

"You don't have to," I say to Maddox once Cecilia is gone. "Obviously. I can—"

"Follow."

He leads me up the stairs. I'm trying to read the title of the book in his back pocket, and he must catch a glimpse of me in the door glass.

"Checking out my ass, Chamberlain?"

My cheeks heat. "The book. I was trying—"

"If you're trying to read the title so you can make conversation, don't bother. I don't do small talk."

"I guessed that. I was actually curious about what you're reading."

A grunt, and then he yanks open the door.

"This is the front door," he says.

"The tour commences."

He walks down an empty hall lined with portraits. "Where you from, new girl?"

"Thought you didn't do small talk."

"It's a long hall. Gotta say something." He doesn't glance back, just strides along, leaving me jogging to keep up.

"Chicago," I say.

"I mean what school?"

I tense. "Nothing you'd know."

"Try me."

"You know many public schools?"

His steps slow. "Uh, no." He glances back. "You *are* a Chamberlain, right?"

I fix him with a level stare. He squares his shoulders and resumes his stride.

"Whatever," he says. "There's only one place you really need to see on this tour." He makes a sharp turn and keeps walking until he reaches another exit. "The back door."

Anger sparks, hard and sharp, and before I can stop the words, I say, "Fuck you."

He turns sharply, looking startled. "Excuse me?"

"Are you saying public school kids don't belong here? Or that I belong on the staff, using the back door?"

He stares for a second. Then he leans back against the wall. "I meant . . ." He waves at the back door. "Escape while you still can."

"Because I don't belong at Westdale." That anger burns white-hot, and deep down, I'm not sure he deserves it, but it feels as if I've been holding in my confusion and fear. All it takes is for someone to suggest I don't belong, and that bubbles over.

He shakes his head. "I just meant you should escape because this place—"

"Everything okay back here?" a voice says behind me.

I turn to see Theo Dubois strolling toward us.

FIVE

Theo nods to Maddox. Then he smiles at me, and my anger evaporates because all I can do is stare.

I've always thought a "thousand-watt smile" was hyperbole. Theo Dubois's smile blinds and spellbinds at the same time. For five seconds, nothing exists beyond that smile and the fact it's for me, and all I can think is *Holy shit, that's a real-life superpower.*

"Liliana, I presume," he says, and again, I thought "forgetting your own name" was also hyperbole, but it takes a moment for my brain to connect the word to me.

"Uh, right," I manage. "I'm new."

"Oh, I know. We have been prepared for your arrival. Welcome to Westdale, Liliana."

"Th-thank you."

"Maddox," Theo says, and I half expect to find my tour guide has escaped, but he's still leaning against that wall like it needs the support. "Mind if I take over?"

"Is that a question?" Maddox waves before Theo can answer. "Never mind. Whatever."

Maddox yanks open the back door, and two seconds later, he's gone.

Theo shakes his head. "Would you believe we were best friends growing up?" He makes a face. "Anyway, the tour. How far did you get?"

"He showed me the back door."

A sharp laugh. "Telling you to get out while you still can? Yep, that's Maddox. Okay, so where do you want to begin? An actual tour? Or a rundown of what to expect at Westdale? Because I don't know where you went before, but *nothing* prepares you for this place."

I breathe slow and steady as my heart races, telling me to just slip away. I don't want this boy's attention. Well, yes, I do, which means I really don't, if that makes sense.

There were always boys like this at my schools, and I gave them wide berth, because if they looked my way, they wanted something. Help with their homework when we'd been young, and then, when we got older, well, they figured shy girls like me would give them whatever they wanted. Only Theo Dubois, with his 4.0 GPA, doesn't need homework help. And the vibes I'm getting are the opposite of predatory.

Because I'm *not* five steps down the social ladder, as I was with those boys in school. I might be new, but I'm an heiress, and that is the strangest feeling. A guy like this looking at me as if I'm a fellow human being, worthy of his time.

And he's waiting for an answer. Deep breath. Play this cool. As if he's just an average guy offering to show the new girl around.

"What to expect, please," I say. "And, possibly, survival tips."

That blazing grin again. "Good choice."

He starts down the hall and shows me classrooms as he asks what I already know about Westdale and runs through the daily schedule.

"And here we have the not-creepy-at-all spiderweb art," he says, waving at the wall with a flourish.

I think he's making a joke about a real spiderweb, but this place is so clean even my mom wouldn't find room for improvement. The web is actual art. It's a giant spiderweb made of silver, inlaid into the polished wood of the wall. It's gorgeous, though I'm not sure I should admit that. In the middle, in place of a spider, there's a woman in a toga weaving. When I step back, I notice that the webbing forms words.

Industry. Art. Science.

"A reminder to us all that we work together to weave a better world," Theo intones like a documentary narrator. Then he leans over and whispers, "Westdale likes its web iconography. Personally, I find it a little creepy."

I smile. "Not a fan of spiders?"

His gaze slants my way. "I should say that I just think it's odd, but yes, it might have something to do with my third birthday party, when I wanted a dinosaur theme, and my mom asked my dad to bring in some of the Jurassic Park animatronics, but he couldn't get them so he settled for an onset tarantula wrangler, and we discovered I am severely arachnophobic."

I bite back a laugh.

He feigns a scowl at me and wags his finger. "Do not mock the childhood trauma. Anyway, they like webs here, to make the point of us all being interconnected. We're working together for the betterment of—if not the world—each other." He resumes walking. "Speaking of which, have they told you about the Optima race?"

"Sort of?"

"And are you running?"

"I'm not sure."

"You should be." He gives me a sidelong glance as we walk. "A 4.0 GPA at a public school. Accepted at every college she applied to, including Ivy League schools, *without* Westdale on her application. Enough awards and volunteer accolades to need an extra page on her application."

My steps slow. "That's . . ."

"Privileged information? Yeah, sorry. I didn't look it up—the Optimas passed it along so I would understand my potential competition."

"Uh, okay."

He pauses at a doorway. "Here's the dining hall. Lunch is at one, dinner at seven. They'll deliver to your room if you're busy with homework, but I'd suggest you don't take that option. It looks bad."

"Antisocial?"

"Yes, but also like you need the extra study time. Westdale is all about appearances." He waves around the room, with its linen tablecloths and gleaming silver. "Food's good. Any dietary restrictions, they'll accommodate."

He returns to the hallway. "Back to the Optima race, I understand that you might not realize how useful it can be. You didn't grow up with it being waved overhead like the brass ring. But you really should consider running."

"My . . . uh . . . lawyer says I shouldn't bother. That I don't need it. Being, uh . . ."

He grins. "A billionaire heiress?"

My cheeks heat. "Apparently."

"Optima is about more than making money." He glances down at me. "So, this is awkward, but do you know who my dad is?"

"Bernard Dubois. And Trinity Nilsen's your mom."

"Ah." His smile seems forced. "Seen me in the gossip pages then?"

When I don't answer, he tilts his head, studying my expression. "Ever seen me before at all?"

"My lawyer told me who your parents are, but I don't follow celebrity gossip. Sorry."

His real smile blazes back. "Damn, *do not* apologize. I love it when people don't know who I am. A chance to make a bad impression all on my own. So, I referenced my dad because he's an Optima. That got him his first gig directing on a big-budget film. If that film had flopped, the Optimas would have gotten him a second chance and a third until he found his footing. The Optimas are the ultimate support network. As the Chamberlain heiress, you won't need to find employment, obviously, but you will need support—if only as a place where others really understand what it's like to be in your position."

He reaches for the door beside us. "Speaking of networking, this is where you'll want to spend most of your evenings."

"Not just for networking, but to look as if I don't need evenings to study."

"You got it."

He pushes open the door, and a girl's voice says, "Excuse me? This room is booked."

He ignores that and walks into a lounge that looks like an old-fashioned men's club, complete with leather chairs and a massive fireplace.

The girl who spoke sits in a club chair, while two other girls sit opposite. It's an arrangement every teenager recognizes instantly.

The queen bee in her hive.

This bee is gorgeous, dressed in the kind of outfit even I recognize as high fashion. I have to dig in my heels to keep from creeping backward and hiding behind the doorpost as I second-guess my cute-goth fashion choices.

She has dark brown skin, a cascade of black curls, topaz eyes behind glasses, and a perfect bow mouth, all set in a heart-shaped face that I'm certain has never seen a zit.

"Allegra Khan," Theo says.

She rises, and even that movement is perfect, as if she's a thirty-year-old supermodel in a teenager's body.

"You must be Liliana Chamberlain," she says, and I can't read her tone. Not warm. Not cool. No hint of inflection.

She doesn't reach out a hand, and I'm not sure what I'm supposed to do, so I just nod and mumble a greeting.

"I'm showing her around," Theo says. "I was saying this is the lounge, where we hang out in the evening."

"It is," Allegra says. "It's also where the societies have their meetings. The schedule is outside the door."

It's an obvious rebuke to Theo, who only says, "I haven't explained the societies yet. These are the Liliths. Allegra, of course. And Polly Reeves." He nods to a girl with blond pigtails, dancing blue eyes, and perfect white teeth. She grins and waves.

"And Isolde Brandt." Isolde is small—about my size—with red curls, pale skin, and a sprinkling of freckles. She smiles shyly.

"Now we will leave the queens in peace," Theo says as he steers me out.

"So that was the Liliths," he says after we've retreated and shut the door. "On Wednesdays they wear pink."

"We heard that," Polly calls with a laugh.

He grins and keeps walking. "There are four societies. Unless you're Maddox Moreno, you'll want to be in one. The Liliths are the top of the ladder. I'd join, but I have this pesky Y chromosome."

"Girls only."

"Yep. The story goes that when the school first opened, the guys formed societies, leaving the few female students to form their own. The Liliths were treated like some cute little sewing circle . . . until the forties, when five Optimas in a row were Liliths. The girls had been biding their time, working out their strategy, and once they took control, they never relinquished it. Forty percent of the Optimas come from the Liliths."

"Is that the point of the societies? Getting one of their group chosen as the Optima?"

"*Everything* is about getting one of your own chosen. Think of our graduating class as a pyramid. The Optima will be at the top. Below them come their society mates. Next come the Optima's other friends and allies. If you can't be Optima, you want to be in the Optima's society, and failing that, you want to be their friend."

"And the Liliths provide the most Optimas."

"Yep. Your mom was a Lilith. In fact, she was the Dux."

"Ducks?"

He grins. "D-U-X. It's Latin for 'leader,' like Optima is Latin for 'best.' And all of the societies are named after Greco-Roman gods, except the Liliths, of course."

"My mom was leader of the Liliths?"

He peers at me. "You didn't know that."

"I didn't know anything about Westdale—or that I'm a Chamberlain—until yesterday."

"Shit." He runs a hand over his face, and when he speaks, it's back to that more serious tone. "I'm going too fast, and I'm being flippant. Sorry. I didn't know."

I shrug. "I'd rather be thrown into the deep end than held back in the shallows." I look up at him. "So how much does everyone know about *me*? About my mom?"

"We were all told you're the daughter of Rosalyn Chamberlain. Most of us know who that is. Not a . . . uh . . . lot of Westdale students leave under, uh, those circumstances. Other than that, they wouldn't have heard much."

"But you were given more, because you're vying for Westdale Optima, and you needed to know about potential competition."

"Yep."

"And that's why I'm getting this tour. Assessing me as competition."

One shoulder rises. "Mostly, yeah. But also, being perfectly honest, I saw you get out of that Jeep, and I wanted to introduce myself."

My cheeks flush, and I'm flattered in spite of myself. I'm also impressed that he admitted he offered this tour to check out potential Optima competition.

I like that.

God help me, I like *him*.

I remind myself that Theo's mom is an Oscar-winning actor, and this is probably all an act, but I'm not sure I care.

Mom always said that charisma is about authenticity. Not flattering or pandering. It's treating people as if you really see them. Talking to them like you're really listening. *Seeming* authentic, even if you're acting.

What Theo has is charisma, and I can concede it's probably an act, but I don't care. I am the person temporarily holding his full attention, and it's glorious. Oh, I know it'll end, but I suspect being the focus of Theo Dubois's long-term attention is more than I could handle. Too much time in the sun when I burn easily.

"But if I'd be your competition, why would you want me to run?"

"Because the competition makes the prize worthwhile." He braces one arm on the wall and leans toward me, his voice lowering. "They say all Optimas are equal, but that's bullshit. Everyone knows which ones had to work their ass off and which glided by in an easy year. This year's competition is . . . underwhelming."

"How many are running?"

"Officially? No one. We don't declare until March first. But everyone knows who plans to run: Me, Natalia, and Cosmo. And Cosmo is going to fold at the first sign of ungentlemanly play."

"Dirty tactics?" I say.

"Cosmo expects a fair fight, which means he's not going to survive, because Natalia is going to fight dirty, and her boyfriend, Jayden, will fight dirtier on her behalf. She's a formidable opponent but not actual competition."

"You'll need to deal with her, but in a fair competition, you'd win."

"Does that sound like bragging?" He shrugs. "Consider it a very healthy self-image. From your credentials, you'd easily beat her, too."

"Which is why you want me to compete."

This grin is a flash of teeth so sharp I swear I see fangs. "I do."

"Because overcoming dirty tactics is fine, but the Optimas want someone who could also win on their own merits." I pause. "So the Optimas choose the winner?"

"Yep. It's based partly on grades, but the professors will also weigh in with personal assessments, and the students themselves will give their feedback in May, which is taken into consideration. That's why having allies is good. In May, the candidates will also be expected to write essays and be interviewed by the current Optimas."

"That's more than the toughest college admission."

"It is." He shifts his weight on the wall. "Here's my suggestion: You and I team up to raise the level of competition. Then, when it comes down to it, we go head-to-head. Whoever wins owes the other."

My gaze lifts to his. "I just got here, Theo. You really think I'm going to believe you want to team up with a total stranger? There's a catch. There must be."

"If I see an opening, I don't dribble around the court thinking it through. Yes, I'm moving fast, but you've walked in mid-game, and I am ready to go."

When I don't answer, he says, "The Optimas had a conference call last night, after they learned you were coming. My dad told my mom, who looped me in with your details. The Optimas have been bored this year. But with you here, they're actually excited. Compared to you, I'm a lapdog with sharp teeth. I can want, but I don't know what it means to *need*."

Do I know what it is to scrabble for scraps? Yes.

Do I want to scrabble right to the top of the heap? Hell, yes.

Theo moves close enough for me to smell his aftershave, and for an unsettling moment, that want and need twists into something deeper as I drink in the smell of him, bask in the heat of him.

I pull back abruptly. I have no time for *that*. I won't until I get where I need to be.

"The Optimas want to see what the two of us can do," he says. "Boy versus girl. Art versus industry. Privilege versus sheer willpower. They're wondering what happens when a Chamberlain doesn't grow up with all the advantages of power and position. Is there something innate that drives them to the top?"

I look up at him. "In other words, if I can beat you, with all your advantages, they can tell themselves *their* privilege isn't such an advantage."

That sharp smile. "Which is what they all want, isn't it? To think they deserve what they have. That they are naturally superior."

"And how do *you* feel about that?"

"My first film got into Sundance. I had three Oscar winners in it. I was thirteen. You think that would've happened if I wasn't Bernard Dubois and Trinity Nilsen's son? If I didn't have access to the best mentors and the best equipment?" He shakes his head. "You ever hear the term 'nepo baby'?"

"Uh, yeah . . ."

"I am the *ultimate* nepo baby. But I'm not going to insist on making a film on a camera from RadioShack, starring kids from my drama class. What would that prove? That I can make a good film based 'only' on a lifetime of living on sets and learning from the best? That's like assholes who call themselves self-starters when Mommy or Daddy bankrolled their first business."

"Okay," I say.

"Okay . . . ?"

"I'll consider running for Westdale Optima."

He pauses, cocks his head. "What convinced you? My nepo baby rant?"

"I appreciate people who understand what they are."

He laughs loud enough to startle a cleaner slipping down the hall. "Oh, then you have come to the right place. Me, that is. Not *this* place." He waves at the school. "Understanding where you fit in the world is rare here. Embracing it is even rarer."

He puts out a hand, and I shake it.

SIX

After that, Cecilia collects me, not batting an eye when she sees me with Theo instead of Maddox. She takes me to the principal, Ms. Dimitriou, and we have lunch while Ms. Dimitriou gives me my schedule and explains the rules.

While I have a vehicle, students can't leave without permission and, even then, only on weekends unless there's an emergency. Weekday evening outings are not allowed. Leaving the property for a walk is not allowed. This is an intensive program and our guardians expect us to embrace it.

"You won't need to worry about Liliana," Cecilia says, and I think she means I don't need to be encouraged to embrace my studies, but then she says, "She won't be leaving the grounds while she's here."

I slowly turn her way. "Excuse me?"

She ignores my tone and addresses Ms. Dimitriou. "Considering her situation, security is very important. People are going to find out who she is, and that poses a risk."

Ms. Dimitriou bristles. "Not at Westdale."

"That's my point. She's safe here, so here she stays, unless I give my express permission for her to leave."

"Is this about what happened on the way in?" I say. "It was a rock."

"What happened?" Ms. Dimitriou's voice sharpens with concern.

"Liliana was struck by a flying stone," Cecilia says. "Obviously it was an accident, but it made me think about her safety. Her grandparents have appointed me as her guardian, and I've decided she should stay locked down for a while." She looks at me, and her voice softens. "Take time to settle in. This is a lot, and you need that space."

"I think I'm old enough to decide what I need. I've been doing it since Mom died."

Cecilia flinches, and I regret mentioning it. Mom was her friend, after all.

"Just take it slow," Cecilia says. "Once news hits that the Chamberlain heiress has been found, I'll need to assess the threat level."

"Are you worried something could happen?" I frown. "Who was supposed to inherit before you found me? Are they a threat?"

She shakes her head. "Nothing like that. The will is structured so that if you weren't found, your grandparents' estate would have been divided among various trusts and charities."

I squirm at the thought that I've taken money away from worthy beneficiaries.

Ms. Dimitriou clears her throat, clearly eager to get back on track. "About the security concerns, for the time being, Liliana will stay on the property." She looks at Cecilia. "Would you like extra security for her?"

"No. For now, I'm just being cautious."

"Well, please let me know if you change your mind. We are more than happy to accommodate. Let's move on to your daily routine, Liliana."

There are thirty-eight students at Westdale this year. Four periods a day, three classes running concurrently, with between ten and fifteen students in each. There are specialties within each discipline—like writing or literature for English—but no electives. Even within the disciplines, my courses have been chosen to align with my future goals.

There aren't any extracurriculars at Westdale. There's no time for them. Instead, there are the societies. Ms. Dimitriou runs through those, and then she gets to the Westdale Optima competition.

"Liliana won't be entering," Cecilia says.

I turn a slow stare on her, but she ignores it.

"I believe the Optimas are expecting her to run," Ms. Dimitriou says.

"I'm sure they are. But it's too dangerous."

Ms. Dimitriou laughs softly. "Dangerous? It's not the Hunger Games, Cecilia." Her voice lowers to a murmur, "Though that might actually make it more interesting."

When Cecilia glares, Ms. Dimitriou gives a tiny smile. "Sorry, that was supposed to be my inside voice. The competition *isn't* dangerous. It's cutthroat, without any actual cut throats. It's the most important part of being at Westdale—the reason many parents send their children."

"Liliana isn't here for that. She's here because her grandparents want it, and she doesn't need to be an Optima. She's a Chamberlain."

"But her grandparents are both Optimas and—"

"And Liliana will not be."

My expression must be thunderous, because Cecilia finally glances over.

"That's not an insult, Lili," she says, her voice softening. "You've been through a lot, and your job here is to focus on the transition. As I said earlier, you don't need to make Optima."

Ms. Dimitriou sneaks me a *we'll talk later* look and then says, "All right. Let's show you to your room."

We climb to the third floor, and Ms. Dimitriou indicates the first door on our right. She shows me how to unlock it with the last four digits of my new phone number and tells me to just ask for help changing it.

When we walk in, my breath catches. My full ride to the state college had included a shared dorm room with common areas, including a washroom that looked like something from my high school. Here, I get a private bedroom, with a private en suite bath. Ms. Dimitriou assures me that I'm welcome to have my own furniture delivered, as many students do.

I look at the four-poster double bed with its thick duvet, the plush armchair and ottoman, the modern desk with an ergonomic chair. I don't even know *what* I'd change.

"We'll let Ms. Dimitriou get back to work," Cecilia says. "I can help you get settled in, but I'll need to go soon, and I believe you have . . ." She checks the schedule on my desk. "Math."

Before I head to class, I consult my map, so I'm not wandering aimlessly. Seeing my class name—Qualitative Analysis and Algebraic Financial Solutions—my stomach clenches. I've taken algebra, of course, and I know what qualitative analysis *is*, but I expected to take it in college.

No, I've got this. I already anticipated putting in extra work to catch up. That happens when you change schools, even in the public system. You're always either ahead or behind.

The lecture hall is set up as a horseshoe. I move toward a guy settling in.

"Are there assigned seats?" I ask.

"No," grunts a voice behind me. "And if anyone says otherwise, tell them to fuck off. Sit where you want."

I glance over to see Maddox. As he walks in, he doesn't look my way. Just heads to the back and pulls out a chair before dropping into it.

I continue to an empty seat—beside the redhead I'd seen with Allegra. "Does anyone normally sit here?"

She smiles up at me. "You do now." She holds out a hand. "Isolde."

"I remember. It's a very pretty name."

"From some opera. The ice queen." She tugs at a red curl. "Doesn't exactly suit me. *You'd* make a better Isolde, with that gorgeous hair."

"Ms. Brandt," a voice says. "May I interrupt?"

Isolde folds her hands on the desk. The speaker is a man in his forties. Dr. Walton. The teacher—or professor, as they apparently call them here.

Everyone quiets down, and class begins.

So . . . math was a disaster. Math has always been one of my best subjects, but here, I was as lost as I'd have been if Dr. Walton had chosen to speak in Finnish. As we leave class, Isolde falls in step beside me and whispers, "That's not what you were studying before, is it."

I'm not sure I dare answer. I've fallen for all the "new girl" tricks before, like where someone seems to be nice and helpful and is only playing with me. Isolde *is* a Lilith, after all.

"It's okay," Isolde whispers. "It's not a standard program. Well, not unless you went to one of the Westdale feeder schools, which you didn't."

I start to breathe, slowly. She's right, of course.

"I've been the new kid a bunch of times," I say. "I just always forget this part."

"I'm happy to help." When I glance over, she flushes. "Sorry if that was presumptuous. I'm sure you can handle it."

I'm ready to say *yes, I can*, but then I see her expression, gaze slightly to the side, as if braced for rejection.

"I'd hate to impose . . ." I begin.

Her face lights up. "No imposition at all. I'm hardly a math whiz, but I used to tutor at my old school. We have a study period before dinner. Oh, and Allegra is going to invite you to sit at the Lilith table." She gives me a crooked, sidelong smile. "Just warning you in advance."

"Thank you. I appreciate it." I smile back. "The tutoring offer and the warning."

She grins. "Anytime. So, what's next on your schedule?"

Next class is English. I'm in Advanced Communication for the Workplace. Even with the "advanced" part, it sounds like one of those classes for kids who can't write emails without text-talk.

I try not to be offended. Sure, I'm a business major, but voracious reading means I've always been at the top of my English class.

When I arrive, I scan for familiar faces. No Maddox, no Theo, no Isolde. Then I spot Allegra, queen of the Liliths . . . and she spots me.

"Move," she says to the poor guy sitting beside her.

He scrambles to another seat. Allegra locks her gaze with mine and motions at the now-empty chair. It's not a kindness or an order. It's a challenge.

Will I sit there? Or will I slink into another seat?

I nod, channeling her own cool, and lower myself beside her.

"Interesting dress," she says.

I tense. I'm supposed to misinterpret that as a compliment and gush my thanks and prattle on about how I just got it and it's not my usual style but I really like it. And then she'll smirk and roll her eyes at her classmates, who all understand that she was being sarcastic.

"Thank you," I say, my voice still coolly polite.

"It needs lipstick," she says.

I start to say that I don't usually wear makeup to school, but that would sound as if I'm insulting her for doing so. So I only nod, and as she studies me, I brace for impact.

"You don't need much makeup," she says. "Your eyes, to make them pop even more. And lipstick with that dress. Red would be the obvious choice, but it won't work on you." She pulls a tube from her bag. "The company sent me this. Definitely not my color." She hands it over. "It'll work with that dress. You should also try mascara. Black. No liner. Don't overdo the goth thing. The dress and boots work because you don't seem the type. It's the juxtaposition that snaps. Lean into it."

I look down at the lipstick. It's still sealed.

"Try it later," she says. "If you hate it, pitch it."

There's a mean-girl trick here. There must be. But what? The lipstick is unopened, so she hasn't tampered with it. She's not telling me to try it on now, which might have left me sitting through class wearing a hideous color.

"Thank you," I say, a little more genuinely.

"Oh, and you'll eat dinner with us tonight."

"I will?"

She meets my gaze. "You will."

I could refuse, but I do need to join a society, and I should check out the Liliths.

Before I can answer, class begins, and it's definitely *not* remedial English for business majors. Dr. Prior's emphasis is on clear and persuasive communication in all forms. Right now they're working on debate strategies, and as someone who spent a year captaining the debate team, I really wish I'd taken this class first.

Dr. Prior looks like a stereotypical English teacher. Tiny and well past retirement age, with a reedy voice and a puff of white curls. Then she slices through our arguments like an Olympic fencer with a razor-sharp rapier. I must be goggle-eyed, because Allegra slides over her phone, open to a Wikipedia page.

Dr. Ester Prior spent fifty years working on political campaigns as everything from communications director to speech writer to media consultant. She also served as "communications advisor" for two former presidents.

Now *this* is who I want for a teacher.

Once class ends, Allegra doesn't ask whether I'll take her up on her offer. She just says, "I will see you at dinner," and walks away.

SEVEN

I meet up with Isolde for math study, and we go to her room. If there's a trick here, I don't see it. It feels like all the other times I've started a new school and one of the quieter girls has offered help. I've found some real friendships that way. I won't jump and say this is another one of those possibilities, but I like what I see of Isolde. She's shy, kind, and patient, and by the end of the hour, she's calmed my fears that I'm in over my head at Westdale.

I think I can get up to speed with some cramming, though Isolde offers to help, and I may take her up on that, if more for the companionship than the tutoring. When you've been the new girl as often as I have, you learn how to spot opportunities for friendship and you know to take them when they come.

I head to my room to get ready for dinner, only to realize I'm not sure what "getting ready" entails at a posh private school. Do we change clothes? Or is that a stereotypical rich-people thing that no seventeen-year-old actually does?

I decide just to "freshen up," as Mom would say, and I start by trying on the lipstick Allegra gave me. Bright pink is one way to describe it. Bubblegum pink is another. I'm going to look like a twelve-year-old, but screw it; I can wipe it off if it's awful.

It's not awful. It actually looks really good. Huh.

I leave the lipstick on, brush my hair, and then head out. The main level is still empty, and I wander around for a few minutes. I'm heading back toward the dining hall when a guy walks straight into my path.

He's white, with dark hair and built like a football player—broad shoulders and biceps shown off by short sleeves. His gaze trips over me, in a cold assessment that has my skin crawling.

"New girl, right?" he says. "You looking for the dining hall?"

"No, I'm fine thanks."

"Well, if you need a tour—"

"Done," a voice says. "By me. Now run along, Jayden. I've got this."

Jayden turns and fixes Theo with a look that would have set my stomach twisting. Theo meets it with an all-teeth smile. He waits until Jayden leaves and then walks over to me.

"Jayden," I murmur. "That's Natalia's boyfriend."

"Boyfriend, guard dog, minion. I suspect he was sent to get a look at the new competition." He nods toward the dining hall. "Let's grab a table."

"Allegra invited me to sit with the Liliths."

"Works for me."

He steers me in. Allegra is already there with Isolde and Polly. I take a seat next to Isolde, and Theo pulls out the one on my other side.

"Lilith table," Allegra says to Theo.

"I see that."

He sits down.

Allegra looks from me to Theo and then says, "If you're implying she needs protection from me, I would suggest she needs to be more concerned about the boy who has very obviously staked his claim."

"Claws in, Allegra," Theo says.

Before she can answer, servers start passing out dinner. As Ms. Dimitriou explained, there are two menu choices each day, and you select at the beginning of the week. Tonight's options are pecan-crusted chicken breast and pan-seared salmon. I'd picked the chicken.

An appetizer salad comes first and everyone waits until our whole table has been served before we begin to eat.

"Do you have a date yet for the Quartz Gala, Theo?" Polly asks. "There's a poll online, you know."

"Oh, I'm sure there is. And don't worry. Once I've picked my plus-one, you'll be the first to know."

She jabs her fork his way, beaming. "You are the best."

Theo turns to me. "Polly is an influencer."

Is it possible for a growl to be cheerful? Then that's the noise Polly makes. "Didn't I just say you were the best? Do you want me revising that?"

"Sorry, Pol." He looks at me. "Polly is an online personality. And *she* is . . ." He bows his head with a theatrical wave. "Amazing."

"She really is," Isolde say. "Her Instagram has over fifty *million* followers."

I blink, unable to even conceive of that.

"Polly is exceptional," Allegra says, with the air of a queen making a pronouncement. "She has parlayed her online fandom into a foundation with a seven-figure income, ninety percent of which goes to charity."

"Wow," I say. "That's . . . wow."

"It'll be a hundred percent to charity someday," Polly says.

Isolde swishes an arugula leaf through some salad dressing. "Why don't you take Polly to the gala, Theo? It'd be great exposure for both of you."

"Hell, no," Polly says.

Theo thumps his fist to his chest. "Straight to the heart, Pol." She rolls her eyes.

He leans toward me. "Once again, my pesky Y chromosome keeps me from all the fun."

"I don't mean like *that*," Isolde says. "You could go as friends."

Polly shakes her head, pigtails bouncing. "Doesn't matter. People would say it's proof I actually do like boys, and that I'm pretending to be a lesbian to spite Daddy Dearest. So, no. Theo will take some lucky person as his date, and I'll get the scoop and he'll appreciate the big reveal coming from a friend."

"I always do," he says. "Because you are? The. Best."

"Right back atcha."

They grin at each other. Then Polly waves her fork at me. "You, Miss Heiress, do not have an online presence. You're a *ghost*."

"It's not my thing."

Theo leans to clap his hands over Polly's ears. "She didn't say that."

"I don't mean like that," I say. "I just . . ." I shrug. "I don't do anything internet-worthy. No one wants pictures of me studying. Or reading books. Or taking long walks by myself."

"That was before you were the Chamberlain heiress," Polly says. "Now *you* get to choose what's internet-worthy. You're a hot girl who'll inherit a fortune. You can make reading sexy if you want. Promote literacy. Chat up your favorite books. Take a stance against book bans. You set the tone. First, though, you need to let me debut you."

"Debut . . . ?"

"Launch you on socials. We need a strategy. Leave it all to me. We'll do a quick interview so your bios are authentic, and then we'll hold the profiles back until I launch you, when—*boom*—hot heiress appears from the ether. It'll be a *moment*."

"Polly?" Isolde says. "We adore your enthusiasm, but you're scaring poor Liliana."

"Nah," Theo says. "The only part that's scaring her is the repeated use of the word 'hot.' I think Lil would rather lean into her brains and her accomplishments."

"No," Allegra says, with that air of pronouncement again. "A girl doesn't need to pick between being hot or smart or accomplished. She can be all of those things. If she chooses to emphasize one over the other, that is her choice. And if the adjective she likes is 'hot,' that is also her choice. *You* don't make it for her."

Theo lifts his hands in surrender. "I stand corrected."

"Theo loves being called hot," Polly says. "It's his favorite adjective. You know why?"

"Because it means everyone underestimates him?" I say. "Dismisses him as a pretty boy?"

Theo grins, just for me, and I feel as if I've won something. "I make such a good pretty boy, though, don't I? It's the same reason Polly loves being called silly."

She rounds her eyes and bobs her head side to side, blond pigtails swinging. "Silly. Vacant. Dumb blond. Waste of space. That's me."

"Then she chews them up and spits them out," Isolde says.

Polly's blue eyes go even wider. "Never! That would be so mean! I'm a nice girl."

"Tell that to the trolls you doxed last month."

"Only because Daddy Dearest sent them after me, and I cannot ignore that." She fake pouts. "*He's* the mean one, not me."

This is the second reference to her father, which I think means I can ask who he is, but Allegra speaks instead, saying to me, "I would strongly suggest you consider Polly's offer. And consider it soon. News of your being here will break. None of *us* will do it. I suspect Theo is already passing along word that whoever outs you will 'disappoint' him."

"So bad," Polly says. "It's like Puritan shunning or Regency cutting. Socially? The worst."

Theo only rolls his eyes.

"But someone will eventually decide the engagement stats are worth upsetting Theo Dubois," Allegra continues. "Once that happens, if you don't have an online presence, the imposters will creep from their holes. If you're online—set up by Polly—you'll be verified. She can fast-track that. You need to claim your online identity before anyone else does."

I turn to Polly. "I'm feeling overwhelmed right now, but I would like to discuss it at some point."

"Whenever you want," Polly says. "And I will promise you the biggest, friendliest launch ever."

After dinner, Allegra says, "You'll come to my room. We need to talk," and no one sees anything wrong with such an imperious summons. Even Theo just shrugs.

"Come back after, and we'll chill in the lounge," he says. "I'll help you put some more names to faces."

We head up to the third floor, past my door to Allegra's. Earlier, Ms. Dimitriou had said we could refurnish our rooms, and nothing in Allegra's is stock. Surprisingly, she's downsized to a twin bed, but that seems to be so she can have more space. There's an armchair and what looks like a drafting table, covered in papers.

"I want to find you another lipstick," she announces when we're inside. "Your skin tone needs less yellow, more red."

I follow her to the bathroom, still wary. She opens a cupboard and pulls out an unwrapped tube of lipstick and also an unwrapped mascara.

"Try these."

I look at the cupboard, which holds more new makeup than a pharmacy.

"They send me things all the time," she says. "As if I'd wear any of it."

I tense, presuming she's saying those are beneath her standards but fine for me. Then I see her own makeup neatly arranged on a shelf. Every item is a brand I've only ever seen locked away, even in the upscale beauty shops where Mom liked to browse.

Simple gold containers with black script.

Allegra by Farjana.

I turn to Allegra. "Your mom is Farjana Khan?"

She unwraps the mascara. "I got my own line for my thirteenth birthday, which is a bit much, but it does mean my makeup is always perfectly suited to me."

"And that you'd never wear other brands."

"Yes. But they're all good, so take whatever you want."

She hands me the wand. "Just a quick flick. Don't overdo it or you'll be leaning into the goth."

I apply it like Mom taught me.

"That works," she says. "Keep it light."

I glance over. "Can I ask about Polly's dad? She mentioned him a couple of times, so I feel as if I should know who he is, but I hate to look him up online."

Her nod says I've earned a point for my discretion. "Polly's father is Owen Culpepper."

I blink. "The . . . uh, I mean . . ."

A humorless smile. "Whatever you were about to say would offend no one at Westdale, least of all Polly. Yes, *that* Owen Culpepper."

Culpepper is one of those guys people love to hate. My dad used to joke that he hated him before it was fashionable. Culpepper is a tech billionaire who shifted into politics, where he courts modern-day Nazis.

I think of Polly, bouncing her ponytails.

I also think of her worrying about people thinking her queerness is performative, meant to needle her father.

And I think of what she said about those trolls being sent by him.

"Polly's from his first marriage, right?" I ask.

"Yes, and to receive proper child support, her mother had to sign an NDA. Polly is the youngest. Once she's eighteen, her mom's free. Until then, Polly is very careful. Not that it matters. Her father sees insult in everything from her dating choices to her charitable efforts. Fortunately, her mother is a wonderful and supportive parent."

"Is her dad a Westdale grad?"

"Hardly." That quirk of the lips. "I can only imagine how much he fumes, having Polly *invited* to a feeder school, when his own very wealthy parents couldn't even get him into one."

She walks into the other room, and I surreptitiously pass the drafting board to see drawings of dresses.

"You're a designer," I say.

"I design. I'm not yet a *designer*." She looks at my dress again. "As I said, that works, but it's not quite right for you. We can do better. I'll send you sketches."

She says this so casually, just like she offered the makeup. Not a favor. Not even a gift. That would imply effort and obligation.

She picks up a pencil and starts sketching as she talks. "What do you know about the Liliths?"

I consider my next words and then decide not to play coy. "I know they're the top society here. Girls only. They produce nearly half the Westdale Optimas. And my mom was, uh, Lilith Dux. Like you."

"Yes." Again, no inflection as she works. "Each society has its angle, so to speak. Their path to success. Do you know the Liliths' specialty?"

"I do not."

"I believe our founders had a very sharp sense of humor. I also believe they knew they were better than the male students. That is no shade on the boys—only that, in their era, to get to here, Westdale women had to be better."

"They named themselves after Lilith, the so-called she-demon whose great sin was that she refused to obey a man."

Allegra finally looks up, meeting my eyes. "Yes. As for our angle, it's something women are usually condemned for. And not sex, though that would also be a correct answer and also associated with Lilith."

"The great seductress. So what else are women vilified for? That'd be a long list. I may need a hint."

She smiles at that. It's a Mona Lisa smile, but still definitely a show of amusement. "Old women, sitting around talking, sharing . . ."

"Gossip."

"Correct. If it were old *men*, they'd be trading information. But if it's women, it's gossip. That is what the Liliths specialize in. Secrets." She sets the pencil down with a clack. "That is the cost of entry to the Liliths. A secret."

"I . . . don't understand."

Her look says she may have overestimated my intelligence. "If you want to be a Lilith, you need to provide me with a secret. About yourself. It proves loyalty."

My eyes narrow. "You mean it *secures* loyalty. Blackmail."

Her brows rise. "That would go against our code. We don't use secrets on each other. It is simply tradition. You provide the Dux with a secret, and she puts it into the vault. It's like . . ." Her lips purse as if searching for a word. "An initiation ritual. Being Liliths, we don't do anything as silly as ask you to run naked through the school."

"Just give away a personal secret."

She eyes me and then nods. "You're suspicious because this is new to you. If you'd grown up as a Chamberlain, you'd know all about Westdale's societies and their rules, and you'd have come here knowing which one you wanted to join and, for the Liliths, the cost of joining. Talk to Polly or Isolde if you have concerns. Even Theo, who would gladly give a secret if it got him into the Liliths, poor boy."

"What if I don't have a secret?"

"Impossible." She continues drawing. "Everyone has done something. Stolen a friend's boyfriend or girlfriend. Stolen a car for a joyride. Stolen a silk blouse from someone's closet. You're a teenager."

"I'm a teenager who's been too busy trying to survive to steal anything more than an extra apple from the healthy snack bin."

The words come out harsher than I intend, and when she turns a slow, steady stare on me, I brace.

Seconds tick past. Then she says, "That was cavalier of me, and I apologize. However, I believe you do have a secret that would qualify. Why did your mother leave Westdale?"

I try not to exhale in relief. This is an easy one. "Because she was pregnant with me."

"When were you born, Liliana? What month?"

"May."

"So your mother left in April 2005 because she was pregnant with you, and you were born in May 2006? Thirteen months later?"

"I . . ." My cheeks heat. Allegra is right, of course.

"This is all new to me," I say. "I didn't even know my mom went to Westdale until yesterday, and I haven't had time to work it out."

"Understandable. But the story is that Rosalyn Chamberlain got pregnant and dropped out. Because no one knew about you, the dates didn't matter. They still don't matter to anyone who doesn't do some basic math and realize the problem."

"Which you did."

An elegant shrug. "It's my business to know what I can about a potential new recruit. But since you don't know why your mother actually left, you can't give me that secret. So, here is my offer. If you want into the Liliths, you'll promise to *find* me that secret."

"Like a layaway plan?"

Her expression says she has no idea what that is, because of course she wouldn't.

"I'd get admitted now," I say, "and owe you the secret when I find it."

"I presume you can do that?"

I actually love challenges like this. I do well in school because I work my ass off, but my true talent is research. I adore solving mysteries, and in the business world, that translates into research. Digging up everything I can on a company, a product, a CEO.

Finding out a secret about my own past? I already planned to, right?

"Can I think about it?" I say.

"Of course." She rips the paper from the pad and hands it to me. On it is a sketch of a dress similar to what I'm wearing.

"If you like it, I'll have it made. My dressmaker comes this weekend, and she can take your measurements. She isn't cheap, but it will be worth it. For the design, I'd only ask that I can take a photo for my portfolio."

"Uh, thank you."

A hand flap says that isn't necessary. I promise to talk to her later, and then I slip out to catch up with Theo and the others.

I find Theo in the lounge, in a large group that I'm grateful to join. By nine, it starts to break up. I doubt anyone really sleeps so early, which means this is when they sneak in more homework. I leave with Isolde while Theo and Polly are deep in conversation. Isolde's room is on the second level, so I leave her there and continue up to the third. As I'm using the keypad on my door, someone says, "You must be the new girl."

I automatically assess tone before responding. I can't tell with this one, so I turn with a pleasant smile.

Behind me stands a girl from my math class, meaning she definitely knows I'm new. She has light brown skin, short dark hair, and piercing golden-brown eyes that make me feel like I have something stuck to my face.

She isn't alone. Jayden has one foot on the landing and the other on the step below it as he leans against the wall, as if still deciding whether to come up.

"Liliana Chamberlain," I say as I thrust out my hand to the girl.

She looks at it like I'm offering a dead fish and says, "I hear you're going for Optima."

I frown. "Who said that?"

"Don't pull that shit. Everyone knows it."

"But you said you heard it. That implies someone said it."

Her eyes narrow. "It's a figure of speech."

"I have no idea whether I'll be competing. I only arrived today. You must be Natalia. You *are* going for Optima, right?"

If her eyes narrow any more, she won't be able to see. "Who told you that?"

"I was told who's expected to run when we declare on March first. You're not Theo and probably not Cosmo." I look over at the guy, standing there, silently. "Also, I already met your boyfriend. That makes you Natalia. Now, while it was nice to meet you both, I—"

"No public school kid is ever going to win the Optima race. Not even a Chamberlain. If you really *are* a Chamberlain, and I'm not so sure. Kind of convenient, how you appeared from nowhere. I'm not buying it."

I shrug. "Okay, you're not buying it. Now, if—"

"I'm trying to be helpful, Liliana. You don't want to run for Optima."

"Oh! Can I guess the rest of this warning? That I don't know what I'm up against, being a poor little public school girl, and the big bad private school kids will eat me alive?"

Her mouth opens.

I cut her off. "I haven't decided whether I'll run for Optima, but scaring me off won't be that easy."

"Maybe you want to make it that easy," Jayden says.

His lips curve into a smile that has my fingers tightening on my doorknob. He moves up that last step and looms over me, so close I can smell dinner on his breath.

Jayden continues, "You know the real difference between public school kids and private school kids? Consequences. Kids at your old school had to face them. We don't. We have the best lawyers money can buy and a school that'll do anything to keep its reputation squeaky clean."

"Hey!" a voice says, and Jayden flies backward down the first step.

Jayden recovers, fists rising. Maddox stands behind him on the stairs. He looks at Jayden's clenched fists. Maddox moves to stand on the same step.

"You really wanna do that, sport?" Maddox says.

"Don't call me—"

"Then back the fuck off or be prepared to use those." Maddox waves at the clenched fists, which Jayden slowly withdraws, even as he glares.

"This isn't like you, Moreno," Natalia murmurs. "Taking an interest in . . . well, anyone."

Maddox cuts his eyes her way and snorts. "Don't pull that shit. I've hauled your guard dog away from his quarry before. You really need to tighten his leash, Natalia. He has a bad habit of cornering people half his size." Maddox moves closer to Jayden; he's leaner, but about an inch taller.

Jayden snorts and waves like he's done with this. Natalia eyes us, her gaze going from me to Maddox, speculating.

Maddox purses his lips, blowing her a kiss, and I bite back a laugh as she flushes and quickly turns away to head down the stairs with Jayden.

As they walk away, I take deep breaths. I stood up to Natalia, and I'd been proud of myself for that, but Jayden spooked me. Now I'm flustered and also annoyed, wishing Maddox had given me the chance to regroup. But also, maybe, glad he had stepped in while being embarrassed that he had to.

Damn it.

When they're gone, Maddox looks at me and shakes his head. "No, Chamberlain."

"No what?"

"No, you couldn't have won that round, and yeah, you're pissed off at needing rescue, but you did. Deal with it."

"I never said any of that."

He waves at me. "Your face. Your eyes. They're screaming it. Don't ever play poker."

"Jayden caught me off guard."

"Yep, because that's his thing. First week here, Natalia saw he'd be useful and snatched him up. She's going to play dirty in the Optima race, and he's her muscle, and he's too clueless to realize he's being used. Stay out of their way, okay?" He waves at the door. "This you?"

I nod.

"Well, go on in. Get some sleep. And . . ." He exhales. "Look, I heard some of that conversation. You snapped back good,

Chamberlain, and I know that seems like the thing to do, but with some people . . . maybe not, okay?"

When my jaw sets, he sighs again and says, "And you don't like that advice either. Fine. Whatever. Just . . . Jayden's right. Nothing sticks here. Be careful, okay?"

He waits until I'm in my room, and I turn, wanting to apologize, to say I know he's just trying to help, but he's already gone.

EIGHT

It takes a while for me to fall asleep, and then it's fitful, me tossing and turning, all the anxieties of the day rushing back. I've been congratulating myself on coping so well, but the truth is that I'm madly stuffing all my fears and worries into boxes and shoving them on a shelf, and once night comes, all those boxes topple down on my head.

I'm struggling to accept that I'm never going back to my old school, my old life. Whenever I've changed schools before I've always had time to say proper goodbyes. Mom and Dad were so careful about that—moving during summer break and telling me at least a month in advance.

Why had we moved so much? I'd never asked. It'd just been part of my life, and it wasn't as if my parents woke me at midnight, telling me to pack my things. But it also wasn't as if my dad had the kind of job where your company moves you around. He'd worked at this and that, usually in an office, and each time we moved, he changed jobs.

I know people can move around chasing work, but Dad never had that problem. When we met his bosses, they always made a point of telling my mom what a great employee he was, how happy they were to have him. But then we'd hit the road again.

Whatever struggles we endured as a family, whatever tensions I felt hearing my parents whispering late at night about moving again, I could hold fast to three indisputable facts:

My mom and dad were both amazing parents.

They loved each other.

They loved me.

As a family, we were outrageously happy, and losing them was . . .

Sometimes I look at myself in the mirror, and I see the cracks, a shattered girl painstakingly pieced back together, those cracks still visible. I want to imagine myself as one of those Japanese bowls repaired with gold. I love the concept of kintsugi—that the breaks make me stronger and better. Someday, I want to put one of those bowls on a shelf and say, "That's me." But it's not me, not yet. My cracks are fixed with the cheapest paste.

What keeps me going is knowing that, as much as I've lost, I *had* more than most people ever get. My parents were incredible, and everything I am today I owe to them. I might be at Westdale because of Mom's name, but if I flourish here, it will be a tribute to what they made me.

And yet, I have questions. So many questions.

When a floorboard creaks overhead, I glance up at the ceiling. Another creak, along with the soft pad of footsteps. I ignore it and return to my thoughts.

Did my father go to Westdale? If everyone thought Mom got pregnant here, then that would seem to mean he attended—

Another creak overhead stops me, the footsteps moving on just as I realize that I'm on the top floor. There *can't* be anyone walking up above me.

No, there must be another level. Or I'm just hearing the creak of a very old house.

I roll over in bed and open my nightstand drawer to take out a notepad and pen. I haven't quite shut the blind, so there's enough light for me to see as I jot down notes.

Whether or not I join the Liliths, I still want to answer questions about my parents. I could start with yearbooks. Look up—

My door makes an odd little noise. A low beep that I recognize but . . .

It's the noise it made when I first tried the keyed combination. I'd typed the default in wrong, and it lit up red with that little beep.

Is there someone at my door?

I go very still, and when I strain, I pick up the faint sound of the buttons being pressed. Another error beep.

Someone *is* at my door. Entering the wrong code.

Because they have the wrong room. Sure, we're supposed to be in bed by eleven on school nights, but when I was talking to the others tonight, they assured me it isn't as if some kind of alarm sounds if we leave our room. Westdale is considered a transitional state between boarding school and college—there's a curfew, but it's your responsibility to follow it, because you're old enough to make your own bad choices.

Someone is returning from another room—talking with a friend or fooling around with a partner—and they tried my door by accident. Except my room is right by the stairs, which makes it hard to mistake for another one. And it's very clearly marked with my name.

After Ms. Dimitriou left us this morning, Cecilia showed me how to change the code and insisted I do it immediately for safety. The "last four digits of your phone number" is a very easy code to crack, especially if that's everyone's default.

What if someone entered that default code, presuming that as a new student I hadn't changed it yet?

What if someone is trying to get into my room, while I sleep?

I tell myself I'm overreacting, but I still slip to the peephole and look out. No one's there.

I pull on sweatpants and tuck in my oversized sleep shirt. I open the door and peer both ways. No one in the hall. No one descending the stairs.

For a moment, I pause, thinking. Then I slip out, creep along the corridor and peek around the corner.

Empty.

I ease along, rolling my bare feet. At the end of the hall, there's an attic door in the ceiling, like in a house we'd rented once, but this one doesn't have any way to lower it.

I'd heard footsteps overhead. Was someone creeping through the attic? The same someone who tried my door?

Okay, I've definitely read too many thrillers. Clearly, whoever came this way must have ducked into one of the bedrooms I passed.

Someone tried to get into my room. Was it just a prank? Or . . .

I don't know what that "or" would have been. But I do know one thing: Maddox is right; I need to be careful. I sleep with the light on that night.

I've just drifted off when someone raps softly at my door.

"Lil?"

My eyes snap open. That sounds like Theo.

It's the middle of the night. Why would Theo Dubois be at my door?

Someone had just tried to get into my room. Someone whose own room is presumably on this floor. Someone who'd know the default door code, because he asked for my phone number.

My stomach clenches.

He'd been too nice earlier today, and I knew that, deep down. Guys like Theo Dubois aren't nice to girls like me, not unless they have an agenda.

Did his story about wanting more Optima competition make sense? No, and yet I've been doing backflips to convince myself it does because I want to justify his interest in me. I know that interest isn't romantic. Sure, he'd said he'd seen me and wanted to get to know me better, and my ego would love to believe it, but I'm not that gullible.

Theo suspects I'll run for Optima, and he's setting himself up as an ally to control the competition. Part of that *could* mean sneaking into my room at night and doing something like planting drugs to knock me from the race before we even declare we're running.

"Liliana?"

Is he trying to get me to *let* him in now? Take another run at whatever he has planned? Because of course I'll let a hot guy in at . . .

I lift my head to peer at the clock: 7:54.

I bolt upright. That can't be right. My alarm was set for seven—

An image flashes. My alarm going off. Me smacking it to silence and then shutting my eyes, just for a second.

Theo is here because we'd agreed to meet at seven-thirty so he could walk me through the breakfast routine.

I yank on my sweatpants, tug at my shirt, and then crack open the door to peek out. Theo stands there, looking sleepy himself, his hazel eyes clouded with concern.

"You okay?" he whispers.

"I accidentally turned off my alarm," I say. "Now I'm late and—"

Theo lifts his hands. "It's fine. Breakfast isn't a served meal. Classes start at eight-thirty. But are you okay? Ma—Someone said your light was on last night. Couldn't sleep?"

"Wired from yesterday."

"It must be overwhelming," he says, leaning in as I open the door another crack. He smells of aftershave, his hair still damp, his eyes softer than usual, as if he hasn't woken and pulled on his armor yet.

I swallow hard. Yesterday, Theo Dubois was *a lot*. But at 8 a.m., standing outside my bedroom door, sleepy and unguarded and worried about me and smelling so good?

Too much.

I have to fight the urge to withdraw into my room. Or to grab him by the shirtfront and *pull* him into—

Where the hell did that come from?

Lack of sleep. Definitely.

"Lil?"

"Sorry. I'm out of it. Thanks for the wake-up."

"Do you eat breakfast?"

I quirk a half-smile. "Most important meal of the day."

A laugh that's far too soft for Theo Dubois. "It is. Can I grab you something?"

"No, I just need a few minutes to get ready. I'll still have time to eat."

"I'll wait for you. Fifteen?"

"Ten."

"See you then."

Breakfast really is informal. Most students just grab and go. We take our plates into the lounge and talk quietly as we eat.

I don't mention someone being at my door last night. Theo had already warned me about Natalia and Jayden, and maybe I should tell about that encounter, but . . .

I need to be more careful about trusting Theo. Last night, Natalia tried to scare me out of the race. Theo could be taking another tact, one that would work far better: charismatic guy befriends the new girl on the pretense of teaming up, and gradually convinces her not to run.

I'm also aware that I can't trust myself. I would love to think "charismatic guy" is never going to work with me. A day ago, I might have actually believed that. But then I met Theo, and I have discovered I am not as immune as I thought.

I'm more concerned about what Theo said earlier. That someone saw my light on last night. I didn't miss Theo saying "Ma—" before rerouting. Theo's redirection seems significant. He was avoiding saying the name, because it's someone he's not supposed to be friendly with.

Maddox.

How would Maddox have seen my light on? And why would he be telling Theo?

NINE

After a quick breakfast, Theo and I head to class—the same class, apparently. We're both in General Science, which really is like what I pictured my English class would be: science for those with no interest in pursuing the discipline. It's mostly tech, which I like, and it'll satisfy the breadth requirement, which is all I need.

Allegra's in the same class, and when it ends, she falls in step with me as Theo stays behind to talk to a classmate.

"It's morning break," she says. "Twenty minutes when we are supposed to go out for fresh air, as if we are wilting violets. All I need is coffee."

We walk into the dining hall, where there's a coffee bar that'd been shut down by the time Theo and I arrived for breakfast, leaving us to the two self-serve espresso machines, which were fancier than anything I'd ever seen.

The machines are still operating, but there's also a big industrial one, manned by a silver-haired barista who moves with the speed of a pro, filling orders while chatting with the students.

"Miss Allegra," he says. "The usual?"

"Please."

The barista's gaze settles on me as he starts Allegra's coffee. "And our new arrival. Miss Liliana. Do you have a favorite?"

"A mocha?" I say hesitantly. "Half-sweet, if you could."

He smiles. "I can do that. Milk choice?"

"Regular, please."

"Dark chocolate or milk?"

"Umm..."

"You're probably used to milk chocolate, so let's go half-dark and see what you think. Whipped cream?"

"Yes, please."

We move down the counter... to a tiered tray of patisserie-worthy baked goods.

"I could get used to this," I say, smiling as I select a tiny cream puff. "An actual barista and—"

I stop. I'm not with Theo. This is Allegra, who has probably never gotten excited over anything in her life, and definitely not for baristas and fancy pastries.

"Sorry if I'm being gauche," I say. "It's all very new to me."

"Gauche." She rolls the word around. "How is it gauche to marvel at going to a school with a world-class barista and Parisian pastry chef?" She sips her espresso as the barista passes it over. "The greater sin, I believe, would be indifference. To accept this as our due."

She takes a mini almond croissant and heads for the door, and I realize this is just how Allegra talks. In pronouncements. I don't think they're meant to *be* pronouncements. They just sound like that, with her cool demeanor and measured way of speaking.

Also, confidence. The confidence of knowing that your words are important and that others will listen.

"The mocha is acceptable?" she says as we walk out the back door.

"It's incredible."

"Enzo is an artist. Tell him you liked it. Let him work with it until he finds exactly the recipe for you. It's not a 'bother.' It is what he does, and he'll be pleased once he's found the one."

"Okay."

"I see you've changed your look today. Is that intentional?"

I brace. "I'm still figuring out my style."

"You don't need one signature style. You can have several." She eyes the vintage peasant top and jeans with heart appliqués. "The jeans, yes. The shirt, maybe. Not the sneakers. You're going for bohemian, yes?"

"Uh . . . sure."

"It works for you. We can adjust the specifics. Starting with footwear."

She continues talking as we walk, and I keep waiting for her to ask what I've decided about the Liliths, but she doesn't. She seems to be giving me time, and that's a relief.

Theo recommends I eat lunch with his society, the Apollos. He says it's a good way to get to know more classmates and also to do a little society-shopping, in case the Liliths don't suit me.

As Theo explains, in the early days, your choice of society was obvious: Lilith for girls; the Apollos for art; Mercury for industry and commerce; Hephaestus for science. Today, the lines are less clearly drawn. Girls can join any society, and if you were, say, a digital designer, you might look at either Apollo for the artistic side or Hephaestus for the tech.

Given that Westdale is a school for rich kids from rich families, Mercury is the biggest society and Apollo is the smallest after the Liliths. It has nine students, with Theo as the Dux. Eight are here today, and I've already met two: Carlee, a writer, and Kai, whose father is the lead singer of a band my parents played on repeat.

The Apollos are all about creativity. The lunch topic of discussion is Taylor Swift, except the usual "love her, hate her" debate doesn't enter into it, and by the end, I couldn't even say for sure who is and is not a fan.

The discussion is about Swift as an artist. Ideas flow so fast and sharp that my brain is popping. I even get a chance to contribute, raising the topic of Swift's issues with her first label and the subsequent "Taylor's Version" albums. I'm interested in that as a fan, of course, but I'm even more interested in it as a future MBA. Where do corporations go wrong in their dealings with artists and how can the relationship be fairer and more mutually beneficial? The Apollos answer my questions from the artist side, and Kai and I get into a wonderful debate.

The afternoon whizzes by, and then it's study period. Isolde has a meeting with the Liliths, so we plan to meet up just before dinner. Until then, I finally get a chance to start pursuing a mystery . . . and to check out what I'm sure will become my favorite room in the school: the library.

Like the house itself, the library is straight out of a gothic novel in the most delicious way—like those online photos that bookworms label "reader goals" but you know the picture is AI because no real library looks like that.

The Westdale library is all dark wood, with stacks to the ceilings, creating endless nooks furnished with massive leather armchairs and embroidered chaise lounges and plush seats with ottomans. Every study desk must be an antique. Some even have those old-fashioned magnifying glasses—the ones on tripods that you set over a book page, and I don't know if anyone uses them or if they're just for ambiance, but I still want one.

Then there are the books. I'm surrounded by the smell of first editions. Okay, maybe first editions don't smell any different, but knowing they're firsts turns that old-book scent into the headiest perfume. I so badly want to browse, but I have a mission: Find my parents in the yearbooks.

Locating the yearbook itself is easy. While Mom didn't graduate, she's there, in all her glory, grinning from her official photo and a half dozen others, and I linger over those, and yes, I cry a little, careful not to let my tears fall on the page.

There's no sign of Will Green in these pages. I've already done an internet search, of course, but it's such a common name that I get endless results, none of them ever about Dad. And searching on his name plus "Westdale" hadn't gotten me anything.

Maybe he lived in a nearby town? Or Savannah? Sure, his accent had been northern and his mom had lived in Vermont, but maybe he'd moved to Georgia? But even now, as I rerun those online searches with added information, I get nothing.

My watch vibrates, my alarm telling me it's time to meet Isolde. I throw open the massive oak library door—and crash into a stranger, sending a book flying from his hand.

"Oh my god," I say. "I'm so sorry."

I pick up the book, and he just laughs softly.

"Liliana, right?"

I nod. We haven't been introduced, but he's the guy Allegra kicked out of his seat in English yesterday. He's tall, with olive skin, brown eyes behind glasses, and a mop of light brown hair.

"Cosmo," he says. "Rumor has it you're running for Optima."

"Rumor has it you are, too."

A wry smile and he says, "Parents," as if that explains everything, which I guess it could.

"I'm not sure if I'll run yet," I say. "I'm just getting a feel for things right now."

"Well, hot tip. Theo Dubois will be the guy to beat. I've, uh . . ." He shifts his textbook. "I've seen you two together. You seem friendly."

"He's been showing me around."

"Just . . . be careful. I like Theo." His cheeks darken in a blush. "I mean, as a person, though, obviously, he's very . . . Er, so, just be careful."

"In case he's setting me up for a fall?"

One shoulder lifts in a shrug. "I'm not saying he would. Just . . . he's a lot more cutthroat—and ambitious—than he seems. We went to the same feeder school in California. Anyway, if you do run, watch your back." He pauses and then hurries on. "But don't let that discourage you. Competition is healthy, right?"

"It is."

"Anyway, nice to meet you."

"Likewise, and thanks for the tips."

"Anytime. I want this to be a fair race. Aboveboard, you know?"

"I do," I say, and I agree, but something tells me Theo is right. Cosmo isn't going to make it through this race. He couldn't even stand up to Allegra yesterday.

How do I feel about that? I should say I feel bad. He seems like a good guy.

But one fewer competitor is still one fewer competitor. And Theo isn't the only "nice" person who's a lot more ambitious than they appear.

After dinner, it's games night, and I play with Theo, Kai, Isolde, and Polly. Then Allegra needs to speak to me, and Theo suggests the library, saying it'll be empty at this hour. One student *is* studying there . . . until Allegra marches over and stands in front of her. The poor girl scrambles up, gathering her things.

As the girl passes me, I murmur "Thank you," and she looks over, as if startled.

"Oh. Uh, okay. No problem."

Allegra follows the girl and shuts the door behind her. Then she turns to me. "You haven't given me an answer, and I know you had lunch with the Apollos today. Is that some kind of negotiation tactic?"

"Uh, no, it's a 'I just got here yesterday and I'm working things through' tactic."

"The Liliths will give you prestige and power. A foot up in the Westdale Optima race."

"And I will give *them* prestige and power if I defeat Theo."

That sets her back, and she eyes me with that look that says she's recalibrating her opinion of me. Then she says, "Female friendships are important. A well-rounded social life will be an asset. If you only have male friends, the Optimas will think you're overly concerned with male attention, easily distracted, however unfair that assessment might be."

I walk over and plunk into a chair. "You don't have to convince me, Allegra. I really am just thinking it through."

She holds up a book pulled from her bag. "Every Dux is expected to keep a journal. It's our history, and only Liliths can read them. This is the 2005 one."

She opens it, and when I see my mother's handwriting, my heart flips.

Another person would tempt me by reading passages and hinting at secrets. Allegra just snaps it shut and waits for my answer.

"I'll let you know tomorrow," I say.

Considering how little I slept the night before, I expect an easy and deep slumber.

Yeah . . . Not when my lack of sleep was due to someone trying to break into my room.

At midnight, I open the window for some fresh air and notice someone is outside, sitting on a bench in the yard. The figure turns and squints up. It's Maddox. He sees me and seems to nod. Then he goes back to chilling, legs outstretched.

I nibble my lip, considering. Then I pull on my jeans with my sleep shirt and head barefoot down the stairs.

The back exit is locked with a code, which we're all given. I slowly open the door. When no sirens wail, I slip out and relock it behind me.

I cross the yard, the trimmed grass cool and damp under my bare feet. Glancing over my shoulder, I see we're directly across from my room, which is how Maddox would have seen my light on if he'd been out here last night. It still doesn't explain why he'd noticed or why he told Theo.

When I'm about ten feet from the bench, I stop.

"I'm not going to bug you, Maddox. I just wanted to say you were right last night. About snapping back at Natalia and Jayden. I should have just dropped it."

"We're good, Chamberlain."

I wait a moment. Then I say, "Do you want me to go back inside?"

"Your choice. Don't mind company, but I don't need it either, if you feel obligated."

When I don't walk away, he pats the spot beside him. I lower myself onto it.

This morning, I'd thought Theo seemed softer, sleepy, and not yet himself. With Maddox, night seems to bring the same change, his hard edges softening.

He holds up a baggie with rainbow-colored candy bears. "Want?"

"Those aren't regular gummy bears, are they?" I say.

A soft chuckle. "They are not."

Well, I guess that explains his mellow mood. When I don't speak, he finally glances over and sees me looking at the bag.

"They're just edibles," he says. "Low dose, and they're actually prescription, but I'm fine with sharing. Just don't tell anyone. My first week here, I got three people asking me if I could get them a little something, because obviously . . ." He waves at himself. "Apparently I look like the school dealer. But you're welcome to one."

"I've . . . never tried anything." When he glances over, I shrug, hoping I don't blush. "I've always had one thing going for me." I tap my forehead. "I guess I was just scared of doing anything that might mess that up."

"Ah, got it." He starts to move the baggie aside, but I reach for it.

"I'll take one," I say.

He peers at me. "If you're trying to impress me, Chamberlain . . ."

"I'm not. I've been kinda stressed, and if that can help, I'm going to give it a try."

He studies me. "If you do, you're stuck out here for the next hour. I need to be sure everything's okay."

"Deal."

I take the gummy. After I eat it, we just sit there, looking out over the lawn for about ten minutes. Then Maddox stretches further to lean his head on the bench back and look up into the stars. When I do the same, he chuckles softly but says nothing.

After about twenty minutes of stargazing, I say, "Can I ask you something?"

"Guess so, now that you've cornered me by making me your first-edible watchdog." He looks over. "Kidding. You can ask, but . . ." He blows out a breath. "Look, let's get this out of the way. If you came out here to ask me about Theo, just say so."

"Theo?"

"You know we used to be friends so . . ."

"I came out to apologize. And my question wasn't about Theo."

He looks over, gaze locking with mine. "No?"

I meet his eyes. "Why would it be?"

"Uh, because he's Theo Dubois? I know him better than anyone here, so . . ." He spreads his hands, the left one nearly hitting me. "I am the Theo Dubois information pipeline."

He looks over. "If you like Theo, tell him. He'll either feel the same or he won't, and if he doesn't, he'll let you down easy."

I round my eyes. "Oh, please help me, Maddox. Theo's just so . . . so . . ." I squee. "*Everything.* Tell me his secrets. How can I get him to like me? *Does* he like me? Can you pass him a note? Please, please, please?"

"You jest, but do you know how many times I've had that? Since fucking sixth grade. Maybe fifth."

"I've been here two days, Maddox. Two days ago I was trying to figure out how to sell our fridge so I could buy food. Now I'm at an elite boarding school with a professional barista."

"Wait, you were trying to sell—"

"Not the point." I jab a finger at him. "The absolute last thing on my mind is getting some guy to like me."

"Not some guy. Theo Dubois."

I mask my unease with an eye roll. "I get it. He's a big deal. Never heard of him before yesterday, but apparently, he's super-special, and if he's talking to me, I should be all . . ." I squee again, and Maddox laughs.

"You're kind of adorable, Chamberlain. That THC is kicking in, huh?"

"I think so. How should I feel?"

"How *do* you feel?"

"Relaxed." I inhale and exhale. "God, that feels good."

"Been a while, huh?" He looks over. "About the fridge . . ."

"It was a dumb idea, okay? There wasn't much left, and yes, obviously you can't sell the appliances in a rented apartment."

"Why not?"

I look over. "Because they come with the apartment."

His brows knit. "They do?"

I sputter a laugh. "No rented apartments in your life, huh? Appliances usually come with the unit. So, selling them would be . . ."

"Tricky?"

"A wee bit."

He bursts out laughing. "That's awesome. I'm sure you could have figured it out, though."

"Eventually."

A moment of silence. Then he looks over. "Am I supposed to say that it really sucks that you had to consider that?"

"I'd rather you didn't."

"That's what I figured."

We stare at the sky again until he says, "So what was your question?"

"Question?"

He sputters. "You've had one low-dose gummy, Chamberlain. You okay?"

I lift my middle finger, and he laughs.

Then I say, "Cecilia said you're supposed to watch out for me, right?"

He tenses. "Right."

"I'm not going to ask why."

"Good, 'cause I wouldn't answer. Yeah, I owe Cecilia, but that's between me and her, and all you need to know is that my debt won you a bodyguard, guide, whatever you want to call it. I know we got off on the wrong foot. I was not, by the way, insinuating that you didn't belong here. It was a joke that landed wrong. Also, not really a joke. This place is . . ."

He looks over at the house, and shadows cross his face before he shakes them off. "Think of it this way. When you ride a bike, do you wear a helmet?"

"Of course."

"Because you like wearing helmets?"

"Uh, no. Does anyone?"

"Okay, so I'm the helmet. You don't want me. You'd rather not need me. But you do. So just put on your helmet."

I stare at him and then sputter a laugh.

"Fine, it was a shitty analogy," he says. "Was that your question? Confirming that Cecilia asked me to look out for you?"

"No, it was . . ." I take a deep breath. "Who can I trust here?"

"No one," he says, without missing a beat.

"So I shouldn't trust you?"

A hard look. "I meant besides me."

"So I shouldn't trust Theo."

He rocks back, and I swear his lips form one word. *Fuck.*

I push on. "Theo has been showing me the ropes, and I'm not sure his reasoning for helping me is sound. You're saying I shouldn't trust him."

"I never said that."

"You said trust no one except—"

"Fuck. Fine. Theo . . ." He runs his hands through his hair. "Theo's good."

"So I can trust him?"

His voice drops, just a little. "Yeah, you can trust Theo."

"Thank you."

He gives me a sidelong glance. "I know I'm not exactly the friendliest guy here, Liliana, but you can come to me about anyone. Like I said, I'm supposed to be your bodyguard, mentor, spiritual guide, whatever." He reaches over, the back of his hand brushing mine. "You're doing good, kid."

I make a face. "Thanks."

"You're welcome. Now enjoy the stars with me. That gummy will wear off enough soon, and you can go to bed."

I slip into my bedroom, and my foot slides on a folder that's been shoved under my door. It's taped shut, as if to make sure the contents stay secure until opened. With my nail, I slit the tape as I walk to my bed. Inside are two pages.

The top one is the printout of a form with the letterhead for Willow Grove Center, in San Francisco. There's a tagline below the name.

Helping Teens since 1965

I frown and glance down, only to stop at the first line.

Patient name: Maddox Alejandro Perez-Moreno

My gaze skims down, over his birthdate and other particulars to "Date of Admission." Two years ago. And then the next part: *Following a breakdown, Maddox was admitted to Willow Grove by his mother. The patient was in obvious mental distress and residential care was determined to be the safest—*

The rest had been redacted before the form was printed. A note in the margin reads: "Thought you might like to know about your new friend. If you want the rest, wait for instructions."

I slap the page down, my blood pounding. Pounding with rage, which I suspect is *not* the reaction the sender intended.

Two years ago, Maddox spent time in a hospital for mental health issues. That's his business. *His.*

Whoever sent this is implying he's dangerous. I know teens *can* suffer from mental illnesses that make them dangerous to others—a friend's older brother had schizophrenia, but it was managed, and clearly whatever Maddox has is also managed. Which means none of this is my business, and I should never have seen it.

I go to slap the folder shut before I can see the second page, but I catch a glimpse. It's another printout, this one of an article. There's a photo attached, and when I see that photo, I freeze.

It's Theo. He's a little younger, and he's snarling, hazel eyes hard, one hand outstretched as if to smack the camera away.

The headline screams *Hollywood Golden Boy Accused of Sexual Misconduct*

The article isn't long. Half of it is background on Theo—who his parents are, the fact he's been a "paparazzi fixture" since birth and, according to this article, has turned into a tabloid fixture for very different reasons. First he'd been photographed dating a seventeen-year-old actress when he was thirteen. Then he was in the tabloids for dating a teen soccer star, the start of his "openly bisexual lifestyle," a phrase that has my hackles rising, as if that's part of his "misbehavior."

There are rumors of DUI charges that went away. Rumors of sexual misconduct allegations that went away. Rumors of trashed hotel rooms that, yep, went away. But now, the article gloats, the Teflon-coated kid is in real trouble because he offered the starring role in his second short film to a twenty-one-year-old actor in return for "sexual favors," which were given . . . and the starring role was not.

I read the article twice, my stomach clenching more each time. I don't care about the other rumors. It's the coercion allegation that has my stomach turning, and I don't want to believe it, but it's right there, in print, listing the actor's name, with quotes from him and from officials confirming that charges have been laid and a lawsuit filed.

What was it Theo said?

I love it when people don't know who I am. A chance to make a bad impression all on my own.

I swallow hard. When he implied he had a reputation, I took that to mean the typical bad-boy stuff I see referenced in this article. A busy dating schedule. Partying. Drinking.

Not using his position to get sexual favors.

There's another note on this one, similar to the first, implying there's more dirt on Theo, and I'll have the chance to get it.

So who sent this?

Who would send me secrets?

The girl who deals in them.

Allegra Khan.

I didn't accept her offer fast enough, and now she's playing hardball, showing me why befriending guys here is a very bad idea.

And the only thing it's actually doing is making me think I want to take a page from Maddox's book . . . and choose no one except myself.

TEN

Yesterday, Theo had suggested we make a routine of grabbing breakfast together. Since he didn't firm up actual plans to meet, I'm telling myself he changed his mind. Which means if I just happen to eat early and miss him . . . ?

I'm at the breakfast room the moment it opens. I grab food, head to the library, and tuck into a corner with my math textbook. Yes, we're allowed to have food and drinks in the library despite it being full of rare books. If we spill something, our families can afford to pay for the damage.

At seven-twenty, I get a text on my new watch.

Theo
Swinging by your room in ten.
LMK if I'm too early

Even seeing his name makes my stomach twist. I want to leave that message unread and pretend I never saw it, but . . .

What had Maddox said?

Don't ever play poker.

I can bristle at that, but he's right.

> **Me**
> Already ate. Sorry

A long pause, and I remind myself that if he's the guy in that article then I don't care whether I hurt his feelings.

If he's the guy in that article.

But he must be, right? It's a legal accusation. If that's the guy he is, I want nothing to do with him.

There's that "if" again . . .

Damn it.

> **Me**
> Getting some math work in.
> Still need to catch up

When he doesn't answer, I silently curse myself. Okay, here I was thinking the pause meant he was trying to figure out why I ducked our informal breakfast date, and really, he'd just accepted my answer and moved on.

I'm about to put away my phone when he starts to type, those three dots pulsing. They stop, and I wait, but then they pulse again, as if he deleted a response and is retyping.

It takes a solid three minutes for him to reply.

> **Theo**
> NP. I know you're worried about math

> **Me**
> I wasn't sure whether
> breakfast was a firm plan

Theo
It's all good. You studying right now?

Me
Yep

Theo
So... not up for company, I'm guessing?

Me
Sorry

He sends a thumbs-up, and a "maybe lunch," and I don't reply.

I want to confront Allegra about the file. I'm hoping to do that at morning break, but she's nowhere to be found. Who I do find, far too easily? Theo.

I'm in line for my coffee when a voice says, "Not stalking you," and I turn to see Theo where Theo had not been before. Behind him is Cosmo, busy studying something on his phone, as if he hadn't just let Theo skip in line, and I'm annoyed on Cosmo's behalf, wanting to tell him that if he's honestly running for Optima, he at least needs to be able to tell Theo Dubois no.

"You didn't answer my text about lunch," Theo says, hands in his pockets. He's smiling, but there's a tension behind his eyes.

"I'm not sure what my plans are."

"Okay..."

"There's a lot to catch up on for classes, and I'm feeling overwhelmed."

"Anything I can do to help?"

"I just need space," I say.

"Space . . ."

"I'm going to keep today free, I think, and study. I know you said it looks bad if we study too much, and I appreciate the advice, but getting caught up is more important."

"And if I offer to bring lunch to the library for you, that'd be a no?"

I shift my book bag. "That's very nice, but you don't need to put yourself out."

"Put myself out," he repeats slowly. "Okay . . ." A pause, and then he lowers his voice. "You can tell me to back off, Lil. I know I can come on strong."

"It's not that."

"Just that you're very busy."

"Right."

He nods and looks away. Thankfully, at that moment, I'm up, and I can place my order with Enzo. I do that, and when I move aside to wait for it, I glance back to Theo, bracing for him to order and move up beside me again.

But all I see is his back, heading out the door.

Theo's waiting for me when I get out of business class. He lifts two fingers.

"Two minutes of your time," he says, his expression unreadable. "Then you can get lunch and go study."

I nod and he leads me down the hall to an empty classroom. Once we're inside, he shuts the door but doesn't push it completely closed. Then he moves so he's not blocking my path if I want to leave, and guilt darts through me.

Does this seem like the kind of guy who'd do what's in that article?

"I don't play games, Lil," he says.

I bristle. "I'm not—"

"I don't think this is a game. But I do think you aren't being honest with me. Cards on the table. That's the only way I play. If you feel chased, tell me, and I'll back off."

"I don't. I'm just—"

"Very, very busy and barely able to look at me."

My cheeks heat. "I'm overwhelmed. That's all."

"Did someone tell you something about me?"

My head jerks up, eyes meeting his even as I curse myself for reacting. "Tell me what?"

He throws up his hands. "Who knows. There's a very long list of things people say about me. Some of it's true. Some of it is not. I'd very much like the chance to explain which is which."

"Can we talk later?"

He pulls back, head tilting as he looks at me. "Are you blowing me off?"

My jaw tenses. "I wouldn't do that. Before dinner. Okay?"

"Okay."

For lunch, I grab a take-out box, which is intended to be taken into the lounge for socializing, not outside for a walk. Or outside to hide, as the case may be.

This does feel familiar, though—early days at a new school when I hadn't found anyone to eat lunch with. I've done the "eat a sandwich in a bathroom stall" thing. But if the weather was decent, I'd take my lunch to go. I just wanted to get in some exercise. Really.

I exit through the north door and then skirt through the gardens to avoid anyone on the back deck. I'm walking and eating a hoagie and daydreaming when I trip over a pot of new seedlings.

"I'm so sorry," I say to the gardener, who is rising from where he'd been working. I scoop the seedlings and dirt back into the pot. "And now I'm making more of a mess, aren't I?"

The gardener laughs softly. "It's fine, Miss N—Miss Chamberlain."

I look up at him. He's maybe fifty, with graying hair and a kind smile.

"I'm sorry, I don't know your name," I say. "I don't think we've met."

"Burt. And we haven't officially met, but I've seen you. You have your dad's eyes." A soft laugh as he fixes the seedling. "You sound like him, too, getting all flustered and apologizing. He was a great kid."

My breath catches, but before I can speak, he says, "I just heard he passed a few years back. I remember him very well. Not the world's best gardener, but he put his all into it, and that's what counted."

I go very still as his words sink in. "My dad worked with you?"

"Sure did. He was taking a year off school, saving up to go to college." He pauses. "I'm guessing he never went."

"He didn't. I came along and then . . ." I shrug. "He was an amazing dad. Never did much gardening, though."

Burt laughs. "I bet he didn't. Got enough of it here. I'm sorry about your mom, too. I heard she passed recently. Man, they were something else. So much in love." His eyes mist. "Too young to fall that hard, I suppose."

I shake my head. "They might have been young, but it lasted to the end."

"I'm glad to hear that, Miss Chamberlain. I really am. And I'm glad . . ." He trails off. "Well, it's good to see you doing so well. Just . . ." He looks toward the house. "Be careful. Please."

I want to ask what he means, but he's already returning to his work.

Now I know why I couldn't find Dad in the yearbook.

It's almost a cliché, isn't it? The heiress and the gardener? Only Dad had been a kid himself, making money for college, and then he'd met Mom and . . .

And what had Burt started to call me? Not Miss Green. Something that starts with *N*.

I remember seeing staff yearbooks in the library. Of course Westdale has lots of old *student* yearbooks, but they also have one shelf—in a less prominent place—for staff, reaching back twenty years, as if it was only in this century that they acknowledged all the work everyone does to keep Westdale running.

The yearbooks are slim volumes, pretty much just photos of the staff, plus pages where students wrote tributes. I choose the right year and leaf through the alphabetical photos to *G* and I *do* find a Green. Or a Greene.

Burton (Burt) Greene. Senior Gardener.

I thumb forward to the *N*s, and there's my dad, leaning on a rake, smiling.

William (Will) Nelson. Junior Gardener.

There's something odd about the photo. Oh, it's definitely Dad. There's no doubt of that. It's a color photo, with his dark blond hair worn to his shoulders in a shaggy look that I would have teased him about. The bright green eyes are my own, as is the dimple on his left cheek.

The odd thing is the photo itself, which seems to have been glued in. Was it put over another one? I scrape the edge and then flip to the previous page, where I can see that it's as if the original photo was cut out.

I take the book to a table with a light and position it underneath. There are marks right at the edge of the cut-out portion. Tiny pen strokes on my dad's side of the page. As if the part that was cut out had writing on it.

Someone wrote on my dad's photo, and the school cut the whole thing out and replaced it.

I flip to the back pages and skim the tributes. There are three pages of them, students thanking and teasing the staff. On the last page, I see Cecilia's handwriting.

Will, you bastard, you'd better take care of my Rose. JK. I know you will. Miss you both already! Ceci

Tears fill my eyes. My dad would never have seen it, obviously, but Cecilia still wrote it, her tribute to him.

As I examine the pages, I notice a couple of oddly blank spots, surrounded by tributes . . . as if those spots hadn't been blank before.

I move the book under the light and see the ghost of writing, hidden under correction fluid. I adjust the gooseneck lamp for a better look—

My phone buzzes, telling me I need to get to Math.

I'm about to put the book back when I pause, find a spot on the shelf behind me, and slide it there instead.

I finally catch up with Allegra. Or she catches up with me, quite literally, as I'm hurrying to the library on the break between afternoon classes. I want a closer look at that yearbook.

"If you're ducking me," she says, "you needn't bother. I won't hound you for an answer. I trust you will make the correct one."

It takes a moment to realize she's talking about the Liliths.

"I've actually been looking for you," I say. "Do you have a moment?"

"I do."

"Let's step outside."

"Must we? It's terrible weather."

"It's sixty-five degrees, and the sun's out."

"Do you know what sunlight does to the skin?"

I shake my head and walk for the side door. She sighs the most delicate of sighs and follows.

"That file you gave me?" I say, turning to face her. "I don't want to know more. You can keep your secrets, and if I do decide to join the Liliths, it'll be in spite of your bullshit, not because of it."

Silence. Then, "Are you finished?"

"Yes."

"Then let's back up. What file did I email you?"

"Not email. A file folder pushed under my door."

Her brows shoot up. "How clandestine. Honestly, Liliana, can you picture that? Me crouching in the hall to push papers under? What was in this file?"

"Secrets."

"Then I certainly wouldn't have been so careless. Secrets about what?"

"About *who*. Maddox and Theo."

"Ah, someone is trying to drive a wedge between you and your early allies. Interesting. I would suggest you look at who that benefits."

I meet her gaze. "I am."

She shakes her head. "Theo is only a threat to me if he lures you into the Apollos, and it's clear he knows—correctly—that the Liliths are a better fit for you. Maddox is only a threat if he lures you out of the race altogether, to join him on the sidelines, sprawled on the bleachers and silently mocking us for doing exactly what Westdale wants, like puppies pointlessly chasing a ball. I can't see you doing that."

"Okay, thank you. Then I think I know who did it." I turn to head back inside.

She glides into my path. "What are the secrets?"

"Do you honestly expect me to tell *you*? The collector of secrets?"

"I've known Theo and Maddox since we were children. We went to the same private elementary school and then Sierra Forks—the L.A. feeder school for Westdale."

When I still hesitate, she lowers her voice. "Is one of those secrets about Jenna Moreno's death?"

I stop short. "What?"

"Maddox's sister. She went here, to Westdale. She died *here*."

I inhale sharply.

Allegra continues, "Jenna OD'd at an off-site party. That's why

Maddox doesn't want to be at Westdale. His mother made him come. So if he seems like just another rich boy playing rebel?"

"He's not," I murmur. "Being here reminds him of her."

"Maddox and his sister were close. When she died, he was out of school for a term and there was . . ."

"A breakdown," I murmur. "That's what—" I stop short.

"That's the secret?" Her face hardens. "What did they say about it?"

"They sent me his intake form for a psychiatric hospital."

Her face goes rigid, eyes snapping with more emotion than I've ever seen from Allegra. "They implied there was something shameful in Maddox needing—and accepting—treatment? That is intolerable, and if it makes you feel differently about him—"

"It doesn't. I was furious at the implication."

That fire is extinguished. "Good. Now for Theo. Was it some sort of equally ridiculous non-secret? Perhaps the fact he's bi?"

"No, I figured that when Polly said he'd be asking some lucky 'person' to the gala. This was . . ." I chew my lip. Then I blurt, "An article saying he coerced an actor into sex. For a part."

"Oh *that*." She rolls her dark eyes. "Do you really think Theo Dubois needs to coerce *anyone* into sex?" When I open my mouth to protest, she lifts a hand. "Yes, sometimes coercion is the point, but Theo's ego alone wouldn't let him sleep with anyone who didn't want him. That particular situation was settled shortly after it hit the news. The actor went to the papers and the police, and then quietly offered to retract his statement in return for a role in Bernard Dubois's next movie. Trinity—Theo's mom—hired a private investigator, who confirmed that Theo's side of the story was correct. He met the actor at a party, and they did leave together, but only to share a car and discuss the actor auditioning for a role. The driver dropped them off separately. They didn't even hook up. It was very clearly a trap."

When I don't answer, she says, "I can send you the article on the retraction. It was, as you might guess, much smaller and less widely disseminated than the accusation."

"Okay, thank you."

"You're welcome. Now about the Liliths . . . ?"

I hesitate. Then I say, "I'm in."

Her head tilts, as if she wants to ask how I came to this sudden conclusion. It's because in this conversation, I caught a glimpse of the girl behind the mask, and I think she's someone I'd like to get to know better.

In the end, she only says, "All right then. Welcome to the Liliths."

ELEVEN

Allegra goes back inside, and I move to sit on the bench and think. Then I pick up my phone.

Me
I'm sorry

Me
Yes, someone said something about you, and I needed to work it out

Theo
Can we talk?

Me
I'd like that

Theo
You busy now?

I tell him that I'm outside, and that I can come back in or we can speak later, as planned. He doesn't answer. He just appears and sits beside me on the bench.

At least two minutes pass, both of us sitting in silence. Then I wordlessly pass him the folded-up article from my pocket.

He opens it and exhales, long and deep. "I should have guessed. That's the one thing that would have you backing off fast." He glances at me. "You could have asked."

"Could I? I mean, yes, I could, but should I?"

Another sigh. "No, you're right. You needed to hear the explanation from someone else. Did they tell you it was a setup?"

"Yes."

He pulls out his phone. "I can prove it. I have the statement from the guy. I know it might sound like I got away with something."

He shows me the statement. I don't need to read it, but I understand that he needs me to. In it, his accuser confesses to the setup, on the condition that his confession means he won't be charged. The fact Theo keeps it on his phone tells me how much the incident upsets him, how badly he feels the need to explain to anyone who heard about it.

Theo fingers the article. "The photo didn't help either, did it?"

"It was concerning. But I'm guessing you get tired of having cameras shoved in your face."

"Honestly, I'm used to it. My parents taught me that there's no point in fighting the paparazzi or you get pictures like this. Give them what they want and hope they move on. But there *are* a few photos like this. I was . . ." He clears his throat. "I was with a guy who wasn't out, and I thought we'd ducked the paps, but we hadn't. I lost my temper."

"I would, too."

He gives me a half-smile. "Thanks." He touches the first paragraph. "I'd kinda hoped for more time before you saw this stuff. Time for you to get to know me first. But someone is making sure

I don't get that, so let's run this down. Do I date guys and girls? Bi, pan, whatever. I like who I like. First date at thirteen with a seventeen-year-old? No, I was fourteen and she was sixteen. Otherwise, yes. Do I date a lot? Well, when you're bi, slut-shaming isn't just for girls. I like dating. I started young. Early bloomer plus a fair amount of opportunity."

I resist the urge to snort at that. One look at Theo Dubois, and I'd say "fair amount" is an understatement.

He continues, "But I know plenty of straight guys who date a *lot* more than I do and don't get called out for it. I won't argue the point in general. I date. Enough said. As for the rest? Do I party? Again, yes, but not as much as this suggests. I drink, maybe more than I should. I don't do drugs—of any kind. Not my scene. Have I done things that have been covered up? Yep. Underage drinking, obviously. One DUI when I was young and stupid. Also a car theft—I took one of my dad's cars without asking, and he called the cops to teach me a lesson, only he called one he knew, so no charges were laid."

He checks the article again. "Sexual misconduct? No. Nothing like that. Trashing a hotel room? It was one room, and I only broke the bed."

There are many ways a guy could say that, to make it absolutely clear how he broke the bed, and all those ways would be creepy. Theo states it like these things happen, which of course makes me think of *how* these things happen and . . .

Is it warm out here? It's the sun, right? Even though we're sitting in the shade?

He continues, "And I not only admitted to the damage but paid for it right away. One broken piece of furniture is hardly trashing a hotel room. But *saying* I trashed it makes a better story."

I'm not actually sure it does. Breaking the bed is a story in itself. Definitely warm out here.

He folds the article and glances over. "Anything else?"

I shake my head.

"I'm not a saint, Lil. I have fun. Sometimes I overdo it. But I'm honest. You don't know me well enough to realize that, but if you aren't comfortable asking me about a rumor, ask Maddox."

"Maddox, the guy who isn't your friend anymore?"

"Yes, but he'll tell you the truth. He never cuts me any slack. You can ask him. Or Allegra—we've known each other forever."

"Okay." I look over at him. "I am sorry."

"You shouldn't be. Turning people against each other is a fact of life here. The only question is who gave you that and why."

"Oh, I know, and I'll take care of it."

He smiles. "I know you will."

I exit English class behind Natalia and then catch up and hand her the folded pages. "Thanks, but I won't be taking you up on the offer. I don't need to know more."

She slows and then walks to the side of the hall as students stream past. Her expression says she's caught off guard and deciding how to play this. Then, with a lift of her chin, she says, "Are you certain?"

"I am."

"You're one of *those*, then."

I don't ask "one of what." I'm starting to see how Westdale students operate. It's on another level from what I'm accustomed to, probably because *they're* on another level. The level where money and privilege have fast-tracked their maturity, so I often feel as if I'm dealing with college kids. I'm supposed to ask what Natalia means and look clueless doing so.

"Guess I am," I say instead and start to walk away.

She gets in my path. "One of those girls who loses all sense of self-respect when good-looking guys pay attention to her."

I only stare, and she pulls back, as if realizing this doesn't quite hit the same when I've already sidestepped the trap.

"Guess I am," I say again.

"I mean it, Liliana. If you honestly think Theo Dubois is into you, then you really are the naive little public school girl you seem to be."

"Ah," I say. "You're one of *those.*"

"One of—" She cuts herself off and glares.

"I *don't* think Theo is into me. I think he's checking out the potential Optima competition. Possibly also bored—I suspect Theo likes the new and shiny. But he's not the guy in that article, and you know it."

"And Maddox?"

"You're saying there's something wrong with a guy needing mental health help after a family tragedy?" I wrinkle my nose. "How very twentieth century of you."

Before she can continue, I say, "Let's make a deal. If you can show me proof that Theo did what's in that article—or that Maddox's issues included violence against others—I will vow to stay out of the Optima race. However . . ." I lean toward her. "If you show me anything false—and I prove it's false—*you'll* drop out."

I extend my hand. "Do we have a deal?"

Her face contorts. Then she rips the pages in half, drops them at my feet, and walks away.

———

After dinner with the Liliths, I slip out to the library . . . and finally get back to my dad's staff yearbook. I take it to a desk and scrape off enough of the corrector fluid on one of the erased notes to see two words, and my breath catches.

Will Nelson

Several words follow. I scrape so carefully that it seems to take forever, and I start to sweat, one drop hitting the book before I wipe it off.

Will Nelson about Annette

I frown. That doesn't make sense. I adjust the book and realize I missed a part before my dad's name. More scraping reveals *Ask*.

Ask Will Nelson about Annette

Annette?

I start scraping the other covered note. I'm moving slower now, the sweat beading faster as my heart thuds. This one is two lines. The first is three words.

Run, Nelson, run.

I work at the second line for what seems like forever, finally revealing the words.

Because if you ever show your face again?

That's it. I reread the two lines. Telling my dad to run, because otherwise . . . ?

Where's the threat?

Wait, there's a little spot I didn't scrape off. I work at it, bit by bit, until I see a tiny circle maybe twice the size of a pinhead. A happy face?

I think of a T-shirt I saw once in a vintage shop. A yellow happy face with a bullet hole in the forehead.

I shiver.

The circle does seem to have something in the middle. I'm peering at it when I remember the antique desk magnifiers.

I hurry over to another desk, set the book down, and move the magnifier onto the page. The image leaps to life, but it's been drawn so small that it doesn't have a lot of detail. A line with other lines coming off it? Like a bug?

"This looks very top secret," says a voice behind me.

I jump, slapping the book shut even as I recognize the voice. It's Maddox, novel in hand, finger holding his place. His boots are off, and I look around for where he'd been sitting.

"Yeah, I've been here the whole time." He points across the library. "You seemed busy, so I wasn't going to interrupt. Then you came racing over to the magnifier, and I got curious." He glances at the desk. "An old staff yearbook?"

"Just research."

His head tilts as he studies me. "You're sweating, Chamberlain. And you look freaked out."

His gaze goes to the book, which I'm holding shut, as if he might snatch it away.

"It's just . . . something," I say.

"Something you don't want to talk about?"

When I don't answer, he rubs his mouth. "Guess I can't push you to spill your secrets when I'm keeping mine about Cecilia. I *am* sorry about that. I'm not trying to be an asshole."

"You aren't an asshole, Maddox. I don't need to know anything you're not comfortable sharing." I look at the book. "And please don't think I'm pretending to keep a secret as some kind of payback."

"What? No. I wouldn't think that." He leans one hip against an armchair. "I just . . ." He exhales. "I've got shit going on, as I'm sure you've realized. Things going on in here." He taps his temple, and I remember the hospital intake form, and what Allegra said about his sister.

I pause, hoping he might say more, but when he doesn't, I glance down at the yearbook. "This isn't really a secret. It's just a personal thing you wouldn't be interested in."

His brows jump. "And you've decided I wouldn't be interested because . . ." He makes a face before I can answer. "Because I'm really good at seeming like I don't care about anything. Yeah, that's my cover, but also, it's this." Another tap at his temple. "Is the school loner a disaffected youth, refusing to engage with a broken system? Or is he just a messed-up kid dealing with bouts of depression?" A strained smile. "One can be both."

He leans toward me. "You don't need to tell me anything. But please don't think I'm not interested. If it upsets you, as it obviously does—"

The library door slaps open, voices rushing through. Maddox curses and ducks back to wherever he came from as Polly bounces in, Theo at her side, Isolde following, and Allegra slowly bringing up the rear, as if she just happens to be walking in the same direction.

"There you are!" Polly says. "You disappeared."

"It's Lil's magic trick," Theo says. "The moment we turn our backs, poof. She's off to the library, in search of better stories than whatever ones we're telling. Stories like . . ."

He picks up the book on the desk, reads the cover, and arches an eyebrow. "*Westdale Academy Staff Yearbook*? Wow. *This* is more interesting than us?"

"Oooh." Polly snatches it. "This is just before we were born. Wait. Is your mom in here?" She answers her own question. "Duh, no, she's a student, not staff."

"It's her father," Allegra says as she walks over. She looks at me. "I presume that isn't a secret?"

"That my dad was the gardener?" I say. So Allegra already knew that. Of course she did. From the expressions on the others, though, she's the only one.

Isolde chokes on a laugh. "The heiress and the gardener? Really? That is awesome. Is he cute? I bet he is."

She reaches for the book, but Polly holds it out of her reach. I take the yearbook and flip to the photo of my father, because if I don't, Allegra is going to smell a secret.

"Yep," Isolde says as I point to him. "Super-cute. Look at those eyes. And that hair." She glances at me. "Is it weird that I'm calling your dad cute?"

"Not when it's a picture of him at our age. He was working for a year before college."

Allegra takes the book before I can stop her. She lifts the book so it's hovering beside my face, looks from it to me, back and forth, and then says, "Yes."

"Yes, what?"

"He is definitely your father."

"Uh, was that in question?"

She shrugs elegantly. "It's always in question."

Isolde nods. "He could have been in love with your mom, and some other guy got her pregnant, but he offered to take care of her and the baby."

"Someone reads too many romances," Allegra says. "But, yes, such a thing could have happened, and it did not. He is your father. She is your mother."

"Congratulations," Theo says. "Allegra Khan has declared your parents are your parents. I'm sure that's a weight off your mind."

Allegra waves a hand at him. "Why are you still here?"

He ignores her. "Come on, Lil. We're going outside. Liliths After Dark."

Allegra casts a pointed look at Theo.

Polly loops her arm through his. He extends his other one for me, and I take it as Allegra leads us out of the library. I try to peek back for Maddox, but he stays hidden.

As the days pass into weeks, I catch up in all my classes and settle into the rhythm of Westdale. Natalia has backed off. Talk of the Optima race has settled. I have breakfast with Theo, lunch with a mixed group, and dinner with the Liliths. When I can't sleep, I look out my window, and if Maddox is on the bench, I join him.

Cecilia and I video chat every other day. At first, I thought she was just making duty calls, but it's settled into a routine that I look forward to. Living at Westdale, it's easy to forget the outside world until something reminds me, like Theo taking a call from his mom or Polly mentioning her siblings. Cecilia isn't a guardian in *that* way, but she's becoming more than my grandparents' lawyer. She comes by with lunch once a week, and we eat in the tiny dining area reserved for parental visits.

When Cecilia first came by for lunch, I figured that meant she lived in Savannah. She doesn't. She's from Atlanta, where Chamberlain Enterprises has its head office and she has a condo. But for the next five months, she's working remotely from a leased apartment in Savannah. Which means she's here for me, and I kinda hate that—hate the idea that my grandparents expected her to uproot her life for me.

"Pfft," she says when I mention it on her next visit. "Do you know how well they're paying me for this gig? I hit the jackpot." Her grin lasts two seconds before it fades. Her voice softening, she adds, "I'm happy to do it, Lili. For your mom. I only wish . . ." She cuts into her pot pie. "I understand that she did what she thought was best for you."

"And you only got an annual Christmas photo?"

She shrugs. "I understood."

"Why did my mom leave Westdale?"

Her fork stops halfway to her mouth.

I lean back in my chair. "Everyone thinks my parents left when she got pregnant. That makes sense. Teenage girl from a wealthy, possibly conservative family."

"Um-hmm," she says around her mouthful.

"You suggested it yourself, but you knew it wasn't the truth. I was born in May, Cecilia. Westdale ends the beginning of June, which means there is no way Mom dropped out early because of me."

"I . . . was asked to perpetuate a misunderstanding."

"By my grandparents."

"No, by your mom." A long pause. Then she sets down her fork. "She messaged me after learning she was pregnant."

"So my parents left and *then* Mom got pregnant and wanted you to tell people that's *why* she left?"

"Your mother dropped out for reasons she did not disclose." Her gaze meets mine. "And that is the truth. She left me a note, but no explanation, and I presumed she'd just gotten sick of the bullshit. But Rose wouldn't turn eighteen until October, and your grandparents weren't letting her run off with a—" Cecilia stops short.

"Gardener," I say. "The point is that my grandparents—among others—objected to the relationship. So . . ." I look up sharply. "Wait. Did Mom *get* pregnant so they'd back off? The damage is done, their little girl soiled, any child they have tainted by my dad being a nobody?"

Her expression answers.

"Seriously?" I say. "Did we hit reverse on the last *century*?"

"Part of the worry would have been that your dad would want money. Having a child with Rose solidified his claim. If your parents were willing to keep running and hiding, that reduced the chance he'd show up with his hand out. As for getting pregnant on purpose, that's not the story I got."

"Which was?"

"That it was an accident. They were getting jobs, settling down, worried about your grandparents finding them, and being less than careful with birth control. Your mom had options, though, Lili, and no compunctions about using them. She chose to keep you."

"Your job was to tell everyone she was pregnant."

"Yes, and your grandparents seized that as an excuse. No one would know when you were born, so the timing didn't matter. They could say your mother got pregnant at school and this boy convinced her to run away with him. They disowned her."

I thump back in my seat. "Disowning? That's a thing?"

"Legally it just means cutting her from the will. Which they could do because of your uncle."

I blink. "I have an uncle?"

"You did. He died years ago. Never married, no offspring, which makes you the heir. The way the family business is structured, they could disown Rose and make James the sole heir. But when he died without issue, it reverted to you, and your grandparents can do nothing about that."

I take a moment, just breathing. "This is a lot."

"It is," she says. "But you don't need to worry about your grandparents. When your grandmother got sick, they took off to Europe for some miracle cure, and they've decided to retire there. You will graduate Westdale and turn eighteen and begin taking your place in the business, which will make the board very happy."

"Who's running the business now?"

"The board. Which is fine—they're very competent—but they'd really like a Chamberlain in charge."

"In charge? Or as a figurehead?"

She smiles. "Does it matter? You can get your foot in that door, learn the ropes, and then throw it open and storm the castle. The fact they *want* you means that door is open, with the red carpet rolled out. Forget your grandparents and how they treated your mom. This is your revenge. Let them just grow old in Europe. Your grandmother has terminal cancer. Your grandfather is seventy-eight—he married later in life."

In short, I won't need to worry about my grandparents re-entering my life, and after what they did to my mom, I don't want them to. Cecilia's right. Let them stay in Europe, enjoying the profits of a family business, while taking no interest in that business—or me.

"Is it possible to get the list of the charities that were supposed to inherit in my place? I know I can't do much to help now, but I'd like it. I want to make it up to them someday."

She smiles, as if I've said the right thing, then takes out her phone and hits buttons. "Done."

"Thank you. About my mom . . . She'd hate me being at Westdale, wouldn't she."

Cecilia makes a face. "Yeah, she would, and if I could have stopped it, I would have. But you're seventeen and your grandparents insisted. I can guarantee you that you're safe. I'm making sure of that."

"I still feel bad that you're stuck in Savannah."

"I *like* Savannah. It was a good time for a change. I recently ended a long-term relationship and was in need of fresh scenery. And I go home most weekends to visit my parents and friends."

I suspect she's putting a good face on a bad situation. Whatever the truth, she's placed her life on hold for me, and I hope I never forget that.

TWELVE

I've researched that symbol from the yearbook, but that's hard when it just looks like some kind of bug. In the end, I need to accept that it's probably something personal that's significant only to the student who drew it.

I *do* find out who Annette is. As Allegra promised, I now have access to my mother's Dux journal. It's not a personal diary; it's her record of the Liliths during her time as Dux. Mostly what I get is a general picture of my mom at seventeen, and goddamn, she was glorious. In her element, organizing and mothering and protecting and also just having *fun*.

As for Annette, it seems she was a fellow Lilith and a friend of my mom's. She'd also been the Lilith candidate for Optima. I don't get much more than that. The journal seems spotty, as if Mom was an infrequent diarist, which isn't really like her, but I'm guessing she became more diligent about stuff as she got older. At Westdale, she was having too much fun to keep a thorough diary, which means all I know about Annette is that she was a Lilith running for Optima, and Mom and Cecilia both liked her a lot.

I also get no hint about why my mom left Westdale. She was here, living and seemingly happy, and then she wasn't.

On another note, I've agreed to let Polly "launch" me on socials, even if I'm not totally sure what that means. For now, it entails giving her all the data she needs and agreeing to let Isolde—a photographer—take pictures of me as we go about our days at Westdale.

I'm finishing lunch with Isolde, Theo, and a few others one day when Polly appears, phone in hand.

"Launched!" she crows.

"I feel like I should crack a bottle of champagne over your bow," Theo says to me.

Polly pulls over a chair and nudges Isolde aside. Then she shows me my launch, which is . . . a single photo on Polly's socials.

It takes a moment for me to recognize the picture as me. I'm in the library, sitting sideways on a chair. I'm wearing the cute-goth dress Allegra's dressmaker made from Allegra's design. My Docs are curled partly under me, my head on the armrest, hair hanging over it as I read a first-edition *Frankenstein*. The angle comes in partly from the side, so you can just make out a sliver of my profile, my gaze so intent on the book that I never realized Isolde was snapping the shot.

What you don't see is that I'm not alone. Maddox is across from me, stretched out in a chair, novel in hand. To an outsider, our joint reading times would look like we just both happened to be there. We don't do more than glance over when the other one reacts to their book. But it always feels like shared time.

I'm not sure I could call Maddox a new friend, a label I'd easily apply to Theo or Isolde. But it's something. It's something small and fragile, becoming more precious by the day.

Anyway, Maddox isn't in the shot. It's just me, unrecognizable, lost in a book. The caption reads:

New friend at WestA! L arrived earlier this month, and we're all so happy to have her.

I peer at Polly. "That's my launch?"

"Don't look so underwhelmed. I am a professional."

She clicks the post to show that it was put up twenty minutes ago and has . . . six thousand likes and two hundred comments? On *that*?

I skim the comments.

Who is she?

If she's at WestA, she's SOMEONE

But coming in second term? Why?

Look at the boots. Daddy's a rock star

Or Mommy

Name starts with L. Who's rock royalty with that initial?

Forget the books, guys, she's reading Frankenstein. Mommy or Daddy is a writer

Guesses follow in a stream.

Polly smiles. "And that is how you do a *launch*. More to come."

Polly posts again two hours later with a picture that shows me properly. The Liliths were outside, talking, and Isolde had been wandering. Then she came up behind me and took a shot just as I turned, my lips parted in mid-speech, eyes dancing with whatever we'd been discussing. Allegra and Polly are out of focus in the background, but it's still obvious who they are.

The post reads:

You guys! So many guesses! So far out in left field! Come on back from the bleachers and meet America's newest billionaire heiress.

Okay, so her fortune is definitely not new, but she just found out she's a freaking heiress to . . . To what? That is the question.

Come on, cyber-sleuths, do your work. For every wrong answer, I'll donate $10 to my foundation. For the right one? Someone takes home $10K from me (though I really think the heiress should pay).

"You are *good*," I say.

"Good?" Polly sputters. "Merely good?"

I smile at her as we head upstairs for study break. "The best." I peer at the screen. "Is that . . . a thousand guesses already?"

"That's why I put the donation at ten bucks each. So I don't go broke. Well, not that I pay. It's from sponsorship money."

"And by putting in a prize for guessing right, you increase the number of guesses overall, which means at ten bucks a pop, you're still going to donate . . . a lot."

"Probably six figures. Which is fine. What *is* money really?"

"I can give you the ten grand for the prize. Cecilia said I can ask for up to that much for petty cash." I pause. "Though I can't believe I just said *petty cash* and *ten thousand dollars* in the same sentence."

"Petty cash? We are posh and proper ladies at a posh and proper boarding school. The term is *pin money*. Next and final post after dinner."

As I'm scraping up the last crumbs of my apple dumpling, someone says, "Holy shit!"

Now, Westdale might be a high school, but it bears only a superficial resemblance to one, and in most ways, it feels more like what I imagine college will be. Unlike my old school, no one is going to start a fistfight in class. Or shout grade-school insults walking down the hall. Or yell "Holy shit" in the dining hall.

So when someone does, I notice. And I notice that half the hall has their phones out.

In the middle of the room, Kai shoots to their feet. They look at me and deliver a long-distance fist bump before yelling at the ceiling, "You are a fucking genius, Polly!"

My gaze sweeps the room. Maddox is at the back, making a rare dining hall appearance, and he has his phone out. He's shaking his head at whatever's on the screen. Then he glances left, and I know immediately who's over there. Theo. Their eyes meet, and there's a look on Theo's face almost like worry, but Maddox shakes his head again and pairs it with the faintest smile and Theo relaxes.

Not friends anymore, right, guys? Yep, that's another mystery I'm working on, building enough data to move forward with my hunch.

For now, I realize they're both looking at me. Waiting to see my reaction to whatever's on the screen.

I finally get the app open. It goes straight to Polly's profile. I click on the latest photo, and my breath catches.

It's me from two nights ago, in the lounge for games night. I'm at the chess table, and I've just won. Isolde caught me leaning back in my chair, laughing, my opponent leaning forward, finger pointed at me, mock angry but unable to keep from laughing.

It's a moment of pure joy, captured and frozen. Two new friends playing chess, the winner crowing her victory.

And my opponent?

Theo Dubois.

The post reads simply: Checkmate.

Then two lines down #LilianaChamberlain #YesThoseChamberlains #TheHeiressWinsAll #AndIDontJustMeanThe Game

I look up, my heart racing as fast as the reactions are climbing. I look anxiously over at Theo, but he shoots me a grin and a thumbs-up.

Then Polly walks in, and the room erupts in applause, Kai leading a standing ovation.

"And you are now launched," she says as she leans over me. "Check and mate."

A few days later, I'm called into Ms. Dimitriou's office. I try not to stress about that. She's checked in on me a few times, but this is my first actual summons.

Her door is cracked open, and when there's no response after a quiet knock, I'm about to withdraw. Then I hear her voice, as if she's on the phone.

"He seems to be doing much better," she says. "I think it'll take this time."

I hesitate. I know I shouldn't be eavesdropping, but I can't help wonder what she means about hoping something will "take." It sounds vaguely sinister.

Her voice drops, emotion threading through it. "Thank you. I really think this hospital can help. He's been through so much, and I try not to blame myself. I was busy with work when he really needed his mom, and he fell in with the wrong crowd."

Oh, shit. She's talking about *rehab*. For her *son*.

I pull back sharply and shake my head as if I can unhear it. That's a secret I'm *not* giving Allegra. It's also a reminder that the adults in my life are people, dealing with their own problems, and a reminder, too, that I blew off my last check-in with Cecilia. She's living in Savannah for *me*, and I can't make her job harder.

I wait out the conversation, and then I rap again, and Ms. Dimitriou calls me in.

When I enter and see what's on her desk, my stomach knot tightens.

After Polly's "reveal," the story exploded in ways I didn't expect. Cecilia knew about Polly's launch and had approved it, while mobilizing my family's PR department to supply approved photos and soundbites and tell would-be interviewers that I'm busy with school.

Yet the photo all the non-business sites want isn't a posed shot of me looking pensive and corporate. It's the one of me and Theo, and Cecilia helped Isolde manage selling rights to it.

It's that photo I'm looking at now, on the front page of a national newspaper's entertainment section with the headline: *Who Is Heiress Liliana Chamberlain?* and the subhead *And Why Is She Playing Chess with Theo Dubois?*

I breathe through my nose, willing my heart rate to slow as Ms. Dimitriou says, "Take a seat, Liliana."

I resist the urge to preemptively apologize for the publicity. Cecilia said it was fine. It *was* fine, right?

Ms. Dimitriou taps the paper. "I like this."

I keep breathing slowly, searching her face for signs of sarcasm.

"It reflects well on us," she says. "Our newest student and our most famous one, playing a game together and looking happy and at ease. Good sportsmanship. Friendly competition. Business and art, working together. It's obviously a spontaneous shot, which makes it even better. The board will be asking Isolde's permission to use it."

My heart rate slows a little, though I'm still wary.

She continues, "You've fit in remarkably well, Liliana. I'll admit, I was concerned. You're quiet and studious, and you come from a very different background, but the fact you've assimilated is both a credit to you and, I believe, to our school."

She folds her hands on the desk. "You know that Optima hopefuls must formally commit to the competition on March first. Which is tomorrow."

"Yes, ma'am."

"Theo already has said he plans to commit, as have Natalia and Cosmo, but you have not, and the Optimas wish to know if you're avoiding it because of Theo."

"No, ma'am. I do intend to formally declare with the others tomorrow."

Which is true. I just haven't said it until now, because I haven't told Cecilia, and I don't want her finding out from someone else. But my new commitment to do better by Cecilia means I need to tell her first.

A quick smile. "Excellent. I would hate to think a promising young woman would refrain from competing with a boy."

"Theo supports me running."

She leans back in her chair. "Good for him. I always worry when one of our art students is the lead contender. They can lack a competitive edge."

"Theo doesn't. Neither do I."

"Excellent. I'll tell the Optimas. They were hoping to video-conference with you. Does eight this evening work?"

My mouth goes dry, but I nod. "Of course."

I'm not freaking out. Really not freaking out. Also trying not to be a little pissed that Theo didn't warn me, but it turns out that he's never video-conferenced with the Optimas.

"I know a bunch of them, though," he says. "And they know me."

"I'm an unknown quantity, and they want to remedy that."

"Apparently. You'll need to prepare."

"Already on it. I'm going to take lunch off and work in the library, doing research. Same during study hours."

"Have dinner with me. Table for two. I'll quiz and prep you." He grips my shoulder. "You've got this, Lil."

I hope so.

———

The video conference feels like one of those "informal" job interviews that isn't informal at all. Every question—right down to "I hear you're a reader? What's the last book you read?"—is another nugget they can dissect for meaning.

Of the twenty-one active members, sixteen are on the call. Half stay off-camera. That includes Bernard Dubois and Marilyn Perez-Moreno, two people I would have liked to meet. My grandparents are also Optimas, but I've been warned they won't be there. Last week, they sent a care package from France, the sort of generic basket you might ask your PA to assemble for the teenage daughter of an important client. There wasn't even a note attached. I've decided I don't give a shit, even if I kinda do.

As the interrogation—sorry, *meeting*—winds down, an older woman says, "It is so good to see you pursuing Westdale Optima, Liliana. It seems only fitting, when your mother was so close to joining us."

I hesitate. "I thought my mother didn't run for Westdale Optima."

The woman smiles. "Of course she did, dear. She was the lead contender."

That's not what Mom's journal says, but I return the smile. "Then I hope to join in her place, however belatedly."

One of the men speaks up. "You thought your mother didn't run. Why is that? Did she say something?"

"No, I just . . . I heard something that I must have misunderstood."

"What *did* she say about Westdale?" he presses.

"Nothing." I give a rueful smile. "I never even knew she went here. But I'm proud to think I'm following in her footsteps."

"Following in her footsteps *and* filling her substantial shoes," the first woman pipes up. "We are delighted to have a Chamberlain in the running again. Is there anything you wanted to ask us?"

So much, but I only smile and say, "I'm sure I'll have plenty of questions, but I'm hoping I won't need to bother you with them."

I'd planned to call Cecilia tomorrow, but I can't risk her finding out that I spoke to the Optimas. I still kind of chicken out by texting the news instead, which gives her a chance to formulate a reply before we talk. Or that's the theory; her response is "call me now!" So I do and she's furious, but when I ask what her concerns are, she doesn't seem to have any beyond not wanting me to "waste" my time. I gently but firmly tell her it's mine to waste, and we go back and forth for a while before she acknowledges that it's also my decision to make. And we leave it at that.

A week later, it's a Tuesday and I'm in the library with Isolde. We're past the tutoring stage, but we've continued hanging out for study period several days a week. It's one of the few times we can be together without others, and I think we both appreciate that. I like hanging out with Theo and Maddox, but I also crave female friendships, and while Polly is great, she's busy with her career and usually only engages in group activities. And Allegra, being Allegra, doesn't "hang out." Which is all fine, because Isolde is more my speed, where we can just chill and chat and get to know each other.

We're supposed to be working on math, but we both whipped through the practice quiz, so we're quietly talking.

I'm sitting in the usual way I sit in the library armchairs—sideways. Isolde is on her back, legs stretched up the wall, red hair fanned out on the floor.

As we talk, she's flipping through social media, and when she holds out a picture, I recognize it from a dozen movie posters. Theo's Mom, Trinity Nilsen.

"Can you imagine this being your *mother*?" she says.

No shade on my actual mom, but I get what she means. What would it be like to have one of the world's most recognizable faces for a mom?

"She's gorgeous," I say. "It's her bone structure. Theo has some of it."

"So unfair. Perfect bone structure should only go to girls. Like a genetic law."

"I don't know. I kinda like it on Theo."

She laughs softly. "I get that. He isn't remotely my type, but I find myself just staring, you know? Like at a painting. He should be an asshole, though. Again, it's like a law. Totally unfair that he isn't."

"I like that, too."

She smiles backward at me. "Part of me wants beautiful people to be assholes, for balance, but it's actually a relief when they aren't." She looks at the photo. "They're talking about what Trinity will wear to the Quartz Gala." She sighs. "I'm never going to that."

"The only invitation I'll get is a request for sponsorship."

"But you could wrangle an invite *with* the sponsorship." She glances over at me. "Make me a promise?"

"That you can be my plus-one? Sure."

"No, just include me on the list when you throw big bashes on your billionaire yacht."

I laugh. "Can you *see* me on a yacht?"

"A small one. Discreet but luxurious. I can definitely see you there, being the perfect hostess, drumming up donations for some cause while Theo charms guests into donating even more. Polly is there, getting it all on socials. Allegra's lounging on some distant deck chair, pretending she's so over all of us, while keeping an eye on us from her perch."

I smile at her. "And you're snapping photos?"

"It'd be nice."

"For a gallery? Or a high-end magazine?"

"Both. First, though, I have to convince my parents not to murder me for ditching a"—she air quotes—"real career."

"Ugh."

"I do not want to go home this weekend. Love my parents, but my brother will be there. Tristan is the perfect example of a dutiful son. I hate him."

"Wait. His name's Tristan? Like Tristan and—"

Her hands shoot up. "Yes. Okay? My parents named us after the opera . . . where Tristan and Isolde are a *couple*. I think they just liked the names. Luckily, most people don't make the connection. Thanks for the reminder, though." She mock glares at me.

"Can you get out of going home while he's there? Make up an excuse?" I tap the textbook lying beside me. "Homework."

"My parents already tell me I do too much homework. My grades are fine, they say. It's the social stuff I need to work on. Why even send me to an Ivy League school if I can't network?"

I lift my head. "Can't *network*? Your friends are Allegra Khan, Polly Reeves, and Theo Dubois. You're a *Lilith*."

She sighs. "I made the mistake of talking about Allegra in the first term. My parents decided she's 'not a real friend.' Same as Theo."

An idea forms. "Cecilia wanted me staying put for a while, but I've been here over a month, and I really want to go out. What if you had plans with me?"

A long pause.

"Or not," I say. "Maybe something else?"

"No, I was just hesitating because . . . Well, my parents may have, uh, mentioned you. They know who your grandparents are and . . . ugh." She rubs her eyes. "This is creepy, sorry."

"No, it's fine. If they'd rather you didn't associate with me, we won't tell them."

"Rather I didn't . . . ?" She flips over and stares at me. Then she laughs. "Wow. I said that all wrong. I mean they've been bugging me about you. They know you're a Lilith, and they've wanted to know if we're friends, which they would freaking love. That's why it's creepy. And embarrassing."

"They do *know* we're friends though, right?"

She glances away. "I've said we hang out. I didn't want to presume anything."

"I consider you a friend, Isolde."

A shy look. "Thank you. But, yes, if you and I were doing something together, they'd totally let me stay here for the weekend. Love them, but they are *networkers*. So where would we go? Oh! Let's look up the entertainment listings for Savannah." She grabs her phone and then stops. "I don't have a car."

"I do." I shrug. "Part of the new heiress package, apparently."

She grins. "That is awesome. Let's see what's going on in the city. We'll ask for passes tomorrow."

———

Cecilia vetoes the night out with Isolde. Even an afternoon out, to see a movie or something, is off the table. I'm furious and humiliated, and we argue, but the problem with communicating by phone is that it's easy for her to duck out of the conversation, which she does.

I apologize profusely to Isolde, who waves it off and pretends that she doesn't really mind going home, but I can still tell it stung, and that hurts.

THIRTEEN

It's Sunday night. Lights out at eleven as usual, and I'm just about to put my novel aside when I get a text on the school messaging system.

Maddox
Need to talk. It's about your mom

Is it wrong that my first reaction is *OMG, Maddox actually messaged me*? My second one, of course, is to try to analyze why that's such a big deal. In the end, I decide it's just because Maddox is one of those people who leaves you never knowing where you stand.

I've spent hours with him reading in the library or out back, talking and staring at the sky together. You'd think that makes us friends, but I don't have his cell number and he hasn't asked for mine. When we pass in the halls, I'm lucky to get a nod of acknowledgment. So yes, having him message makes my heart flutter.

I check out the window. The bench is empty.

Me
Meet out back?

Maddox
Basement

Me
???

Maddox
Found something in the basement, Chamberlain. You wanna see it or not?

Me
Be right there

Maddox
Midnight. Staff's still here

Me
Right. See you then

I'm sorely tempted to sneak down to the basement early and try to find what he's talking about on my own. Yep, that's me—always wanting to be one step ahead. But with Maddox, I want to let him show me what he's found, because that too is a big deal. I've mentioned my mother and her Dux journal and how badly I want to know more about her time here, to figure out why she left. And Maddox found me something.

Does that mean he went looking? He must have. He'd seen old books or something down there and returned in hopes of finding information on my mom, and that's huge. It really is.

Maddox seems to enjoy our time together, but he's not Theo, who has made it very clear that he wants me around. With Maddox, there is always a worry that his pact with Cecilia means he feels obligated to be nice to me. He hasn't mentioned his sister, even though we've talked about my parents' deaths and my grief. He's put up a barrier that I can't cross, and I really want to.

Now he seems to have gone looking for answers to my questions, and that hour passes so slowly. At 11:55 p.m., I'm up—already dressed—and slipping out my door.

The staff leaves at various times during the evening, with the last ones departing around eleven. There are still guards, of course, but they're on outdoor duty. Students aren't confined to the house—as evidenced by Maddox being able to sit outside, undisturbed—but if you tried to actually leave the grounds, you'd be stopped.

Outside my door, I listen for sounds of life. There are none. Everyone is supposed to have been in their rooms an hour ago, and it seems they are.

Getting to the basement means going down a whole lotta stairs. I pass the second floor—also bedrooms—and exit onto the first, where most of the common rooms are located. Part of the basement is also common areas—namely, the archives and the media room. But I'm guessing that's not what Maddox means, and I head straight for the door into the off-limits sections.

It's cracked open.

I push the knob, and the door creaks wide. When I reach for the light switch, I almost expect it not to do anything. Creepy basement. Squeaky door. Of course the lights won't work. They do, though, and I walk into a hallway with three closed doors. I mostly shut the one behind me, though I leave it open a half-inch because while I really can't see Maddox locking me in as a prank—or even *playing* a prank—I'm being careful.

I continue along the hall. The first door opens into a room with manacles on the wall and dried blood on the floor and . . .

I'm kidding, of course. It opens into the furnace room. The next door reveals additional machinery, most of it very old and probably unused. That leaves the final door, and as I approach, I realize I should have started there, because it's open a half-inch, with light beyond.

I push the door. It does not creak, sadly, but it does open to another staircase, this one a classically creepy wooden stairs.

"Maddox?" I call down.

There's definitely a light on, and maybe I've read too many scary stories, but I am not waltzing down those stairs until I'm sure he's there. I take out my phone, open the school messaging app, and type.

Me
I'm at the top of the stairs. Where are you?

My message pulses and then a "Not Delivered" warning pops up.

I frown down at the phone. Then I see the "no signal" symbol. Okay, it makes sense that I wouldn't get a cell signal down here, but when I tap the Wi-Fi indicator, it just spins. From somewhere in the basement comes what sounds like a voice. Maddox's voice. It's muffled, so I take two steps down.

"Maddox?" I say.

A reply, but I still can't hear his words. It definitely sounds like him, though.

Damn it. I do not want to go down there until I'm sure.

Really, Chamberlain, what do you need? A formal invitation by carrier pigeon?

I take another step. Then a stair creaks behind me, and I start to turn when something hits me between the shoulder blades, hard, knocking me forward, and I'm still turning, which means my feet tangle. I catch one glimpse of a figure slamming the door and then I'm plummeting down the stairs.

My hands shoot out to grab something, anything, as I fall, my hip striking the edge of one stair, my shoulder whacking into another. I start skidding headfirst and manage to . . .

I don't even know what I do. I flail and somehow that stops me before my head hits the concrete floor below.

I lie there, on my side, pain and panic slamming through me. Then, very slowly, I roll onto my stomach, looking at the floor a few steps down. I get my palms on the step and brace myself, but I don't know how to rise from this position, and I'm afraid of tumbling the rest of the way.

I squirm and twist until—after what seems like forever—I'm crunched up sideways on the stairs and I can get my feet down. I don't stand. I just keep pushing until I'm sitting there, leaning over my knees, my heart racing as I catch my breath.

The flashed image from above shoots back.

Jayden.

That's who pushed me.

That's who could have killed me.

I start to shiver, and I can't breathe, my chest heaving as fresh panic thrums through me.

I could have died. If I hadn't caught myself, my head would have smashed into the concrete below, and even if I survived, I could have suffered brain damage and—

Rage licks at the heels of the panic.

What the hell?

What the absolute fucking *hell?*

Someone just tried to *kill* me.

I take a moment to catch my breath. Then I rise, and I would love to say I march up the stairs, but it's really more like hobbling, my hand on the banister, my breath coming hard as I pull myself up.

I grab the doorknob and—

The door is locked.

I let out a string of curses. Then I take a deep breath—gasping as pain shoots through me—before I lift my phone and . . .

And I see the "no signal" warning.

No cell signal. No Wi-Fi.

I fight the panic and struggle to focus. Jayden is in Hephaestus. Theo said his parents run a tech company. Cutting off communications would be no problem for him. Nor would hacking the school messaging system or setting up a speaker to play a voice clip of Maddox.

I look at the messages again.

I hadn't questioned them. They sounded like Maddox—the tone, the abrupt sentences. Yet anyone who's had contact with him would know that's his style. Same as anyone at Westdale could guess I'd want information on my mother. The thing that had made me not question it, though, was calling me by my last name. But all Natalia or Jayden had to do was eavesdrop on one of the rare occasions when Maddox and I talk in the halls.

So I have no phone signal, I'm injured, and I'm locked in the basement.

I lift my fist to bang on the door. Then I stop. Who am I going to summon by banging? There's no staff, and the students are at least two floors up, in rooms with soundproofing for privacy. The only person who might answer is Jayden . . . who could realize I'm still alive and come back to fix that.

I want to laugh at the thought. Of course he wouldn't *murder* me.

But he almost did, didn't he? It's not as if he grabbed my shoulder, and I accidentally fell. He shoved me hard. If he just wanted to give me a scare, he could have locked the door behind me.

He tried to kill me.

Over a high-school competition.

I hear Ms. Dimitriou's voice.

Dangerous? It's not the Hunger Games, Cecilia.

Yes, but that doesn't mean contestants can't go too far.

I close my eyes and refocus. I don't want to shout for help until I'm sure someone—who is *not* Jayden—will hear me. Staff start coming in around five, which I know because the earliest we can grab coffee is six. Even if they don't hear me then, Jayden can't mess with the Wi-Fi after everyone starts waking up. That means I only need to wait . . .

I check my phone.

Five hours? Maybe six?

I head downstairs. Then a noise comes from deeper in the basement and I stop short.

Am I sure shoving me down these stairs was the extent of Jayden's plan? What if someone's down here? Someone who might hurt me if the stairs didn't do enough.

Earlier, I'd heard Maddox's voice.

No, that was a trick. A recording or something.

Am I sure?

My insides lurch at the very thought of suspecting Maddox. It's not just that I've come to trust him. It's the idea of suspecting someone I know spent time in a mental hospital, as if deep down I'm still worried. That's not it, though. If I suspect him, it's because I'm afraid I've misplaced my trust, been too eager for friendship.

My instinct says he'd never do something like this, but even if what I heard was a recording, that doesn't mean there isn't someone down here. Probably Natalia. She had her minion shove me down the stairs, and if that's not enough to scare me out of the Optima race, she's hiding, waiting to do more.

I climb up the stairs, wincing at the pain, and check the door. Then I check my phone. Still no signal.

The sound comes again—a *thunk*, deep in the bowels of the basement.

I should stay here at the top of the stairs. Don't let myself be drawn in deeper.

But does that do any good? I can't escape, and if Natalia is waiting for me, she'll eventually come out. Better to find and confront her.

My hip throbs as I shift my weight, considering. Then I turn on my cellphone flashlight and slowly walk down the stairs. At the bottom, it looks like any old basement with a concrete floor and semi-finished walls. Smells like an old basement, too—that musty odor.

The sound seemed to come from the far end of the basement. I look around for a weapon, but the hall is spotless. I start forward, rolling my feet, making no noise.

I reach the end just as another sound comes, a whooshing that echoes from behind a closed door. I take a deep breath and throw it open—

It's a room filled with storage boxes. My breath quickens. If Natalia is hiding here, she could be anywhere.

I take my time moving through the room, checking behind each stack. Minutes pass, seemingly endless minutes, and sweat trickles down my forehead as my heart races. There are so many boxes. So many places to hide.

I finally reach the last stack, and there's nothing behind it. I stand there, catching my breath, thinking hard, when another *thunk* nearly has me jumping out of my skin. The noise comes from overhead, and I look up sharply. All I see is a ceiling. Then comes the *whoosh* I heard.

Water.

The *thunk* of a pump followed by the *whoosh* of water running through pipes. Somebody using the bathroom. Flushing the toilet and then washing their hands. The plumbing must be in the room above.

I shake my head as I relax. Then I tense again. While I've identified the mysterious sounds, that doesn't mean I'm alone in the basement.

The next room I enter is also storage—furniture wrapped in plastic. I search it and then move on to the next. When my phone flashes a warning, I glance down to see that the battery is at ten percent. Right, because I usually plug it in when I go to bed.

I don't dare drain the battery and risk being trapped down here even when the Wi-Fi comes back on. I put my phone in low-power mode and rely on the overhead lights, which makes searching tricky. Shadows lurk behind every storage box and covered chair.

I conduct a full sweep, and I'm about to move to the next room when I spot an old screwdriver on the floor behind a cabinet.

Well, I *was* looking for a weapon.

There's a gap behind the cabinet—which is how I saw the screwdriver—but it's too narrow to reach into. To get the screwdriver, I need to move the cabinet, and I can't imagine that's happening, but when I tug, it shifts easily, as if it's empty. It's still not feather-light, and my battered body screams as I pull, but soon I've yanked it far enough forward to reach—

There's something behind the cabinet, and when I see what it is, I rub my eyes, certain this is proof that I'm actually asleep, that I drifted off and dreamed the message from Maddox and everything that followed.

Because what I see is a tiny door.

It's a hatch—about three feet high and narrow.

I move the cabinet until I can clearly see the little door. There's no handle, and I push on the wood, but nothing happens. I also notice something on the back of the cabinet. Old duct tape that's flapping free. I frown at that. Then I look between the hatch and the screwdriver on the floor, and I give a soft laugh.

The tape used to hold the screwdriver. Considering the amount of dust, it held it on there a very long time ago. Eventually, though, it fell off. And why was a screwdriver taped to the back of the cabinet? Because it's used to open the hatch.

I test my theory by wedging the screwdriver into the gap around the little door and prying, like a crowbar. Sure enough, the door pops open . . . and dust rolls out, and I back up, eyes watering as I hack enough to make my battered ribs scream.

Once I've recovered, I turn on my cellphone light, crouch—my injured hip complaining about that—and crouch-walk through the door. It leads to a room. A very small room, maybe ten square feet, but inside, I can straighten. As I turn, I see a flashlight on a little table near the door. It's very old and very heavy and, unsurprisingly, doesn't work, but there are also matches and a candle.

I light the candle and shine it around. The first thing I see is some kind of art on the far wall. I walk over and peer at it.

Not art but a symbol. A circle painted in red. And, yes, of course my brain screams *painted in blood!*, but the red is too bright for that.

Inside the circle is . . .

A two-headed scorpion.

I pull up the photo I took of the magnified symbol in my dad's yearbook. The one someone drew beside the vague threat against my father. It looked like a bug, but the parts match a scorpion—a line for a body ending in a curved one for the stinger, six lines for legs, and two longer forked ones for pinchers.

I take a photo of the wall symbol. Then I look around. There are mats on the floor, like the kind preschoolers sit on. They're arranged in a circle around a metal thing.

I crouch by the "metal thing." It has a grill, and when I open it, inside are very old ashes. The word *brazier* springs to mind. A little metal cage that holds a fire.

At this point, maybe I should freak out. Two-headed scorpion painted in red on the wall. Mats arranged around a brazier. It screams "dark ritual." But it's also all very old and seems long abandoned. I can see my footsteps in the thick dust, and I know no one has been down here in, well, decades probably.

I crouch by the brazier again. It's about eighteen inches in diameter, and the grill comes off. When I remove it, I see more than ash inside. There's paper. Burned pages.

I sift around for something big enough to read and finally find one scrap. I pull it out, but all I get is a date.

May 10, 1956.

There's the top edge of a handwritten line below, which makes that date look like the header on a journal entry. It's lined paper.

Like a Dux's journal?

I dump out the contents of the brazier. It's mostly very well burned, but down at the bottom, I find another scrap with two words: *Janus Society*.

There's part of a date under that, too. It looks like it's also 1956.

The Janus Society? What is the—?

Footsteps pound on the stairs, and I leap up.

Jayden. He's peeked in and seen that I'm gone and now he's running down to find me.

I grab the screwdriver and hurry through the hatch as fast as my battered body can move. Steps pound down the hall now, and they sound like multiple sets. Natalia *and* Jayden?

I grip the screwdriver as I creep toward the hallway.

"Liliana!" a voice bellows.

Theo?

I step into the hall, and the first person I see isn't Theo. It's Maddox. He runs for me, with Theo right behind him.

"I'm okay," I say.

Maddox holds me at arm's length and as his gaze trips down me, his face hardens. "You are *not* okay."

His hands move to my shoulders, and when I wince, he loosens his grip but his mouth tightens. Theo hovers behind him.

"What happened?" Theo says. "Who did this?"

"Jayden. He pushed me down the stairs."

"Jayden *pushed* you?" Maddox explodes.

Maddox wheels, and I tense, expecting to see Jayden there, but no one is behind him. No one at all. Theo is already running up the stairs two at a time.

"Theo!" Maddox says. "Get back here! Do not—"

Theo hits the top and disappears, footfalls thudding. Maddox lets out a string of profanity. Then he turns to me. "I need to stop him before—" He cuts himself off. "No, I'm not leaving you. He's a big boy. Can you walk?"

I remember that tabloid photo. The rage on Theo's face. "Go after him."

"You're hurt. I'm—"

"I'm right behind you."

More cursing. "I don't want to leave you, but he—"

"I'm *right* behind you."

FOURTEEN

Maddox still takes my arm, guiding me, which means I need to move a whole lot faster than I'd like. He won't abandon me, though, and I need to appreciate that, even if I'd really rather he ran after Theo.

We make it to the main level when we hear Theo slamming his fist against wood far above us.

"Jayden!" he bellows. "Open this door!"

Maddox curses more, and I push him off, saying, "Go to him. Before this gets worse."

More banging. "Jayden!"

As Maddox races up the stairs, he shouts, "Do *not* open that fucking door, Jayden."

I reach Jayden's third-floor room just as he opens the door. Theo barrels through, and there's an *oomph* as he charges into Jayden. By the time I get there, Maddox is hauling Theo off Jayden as Maddox snarls, "Do you want to be expelled *with* him, Theo? *Stop. Now.*"

When that doesn't work, Maddox says, "Lili is hurt, and she needs a doctor, but instead of getting one, I'm dealing with your dumb ass."

Theo jerks up . . . just as Jayden swings. Maddox catches his wrist midair and holds it. Jayden tries to yank free but can't.

Still gripping Jayden's wrist, Maddox leans over him. "I might be pulling him off you, but that doesn't mean I don't want to snap your damn wrist myself. And I don't really give a shit if I get expelled. So go ahead and see how far you can push me."

Jayden's jaw sets, but he grunts and looks away. Maddox releases his grip and turns to Theo.

"He'll get his. Now go find a night guard. I'm calling Dimitriou and getting a doctor for Lili."

Theo lopes out. Doors all along the hall have opened. As Maddox yanks Jayden's door shut, he waves at Allegra.

"Make sure he stays in there," Maddox says.

"Me?" Allegra says.

"Tell him if he opens that door, you'll spill his secrets. And don't tell me you don't have anything on him."

Maddox steers me toward the stairs as he places a call on his phone. I don't listen. The adrenaline rush is subsiding, and my brain whirs as he finishes his call and leads me to the lounge.

"Sit," he says, helping me onto the sofa. "The doctor will be here in a few minutes. Rest and tell me what you need."

I do sit, but I also glance up, meeting his gaze. "So you and Theo aren't friends anymore, huh?"

He looks at me. "Really? That's what you want to talk about right now, Chamberlain?" He shakes his head. "We'll discuss that later. For now, tell me what happened."

Maddox and Theo didn't just happen to find me in the basement. Maddox figured out that his school account had been hacked when he got an alert. Like Jayden, Maddox is a tech guy . . . at least in the sense he comes from tech money and has an aptitude for it if not an interest. His mother has made him very cybersecurity aware, so if there's any unexpected activity on his accounts, he's alerted. In this case, he didn't actually see the alert until he woke after midnight and checked something on his phone.

That sent him into his school account, where he realized messages had been sent to me about meeting in the basement. He notified Theo, which is totally what you do with your "former" best friend.

I don't tell them about the secret room. I need to work that through first, and I wouldn't have time to explain anyway before Ms. Dimitriou and the doctor arrive.

The doctor assesses me and gives me some painkillers and light sleeping meds, but I only have bumps and bruises, and he doesn't see any need to take me to the hospital.

"You're a very lucky young lady," he declares.

He's just finishing up when Cecilia arrives . . . and chaos descends on Westdale Academy.

Of course, Jayden denies everything, but I identify what he'd been wearing, and his door lock shows he went inside five minutes after I tumbled down the stairs.

Did he really try to kill me? Cecilia doesn't think so, because when she told him he'd be charged with attempted murder, he erupts in what seems like genuine panic and confusion. Kill me? No. He'd only meant to push me down the stairs. Cecilia mutters a lot about teenagers and prefrontal cortex development and bad decision-making skills.

By then it's morning, and I spend half the day resting—doctor's orders—and half in meetings as everyone tries to negotiate a settlement via video chat. Jayden's parents try to claim that, since their darling boy didn't seriously injure me, he should just . . . I don't know, be given a few days off to think about what he's done?

Yeah . . .

The final decision is that Jayden is expelled from Westdale. No charges will be laid, but Jayden signs a confession, which will go into his file and, if he ever contacts me or sets foot on the property again, that confession will ensure he never gets into any decent college.

Then there's the matter of Natalia. Jayden says it was her idea to lure and lock me down there, and she'd told him to do "whatever it takes" to scare me into dropping out of the Optima race.

Of course, Natalia denies it.

Except . . .

I don't like the way Natalia reacts. It's too much like how Jayden responded to being accused of trying to kill me. Shock and confusion first, as if this is some kind of joke. Then panicked denials. According to Natalia, Jayden must have acted alone. She never told him to lure me into the basement. She certainly never said to "do whatever it takes." She begs to be allowed to talk to him, so she can straighten this out, but he won't speak to her, and he sticks to his story.

When Jayden was shocked that Cecilia thought he tried to kill me, everyone decided he'd clearly made a mistake. When Natalia is shocked at being accused of orchestrating it, everyone decides she's clearly lying. Since it was Jayden who pushed me, Ms. Dimitriou consults with Natalia's parents and rules that she can just transfer back to her feeder school. The story will be that her parents needed her closer to home for a family emergency.

I'm satisfied with how it's handled for Jayden. I don't think he meant to kill me, and I just want him far away, which they're making sure happens.

But Natalia?

I don't like what happened with Natalia, and later that day, when I venture downstairs for a coffee, she lunges out as if she'd been lying in wait, and I nearly trip down the stairs a second time.

She stands on the landing with her arms crossed. "How'd you do it?"

"Do what?"

"Lure Jayden away."

I blink. "He lured *me*, Natalia. He sent me a message—"

"Oh, I heard how you two set it up. I want to know how you lured him away from *me*."

"How I—? You think I *seduced* him?"

She moves into the light, and her eyes are red from crying. "Theo Dubois went from 'I don't date at school' to falling all over you. And Maddox? Rumor is he's ace because he doesn't look at anyone—guy or girl—and now he's sneaking off to star-gaze with you? Everyone wants to know how you did it."

I'm tempted to snap that I give really good blowjobs, obviously, but those reddened eyes won't let me. Nor will the way her lip trembles even as she's hurling accusations.

"I've made friends, that's all," I say. "New-girl novelty. It's second term, and kids are bored. But I haven't had any contact with Jayden. You honestly believe we set this up together?"

"Duh. Look at you. A few bruises? A scrape on your cheek? You didn't fall down the stairs. Or you didn't fall down very many. You and Jayden collaborated to get rid of me."

"But he's gone, too. Expelled."

"It's the price he was willing to pay. Once you're Optima, he can cash in his chit. That must be what you promised him. Whether you plan to deliver is another thing."

"If you weren't in on it, then you need to be sure everyone knows—"

"Natalia?" It's Allegra, coming from her room behind Natalia. "I don't think you want to be caught harassing your victim, do you?"

Natalia spins on her. "I had nothing to do with what happened. I've been set up."

"No, you've been caught, and you're trying very hard to play your own victim card, but no one's buying it. Would you like me to talk about how you used Jayden to convince Kai not to even *consider* running for Optima?"

Natalia's mouth works. Then she says, "That was different. Kai wasn't committed, and we just gave them—"

"A little scare. Like you gave Liliana." Allegra lifts her fingers in a tiny wave. "Buh-bye, Natalia. You lost." She turns to me. "What are you doing out of your room?"

"Getting coffee. Is that allowed?"

"I would have suggested you call one of your boys to deliver it, but if I accompany you, you may get coffee."

"You're my bodyguard now?"

She sniffs. "Hardly. The threat has been handled. Now you need to handle the fallout—curious classmates who will fall over themselves to ask how you're doing, while praying you drop a tidbit of juicy gossip."

"Gossip that rightfully belongs to my Dux?"

"Correct. Now come."

I glance back for Natalia, but she's already disappearing into her room.

I don't get much time to myself that day, but when I do, one question looms.

What is the Janus Society?

That secret room hadn't been touched in decades. Is it a defunct society? It seems so, and if that's the case, then it doesn't concern me.

But still . . .

A hidden room with a mysterious double-headed scorpion, burned journal entries, and evidence of a fifth society? How am I *not* supposed to be curious?

Two scorpion heads.

Two "faces."

Janus is the two-faced god. I look him up, but I can't quite find what he stands for. Passages, bridges, time, beginnings, change, and transition are all mentioned, but it's the same as any of the societies, where they've chosen a figurehead who is associated with their area of interest, among others. The Mercury Society is about commerce, and Mercury is the god of shopkeepers and finance. He's also the god of travelers, luck, and thieves, which have nothing to do with business. Okay, fine, I can make a joke about price gouging and highway robbery, but the point is that the Janus Society has chosen Janus for one of his aspects, and I won't figure out which that is without more information.

Theo has been checking in on me all day, while Maddox vanished once the doctor arrived, and I haven't seen him since. The sensitive part of me wants to read too much into that—that Maddox only helped earlier because those messages implicated him in Jayden's scheme. But I saw his face when he came running down that basement hall. His panic. His outrage. And, later, his fury. He's backed off because someone else is on Lili-duty. His so-called former BFF.

Still, when I get a text during study hours, and it says, "This is my number, thought you should have it," my heart does a little dance. Then I remember it doing the same thing for the fake messages. Before I can say anything, he texts again.

Maddox
You always take the yellow gummies

Me
I like lemon

Maddox
Bullshit, Chamberlain.
You take the flavor you think I won't want

Maddox
I'm going to start removing colors until
I figure out which one you really like

I smile and shift to sit cross-legged on my bed. He's proving it's him, but also, however unintentionally, proving something else, too. That he notices what I do. That he understands why I do it.

Maddox
Those four walls closing in yet?

Me
They are. I'm considering going down to dinner, but I'm not sure I dare

Am I hoping he'll invite me to a private dinner, take our food someplace quiet? Of course I am. And my heart sinks at the next text.

Maddox
I'd suggest room service.
You don't need everyone's bullshit

Me
Okay

Maddox
But if you're bored, meet me
behind the carriage house in 10

Me
Uh . . .

Maddox
Fuck. Right. After last night, I can't be
luring you out of the house. Hold on

Less than five seconds pass before I get another text.

Theo
Carriage house in 10?

I grin and send back a thumbs-up.

FIFTEEN

Theo catches up before I reach the old carriage house, where I can see Maddox waiting.

"Is this where you guys finally admit you're still friends?" I say.

One corner of Theo's mouth quirks. "You're too good of a detective, Lil."

"No, you two are just really lousy at hiding it. I'm not sure why you're pretending you aren't friends, but it's none of my business, especially if it's . . . more than friendship."

"More? Ah." A look that almost seems like regret before it vanishes in an easy smile. "Nah, nothing like that. We're friends. Very good friends."

I head toward Maddox, who says, "We shouldn't be out here for long. I've set a timer for fifteen minutes."

I look at Maddox. "You recruited Theo to help look after me, right? To keep your promise to Cecilia."

"Yeah, that's why I showed you around that first day," Theo says. "I saw Cecilia heading for Maddox with you, and I knew I'd be better at giving the tour. And I wanted to help him look after the new girl because it's really not his thing."

"Oh," I say, and hope I hide my disappointment. "Okay, so is there some other way we can do this? I understand you owe

Cecilia, Maddox, but you guys really don't need to pretend to be my friends to do that."

"Pretend?" Maddox says, face scrunching up.

"Uh, Lil?" Theo says. "It's been over a month. I'm not still having breakfast with you every day because of Cecilia. And Maddox isn't sharing his gummies with you because of Cecilia. Though . . . not sure I'm keen on that part. They are prescription. I'm not even sure *you* need them, Mads."

Maddox makes a noise, as if warning Theo off, and now it's Theo stuffing his hands into *his* pockets, looking something I've never seen Theo look: abashed.

I'm drinking all this in, like I did earlier, the way they act around each other when they stop pretending they barely talk. The vibes are so different. *They're* different.

"As you figured out, we're obviously still friends," Theo says. "As for the charade, it's because of the Westdale Optima thing. Maddox and I knew we'd be expected to compete, and we don't do that."

"Compete?"

Theo's expression goes firmer than I've ever seen it. "We've been friends since we were, what, five?" He looks at Maddox.

"About that."

"And when you're high achievers from high-achieving families—*rich* high-achieving families—everything is . . ."

"A fucking competition," Maddox mutters.

"Even when the other person is your best friend. Even when you aren't into the same things. *Oh, Maddox, I hear Theo's doing really well in basketball. Why don't you try out for soccer—your cousin played for Barcelona. Oh, Theo, I heard Maddox won the short-story competition at school. Directors should also know screenwriting—why don't I hook you up with a mentor?"*

"Fucking endless," Maddox mutters.

"And we *hate* it. So we refuse to compete with each other." Theo looks straight at me, like he's saying something I might not understand.

I nod. "You decided Theo would go for Optima, and Maddox would reap the benefits if he wins. And it helps if you don't appear to be friends anymore?"

Theo glances at Maddox. "We . . . went through a rough spell a couple of years ago. We worked it out shortly before we came to Westdale, but we decided to keep faking it."

My gaze moves from one to the other. Theo has this slightly wide-eyed expression, selling the honesty a little too hard. Maddox isn't even looking at me.

"And that's it?" I say. "Theo aiming for Optima is the entire reason for the charade?"

"Pretty much," Theo murmurs.

"Pretty much," I repeat. "Weird, because it seems like a lot of work to win something that Theo was already the lead contender for."

Maddox meets my gaze. "Yeah, there *is* more. We're just not ready to talk about that."

"We promise it has nothing to do with you," Theo says.

Maddox gives him a look, and Theo gestures, almost like private sign language, though my interpretation is something like *What the hell do you want me to tell her?*

Maddox locks gazes with me again. "We aren't using you. I promise that. It currently has nothing to do with you, but if that changes, we'll let you know."

"Just . . . give us time," Theo says. "It's tricky."

"And you don't know me well enough yet." I hold up my hands against Theo's protest. "That's a fact. I didn't ask what this other thing is. I'm not owed answers unless I'm in some kind of danger because of it."

"You're not," Theo says firmly . . . and Maddox gives him that same look, which earns him more dramatic Theo gesturing.

"We will make sure it *doesn't* affect you," Maddox says. "For now, that's all I'm comfortable saying."

"And that's fine. Really." I look from one to the other. "I'm not trying to interfere here. That's part of why I wanted to understand what's between you two. So I don't interfere."

"You're not," Theo says. "I'm at school with my best friend and need to pretend we're barely on speaking terms. That's rough." His voice softens. "You're helping, Lil."

"I just want you both to know I'm not shoehorning my way into your club."

Theo grins. "No? We have a clubhouse."

I laugh and shake my head. Then I see the look on Theo's face.

"Wait," I say. "You actually have . . . ?"

"A clubhouse? Of course. Messaging is fine, but we're not going a year without talking." Theo leans toward me. "Slip out during study hour tomorrow. Meet us here."

"And time's up." Maddox lifts his watch as the timer goes off. "I'll go around the side. You two can just head in the back door—and if anyone wonders what you were doing out here together?"

Theo's grin grows. "Let 'em wonder."

I eat in my room, but I'm not alone. Isolde and Polly show up with trays, and we have a private dinner party. Allegra joins us after she eats, because apparently, eating in bed is really not an Allegra thing. Theo comes by later with junk food and booze.

I'm about to open a canned cocktail when I get a text from Maddox telling me to check my pain meds and make sure they're compatible with alcohol, and I have to resist looking around for hidden cameras. But as I read the text, Theo quickly says the same thing, and I know exactly what happened. Theo said he was bringing booze; Maddox warned him they might not go with my painkillers; Theo forgot to mention it until he saw me checking my texts, Maddox having known he'd probably forget.

I have to smile at that. I'd moved around too much as a kid to still know anyone from childhood, but I love that dynamic in books—the lifelong friend who understands you better than anyone—and I love seeing it playing out with Maddox and Theo. Maybe I should be envious. I could even be jealous. I'm neither. I'm happy for them, and "secretly still BFFs" is a much better story than "former BFFs who don't talk anymore."

After the Liliths leave, Theo brings me a hot-water bottle, which he says I might need for my aches and pains. He also checks what the doctor gave me, and suggests I take the sleeping pill if I need it. Then he brings me both a pitcher of water and a bottle of juice. It's all super-sweet and considerate. Is it any less sweet or considerate when I see him consulting a list that I suspect came from Maddox?

No, it is not.

The next day, I head outside during study period. Theo is waiting for me behind the carriage house. Maddox has gone on ahead.

To get to the clubhouse, we have to walk through a stretch of forest to an open wildflower field. Theo explains that it had once been a pasture, back when students brought their horses with them. Even after the era of cars, many had their own horses. That ended about twenty years ago. Oh, rich kids still ride—I remember that newspaper photo of my mom—but the school isn't going to tend their horses for them. It's one of many over-the-top luxuries that Theo says his dad waxes nostalgic about, complaining that tuition has continued to rise while perks disappear.

There's a reason for this history lesson. The clubhouse is located in the old stables. The main part has been hollowed out and serves as a garage for student cars. But there's no longer any need for the apartments over the stables where the grooms would have lived. They're all boarded up. Except for one . . .

The clubhouse.

The minute I see it, I have to bite back a laugh.

I've seen photos of mansions, the kind of thing people pass around online as examples of excess, and I remember one of a teen boy's "leisure room." Plush couches, custom-made gaming chairs, a wall-sized TV, and every gaming system known to man. It had multiple temperature-controlled fridges, vintage pinball and arcade games, and walls covered in posters of women that required discreet blurring.

This is the down-market version, the kind normal teen boys might have.

There's a shabby loveseat and a ratty recliner, a monitor with a crack in the corner, a dented bar fridge, and a game console older than the one I sold for fifty bucks. No posters of women, dressed or undressed. No decorations at all . . . unless you count the pyramid of beer cans in the corner.

"Oh my god," I say. "This isn't just a clubhouse. It's a movie set." I turn to Theo. "What are you filming? A don't-hate-the-rich PSA? 'Theo Dubois and Maddox Moreno Are Regular Guys, Just Like You'?"

Theo flips me a cheery middle finger. "We found it like this. Needed some dusting, but it cleaned up fine."

"Did you inherit the beer-empties pyramid, too?"

"Nope. That's all mine." He opens the fridge door to show off a selection of cans. "Take your pick."

I reach past him for a soda. "I hate beer."

Maddox, who is slouched on the loveseat, holding a game controller, lifts his free hand.

"Beer or Coke?" I ask.

"Coke," Theo says. "He makes me drink alone."

"I can't drink with my meds," Maddox says evenly.

Theo shifts, as if holding back a grumble, maybe something else about Maddox not needing them.

Theo reaches past me for a beer. I take out a soda for Maddox and then get a better look at him. He's in the shadows, where he's always most comfortable. He wears a T-shirt, his lean muscles visible, and he's slouching, long legs stretched out, motorcycle boots resting on a milk crate. When he turns back to his game—one of the old *Zelda*s—his dark hair curls over his face and spills onto the couch as he reclines.

At a soft noise beside me, I turn to see Theo smirking. He waggles his brows, and I realize it must have looked like I was checking out Maddox.

Okay, I *was* checking out Maddox.

Without turning from his game, Maddox pats the spot beside him, just like at the bench, and I slide into it and hand him his soda. He pops it open with one hand and shifts, making sure there's room for me, our legs brushing. He reaches to squeeze my knee, just a quick gesture of reassurance, but Theo makes that damn noise again, and when I look over, he's smirking that damn smirk, like a matchmaker whose work here is done.

I do not understand Theo Dubois. One minute he seems to be flirting with me, and the next he's nudging me toward his best friend. Which is it?

It must be the latter. He's matchmaking, and the flirting is my imagination, because no guy is going to do both, right?

Right?

Maddox reaches beside him and picks up another controller. "You play *Mario Kart?*"

"I do."

"Theo? Grab the cartridge and the third controller."

Theo pops *Zelda* out and *Mario* in—the cartridges make it a very old system indeed. Then he plunks down on my other side.

"Theo!" I say. "This is a loveseat, not a couch."

"Just scooch over."

"I can't scooch anywhere except Maddox's lap."

I regret that as soon as I say it.

Theo gives a low laugh. "Guess Lil's sitting on your lap, Mads. How will you ever survive?"

"Ignore him," Maddox says and shifts, with his right arm going up along the back of the couch, controller held in his left hand. "There. You've got a bit more room."

I ease over under his arm, which he rests partly on the sofa, partly on my shoulders. Theo pushes back until he's seated, though I'm right up against him, too, from knee to hip to shoulder.

"There," Theo says. "See? It works."

Maddox shakes his head. "Leave her alone and start the damn game."

SIXTEEN

I spend the next few days continuing to heal while obsessing over my mini-mysteries whenever I have time . . . between classes and homework and socializing, which means I don't get nearly enough opportunity to pursue them properly. None are urgent, though, so I prioritize appropriately.

The basement scorpion seems to be the one in the staff yearbook, following a message threatening my father. There are *two* threatening messages, and someone also defaced his photo. Then the school replaced the photo and covered up the messages.

I also haven't overlooked the fact that my father's surname isn't what he went by. He borrowed it from his supervisor, Burt Greene. A simple and common name.

Run, Nelson, run. Because if you ever show your face again?
Ask Will Nelson about Annette.

The first is a threat, but it can't be because my dad "got" my mom pregnant, since that wouldn't have happened yet. Also, that symbol makes me nervous. It's as if the symbol *is* the threat.

The second warning is an accusation about Annette, the Lilith who'd been running for Optima that year.

There's no last name for Annette—not in the yearbook or in Mom's Dux journal. I can ask Allegra for the roster, which would seem a simple thing, but with Allegra, nothing is simple. Better to find this on my own.

The obvious place to look is Mom's yearbook, but when I went to the library to check again, it was gone.

The yearbooks—like all the library's rare books—can't be removed from the room. Yet someone did. Who? It could be anyone, frankly. There's no security system. No formal check-out system either. Sure, there are first editions that must be worth thousands, but this is an elite private school. No one here would steal. Or, at least, they wouldn't steal books.

When that yearbook doesn't turn up and internet searches on Annette and Westdale bring back nothing, I have only one clear resource. And, if I'm lucky, that same route might help me find the Janus Society.

I tap on Allegra's door during study hours.

She opens it and says nothing.

I whisper, "I know it's quiet time, but I'd like access to the Lilith's archives."

"Be more specific."

I try for a casual shrug. "All of it? I'm trying to catch up."

She retreats into her room, but I presume the open door means I can follow. By the time I enter, she's already back at her drafting table, working on a new design.

"I'm not granting you carte blanche access to the archives, Liliana. You haven't been pulling your weight in the Liliths."

I fall into the armchair. "I haven't missed a meeting or a photo shoot or—"

"You have provided me with nothing. Not a single secret." Her pencil moves faster, gaze on her design. "Polly finds things on social media. Isolde is good at overhearing gossip. What have you brought?"

"Uh . . ."

She keeps working. "Tell me who Theo is taking to the Quartz Gala."

"I have no idea. He's never mentioned it."

"Then find out. Polly wants to know."

I shake my head. "I wouldn't do that to a friend."

"A friend? Or a boy? Even when it would *help* a female friend?"

"Cut that shit out, Allegra. By now you should know goading me about choosing guy friends over my girl friends doesn't work."

"How about your mother's secret? Are you investigating that?"

"It's why I need access to the archives. To follow up on what I've found so far."

She eyes me and then says, "Which is?"

I shake my head. "This is my family history. I'm not sharing anything until I'm sure it's connected to the secret."

"Fine. I will get you into the archives."

Ms. Dimitriou is the one who actually needs to get us inside. All society archives are kept in a lower level chamber, accessible only by both a code and a fingerprint scan. If I find this a bit much, Ms. Dimitriou seems even more amused at what she has to go through.

I think the whole secret-society thing amuses her, like we're kids playing a game. Which maybe we are. I think of that secret room downstairs, and how it's creepy and strange, but also . . . kinda cool? Maybe I'm inhabiting my goth look a little too much, but if Allegra decided the Liliths should hold meetings in secret rooms with candles, where we all swear blood oaths, I'd go for it.

I really need to suggest that, just to see her horrified expression.

I'm sure the extra security on the archives is just the school "humoring" us, acting as if the archives are as valuable as the members believe them to be. If so, they don't know much about the Liliths, because I suspect, if they read our archives, they'd burn them. I can only imagine the dirt we have on past Optimas.

The admin can't read our archives, though, because *that* key is entrusted to the Dux. It's some kind of special key, too, which Allegra says makes the lock unpickable. I do note that the other society cases seem to have regular locks.

Interesting. Especially when the principal has to leave me alone in this room so I can access the Lilith records in private. Once, when Dad briefly worked at a locksmith, he taught me everything he was learning, just for fun. Lock picking might not seem the ideal pastime for a twelve-year-old, but my parents knew they didn't need to worry about me making a career of it. And it does mean that with a few makeshift tools, I *could* open those other society locks.

I wait until the door shuts behind Ms. Dimitriou. Then I check for cameras before I set my bag down in front of the door, so if anyone enters, I'll be warned.

Each society has a bookcase-sized cabinet for their archives. They're all marked. Lilith, Apollo, Mercury, Hephaestus. Four. No sign of a Janus, which seems odd. Even if they're a defunct society, wouldn't they have archives?

I set that aside and open the Lilith bookcase.

Step one: Find Annette's surname.

I just need a roster for 2005. Seems easy enough, but there isn't a book of members, which means that list must be in something else.

There's a full bookcase of archives, at least half of them labeled "Housekeeping Hints and Tips." That's early Lilith humor. The "hints and tips" are the Lilith secrets. I know the roster won't be in there, but I can't resist pulling one out, opening it and—

It's in code.

I laugh to myself. Of course it is. The Liliths weren't just hiding all their hard-earned secrets behind a fancy lock.

There are also account books, and I'm not sure why, since we don't do anything requiring money, but when I look inside, I see that the Liliths used to hold parties. Apparently, being the sole female society, they were expected to host teas and brunches for visiting parents and alumni. That ended in the sixties, when they must have rebelled with the rise of women's rights.

Hmm. If I were a membership roster, where would I hide?

I reach one title and laugh. *Burn Book*? Really? Please tell me this is someone's idea of a *Mean Girls* joke.

I pull it off the shelf and realize it's been rejacketed. The outer cover is only maybe twenty years old. Inside it's much older.

I flip to the first page and see sketches of three girls from 1896. Beside each is a name and a secret.

Alma Walker—takes both desserts and only eats a few bites of each

Edith Chamberlain—sneaks coffee from the teachers' kitchen, sometimes adds whisky

Juliette Brandt—leaves a stench in the chamber pot and claims it was one of the boys

They're tongue-in-cheek secrets. The Liliths poking gentle fun at each other. Juliette must be a relative of Isolde's. I'll need to tell her about it, give her a laugh.

Edith Chamberlain must be an ancestor of mine. I touch the sketch and think I see something in it that I recognize. A mischievous smile that reminds me of Mom.

I flip through the book. Each page is a year, with sketches giving way to photographs, black-and-white and then color. And always, that gentle secret.

A burn book indeed.

I flip to 2005. Mom is there, grinning.

Rosalyn Chamberlain—cheats at cards but still loses

I choke on a laugh. True. Mom always said it didn't matter if she cheated, since she never won anyway.

And there's Cecilia, her hair blown straight, making a face for the camera.

Cecilia Robbins—supplier of fine intimate feminine products

Beside that someone has drawn . . . what is that? A tampon? I squint. No, it's a . . .

It's a vibrator.

I shake my head. Definitely not asking her about that.

No, I might, just to see if I can finally fluster the unflappable Cecilia.

There are two other girls on the page. And then the one I'm looking for. The photograph shows a shy-looking girl with dark hair, pale skin, and freckles.

Annette Donleavy.

Her secret has been slashed out. Not coated in correction fluid but covered with black marker. I put my phone flashlight in front of and behind the page, but it's been thoroughly erased. And on the back of the page, I can see the marker bled through a little and the Liliths left that spot blank, meaning it was erased before the next year added their pictures.

I take a photo of the page for Mom's year. I have Annette's surname. Now on to the next reason I wanted archive access: looking for any mention of Janus.

I flip through the Lilith Dux journals from the fifties and find nothing. From there, I skim backward in time, and after an hour, I'm all the way to 1913, without finding any mention of Janus. Then my phone buzzes with a message.

Theo
Got a question for you

Me
K

Theo
Behind the carriage house in 5

Me
I'm actually in the middle of something

There's a long pause as a red dot pulses, meaning he's typing. It stops. No message comes. It starts up again. Stops. As if he's typing, erasing, re-typing.

Me
Is it important?

The dot pulses. Stops. Pulses again.

Theo
Nah. Later?

Those typed and erased messages tell me that he doesn't want to wait, but the question isn't critical enough to interrupt my study break.

I look at the Dux journals. If I haven't found anything by now, I won't. I message back saying I'll be there in ten minutes, and then I text the principal, to let her know I'm done.

When Ms. Dimitriou retrieves me, I show her the inside of my book bag. She didn't ask, and she seems amused that I feel the need to prove I didn't steal anything, but I don't want anyone claiming I did. Also, I may be establishing my honesty creds, in case I ever do swipe something from in here.

Before we leave, I say, "Can I ask a question about the societies? I found something about one called Janus."

Her frown tells me she doesn't recognize the name.

I continue, "Are there any defunct societies?"

"Not that I know of. You can check the school history books." She tells me where to find those and then offers a wry smile. "They may be a bit dusty. I doubt anyone reads them."

"Okay, thanks."

When I near the carriage house, I rub my face, hoping to erase any sign of distraction. Theo's obviously excited about something, and I don't want him feeling as if I'm only grudgingly here.

"Hey," I say.

He flashes his spellbinding grin, and Annette and the Janus Society tumble from my brain.

"I didn't pull you away from anything important, did I?" he asks.

I flutter a hand. "Homework. What's up?"

"What do you know about the Quartz Gala?"

I go still. Shit. Did he find out what Allegra asked me to do? I look up at him, but he's clearly brimming with happy news.

"Nothing?" I say. "Except that Polly really wants to know who you're taking."

"She's been pestering me, but I've been holding off, working up to the point where it won't seem too weird."

"What won't seem too weird?"

"You wanna go?"

I blink. "Do I want . . . to go . . . ?"

He props one elbow against the stone carriage house. "To a movie, Lil. I'm asking you to a movie." He shakes his head. "The gala. Obviously."

Before I can process that, he says, "Maddox is ready to tell you about the other thing. What we're up to at Westdale. He's letting me handle it, and the gala would be the perfect place for that. Guaranteed privacy, away from this place."

"Okay . . ."

"Also, I really wanted to ask you, so that part just makes a good excuse."

"Is this a society event? A Hollywood party? Either way, you probably don't really want me there. The fanciest thing I've been to was a school semi-formal."

"It's just a fundraiser. For the Quartz Gallery in Atlanta. A day trip. I can't guarantee Cinderella will be back by midnight, but I can guarantee our car won't turn into a pumpkin."

"Cecilia doesn't want me leaving Westdale."

"I've talked to her and Dimitriou. It's up to you now."

"When is the gala?"

"March twenty-third."

"This weekend?" I sputter. "I need a dress and shoes and—"

"It's Monday. We have enough time if you say yes now. I'll lead you through all the rest. So yes?"

I nibble my lower lip.

He bends down, close enough for me to feel the heat of him. "Eventually you're going to need to do stuff like this, Lil. Polly launched you on socials. I can launch you in society. Do you trust me to do that?"

"Of course."

"So . . ."

I take a deep breath. "Okay."

He pulls me into a hug so fast I don't see it coming, and by the time I do, he's released me and he's grinning like I just agreed to let him win Optima.

"Don't worry," he says. "You'll be with me. Safe as houses."

"What does that even mean?"

"No idea," he says, and steers me toward the house. "Now I need to get you on the guest list and tell my mom who I'm bringing so she can stop pestering me. She's as bad as Polly."

SEVENTEEN

After that, I don't get a chance to research Annette Donleavy. That doesn't mean I don't fret about it. Her "secret" is erased, and someone wrote "Ask Will Nelson about Annette" in the yearbook. What if my dad had a thing with Annette before he fell for my mom? That would explain both the message and the missing secret, which might have been removed because it was more cruel than teasing.

Do I care if my dad hooked up with Annette before getting together with Mom? Of course not. And that's just wild speculation anyway, trying to figure out what might connect the two. It's the kind of thing that would have been a high-school scandal, but in the larger picture, it's just regular life, where dating means testing possibilities.

I do find time to skim through those history books Ms. Dimitriou mentioned, but I see no sign of a Janus Society. Anything on the societies follows what I've been told. There were three main ones: Apollo, Hephaestus, and Mercury. Then the Liliths rose to occupy full society status after the turn of the twentieth century. That's it.

I need to set both mini-mysteries aside to focus on preparing for this gala. Also, it's freaking terrifying and I don't know how Theo thinks I can pull it off and what if I embarrass him and—

Breathe.

Would I rather he asked someone else?

Shit.

With each passing week at Westdale, I've gotten to know Theo better, and my feelings get more confusing.

Is what I feel just friendship with sparks of lust? My libido waking up and saying *Well, hello* every time Theo fixes me with a certain look or flashes a wicked grin or lounges, stretching, his shirt riding up from his jeans—

Stop.

It's just lust, right? Because I'm seventeen, and I've been too busy for dating, and all that repressed energy—

Repressed energy? What am I? A horny Victorian maiden?

I accept that I have a physical reaction to Theo and that it must be just hormones, because I have the same reaction to Maddox. So it's me, not them, right?

I shouldn't be lusting after male friends.

But I don't mean to, and I'm as discreet about it as possible, and I can't help how my body responds, and I'd certainly never *act* on it.

So it's fine, right?

And it can't be more than friendship, because if it was, I wouldn't feel the same way about both of them. Except the way I feel with Theo isn't a mirror image of the way I feel with Maddox. It's different, but also equal and—

Nope, I'm not doing this. Not analyzing. My brain and body are just confused by the nearness of two very attractive male friends. Wires are getting crossed, and I need to keep them separate because otherwise, it's weird.

I will go to the gala with Theo and try not to be secretly pleased he asked me. I'll remind myself that he has a reason, even if he admitted that reason was only an excuse.

Damn it.

Anyway . . .

I'm supposed to meet them at the clubhouse tonight to finalize plans, and I'm glad Maddox will be there, because I want to be sure he's okay with this.

That he's okay with Theo telling me their secret? Or that he's okay with Theo taking me to the gala?

Damn it.

I arrive to find Maddox alone, stretched out on the loveseat reading his latest novel. He swings his legs down and pats the cushion before rising to get us both a soda.

"Theo will be here in ten," he says.

I sit on the loveseat, and he plunks down beside me, handing me a can.

"Theo says he had to do something, but I think he's giving you time to confess that you really don't want to go to the gala." He pops the can open. "If that's the case, I'm going to try talking you into it." A sidelong glance my way. "Theo really wants you there, if that wasn't obvious."

"He seems to, but . . ."

Maddox tilts his head. "But what?"

"Nothing."

"He wants you there, Chamberlain. He wouldn't have asked otherwise. It'll be a good break for you and a good introduction to society bullshit. You'll both have fun. But also . . ." He gulps soda and then sets the can aside. "Having you there will make it easier on him. I know he probably seems like he loves this shit, dressing up, mingling, being the center of attention. He does . . . and he doesn't. I know that probably doesn't make sense."

"He likes it in small doses. He's good at it, but the constant attention is exhausting."

He tilts his head, gaze meeting mine. "You've noticed that."

I shrug. "I've seen how he reacts to social media. He's happy to hear his likes and comments are skyrocketing, but he doesn't actually go on himself. He leaves it all to his social media manager."

"Yeah. Theo enjoys the power that comes with being Theo Dubois. The doors it opens. The roads it smooths. But it is, like you said, exhausting. The older he gets . . ."

Maddox stretches out. "When he was a kid, he *loved* the attention. Every time he appeared with his mom or his dad, people fawned over him, and he ate it up. He didn't even mind the paparazzi. He thought it was cool, everyone wanting photos of him. But now?"

Maddox shrugs and glances at the door, as if to be sure Theo isn't going to walk in. "He hates that it's all about the photos. That he's the kid of two huge Hollywood names, and he looks like a movie star himself, and that's what all the attention is about."

"I found one article that was supposed to be about his high-school basketball team," I say. "But it was all about Theo, and it *still* barely mentioned his scoring stats or that he was chosen MVP. It just gushed about his family connections, and there were *so* many photos."

"Yep. So what I'm saying is that having you there will help. You don't know *that* Theo Dubois. You know the one who hangs out here and plays video games and goofs around and is serious about school and his ambitions. So just . . ." A door closes downstairs. "I can give you pointers later, tell you what to expect."

"I'd appreciate that. I'm kinda terrified."

Maddox squeezes my hand and gives me that rarest of gifts—a Maddox Moreno smile, crooked and real. "You'll do fine."

"'Course she will," Theo says as he comes in. "She'll be with me."

Maddox only shakes his head. His hand is still on mine. Theo notices and grins . . . and then goes to drop into the tiny sliver of loveseat beside me.

"No," Maddox says, in the same tone one might use for a wet puppy trying to jump on the sofa. "Stop crowding Lili."

"She can sit on my lap. Or yours. Choices. Everyone loves choices."

"Or . . ." I say, getting up. "I can sit on the recliner."

I drop down into it. "So, what are we discussing?"

"The fact that Theo has no concept of personal space," Maddox says, looking down at his lap, with Theo's feet now on it as he stretches out across the loveseat. "And that his shoes have very old horse shit on them."

"Want my head there instead?" Theo asks.

My breath catches, waiting for Maddox's reaction, but Maddox only shakes his head, yanks off Theo's sneakers and pitches them across the room. Then he lets Theo's feet drop back onto his lap.

"Is *that* smell any better?" I ask.

"Yeah," Maddox says. "The rest of us get foot odor, but Theo Dubois smells like fucking roses. Now, if he's done goofing around, I think Lili will want to talk about her costume."

"Costume?" I say. Then I laugh. "Ah, you mean my fancy dress for the fancy-dress ball."

Maddox twists to look at Theo. "What exactly have you told her about the Quartz?"

"That it's the Quartz," Theo says.

Maddox mutters a curse. Then he looks over at me. "Do you know what the Met Gala is?"

I go still, heart thudding. "Yes?"

"It's like that, only on a much smaller scale. It's a fundraiser with some Atlanta old money and a whole lot of Hollywood. There's a theme."

I stare at Theo. "You did *not* say that. I was already freaking out over getting a dress in time. A *themed* dress? I-I can't."

"You can," he says. "I don't have anything yet either."

"Because you're a guy. You can just add a fancy hat to your tux and call it a costume."

"Pfft. Theo Dubois does *nothing* by halves. We're going in a couple's costume."

I look at the stack of game cartridges. "Mario and Luigi?"

Maddox chokes on a laugh. "Oh, man, I *would* pay you two to show up at the Quartz as Mario and Luigi."

"She's a billionaire," Theo says. "You can't pay her. You need to offer a service. If you want suggestions—"

Maddox presses his cold can against Theo's instep, making him yelp.

"Sadly, no," Theo says when he recovers. "We can't do Mario and Luigi."

"What's this year's theme?" I ask.

Theo makes a face. "Mads mentioned it's kind of a cut-rate Met Gala, and they really need to work on their themes. This year's is beauty."

I stare at him, waiting for the punchline. When he says nothing, I say, "Beauty? With a party full of gorgeous Hollywood stars?"

"Think of it as a challenge. I already have an idea. Beauty and the Beast."

"So I'm Beast?" I say.

Theo chokes out a laugh. "Clearly, you would be Belle, with her books, which fits."

"And you'd go as a beast?" Maddox says. "The guy everyone wants a photo of will be hidden behind a mask?"

"Nah. I'd love to pull that stunt, but not at a fundraiser. I'll be a sexy beast." He leans his head back to look at me upside down. "Think I can pull that one off, Lil? Sexy beast?"

I'm pretty sure my cheeks flush, but Theo doesn't notice because Maddox makes him yelp with the cold-can-on-instep trick.

"There will be a dozen Beauty and Beasts there," Maddox says. "It's the obvious combo."

"What if we *did* reverse it?" I say. "I don't mind being hidden behind a mask. In fact? *Please* let me hide behind a mask."

Theo shakes his head. "Nah, sorry, Lil. This is about launching you. And the internet is misogynistic as hell. You'd get hit with bullshit about how you must look better with your face covered."

"Okay, so beauty . . . I don't even know where to start with that."

"Byron," Maddox says.

We both look at him.

Maddox waves at me. "Lili likes the cute-goth look. It works for her. Juxtaposition. All that's best in dark and bright."

When we just stare, he thumps his head back. "Fine. Ready?" He takes a deep breath and rams through the poem like he's reciting the alphabet. "*She walks in beauty, like the night / Of cloudless climes and starry skies; / And all that's best of dark and bright / Meet in her aspect and her eyes.*"

He glares at us. "Don't make me recite the whole thing."

"You say it with such heart, such feeling," Theo says.

Maddox flips him the finger. "I wouldn't need to recite it at all if I weren't dealing with uncultured boors."

"Hey, I know the poem," I say. "I just blanked. It's gorgeous, but I have no idea how to translate it into a costume."

"Allegra will."

"Does this mean I get to be Lord Byron?" Theo sits up. "Mad, bad, and dangerous to know?"

I glance over. "He was also chased out of England for his scandalous behavior and enormous debts."

"Goals," Theo says.

"Does this work for you, Lili?" Maddox asks.

"It does."

"Then I'd suggest you two go talk to Allegra while I finish my book."

"Yes," Allegra says to Theo and me after the obligatory grumbles about the timing. "I will design a dress for Liliana."

"And this fulfils my obligation?" I say. "Since I told you who Theo's taking to the gala before anyone else knows?"

She gives me a hard look.

"What?" I say. "Technically—"

"I will accept it as a down payment. I'll design your dress and recommend the makeup and accessories to complete the look. In return, you will be very clear who's responsible for your outfit."

"You'll get all the credit," I say. "For both our outfits."

She turns to Theo. "Not yours."

"What?" Theo says. "You won't turn me into Lord Byron?"

"You're already halfway there."

"I'll take that as a compliment."

"It's not supposed to be. I design dresses, not costumes. You have all the Hollywood connections, and you can easily find a historical costumer. Then put them in touch with me so we can include complementary elements in our designs."

The rest of that week is spent in gala-prep. Well, gala-prep squeezed into already busy school days. And gala-prep includes getting ready for my society debut. The guys can reassure me that the Quartz is much smaller than the Met, but it still feels like being flung into the deep end when I can't even dog paddle.

Seven times, I work up the courage to tell Theo I can't do this. Four times I talk myself down. Twice, Maddox talks me down. Once, I just curl up in bed and whimper until the feeling passes.

What gets me through it are three things: One, knowing I need to appear in public sooner or later, and I kind of like the idea of "hiding" in a costume when I do it. Two, knowing this is a big deal to Theo, and I'd never let him down. Three, knowing Maddox wants me there for Theo, and I'd never let *him* down.

Theo's mom asked us to join her for brunch before the gala. His mom . . . who is one of the most recognizable faces in the world, a woman with Oscars for Best Actress *and* Best Supporting Actress, a woman I've seen on screen since I was a little girl, staring up at her in a movie theater and thinking she was the most beautiful woman imaginable.

Now I'm supposed to meet her for brunch? When I'm going to a party with her son? As his date?

When Theo mentioned it, I immediately ran to the bathroom

and threw up, which answered his question. He sent his regrets—so much studying, we'll see her at the gala, kiss-kiss.

Car service picks us up at Westdale and drives us to an Atlanta hotel. We're snuck in the back and whisked up to our separate suites, where teams wait to get us gala-ready.

The next few hours are like every movie-makeover scene times ten. A mini-salon has been set up in my room, and the team starts by washing my already clean hair. Then my face is . . . I don't know. Scrubbed? Peeled? Waxed? All of the above? My brows are reshaped. My hair is trimmed. I get a full mani-pedi, and the whole time, I feel like a doll, propped up in a chair while everyone works on me.

Once all that's done, I'm outfitted in the first layer of my costume, a dark-blue sheath that's nearly black. It's adjusted until it's so tight I might need to be cut out of it later.

Then it's time for makeup and hair. The makeup is more like face paint—it's part of the costume—and it takes an hour.

Next the costume's top layer is added, followed by more primping and adjusting and tweaking, before I'm declared ready.

I haven't seen myself yet. That's one way this room differs from a salon. No mirrors.

Finally, my makeup artists send me into the bedroom to see the end result. I expect they'll follow me for my reaction, but thankfully, they don't.

I half shut the door behind me. Inside, there's a big three-way mirror. It's angled so I can't see myself yet, and I approach it the way one might a wild animal.

What if it's awful? What if they put in all that work, and it doesn't live up to Allegra's vision because *I* don't live up to it? Everyone can only work with what I give them.

I slide in front of the mirror and—

A stranger looks back—a huge-eyed grown woman—and I want to flee. To race out of the mirror's eye until my heart stops thumping.

I take a deep breath and force myself to look at the gown first. There's the simple sheath dress, which has found curves where I didn't think I had any. It's also very short. Like "barely covers my ass" short, and my face heats seeing it. At least the second layer helps, even if it's pretty much see-through. It's that same blue-black color, diaphanous with silver threads that sparkle like stars in a night sky. Because it's sheer, you can see my skin under it, so pale I glow.

For footwear, I have sandals with laces that go up my calves. The heels are low and chunky, suitable for a girl who's never worn stilettos. I wear silk gloves with straps weaving up my forearms to match the sandals, and under those straps, my skin is luminous.

I slowly lift my head to see my face and my breath catches. I've seen myself in makeup, obviously, but this is different. The artist contoured my face with exaggerated shadows to embrace the "dark and bright" motif. Makeup makes my oversized eyes even bigger and their green even brighter. My lips are goth-dark, and there's smudged color along my hairline, as if my face is partially in shadow. Whatever they put on for powder sparkles when I move.

My hair is the least "done" part of me, left down and curled into soft waves at the front. It's a simple showcase for the fancy headpiece, which is a glittering black tiara woven into my hair.

Soft footfalls sound, and before I can turn, a voice murmurs, *"She walks in beauty, like the night / Of cloudless climes and starry skies."* Theo appears behind me, his hands clasping my upper arms softly as he bends to kiss my neck. *"And all that's best of dark and bright / Meet in her aspect and her eyes."*

My eyes glitter—and not from makeup—as I quickly blink back tears.

He squeezes my arms. "You look *incredible.*"

"Don't you dare make me cry. Someone spent a half hour on my eyes."

He kisses my neck again, and a shiver runs through me, and I know he's just being . . . gallant? Chivalrous? But I still feel the heat of his lips long after he moves away.

I turn and step back to get a look at *him.*

He model-turns. "Not bad for a guy who's been dead for a few hundred years."

I whistle. "Wow, Allegra is going to be *pissed* that she can't take credit for this."

"Her own fault. She had her chance to dress Theo Dubois."

The costume designer went for vibes rather than authenticity, and his outfit is the better for it. He has the wide white collar and flowing cravat we saw in paintings. And he wears a burgundy coat, like many of the portraits. But the coat is a modern-vintage crushed-velvet fitted jacket, and the snug trousers are definitely not eighteenth century. I have no idea if the knee-high black boots are, and I don't care.

A makeup artist has worked on him, too, with smudged eyeliner and a faint red on his lips that may not be period-appropriate but definitely screams Romantic poet. His hair has been styled to turn his waves into soft curls that tumble over his forehead. The most impressive part, though, is the color. The stylist didn't darken his gold locks to match Byron's hair—instead they added black streaks, making his hair look like art.

"You like the hair?" he says. "Dark and bright, but also, tarnished gold, suitable for a bad-boy poet." He grins. "And maybe for me, too."

"You look amazing."

"Then I look like I belong with you." He takes my hand and lifts it to his lips with a half bow. "Before we go, though . . ."

He takes out his phone from a hidden pocket and hits a button.

A moment later, Maddox appears. "Finally. I thought I was going to have to look up photos online."

"Art takes time. And this is art . . ."

He turns the phone toward me and pulls back so Maddox can see as I twirl for him.

"*Fuck*," Maddox says. "That's . . ."

"Your idea," I say, grinning as I move back to the phone.

"My high-level concept. Not my execution."

I take the phone and back up to show him Theo. "And the Byronic hero himself."

"Adequate," Maddox says.

Theo lifts both middle fingers.

"I'm kidding." Maddox's voice softens. "You look good, buddy. Really good. You two are going to *slay*."

"That is the plan," Theo says. "Now, I need to run and do something. You keep Our Lady of Dark and Bright company."

Theo lopes off, shutting the door behind him.

When I frown, Maddox chuckles. "That's his not-very-subtle way of giving us a moment. In case you have any last-minute concerns."

I inhale deeply. "Trying not to. The outfit helps. It's like hiding behind cosplay. I can be someone else. Someone who belongs at this party."

"You're an heiress at a fancy fundraiser, Chamberlain. You *belong* there."

"You know what I mean."

His voice softens again. "You've got this. Theo is right there, and if you need a moment, go to the restroom and call me. I'll be awake until you're back."

My eyes prickle again. "Thank you."

"It's going to be a roller coaster. You'll see some sides of Theo you don't see at Westdale. But whatever happens, he really wants you there. Remember what I said?"

"If he gets stressed, find a quiet place and let him vent."

"If he gets stressed, he also might drink. I have my edibles, and he can mother-hen about that, but he has his pressure valve, and it's a good strong drink. Or three. Cut him off at two. Let him get tipsy enough to forget why he's stressed. But not drunk."

"Would that be . . . a problem?"

"Like violent drunk? Never. More like the walls come crashing down, and you might be ready to see that, but I don't think he's ready for you to see that. One drink, fine. Two drinks, okay. Then cut him off. Invoke my name if you need to. But unless anything goes wrong, he's not going to drink. Focus on having a good time. That's what he wants, and what I want for both of you."

"Thank you."

EIGHTEEN

In my old life, I didn't read celebrity magazines. I have my favorite stars, but I admire them for their work and leave them to their private lives. So I've never watched an Oscar ceremony or followed the Met Gala coverage. But I still know this scene: that moment when the fancy car pulls to the curb, and the occupants step out onto the red carpet.

Before the car reaches the front of the queue, Theo sends Polly photos of us in our gala costumes, so she can "break" the story ahead of everyone else. Then the car stops, and he's getting out of his side, coming around to mine, and the cameras are flashing.

There's also screaming from a cluster of tween girls who seem ready to faint. One has a sign reading "Theo, we love you!"

I look at those girls, nearly crying with excitement, and the cameras jostling for position, everyone desperately trying to get Theo's attention.

My door opens before I know it, and I freeze. Theo leans in, whispering, "If it's too much, smile and recite business stuff in your head."

"Business stuff?"

He shrugs and smiles. "Don't ask me. I'm an art guy."

I laugh softly . . . and then I realize the cameras are already flashing, getting shots of us during a private moment that is not private at all. I take a deep breath and let him help me out. A breeze ripples my dress, and I bite my lip, praying it doesn't flip up.

Theo leads me to the carpet and then lifts my hand high, turns to me, as if showing me off to the cameras . . . and recites the whole damned poem. Right there. He doesn't whip through it like Maddox did. He doesn't say it softly, like he did in the hotel room. He emotes it—every word, every inflection, every nuance perfect, having obviously practiced.

Cameras flash and people surge against the velvet ropes. When Theo finishes, he leans in to kiss my forehead—to the renewed screams of the tweens—before leading me up the carpet.

"You didn't warn me you were going to do that," I whisper.

"Because you'd have told me not to."

I only hope my cheeks aren't as red as this carpet. I'm pretty sure my eyes are glowing, though, as I float down that carpet, barely noticing the flashbulbs all around us.

We've been at the gala for nearly an hour. This is the part that terrified me, but it passes in too much of a blur to even register.

Any society people here don't come over to greet the new Chamberlain heiress. On the one hand, that's a relief, but on the other, I can't help feeling snubbed.

If those people are here, they're staying well away from me. The guests we do see are Hollywood. Fifty percent are faces I recognize from the screen. The other fifty are from behind those screens: directors, producers, studio execs. They hug—or fist-bump—Theo, and he introduces me and I say hello and they say how lovely my outfit is and I find something to compliment on theirs, that being a trick Polly taught me, finding one specific thing rather than a general comment.

We're moving across the floor when Theo pulls out his phone. "My parents are pulling up."

I swallow, not daring to speak.

"We'll give them time to get in," he says. "Then we'll catch up with Mom first."

He catches my expression. "It's just my mom, Lil."

"Even if she was 'just' your mother, that wouldn't make this easier. You know that, right?"

He squeezes my hand. "It's my father who's the asshole, but we'll put off that introduction for now."

Five minutes later, we're walking up to Trinity Nilsen. *The* Trinity Nilsen.

She's dressed in a stunning gown with pastel watercolors, subtly striped, and it reminds me of something that takes a moment to click. A sunset. It's a gorgeous sunset over the water, her interpretation of the beauty theme.

She has Theo's gold curls, a delicate face, and makeup so flawless that you question whether she's actually wearing any. She's in a side hall, checking one earring in a pocket mirror. Then she hears us and looks up, with hazel eyes that are the exact match of Theo's.

My steps slow, and Theo's arm firms around my waist, guiding me forward.

"Liliana." Ms. Nilsen moves to take my hands in hers. "Theo has told me so much about you. May I?" She puts out her arms, and I can only nod dumbly as she pulls me into a hug.

Then she turns to Theo and beams, and it's his smile, that spellbinding one. She pulls him into a tight hug and I hear her whisper, "I'm so proud of you, baby."

She steps back and tugs me over to see us together. "You both look amazing. I saw a clip of your poetry recital, Theo." She sighs. "I haven't heard you do that in years. It was beautiful." Another quick hug for her son. "I won't keep either of you long. I just wanted to meet Liliana."

"It—It's good to meet you, Ms. Nilsen."

Theo leans over and stage-whispers to his mom, "Lil's a little nervous."

"Then don't tease her," she says to him. Then to me. "Call me Trinity. Anyone who makes my son this happy is on a first-name basis." She eases back, her smile fading a little. "Did I hear you're both going for that Optimus title?"

"*Optima*," he says, with the sigh of any teenager whose mother gets the lingo wrong. "Lil and I are running neck and neck."

Her smile falters more. "Just . . . be careful. Both of you. Sometimes, in a relationship . . ." She trails off, sadness shadowing those beautiful eyes. Then she tosses it off, looking like Theo when he shoves away a troubling thought. "It can be complicated. That's all."

"My ego will fully survive being beaten by a girl," he says. "I have this mom who'd kick my ass if I sulked."

They exchange a look of such genuine fondness that something in me settles. After Theo called his dad an asshole, I'd been worried, but *this* relationship is obviously a good one.

"Just be careful," she murmurs. "Don't let friendly competition get in the way."

"I know," he says. "For now, Lil and I are having fun running against each other. If that changes, I'll reassess. You know how I feel about competing with people I care about."

"I do." That shadow again. "And how is Maddox? Are you two talking?"

He pats her arm. "We'll work it out. Stop worrying."

Trinity looks at me. "Do you know Maddox?"

I smile. "I do. He's been great, helping me adjust. Though I probably shouldn't say that. Ruin his rep."

Her smile returns, warm and genuine. "You're right. He'd hate it. But he's a lovely boy with the best heart." A glance back at Theo, who lifts his hands.

"Yes, Mom, Mads and I will work it out. Just give us time." He leans to kiss her cheek. "Now I'm going to drag Lil out for more meet and greets."

"Your dad will expect to see you," she says, her voice low.

"I know. We'll do a drive-by."

Things get rocky after that. The booze is flowing, and from the looks of a few people who corner us, the drugs are flowing, too.

Two people make a point of saying they've heard Theo turned eighteen in January. It seems strange that they want him to confirm that, until Theo grumbles about older guys checking me out and wanting to hang a "She's seventeen, assholes" sign on me. Then I understand the comments about him being eighteen, which are super-creepy considering that both people who pressed for confirmation were on the far side of thirty.

When a guy I definitely recognize from TV starts cajoling us to come party with him—while bragging about how soundproof his hotel suite is—Theo decides it's time to pay that duty visit to his dad.

First, though, he's flagged down by a studio exec eager to talk about Theo's future film plans, and I know Theo will want to have that conversation, especially since the exec is sober. I spot the restrooms and whisper that I'll slip off. Theo hesitates, but the hall is right beside us.

I find the restroom, where two young actors are doing coke at the sinks, and I get in and out as fast as I can.

Heading back, I turn too soon and don't realize it until I find myself in a service hall. I circle back, and by that point, I'm worrying that I've been gone too long and Theo will be looking for me. I'm also worried that stepping away from his conversation with the studio exec might have looked as if I was bored rather than being respectful. Yes, I'm out of my element and overthinking everything. The absolute last thing I want to do is embarrass Theo. I need to get back to him . . .

A door shuts behind me. Startled, I wheel and stare in confusion at a door that hadn't been there a few minutes ago. I'd been walking down a hall, so why is there a closed door behind me, blocking where I just came from.

I quickly see my mistake. The hall has a fire door that can be closed in an emergency, and it somehow swung shut after I went through.

Apparently, I took *another* wrong turn. Great.

I head back. I need to get past the fire door and then make a left. That should take me to the restroom, and I can find the way back from there.

Now I really do need to worry about Theo worrying. I reach for my phone and . . .

And it's with Theo, because I don't have pockets. I really need to talk to Allegra about that. Dresses need phone pockets.

I reach the fire door and push—

Nothing happens. I push harder, and it doesn't budge.

A tiny seed of panic sprouts deep in my gut. I'm locked in. The fire door somehow shut behind me and locked me in, just like when I was locked in the basement and—

And what? That was Jayden, who absolutely could not get access to the Quartz Gala. I just walked through a door I shouldn't have, which triggered something to shut it.

I take deep breaths, and then I push on the door again. When it doesn't budge, I resist the urge to bang on it. I am *not* causing a scene while I'm here as Theo Dubois's guest. If I do, I'll wake up tomorrow to online stories that I got drunk and locked myself in a back hall.

I turn around and head the other way. There's a corner up ahead, and I can hear the distant voices of the gala.

Picking up my pace, I hurry toward that corner. My sandals clack loud enough that I'm sure everyone at the party can hear them, and I slow just in time to hear a footstep behind me. I start to wheel—

Hands grab me from behind, one going over my mouth. The shock of it has me reeling back. The person starts to drag me, and I snap out of my shock and flail, kicking backward.

My kick hits empty air. I grab at the hand, yanking, but it's a viselike grip, and they're dragging me toward an open door—a door that had not been open earlier.

Then there's a loud boom behind us, and the person dragging me goes still.

"Hey!" a woman's voice calls. "Who shut this?"

She pounds on the fire door. The person holding me loosens their grip, as if twisting to see what's happening.

I bite down hard. My attacker yelps, and I'm free and flying along the hall, skidding around the corner. The voices ahead come clearer now, and I hope that means this hall opens into the party. I can't hear whether my pursuer is following—my heart pounds too hard to catch footfalls.

I turn left at the next corner, only to hit a dead end. I spin around and—

"Rosie?"

I shrink back. The hall is dimly lit, and the man stands at the junction I just rounded. He's in his mid-thirties with dark hair, and his face reminds me of someone, but I don't have time to stop and wonder who. I back deeper into the shadows, my hands still lifted to ward him off.

He frowns, and his words slur. "Rosie? I'm not going to hurt you. I'd never hurt you."

He steps unsteadily toward me. His pupils are huge, as if he's high.

"I heard you were . . ." He swallows. "Dead. Are you a ghost?"

Rosie. He called me Rosie.

I creak out the words, my voice as unsteady as his steps. "If you're mistaking me for Rosalyn Chamberlain, sir, I'm her daughter, Liliana."

He stops. Frowns. Sways. "Liliana." He rubs a hand over his mouth. "You look so much like your mom." His gaze moves over me. "God, you're beautiful."

I creep back more as my heart pounds. "I need to get b-back to the party, sir."

"You look just like her."

He keeps coming at me with a look that makes me feel as if bugs are crawling across my skin. Like I somehow lost the sheath of my dress, and I'm wearing only the sheer top layer.

"Sir?" I say. "You've mistaken me for my mother."

"You're so pretty, just like her."

"P-please let me get back to the party. I won't tell anyone you grabbed me. It was an accident. I know that." I don't think it was, but I need to give him an excuse.

He stops and frowns. "Grabbed you? I never touched you, Rosie. I just saw you run around the corner—"

"Whoa!" Theo comes running up behind the man. "What the hell?"

Theo is between us in a heartbeat, and that's when I understand why the man looked familiar. His hair might be dark, but he has Theo's facial shape and eyebrows.

Theo's father? No, Bernard Dubois is in his fifties.

"Theo." The man straightens. "I was just talking to—"

"You cornered her in a fucking hallway." He turns to me. "This is Charles Dubois. My uncle. He's sorry for scaring you, and he'd like to blame the fact he's high as a kite, but he always is, so that's no excuse."

In a blink, Charles's body language shifts, his face going hard as he advances on his nephew.

"You condescending little prick. Go run and hide behind Mommy. I'm talking to Rosie."

"Fucking hell." Theo gives him a push. "You're even more wasted than usual. Back up and let us through."

"This is your date?" Charles says.

"Yes, this is Liliana Chamberlain." Theo's arm goes firmly around me as he steers us past his uncle.

"You're wasting your time, boy," Charles calls after us. "She won't stay with the likes of us. The first low-bred, half-illiterate nobody who smiles at her is getting between her legs. Just like her mom. A fancy whore but still a—"

It happens before I know it. Theo turned as his uncle started to speak, and it was a slow pivot until those final words, and then, suddenly, he has Charles against the wall. Theo is a couple of inches taller, and as his uncle squirms, it's obvious Theo is a whole lot stronger, too.

"You will never speak about Liliana like that again," Theo says, his words slow and measured. "You will never speak about her mother like that again. Is that clear?"

"You're a child, Theo," Charles spits. "Stop pretending you have one iota of power—"

"Should I tell my dad he really needs to conduct a full audit of his company, with special attention paid to . . ."

He whispers something in Charles's ear, and his uncle pales.

Theo drops him and walks back to me. As Charles recovers, he rolls his shoulders and stretches his arms. From under his right cuff, a tattoo appears. A scorpion tail.

Charles scowls at me and adjust his cuffs to cover it. Then he turns and strides off.

NINETEEN

"I didn't know he'd be here," Theo whispers as we return to the main room. "I would have warned you."

I barely hear him. All I see is that scorpion tail.

"Lil? Shit. Did I scare you?"

"What?" I shake it off. "No."

"But *he* did. He cornered you. Did he touch you?"

I think of that hand over my mouth, of what could have happened if someone hadn't banged on the fire door.

Theo's voice rises. "Lil? He touched you? What—?"

"N-no," I say. I'm safe now, and I can't bring myself to tell Theo that his uncle grabbed me. "He just startled me. He was pretty out of it."

"He's always pretty out of it. Ogling you like that, though? I'm so sorry."

"He mistook me for my mom."

"Which makes it even creepier."

"They went to Westdale together? That's what it seemed like."

"Yeah. I'd heard that. Which is why I would have warned you he was here. When he found out you were at Westdale, he reached out for, like, the first time in years. Asking me about you. I said he was being creepy. He got pissed off and said he wanted to be sure you were doing okay because he and your mom were close." Theo leans down. "They were *not* close. At least not in the way he's implying. I asked a few more questions, which Charlie dodged, and my read is that he liked your mom, but she fell for your dad."

Theo starts to say something else and then a movement catches his eye. "And there's my father. We'll talk to him soon. First, let's get you someplace to rest for a moment."

I shake my head. "I'm fine. You need to introduce me to your dad."

"Are you sure? We could sit down—"

"After we talk to him. Please."

Bernard Dubois is looking for someone. Someone who isn't us, because when he sees Theo, his mouth tightens, as if we're an unwelcome interruption.

"Theo," he says. "And . . . Lillian?"

"Liliana," Theo corrects.

"The Chamberlain girl."

Bernard barely glances at me, which I guess is better than his brother's ogling, but I definitely feel that snub as his attention moves on without even a greeting.

Theo whistles and snaps his fingers. "Over here. Where I am introducing you to someone who is very important to me."

That gets his father's attention, but with an eye roll. "Of course she is. How long have you known her? A week?"

Theo's holding my hand, and when his tightens, I squeeze back, asking him to let it go.

"I just wanted to say hello," Theo says. "Introduce Lil and . . ." Theo's jaw goes rigid, eyes snapping as his dad resumes looking around, obviously done with us.

"If you're looking for Mom, I saw her over by the ice sculptures."

"Who?" Bernard's attention swings to Theo, face scrunching in confusion.

"My mother? Your wife? That's who you're looking for, right?"

Bernard's disgusted snort startles me.

Theo's face hardens. "That was a joke, Dad. I know you aren't looking for Mom. So who is it these days? Marguerite? Or has she been replaced already by some younger, more naive starlet?"

Bernard slowly turns to face Theo. "There is a saying, boy. Pots and kettles? Ever heard it?" He looks at me. "Dubois men aren't good at monogamy, my dear. A little tidbit you might find helpful."

Cold fury radiates from Theo. "Don't compare me to you, *Dad*. In my case, all parties are aware, all parties are accepting, all parties are consenting. My mother is none of the above."

With that, Theo turns on his heel and leads me away.

"Holy shit, did I just do that in front you?" Theo whispers as we walk, his voice strained. "I'm so sorry, Lil. I couldn't even hold it together for two *minutes*."

"It's fine. Let's just—"

"First my uncle and now my father."

People are starting to look over. Theo's face pales, his expression stricken as I lead him through clusters of partygoers.

"It's fine, Theo," I whisper. "But can we go sit someplace for a moment?"

"Oh. Yes. Sure. Just . . ." His eyes go to the bar. "I'll get us some drinks."

"Oh . . . um . . ."

"I know a place we can sit. I just really need a drink."

I take a deep breath and remember Maddox's warning. Theo is stressed, and I should let him have that drink and just make sure he doesn't have more than two. "Go ahead."

"Can I get you something? Maybe champagne?"

I smile at him and hope it looks reassuring. "Sure. I'll take champagne."

The bartender doesn't bat an eye when Theo orders. Not even when he wants a whisky, straight.

"Thank you, man," Theo says when he takes the drink.

"No problem." Then, before Theo can back away, the bartender blurts, "I've seen your short films. Great work. Really. I mean that."

Theo blazes his thousand-watt smile. "Thank you. Actor?"

"Y-yes."

"If you see me casting, remind me I met you here."

"Y-yes. Thank you. Really."

The guy flushes and stammers in a way that'd make sense if Theo was fifty-something Bernard Dubois and the bartender was a college kid. But it's eighteen-year-old Theo and a guy who has to be in his late twenties. I don't think this will ever make sense to me. The power in play here. The power *of* power.

Theo finishes his drink before we get five steps. Then he grabs another from a tray as we pass, and my stomach flutters, but he doesn't touch it, just leads me past a rope marked "No Entry" and into the gallery rotunda. When we see a guard, the guy only glances our way.

Theo calls over, "We'll behave. If we don't, I'm—"

"I know who you are, sir."

Sir. From a guy twice Theo's age.

Theo flashes his smile and tucks a bill into the guard's hand as we pass. "I *will* behave."

"I would appreciate that, sir."

Theo leads me up two levels on the rotunda stairs, and then expertly weaves through galleries until we reach the Old Masters. There, he sets down his drink, takes mine, puts it aside, lays his hands on my shoulders and says, "I'm sorry."

"Please stop apologizing." I push past memories of my scare with his uncle and focus on the rest, on being with Theo. "I had a good time. An *amazing* time."

"Until I fucked up."

"*Theo.*" I take his hands and hold them as I look up at him. "I'm fine. The person I'm worried about is you. Are *you* okay?"

He drops onto a bench, and I sit beside him.

"I told myself everything would be all right, and then . . ." His shoulders slump. "Even with my mom. She worries about me and Maddox, and I can't tell her the truth, and that feels . . . it feels cruel. She gets enough of that from—" He swallows.

"She'll know soon. Once the term is done, you can tell her you guys made up."

"And then Charlie. Here I am, worried about anyone being shitty to you, and who does it? My own uncle. And my dad never even said hello to you. I should have told Mom I couldn't find him. But then she'd worry we were fighting, and sometimes, Lil?"

He twists to face me. "Sometimes I wish I did fight with my dad. Isn't that what normal guys my age do? Butt heads with their fathers? My dad and I just snipe at each other and it feels . . ."

He runs his hands through his hair, some of the black flaking off. "I'd say it feels juvenile, but it actually feels the opposite. As if he doesn't see me as his son. I'm another grown man he can push around. Or, worse, I'm a competitor, just like . . ." He drops his head. "Fuck."

I inch closer and put my arm around him. He twists to face me, but it's awkward, and then he scoops me up and says, "Okay?" and I nod and then I'm on his lap, and his arms are around me, his face against my shoulder. I put my arms around his neck and he exhales, his breath warm.

We sit like that for a minute, and then he says, "I don't want to unload on you, Lil. I'm afraid I'll scare you away."

"I'm not going anywhere." I glance at him. "You said your dad makes you feel like a competitor?"

"He was incredibly supportive with my first film. It felt like a breakthrough. Mom was so relieved, especially when he was proud of how well my film did. But then along came my second one, and I realized . . ."

He shifts so we're facing each other. "He thought the first one was a fluke. I was thirteen, and I had a lot of help, and everyone thought it was cute, this little kid playing filmmaker, and Dad presumed that's why it got into Sundance. But then I did the second one with far less help, and it did even better, and suddenly . . ."

"You're competition."

"Which is absurd. I'm a kid with two short films. He's made twenty-six movies and shattered box office records. But he did the same thing with . . ." His voice hitches. "My mom."

I lower my voice. "He sees her as competition."

"Which is, again, absurd. He's a director. She's an actor. They *shouldn't* be competing for anything."

"Except fame."

"It's not even fame, Lil. It's status. Success. Power. You'd think my dad has enough, but it's *never* enough."

He adjusts me, making sure I'm comfortable. "Dad gave Mom her first starring role. Not sure if you knew that."

"I'd heard it."

"He didn't 'discover' her. She was making a name for herself, and he snagged her early on. They fell in love. Got married. At first, Mom acted only in his movies, like in the old days, when you'd be under contract with one studio. Then Dad 'let' her take a role in a friend's film . . . and she won her Supporting Actress Oscar. After that, she was being offered leads and didn't have time to play the girlfriend in *Big Guns and Explosions Part Four*, or whatever Dad was pumping out. And then, all of a sudden, she's unexpectedly pregnant. Whoops. Don't know how that happened."

Theo bites his lip. "I have my theories, obviously. I was born, and Mom had to slow down and take jobs with Dad again, because he'd accommodate her on set. But then I get a few years older, and Mom finds an amazing nanny, and she can take us both on set, and she doesn't want the roles Dad's offering."

"The girlfriend in *Big Guns and Explosions Part Seven*?"

"Hardly," he snorts. "By that point, it'd be the girlfriend's *mother*, 'cause Mom had turned thirty. And that's when the fights started. Dad wanting more kids, Mom wanting to wait a few years, Dad asking me if I want a little brother or sister . . ."

I inhale sharply. "That's wrong."

"It is." Theo reaches for a sip of his drink. "Which is not what I'm here to talk about. But I'm going to use it to segue into something that may require the rest of this drink. And you might want to take a big gulp of that champagne."

"Uh . . ."

Despite his words, he sets down his glass without finishing it. "When Dad took his potshot at me, do you understand what he was saying?"

I mock-glare at him. "I'm not twelve, Theo. He meant you don't do exclusive relationships."

"But the way he said it makes me seem like some kind of fuckboy. I do *committed* relationships, Lil. They're just not *exclusive*. By mutual agreement, of course."

"Okay." I arch an eyebrow. "Was that the awkward part? If so, I'm wondering how sheltered you think I am."

"We are about to find out."

"Uh . . ."

"I've mentioned that Maddox and I don't compete." He meets my gaze. "Ever. For anything."

"Okay."

He studies my expression. Then his lips twitch. "I really do need to spell this out. Let's start with a story. Twelve-year-old Maddox and Theo. Cute girl at school who makes it very clear she likes both of them. I kiss her. Maddox kisses her. We compare notes."

I sputter. "You compared notes?"

"We were twelve. After that, though, she started expecting us to compete for her. Like, who could take her to the best places. Who could buy her the best gifts. But we don't do that. So we flipped a coin to decide who'd keep dating her."

Now I'm choking on my laugh. "Seriously?"

He lowers his voice conspiratorially. "We weren't really that into her. Anyway, I won, and she was furious. She'd read about love triangles in books, and Maddox and I were supposed to fight for her. Instead we shrugged and walked away."

"Because you don't compete. Which makes sense. I've read those stories, too, and they can be fun in fiction, but in reality, someone is going to get hurt."

"Which is completely unnecessary."

"I agree," I say. "If the competitors are, say, siblings or good friends, she shouldn't get into a romantic relationship with either of them."

"Uh . . ." He presses a thoughtful finger to his lips. "There is another solution."

I frown. "What?"

He looks me in the eye. Sighs. Shakes his head. "Looping back to what we just talked about. Committed non-exclusive relationships."

"Ah." I smile. "That'd work. All parties knowing. All parties agreeing. All parties consenting."

"Exactly." A pause. "Would *you* ever date two guys at the same time?"

I shrug. "Theoretically, sure. I always thought it was weird that kids jump straight into monogamous relationships. My friends would go out with a guy once and suddenly they're exclusive. I always wondered if it's a cultural thing or just insecurity—not wanting to share."

"Don't look at me. Since I am non-monogamous, I do not expect—or need—monogamy."

"But it is weird, right? At our age, we're figuring out what we want in a partner. Or even if we *do* want a partner. Dating more than one person makes sense."

"It does. And I'm really glad you think that."

When I frown, he stares at me. Just stares. Then he thuds his head onto my shoulder and reaches for my champagne flute. "Have some of this, Lil. I think you'll need it."

I take a sip to humor him.

"Do you like Maddox?" he asks.

I choke on the champagne. He pats my back and then says, "More is obviously required. Another sip."

I roll my eyes but do it.

"You like Maddox," he says. "And don't do the 'as a friend' bullshit. You like Maddox. You're both doing that cute thing where it's obvious you're into each other and you're both certain the other one doesn't feel that way. Very middle-school, Lil."

"Maddox has never given any—"

"You two are practically holding hands when you sit together. Middle-schoolers know what that means. *Middle-schoolers*." He waves at the champagne flute. "Have another sip before your face lights on fire."

I take a sip. Possibly a gulp.

"And me?" he says.

"Wh-what?"

"I think you like me," he says. "I *know* I like you. I've been very obvious about it. If you only want to be friends, that's cool. If you only want to be friends with Maddox, then you need to let him know, but also, that's your choice. Neither of us hangs out with you because we're hoping for more."

"Okay..."

"If you want neither of us, we'll survive. If you want one of us, we could work it out. There is, however, a third alternative."

I blink at him, my brain swirling from the champagne.

He groans. "By this point in the conversation, please tell me you know where I'm going with this."

"Date... both of you?"

He slaps one hand on his thigh. "Finally. I thought we were never getting there."

"I can't—I mean, I could—" My cheeks burn. "But I can't just *decide* that."

"Sure you can."

I sputter. "Are you seriously proposing this without asking Maddox what *he'd* want?" I pause. "*Have* you asked?"

"Not outright. He'd do what you're doing, sputter about how you might not want to and how do I even know you like him and..." Theo throws up his hands. "I need to start somewhere, or the three of us will be circling one other until the next century."

He puts his hands on my shoulders. "You said you can't just decide you'd date us both. But you can. For *you*. I can decide it for me, which is obviously a yes. And Maddox can decide it for himself, and if he says he needs exclusivity, then you have another decision to make."

"I'm very confused."

His hands rise to my face, cupping my cheeks. "I know. But this didn't come out of nowhere, Lil. I think you realize that. So take some time and think about it. Can you do that?"

I nod.

"In the meantime, can I kiss you?"

TWENTY

I blink. "Kiss me?"

"Is that a no? Because the pattern was established five years ago. I kiss you. Then Maddox kisses you."

"And you compare notes?"

"Nah, we aren't twelve. But I will ask one thing." He leans in to my ear. "Please don't make us flip a coin. That's just weird."

"And I can't make you compete with gifts?"

Theo waves. "I brought you to the Quartz Gala. Unless Maddox can get you into the Met, I win." He pauses. "No, wait. I could get you there, too. Also the Oscars, Sundance, Cannes. I think Maddox can get you VIP tickets to the big tech shows."

"I might like tech shows. I could wear a full costume, with a mask."

"Uh, that's Comic-Con, Lil. Which, again, I can totally get you into." He leans his head onto my shoulder, arms tightening around me. "We'll put the kiss aside for now, because while you're being very patient, I know you want to hear what I promised to tell you. The excuse for the gala trip."

Right. I'd totally forgotten that. "Why you and Maddox are really playing not-friends."

"Yep, and when I'm done, I probably won't get that kiss, which is why I was trying to sneak it in. Also, possibly sweetening the pot with the idea of getting to date two very fine guys . . . if only you forgive them for one very lousy trick."

"Uh . . ."

"Remember that we decided all this before we got to know you." He clears his throat. "I don't give a shit about being Optima."

I blink at him. "What?"

"I *would* like to win, but only to tell those fuckers I'm not joining their little circle-jerk."

I slowly climb off his lap, still processing what he's saying as I sit down beside him. "So you—"

"Lied. Not going to dance around it. I lied." He exhales. "Okay, that's the confession out of the way, and now the context. For that, we need to roll back. What do you know about Maddox's sister, Jenna?"

I take a moment to segue, while knowing it's not really a segue—he's suggesting these things are connected.

"I heard she died," I admit. "Someone told me, and I hated knowing when Maddox obviously didn't want that."

Theo shrugs. "It's not that he didn't want you to know, Lil. It just wasn't exactly going to come up in conversation. I'm glad you know, though. It helps. For understanding him. Where he's at. So what *do* you know?"

"Only what I was told. That Jenna was a Westdale student. She went to an off-site party and died of an overdose. It hit Maddox hard, and he didn't want to come to Westdale, but his parents made him."

"Maddox *did* want to go to Westdale. He just doesn't want to *be* there."

I want to ask what Theo means by that, but he keeps talking.

"If he had refused, his mom would have insisted. Not his dad. His parents split long ago. Dad's fine, but he works for the government, posted overseas."

"He doesn't talk about his parents."

A humorless smile. "What's there to say? Dad's mostly MIA. Maddox barely talks to his mom since Jenna died. His sister *was* his family."

"So she *did* die of an overdose."

"According to the coroner's report. We also have a contact in the legal system who confirms it. But 'overdose' might not tell the whole story."

"Because Jenna didn't do drugs?"

A soft laugh. "Oh, she did. Recreationally. It's how she blew off steam. And not Maddox's prescription edibles either. She *partied*. And she experimented. The official story is that it was an accident. She shot up heroin at the party, and her batch was laced with fentanyl."

My heart beats faster, thinking of this girl, Maddox's sister, just wanting to have some fun, try new things, explore. And then she was dead, and everyone was going to blame her, just another kid doing something stupid.

Theo continues, "I *could* buy the official story, but I'm not going to because Maddox is my best friend, and he has questions, and I want him to have answers."

"What are his concerns?"

"One, Jenna didn't do heroin. She was needle-phobic. She also never took anything she considered too addictive, and heroin is at the top of that list. She might have been a party girl, but she was *very* responsible."

"Like Maddox. He acts like he doesn't care about school, but he's never late with an assignment."

"Yes. He also doubts Jenna went to any party, because when he spoke to her earlier that evening, she said she had a project and was planning to pull an all-nighter. Maddox says she'd never skip out for a party, and she'd never lied about going out before. In fact, she always sent him the address because she insisted on knowing where *he* went, for safety."

"Sounds like a good sister."

"She really was. Maddox's other argument is that getting Westdale passes is tough, and he can't see them granting her one to leave so late. She was in her room, video-chatting with Maddox at eight."

My gaze flies to his. "They gave her a pass? That's on *record?*"

"It is. The pass says she said she was going to a movie in Savannah with local friends, leaving at six and back by eleven. It's signed, allegedly, by Jenna."

"*Allegedly?* You think it's forged?"

"Maddox does."

"If Westdale forged an evening pass, after a girl *died* off-site—"

Theo lifts his hands. "If Jenna snuck out and died, there'd be a huge uproar about security. By claiming she had a pass, Westdale could be covering its ass. But, yes, Maddox thinks it's suspicious. When I said he doesn't want to *be at* Westdale, but he wanted to *go to* Westdale, that's what I meant."

I rock back. "He believes Westdale had something to do with Jenna's death. He hates being where she died, but he's there to investigate her death. With your help."

"Yes."

I sit with that for a second. "That's why you're faking the not-friends routine. So no one catches you whispering and conspiring, but also so you can investigate independently. If you ask questions, no one thinks you're asking for him, because you aren't friends anymore. If you take an interest in, say, the process of issuing passes, they won't connect it to Jenna."

"Yes."

"Okay." I think some more. "But how did befriending me help you with this case? Because it must, if this is your explanation."

"It's more like an incidental connection. Cecilia claimed Maddox needed to help you because he owed her for getting him out of trouble. That's half right."

I squeeze my eyes shut. "Cecilia didn't get him out of trouble. Maddox doesn't *get* in trouble. Even his edibles are prescription."

"After Jenna died, Maddox found Cecilia's business card in his sister's things. He knew Cecilia does legal work for Westdale. Jenna having her card seemed suspicious. Turned out to be something completely unrelated, but Cecilia was . . ."

He shrugs. "Cecilia is badass and takes no shit, but she has a soft spot for kids with problems, especially Westdale kids. She figured out that Maddox was concerned about Jenna's death, so she gave him everything she could."

"Does she think he has reason to be suspicious?"

"She never says. That woman plays her cards so tight to her vest they're practically glued on."

"So she asked him to watch out for me in return for what she's given him on his sister."

I remember that first day, when Cecilia and I drove up, and Maddox just happened to be reading on the front steps . . .

which I've never seen him do since. He knew Cecilia was coming and why.

"Did she ask you to help out, too?" I say.

"Nah. Maddox asked because . . ." Theo rubs his mouth. "Jenna's death has made him super-careful. He thought it was strange how Cecilia stressed that she wanted him looking out for you. Not just showing you around but watching over you, reporting any trouble, however small. Cecilia's concern made *him* concerned, so I came up with the Optima competition idea to explain why I was being helpful."

"You could have just pretended I was irresistible," I say with a smile.

He laughs. "You'd have run the other way." He looks at me. "So that is why we were both watching out for you, but it's not why we were *hanging* out with you. Our attention could have tapered off once everything seemed fine, except by then we *wanted* to be with you. In case that's not completely obvious."

Silence sits there, between us, until he says, "I'm sorry, Lil. For lying."

There's a moment where I'm not sure what he means. Everything else he's said has buried that lie, and I dig it out again now, examining it from every angle.

Does it make any difference *why* he got to know me? He admitted to having an ulterior motive from the start, and if that actual motive was a lie, it's not as if the truth was something dark and devious. He'd already confessed he started hanging out with me to help Maddox. It's just the reason that's different. He didn't do it because Maddox owed Cecilia; he did it because Maddox was worried, and that's the best reason of all.

"Lil?"

I turn to him, seeing his worry etched there, his breath coming slow and shallow, as if he's waiting for me to stand and walk away. And I do the only thing I can think to do. I lean over, and I kiss him.

Then I realize my mistake.

I don't know how to kiss.

Okay, yes, I've kissed boys, but we're talking middle-school kisses and a few times when a male friend tried to kiss me. This is Theo Dubois, who has *all* the kissing experience, plus experience in things I haven't gotten anywhere near and, oh god, this is going to be so embarrassing and I should stop before he realizes . . .

Except he doesn't seem to realize anything's wrong because I'm doing fine, following his lead.

Only then it's like someone tossed me in the water, and I started dog-paddling instinctively, only to remember I don't know how to swim, whereupon I stop swimming.

My lips stop moving.

Theo pulls back, his breath coming fast, his pupils dilated. "Lil? No?"

Do it, Liliana.

Do not think about the thing.

Do *the thing.*

I kiss him again. It's like ballroom dancing, right? I can just follow his lead. Or that's the theory, but once he's kissing me again, my brain shuts off, which is probably for the best.

My arms slide around his neck, my body pressing to his, and he makes a low noise, like a groan. His hands slide to my ass, as if he's going to pull me back on him. Then he stops and murmurs what sounds like an apology, and there's part of me that wants to climb onto him anyway, straddle him and feel his hands on my ass, under my skirt . . .

And there's part of me that says no, he's right, slow down, I'm not ready. I'm nowhere near ready.

So I just kiss him. His hands are around my waist, mine around his neck, and I kiss him until I can't breathe and I still don't care.

Finally, I give a little gasp that may be my body's panicked cry for air, and he pulls back, his chuckle vibrating through me. Then he hugs me. Just holds me tight, his body warm, his heart beating against my chest. When he lets go, his hands move to cup my cheeks.

"You won't regret this," he says, his voice rough. "I promise that." He presses his lips to mine, his hands still cupping my cheeks, thumbs stroking my face, kissing me until his watch vibrates with an alarm.

He pulls back and sighs. "And that's our sign."

"The ball is done? Our coach about to turn into a pumpkin?"

"Nah, but *we'll* turn into pumpkins if we aren't back by two. I need to call the driver." He smiles. "It'll take him a few minutes to get here, though, so if you have any idea how to fill the time . . ."

I smile back at him. "I do."

We've been in the town car for two hours, with just over an hour to go, Westdale being, well, *west* of Savannah and therefore closer to Atlanta.

Before leaving Atlanta, Theo had the driver stop for takeout at his favorite local burger place. We'd both removed our makeup, already smeared from kissing. After we both ate and sent some texts, Theo started drifting off. Now he's asleep, with me up against him, the remnants of our meal lie scattered around us.

I keep thinking through everything Theo told me about Jenna Moreno.

Did Westdale forge the pass to avoid the hell that would rain down if a student snuck out and OD'd at a party? Has everyone jumped to the conclusion that it *was* an OD because Jenna was a party girl? What if someone at the party injected her?

I had a friend who was needle-phobic and practically had to be sedated. I can't imagine that friend *ever* injecting herself with drugs. But was Jenna *that* needle-phobic?

Did she fudge the truth for her little brother? Did she lie about staying in with homework? Did she finish early and sneak out?

What if she never went out? What if someone at Westdale killed her? And if the police claim she OD'd at an off-campus party, that's a cover-up.

The whole *thing* smacks of cover-up. Jenna was a known party girl. What's the obvious explanation for her sudden death? An overdose . . . off-site, of course, where Westdale couldn't be responsible, especially if they gave her a pass to see a movie with friends.

I want to look up her death online, but first I need to hear Maddox's version. Theo said he'll be at the clubhouse, and we'll sneak back there after the night guard confirms we've returned. Because that's the routine.

The night guard needs to confirm the return of all students who leave. And the school will have records of when we left because, duh, gated entry.

So how would Jenna—?

That's a question for Maddox, and I'm sure he'll fill me in.

I have my phone in hand, browser open, as if I'd subconsciously been preparing to research Jenna's death.

There is something else I can look up. Another Westdale student.

Annette Donleavy.

The search engine tries to direct me to Annette "Dunleavy." Donleavy is apparently rarer. In fact, it's so rare that an initial search brings back nothing but results that mention two different people: an Annette plus a Donleavy.

I switch to a slower but more accurate search engine.

As I'm waiting for the results, I remind myself that Annette will be thirty-six or thirty-seven, and if she's married, she may have taken on her spouse's name. Results under her maiden name could be sporadic and—

Obituary for Annette Marie Donleavy

My heart sinks. I click on the link and a photo fills the page, one of a girl with dark hair and a smattering of freckles.

It's the same photo from the yearbook. Odd that they'd use such an old picture when she must have died years later—

Annette Marie Donleavy. 1987–2005.

I inhale so deeply that Theo stirs against me. I turn to kiss his shoulder and then pause, struck by how automatic that instinct was.

I want to stay there longer. Kiss him again, snuggle in and be a girl with a guy in the back of a car, my heart soaring with hope and possibility, forgetting—for a moment—what's on my phone screen.

I take a deep breath. Then I look at my phone again.

Annette Donleavy died the year my parents ran from Westdale.

Maybe she died after graduation and—

Funeral to be held March 12, 2005.

My fingers tighten on the phone.

The obituary contains only the barest smattering of facts, mostly dealing with the service, and the usual "survived by" list of relatives. There's nothing about Annette herself beyond trite phrases like "taken too soon" and "claimed by the angels." As for cause of death? "Died unexpectedly."

Does that mean suicide?

Using her death date, I dig deeper. It takes a while before I find any mention, and when I do, it's in a community paper for a town near Westdale, and it doesn't even get her name right, listing her as Annie Dunleavy.

"Annie Dunleavy" died in a single-vehicle accident on March 7, 2005. She was the driver of said vehicle. There were no other occupants. The accident was believed to have occurred in the wee hours of the morning, and the car was found early that morning. "Miss Dunleavy" was a student at the very exclusive Westdale Academy. Calls made to the school for a statement were not returned.

Annette died on a back road between Westdale and Savannah, on a Wednesday, which means she was out on a weekday night, which is not allowed.

Annette Donleavy was a Westdale student who died in an accident, under circumstances that don't make sense.

Just like Jenna Moreno.

"Cecilia," I say, harshly and loudly enough that Theo startles.

"Hmm?" he says, rubbing his eyes.

I hesitate, knowing I should tell him to go back to sleep. But we're only about twenty minutes from Westdale.

"I know why Cecilia helped Maddox with his sister," I say.

More eye rubbing, combined with a yawn. "Why?"

"I've been looking into a girl named Annette Donleavy. She was a Lilith at the same time as my mom and Cecilia. I saw her name in conjunction with my dad, which made me curious."

Theo adjusts, sliding his arm behind my back. "Your dad?"

"I'll get to that. The point is that I was curious but not alarmed. Just a little mystery that I hoped would shed more light on my parents' time at Westdale. I was doing that by searching on Annette just now. She died the year she was at Westdale."

Now he straightens. "What happened?"

"I only found this." I show him my screen. "It's a very short article from a very small paper that didn't even spell her name right. According to it, she died in a single-vehicle accident late on a Wednesday night. No witnesses."

"Shit." He puts his window down for fresh air as he shakes off sleep. "So Cecilia knew her. They were in the Liliths together."

"Yep, which I suspect means Cecilia wasn't just helping Maddox out of the goodness of her heart."

"Jenna's death reminded her of Annette's."

"And that's also why Cecilia won't give an opinion on Jenna's death. She—"

I lean toward the window as we pass the Westdale gates. "We'll see Maddox in a few minutes. We can talk more then." I look at Theo. "Is that okay? Or would you rather hold onto this?"

"Personally? I'd rather not give him this until it seems to definitely mean something. But I don't want to keep it from him."

"I agree."

"And on the topic of Maddox, I've told him everything."

"Everything about . . . ?"

"Tonight. We were messaging earlier while you were chatting with Polly. I told him about my uncle, my dad, my meltdown, our kiss."

"Wait. What?"

Theo sighs and slumps against the seat. "Couldn't slip that last part by you, could I?"

"Uh, no."

"I wanted to be the one to tell him."

"What exactly did you say?"

"That you and I talked. And then we kissed."

"I asked what *exactly*—"

"That's between me and Maddox. What you need to know is that he is aware that we kissed and we intend to keep kissing, within a nonexclusive relationship, and he's fine with that."

"Fine how? Okay with it? Not thrilled but accepting? Or actually fine or—?" I stop myself and take a deep breath. "You're right. It's between you and him."

"And he"—Theo tilts my face to his—"is fine with it. We've been best friends since we were five, Lil. That's why I let him know quietly and privately. So I could get his honest reaction. And I wouldn't have kissed you at all if I didn't know he'd be okay with it—that he expected it."

"Okay. Sorry if I freaked out."

"Oh, I expected *that.*" He leans over, lips coming to mine. Then the driver rolls down the divider, making us both jump.

"They asked for a ten-minute warning before we arrived," she says.

I'm about to ask what she means when the car stops, and Kai is there, pulling open the door, Isolde and Polly behind them, at least a half dozen others on the front steps.

"*Finally*," Isolde says. "Tell us everything."

I glance at Theo. This is not what either of us wanted to do right now, but our friends are waiting, having stayed up to get the scoop on the gala.

I message Maddox.

Me
We've been waylaid by a welcoming committee

Maddox
Yeah, I snuck past them.
See you when you get here.
I'll save you a soda

TWENTY-ONE

We get through the update and then Theo's teasing me about yawning, which I'm not, but it's a signal to everyone that we need to get to bed. We head upstairs, and Theo leaves me at my door, saying he'll see me for brunch.

As I'm shutting the door, a guy I don't recognize just from his voice says, "Wow. Take her to the hottest ticket in the country tonight and you're sleeping alone afterward? What does it take with some girls, huh?"

There's scuffle, then, "Hey, sorry, man. Really. I was kidding."

I peek out. I still can't see who it is, only that Theo has him against the wall, but unlike with Charles Dubois, Theo isn't holding him there. He's just backed him up. Then he shakes his head and walks away as the guy keeps sputtering apologies.

I withdraw, change into my sweats, and wait until there's a tap at my door. Then I join Theo, and we slip down the empty halls and out the back door.

Maddox is in the clubhouse, stretched out on the loveseat, which apparently opens into a bed. He's wearing a tee and sweatpants, his eyes closed until we walk in.

"Hey," he says. "You guys still up for talking?"

"Are you?" Theo says. "You look all comfy. Not sure an open bed is really the message you want to send right now."

A middle finger from Maddox, who then looks at me. "You want it folded up, Chamberlain? It's clean—I used to sleep out here sometimes, so I replaced the mattress and cover. I just figured you might want to stretch out."

"That is exactly what I want to do." I crawl onto the mattress and lay on my back, sighing as I shut my eyes. "Thank you."

"Recliner," Maddox says.

I peek to see Theo with one knee on the mattress, Maddox pointing at the chair.

"Hey, I'm tired, too," Theo says.

"The recliner reclines. It's right there in the name."

"Didn't we have this talk earlier? I could swear we had a talk—"

"Not about you crowding Lili when she's trying to rest on a very small mattress."

"I could get us a fold-out full-sized couch."

"Go for it."

Theo grins. Maddox ignores him, and *I* try to ignore the heat rising in my cheeks.

Maddox flips onto his side, facing me. "Theo told you about Jenna."

I nod.

"He said you'd already heard it from someone, so I'm sorry if you felt you had to pretend you didn't know. I wasn't keeping it from you. It just isn't something I bring up. I'd have been fine with you knowing. Relieved, actually."

"I still feel bad about knowing."

A crooked smile. "Yeah, you're really good at feeling bad."

I roll my eyes. Then I say, "I'm happy to help. Investigating, that is. I'll need to get details from you, but we can do that tomorrow. For now, there's something *you* need to hear."

I glance at Theo, who's quietly listening. He nods, and I tell Maddox about Annette.

Maddox doesn't jump on Annette's death as proof that something is going on at Westdale. He listens, considers, and then says, "Yeah, that explains why Cecilia has been helpful. She has questions of her own."

"Which I'm going to confront her with. Unless that's a bad idea."

"Nah, go for it."

"I will. There's more, though, which I didn't get a chance to talk about with you, Theo."

I tell them about the connection to my dad, through that yearbook.

"Huh," Maddox says. "So . . ." He lays his head down, dark eyes on me. "This might be awkward, but it sounds as if, well, um, maybe your dad and Annette . . ."

"Hooked up? Hopefully that'd mean he wasn't exclusive with Mom. But it's also possible that he cheated on her."

"Nah," Theo says. "Cheating on your mom doesn't fit that yearbook message. Dumping Annette for your mom would. Still weird, considering that Annette was already dead when it was written."

"Unless someone blamed my dad for that. Single car accident. It could, well, it could be suicide."

"Either way, he could have been blamed," Theo says. "He leaves Annette for your mom, and when she dies, everyone blames him, and it's so bad that your parents take off."

"Maybe? But there's another weird thing with Annette, unconnected to my dad." I prop myself up so I can see them both. "In the Lilith journals, Mom wasn't the Lilith candidate for Optima. That was Annette, and Mom supported her."

"Okay," Maddox says.

"But when I had that video call with the Optimas, they very clearly said my mom was running. I even questioned it, and they were adamant. Mom was running for Optima."

"So the next awkward possibility . . ." Maddox begins.

"Is that Mom was running for Optima and only pretended to support Annette. But even other Liliths can't read the current Dux's journals. Who would she be lying to? If she ran for Optima, she had to declare first. And I honestly can't see Mom *wanting* to be Optima."

They wait for me to go on.

"Mom always said she wanted to be a mom and a wife," I say. "That was her goal. Marriage and motherhood. She used to joke about being born in the wrong generation, and how at one time in her family, being a wife and mom would have been a full-time job. I thought she just meant older generations of stay-at-home moms, but now I realize she probably meant Chamberlain wives. The wives of rich and powerful men."

"Managing big households," Maddox says. "Hosting big parties. Supporting big careers."

I nod. "And that's what she did, on a much smaller scale. She was super wife, supermom, and it made her happy. After Dad died, she had to get work outside of the house, but it was a struggle and . . ."

My voice drops. "I guess she was a little lost. She wasn't a wife anymore, and she couldn't afford to be a full-time mom."

I take a deep breath. "My point is that Mom *wouldn't* have wanted to join the Optimas."

Theo says, "Maybe she said she was running to scare others out of the race for Annette's sake."

"Except Annette died on March seventh. After she declared her intent to run. I really need to talk to Cecilia."

"Tomorrow," Maddox says. "For now, we need sleep. Should we head back to the house? Or set an alarm?"

"Am I stuck on the recliner?" Theo asks.

"Yep."

Theo mutters, but he ratchets out the footrest, and we settle in.

I crash hard, only waking to the vibration of Maddox's watch alarm. I open one eye to see him stretching, arms over his head, tee riding up, and I lie there, watching until I realize he can see me in the reflection of the TV screen. Before I can look away, he flips onto his side, the corner of his mouth crooked, hair falling over his forehead, one eye hidden, the other glittering.

"Morning," he says.

"Good morning."

He lies there, one arm under his head, watching me with that lopsided smile. I reach out, moving slowly, waiting for any sign of him tensing. Then I gently move the hair back from his hidden eye.

"Better?" he says.

"Mm-hmm."

"You looked amazing last night," he says. "And you look amazing right now."

My cheeks heat.

He shifts closer, leaning in to whisper. "You're shit at taking compliments, Chamberlain. I'm not really complaining, though. You *are* adorable when you blush."

"Good thing I do it a lot then."

"Like I said, I'm not complaining." He puts his fingers under my chin, tilting it up just a little. "I really want to kiss you, but I'd like to talk first. Later." His gaze shifts. "When there's not someone five feet away, bound to wake up at any moment and put his two cents in."

"Two? It's at least five."

A soft chuckle. "It really is. So . . . later?"

I nod.

He continues, "I'm guessing you'll have brunch with Theo, then talk to Cecilia, after which I'd like an update, so . . . maybe this afternoon? Then I can bring you up to speed on Jenna's case."

"Perfect. Where? Here?"

"There's a pond. Wildflowers popping up. A freshwater spring."

I lift myself up on one arm. "Why have I not seen this pond?"

"Because you're at a school full of teenagers who don't go beyond the back lawn? Why do you think they haven't found *this* place either? They don't wander."

I smile at him. "But you do. Wandering through the forest and haunting the pond, like a Romantic poet."

"Not Byron, I hope."

"Pfft. No. Byron was wild, flamboyant, charming, and a little bit broken."

His gaze flits to Theo, still partly in his Byron costume. "Yeah." He watches Theo for another minute and then shakes it off and says, "Time to wake Sleeping Beauty. We need to get to the house before anyone's up."

We're in the house by six. Normally, Theo and I would have Sunday brunch at nine, but we reschedule for ten so we'll have a few hours to rest. Only I can't sleep.

I'm alone in this massive building. I can hear its old-house creaks and groans, and the distant flush of toilets, but there's a lack of nearby warm bodies and soft breathing to distract me, so all I can think about is Annette and Jenna.

By seven, I'm awake and making notes. First, I write them down on paper, which helps me organize my thoughts. Then I type them into a secure app and shred the physical pages.

At eight, I text Cecilia.

Me
Something came up & I'm concerned. Need to talk. 11?

It takes her less than a minute to reply.

Cecilia
10? Could do after 2 but sounds important

Me
Sure. 10

I message Theo and say I can't make brunch at ten. I expect he's asleep with his phone silenced, but he messages right back asking if nine works. I say yes and return to my notes.

TWENTY-TWO

Theo and I usually do Sunday brunch at nine because it's the earliest slot so it's the quietest. That's not the case today, because everyone who *is* there wants to talk about the gala, so we end up at a big table, answering questions.

I zip up to my room at 9:45.

"I saw pics of you and Theo at the Quartz," Cecilia says when the video call connects. "Damn, that was some outfit. And red-carpet poetry? That boy is *working* it." She takes a deep breath. "But you didn't call to catch up. I could hope you're calling for help with boy drama—I give the *best* advice—but I know that's not it. I also saw that Charles Dubois was there. Was he an asshole to you?" A pause. "God, tell me he didn't hit on you."

"He was wasted and temporarily mistook me for Mom. Theo sorted it."

"Good, so this call isn't about that, I take it. What's wrong?"

"Nothing's wrong. Just a concern."

"Oh?"

I study her expression. It's calm, but I don't miss the tightness in her voice. She's on high alert for "concerns."

"Annette Donleavy," I say.

She rocks back as that bomb lands.

"I'm going to call you back," she says.

Thirty seconds later, a video call comes from an unknown number. I tentatively click, but it's Cecilia.

"This line is more secure," she says.

"You need a secure line to talk about Annette?"

She waves that off. "Just a lawyerly precaution."

"I know about Annette. I also know about Jenna Moreno."

A slow nod. "I wasn't averse to you learning about Jenna. In fact, I recommended it to Maddox weeks ago. He wasn't ready, but I'm glad you know."

"Why?"

The question catches her off guard. "You two have become friends, and I thought you'd want—"

"That's not the reason."

She gives a sharp laugh. "You don't give me an inch, do you, Lili?"

"I don't give *anyone* an inch. If I seem to, it's just not useful for me to confront them yet."

"Fine. You've said you like solving mysteries, so maybe you could help him. Your next question will be whether I think there's a mystery to be solved. I have no idea, but I believe Maddox needs answers."

Nice answer. Also, the same one Theo gave.

"I think there's more to your concern," I say, "but we'll get to that. For now, yes, I know about Jenna, and Maddox is going to share what he's found. I might want to talk to you about that after I've processed it."

"There isn't much to process, Lili. But, yes, I'll be home after two."

"One quick question before we talk about Annette."

She relaxes, as if I've given her time to prepare. "Shoot."

"You said before you don't know why my parents really left," I say. "Could it have had anything to do with Annette's death?"

A pause, and then, "Continue."

Not the answer I expected, but when she says it, I almost smile. Typical lawyer. She's going to find out what I know before responding.

"Annette died in March," I say. "Single-vehicle accident. No witnesses. That's always suspicious, but it also does happen, and I can come up with ten reasons why a Westdale student might sneak out and drive to Savannah along back roads. If there's an accident—teen driver who is either inexperienced or driving recklessly—on a road like that, it could be a single vehicle, no witnesses, the accident not found for hours."

"Yes."

"Was it her car?"

A pause. "Annette didn't have a car. It was your mom's. An antique convertible."

That gives me pause, but I push on. "Did Annette have a pass?"

"She did not. One of the guards was let go immediately after Annette's death. It's presumed he was fired for allowing her to leave without a pass."

I focus on my breathing and try to sound casual. "Any chance Mom was driving?"

"Rose didn't drive."

"Mom had a car that she didn't drive?"

"You also have a car that you don't drive. It's a rich-kid perk. She *could* drive, but she had no interest in it."

That tracks, actually. We only ever had one vehicle, and it was mostly Dad who drove it.

I continue. "So someone could have been in the car with Annette, though if it *was* my mother, she would have been a passenger."

"Yes, but if your mom went out with Annette, she'd have told me she was leaving the grounds. She always did, even when she was sneaking off with your dad."

"What was up with my dad and Annette?"

Her frown is immediate and genuine. "Your dad and Annette?"

"Right. What was their connection?"

"Your mom? I mean, Annette knew they were dating." Her frown deepens. "Are you thinking she told someone about your parents? She wouldn't have. Annette kept her head down. She was a scholarship kid."

"I thought Westdale didn't do that."

"They tried it for a while. Annette was one."

"So my dad and Annette never had a thing?"

She stares and then bursts out laughing. "Definitely not. Your dad met your mom on, like, day three, and I don't think either of them ever *noticed* anyone else after that. It was like something out of a book. I teased Rose mercilessly, of course."

"If Annette was a scholarship kid, is it possible she knew my dad from before Westdale?"

"Nah. He was from Vermont, and she was from the West Coast. Seattle, I think. They *did* talk. They were both smart blue-collar kids heading to college. Zero romantic vibes. Trust me on that. If I'd seen them from Annette, we'd have had a chat. If I'd seen them from your dad, I'd have kicked his ass. That night, we believe

Annette left to see a boy she met online. She'd talked about one."

"So there was nothing between Dad and Annette?"

"Where is this coming from, girl? Holy shit, it wasn't creepy drunk Uncle Charlie, was it?"

I think about the scorpion tail on Charles Dubois's arm. And the scorpion beside the warning in that yearbook. And the scorpion in that secret room.

"What society was Theo's uncle in?" I ask. "Janus?"

Her brow furrows in obvious confusion. Then she laughs. "Still figuring all that mythology nonsense out? Yeah, old white guys really like the Greeks and Romans. The societies are Apollo, Hephaestus, Mercury, and Lilith."

"Is Janus a retired society then?" I ask.

"I don't think there are any retired ones, though I'm certainly no expert in Westdale lore. As for Charlie, he was in Mercury. He didn't inherit any of the family artistic talent. His plan was to go into business and support Bernard's career that way, which I think is what he's doing these days."

"There's a comment about Annette and my dad in the staff yearbook. My dad's photo was defaced. I could see where it'd been cut out and pasted back in, with some stray pen marks."

"Yeah, I don't doubt it," Cecilia says. "As you probably saw with Creeping Charlie, there was some hate after kids realized who Rose left with. Half the male students spent the next week blustering and whining. Most-eligible girl in school runs off with the gardener. It was kinda epic."

"I bet. So Dad's photo had to be replaced, and there were also two comments. They'd been covered up, but I scraped off the whiteout."

She smiles. "Of course you did."

"One said 'Run, Nelson, run. Because if you ever show your face again?' And that was it."

"Couldn't even think up a threat? Yeah, my money's on Creeping Charlie for that."

I make a noncommittal noise. Then I say, "The other said 'Ask Will Nelson about Annette.'"

She stops, water bottle halfway to her lips. Her brows knit. "Ask your dad about Annette?"

"It wasn't the same handwriting as the other message."

"Huh." She leans back, office chair tilting. "I don't know what to say, Lili. If anyone was saying shit about your dad and Annette, it was just that: shit. Maybe a rumor?"

"About a romance?"

"Girl, you are *hooked* on romance, aren't you? Anything I should know about in your own life? Maybe after that gala?"

I ignore her and continue. "What else would the note mean?" I stop. "Annette's death?"

Cecilia throws up her hands. "Who knows. It was a message written by a seventeen-year-old. Don't expect it to make sense. Someone threw out a wild and vague accusation, hoping to stir up shit, and all that happened was some poor staff member had to white it out."

"Do you think Annette *did* die in a single-vehicle crash?"

"I do not know."

"But combined with Jenna Moreno's overdose, you believe it's suspicious." I pause. "Are there others?"

"Other students who've died at Westdale? Of course. It's been around for a very long time. Also . . ."

Her voice lowers. "It's a very high-stress situation. Westdale kids are the best of the best, from parents with very high expectations. No matter what they do to prevent it, the school loses someone to suicide every few years. There have also been DUI deaths, alcohol-poisoning deaths, drug-use deaths. Kids self-medicate for stress, the same as adults. And for teens at Westdale, that stress starts much earlier."

I think of Theo, drinking at the gala, and Maddox with his edibles. Even I'd taken Maddox's gummies to relax.

"You've dug into this," I say. "Deaths at Westdale."

"Yes."

"Can I get the names of the deceased? Or do I need to find them myself?"

She sighs. "We'll see. But we aren't talking about students dropping like flies. Including suicide, the stats work out to one every four years, with higher numbers before there were mental health resources." She checks her watch. "My parents and I are heading to church soon. Any other questions?"

"Your parents? Are you in Atlanta this weekend?"

"I am."

I pause. "Does that have anything to do with *me* being in Atlanta this weekend?"

"Is that your question, girl? Because I really need to go."

"Fine. Do you think the school is behind Annette's or Jenna's death?"

"The *school?*" She bursts out laughing and then erases it with a grimace. "That was rude. You just looked so serious and . . ." She clears her throat. "Do I fully believe the official versions of Annette's and Jenna's deaths? I do not. But if either one is suspicious, it's not Westdale you'd be looking at."

"They *have* covered it up."

"No, they covered their asses."

That's exactly what Theo said about Jenna's possibly forged pass. And it does make sense.

"So who would we be looking at?"

"That's the problem, kiddo. I have no idea."

TWENTY-THREE

Before we wrap up the call, Cecilia promises to get whatever she can on Annette's death. Then I follow Maddox's directions to find him at the pond, gazing out. I can see his profile, and I pause to watch him unguarded, his posture relaxed, hands in his pockets.

I ease over so I can keep watching him as I approach.

"You checking me out, Chamberlain?" he says without turning.

When he does turn, he gives me that quarter-smile. "I shouldn't tease or you'll stop doing it."

"I don't think I could."

His breath hitches at that, and I'm glad I said it. He flushes, and then that smile quirks higher and he walks over, takes my hands in his, leans down, and kisses me.

It's a gentle kiss, tentative at first and then a little more, but not much—not enough—before he eases back, still holding my hands.

"Hey," he says.

"Hey."

Another kiss, still gentle, still slow, still ending much too soon. He leans down. "Fair warning, I'm not very good at this."

"You seem fine to me."

A hint of a smile that doesn't reach his eyes. "I'm not Theo."

"Are you supposed to be?"

A soft chuckle. "I just mean Theo's better at this. All of it. He was an early bloomer. And I . . ." He leans toward my ear again, as if to break eye contact. "By the time I was ready to date, I was fourteen, and then Jenna . . ." He pulls back, making a face. "Fuck, I'm fumbling this. Shocking, huh."

He drops one of my hands to push his hair back, and I can feel him withdrawing, the walls slamming into place.

I meet his gaze. "I've been on a grand total of three dates. All with different guys because they were terrible. Last one was in my junior year. After that, I told myself I was just busy. Much too busy."

He relaxes, that smile returning. "Yeah, same here. Much too busy."

Taking my hands, he pulls me into another kiss. It lasts longer but stays slow, and I decide I like that. A kiss I can sink into instead of plummeting headfirst.

"This okay?" he says afterward.

"Uh-huh."

"And is *this* okay?" He meets my gaze. "All of it?"

I look into his eyes. "Yes."

Another kiss, and I think I could do this all day, slow kisses and quiet talk.

"If you change your mind . . ." he says. "At any time. About me. About . . . everything."

"Same goes for you."

That smile touches his eyes. "I'm good." He leans in and whispers, "Really good," before kissing me again.

We're stretched out by the pond, hips touching as we gaze into the water. I ask about Jenna. Theo painted me a light portrait, but

I'd like more, and Maddox is happy to fill in the picture of a sister who seemed nothing like him and everything like him. The wild party girl, but also the clever one, the responsible one, those parts overlooked—along with her kindness and caring—by those who only saw the wilder bits. Like Maddox's heart—and brains—are missed by those who see only a sullen loner.

As for Jenna's death, he tells me what he's found and promises to send the encrypted files.

"Somehow, I thought just coming to Westdale would be enough," he says as he plucks at a wildflower. "That someone on staff would see me and know I was her brother and they'd start acting weird, proving they knew more than they'd let on."

"Hasn't happened?"

A snort. "Nope. Seems detective work takes actual detective work. I *have* done some. So has Theo. But you're probably going to laugh when you see how little we got."

"Never." I glance over. "Any clues?"

"Not a single one. We got hold of the pass, and it looks like Jenna's signature. Theo chatted up the guards, but the guy who was on duty that night is gone. Nothing suspicious. Like your dad, he was just here for college money, and he got it and went to school overseas."

"Anything you checked out is something I don't need to."

I rest my chin on my folded hands as I watch a heron fishing. Maddox leans my way, head touching mine as he tells me about the wildlife he's seen here, and we talk about that, conversation languid, flowing easy and slow as the brook that feeds into the pond.

After a bit of that, I tell him everything Cecilia said about Annette, and we talk it through.

Is it significant that Annette was driving Mom's car?

Is Cecilia right to shut down our speculation over my dad and Annette? I think her reaction seemed genuine.

I also tell Maddox how Cecilia reacted to me thinking the administration had covered up murder, and he agrees with Cecilia. What I suspect Westdale of—forging a pass in Jenna's case, firing a guard in Annette's—can be explained as Westdale covering its ass . . . from security slipups, not murder.

With the murders being fifteen years apart, if one person is responsible for both, the staff would be the obvious suspects. The second possibility would be an outsider who kidnapped the girls, killed them off-site, and staged the deaths as accidents.

I'll compile a list of staff who were here that long, but I'm also aware that even if one of these deaths was murder, it doesn't mean they both were. Or that they're even connected.

What if another student was driving that car with Annette?

What if another student talked Jenna into injecting heroin at the party?

That would make the person culpable, but it's not cold-blooded murder.

Could Annette or Jenna have been murdered by a student? Not a car *accident*. Not a consensual drug injection?

"Annette was running for Optima," I say. "But not Jenna, right?"

"Definitely not. She had zero interest. Like me."

I'm quiet, both of us idly playing with a blade of grass, flicking it back and forth. "You were never interested?"

"Nope."

"Theo says you'd have been stiff competition."

"I have no idea what I want to do with my life, Lili. I mess around with writing, but I don't see a future in it. I'm good at coding, but I'm really not interested in that, however hard my mom pushes. She wanted me to run for Optima. That was her big dream—that I'd join her there."

"Did she push Jenna?"

He snorts, and it's derisive, but there's pain and anger in it. "Our mother wrote Jenna off years ago."

He locks my forefinger with his, tugging at it, playful but also taking a moment before saying more. "I don't think I'm any smarter than Jenna. I just applied myself more. Way back in middle school, when I brought home straight A's while Jenna got B's and a few C's, Mom made her choice. Even when Jenna later got the grades to attend Westdale, nothing changed."

"I'm sorry."

"Jenna didn't care. The way her brain worked . . ." He tilts his head. "It was actually more like Mom's than mine is, which is ironic. I can code. Logical reasoning comes easy to me. But I prefer literature, history, writing. Jenna *only* liked coding. She was brilliant at it. She didn't need Mom's support. Or the Optimas. She'd have gone into tech and made her own fortune."

We sit quietly, playing little hand games, physically connecting and reconnecting as our minds wander down dark paths.

"So no," he says, finally. "No one murdered Jenna to clear the way to Optima. Have you looked into who eventually won it your mom's year?"

"A financial whiz. I talked to him briefly in the video chat with the Optimas."

"Likelihood of him being a killer?"

I laugh softly. "Having never met a killer, I have no idea. He was very soft-spoken. Really just popped off mute to say that he remembered my parents and was sad to hear of their passing. He talked about both of them. Not much, but it felt genuine. I'll still ask Cecilia if there could be any link between him and Annette."

"Like a way for him to get Annette into the car." He pauses. "Did your mom know Annette borrowed it that night?"

"According to Cecilia, no, but all their friends knew where the keys were kept and were welcome to it."

More silence, Maddox entwining his fingers with mine.

"There's something else," I say. "Something unconnected but weird. About Westdale."

"Shit. Did you find those skulls piled up in the basement? I thought I got rid of those."

When I glance over, he says, "That's a joke, Chamberlain. Obviously, I hope."

"Well, actually, it is something I found in the basement the night Jayden locked me in. A secret room."

His brows jump up. "And you didn't say anything? What about me suggests I'm *not* the guy you'd tell about a secret room?"

I lower my voice to imitate him. "Uh, yeah, Chamberlain. It's a big house. It has unused rooms."

"Unused is different from secret, and I trust you to know the difference. So spill."

I tell him about the room. When I finish, he says, "Shit. That's . . . Is it wrong to say that's cool?"

I laugh under my breath. "Exactly my reaction. I kinda love the vibe. I don't think I could convince Allegra to hold our meetings down there, though."

"Yeah, that ain't happening. But I need to see it. Tonight?"

I smile. "Tonight."

We've decided not to take Theo with us. I agonize over that, maybe more than I should. I'm navigating territory that seems to come so easily to the guys. Maybe it's because I've grown up in a culture where girls are taught to be very careful not to make their boyfriends jealous. I've had friends who'd lie about *talking* to another guy.

If I'm dating two boys, I feel as if I need to bend over backward to ensure they're getting equal amounts of my attention and that neither ever feels left out. But that's not solely my responsibility. I need to trust that if there's a problem, they'll let me know. And I do trust that if Maddox wants us to explore the basement, he's not shutting Theo out. The truth is that Theo isn't going to get excited about a secret room. And, as Maddox knows from growing up together, Theo hates basements—they have spiders.

To prove that I'm overthinking it, when Maddox and I make our plans, he tells me that he let Theo know we were busy tonight, chasing a clue, and we'd fill him in later. Theo was fine with that.

Maddox also foresees and fends off another potential issue. After Jayden shoved me down the stairs, Westdale decided they needed to do more to keep students out of that subbasement. So far, though, they've only put on a latch, and when we see it, Maddox pulls a multi-tool from his pocket.

"I checked it earlier," he says as he unscrews the latch.

Thankfully, I wasn't entirely unprepared for this journey. I charged my phone *and* brought a flashlight, and once we start descending the stairs, I check my phone to make sure I have reception. My cell signal is weaker, but it's still at several bars, and my Wi-Fi is excellent.

I lead Maddox straight to the storage room with the secret hatch. As I enter, I curse under my breath.

"What's wrong?" he asks.

I wave. "I forgot to re-hide the hatch. It was behind that cabinet."

"Well, if those footprints in the dust are any indication, no one else has found it since."

I follow his cellphone light beam and see what he means. The only tracks through the dust are mine.

"I guess that makes sense," I say. "They didn't need to come down here to investigate my story, so they probably never came down at all."

"And the fact they didn't suggests they don't know there was anything here for you to find."

"Or they don't care. Just rich kids and their secret-society games."

I show Maddox how the hatch had been hidden, and how the screwdriver had been used to open it. He examines the old tape on the back of the cabinet and agrees with me that the state of it—and the fact the screwdriver had fallen off—suggests no one had been down here in a very long time.

When I lead him through the opening, he puts his sleeve over his mouth to stifle a sneeze.

"The cleaners have *definitely* not been in here," he says.

"It smells like it hasn't been opened in decades, and I couldn't see any footprints in the dust."

He crouches. "Thick dust, too. That really does suggest it hasn't been used. If the room has been closed up, the usual particles—like dead skin cells—aren't coming in to make dust."

"Look who's showing off his science guy creds."

He rolls his eyes and continues shining his light around. He takes in the candles and the brazier and crouches beside it, poking at the burned paper bits. It's only when he stands that he sees the scorpion on the wall and gives a start.

"Shit," he says. "Okay, it's official. You're tough as nails, Chamberlain."

My cheeks heat. "Not exactly."

He gives me a look and his voice softens. "You spent months living alone after your mom died. You are hardcore, Lili. But right now, I mean this." He waves his light around. "The secret room. The candles. The weird little altar thing with burned paper. That's creepy enough. But a scorpion drawn in blood? I'd have been out of here in two seconds flat."

"It's not blood. Just red paint."

"Which you needed to walk up to and check out to discover, while I'd have been hightailing it out that hatch." He walks over, puts his fingers under my chin, and lifts my face, touching his lips to mine. "You really are something else."

I make a face.

"Yeah, yeah, you're also still shit at taking compliments," he says. He points at the symbol. "Do we know what that is?"

I tell him about the scraps I found in the brazier—with the dates and the words *Janus Society*.

"Never heard of it," he says.

"I've looked it up *and* asked around. Blank looks from Ms. Dimitriou and Cecilia, nothing in the Westdale archives. As for the symbol, I saw a tiny version of it on that message in my dad's staff yearbook."

I show him the photo on my phone.

Maddox frowns at it. "Maybe I'm reading too much into it, but it seems like that symbol *is* the threat."

"That's what I thought. And I saw a scorpion somewhere else, too."

I tell him about the tattoo on Charles Dubois's arm.

"Huh," he says, rocking back on his heels.

I hold up my hands. "I might be wrong. I only saw the tail, so it might just be a regular scorpion, nothing to do with this symbol."

Maddox eyes the symbol. "It's pretty distinctive. And I know I've seen the tattoo, though I haven't really looked at it. Charlie has a few, and Theo snarks about them. Charlie is . . . Well, he's a corporate guy. Not an artistic bone in his body. Theo thinks he got the tats in college to try to look more Hollywood, but they really don't work for him. Most times these days, he keeps them covered. We can ask Theo, though."

Maddox returns to the brazier and pokes around in it. "There are other pieces of paper with writing. Probably a wild goose chase—and it's not like we have a ton of free time—but . . ."

"Let's gather them up. Maybe I can piece them together."

We're heading up the stairs when I stop short.

"Oh!" I say. "The audio."

"Audio?"

I glance over my shoulder, looking deeper into the subbasement. "When Jayden lured me down here, I could have sworn I heard your voice. Obviously it wasn't you—and I couldn't make out words. It was just enough to convince me that you were down here. It must have been a recording, but I forgot all about it." I shine my light down the hall. "Do you think it's still here?"

"Let's find out."

TWENTY-FOUR

We find the recording. Jayden got kicked out so fast that he never had time to retrieve it. And since he was already being expelled—and had confessed to luring me—maybe there was no point bothering with the recording.

It's a tiny speaker with a prerecorded clip. Maddox says it can be triggered by a Bluetooth connection. It can also be triggered manually. We do that.

"Yeah," Maddox's voice says. "That tracks. Let me see if I can—"

It ends there.

"That's definitely me," Maddox says. "No idea who I was talking to."

"Jayden or Natalia?"

"I never talked to Natalia. And I'd only ever spoken to Jayden when I was telling him to back the fuck off someone. I sound calm there." He frowns, plays it again, and shakes his head. "Let me take it. I'd like to figure this out."

"You take the audio clip, and I get the burned paper. Two more mini-mysteries for our copious free time."

The next morning, I'm called into the office at the start of lunch. I don't know what it is about school-office summons, but even though I have never been called down for any misconduct, my gut goes cold every time, my brain racing through every minor misdemeanor I've committed.

Okay, at Westdale, I might have more reason to worry, given that I've been hanging out in a secret clubhouse, poking around the basement, and investigating the death of two past students.

I get to Ms. Dimitriou's office to find Theo already there. He shoots me a thumbs-up, too low for the principal to see, and I exhale under my breath.

"Liliana," Ms. Dimitriou says, "I was just telling Theo how delighted the board is by the publicity you two got this weekend."

"Oh? Uh, that's good," I say as I slide into the chair.

She beams. "It is wonderful to see two young people getting so much positive press. Of course, Westdale doesn't *need* that press. We are known worldwide for our stellar education. And it's not as if we need to drum up admissions."

She gives a little laugh, and we oblige by smiling.

"Still," she says, "a positive light on our school sheds a positive light on our graduates." She lifts her phone and flips through the screen. "You were both commended for everything from your poise to your articulate conversation to your fundraising efforts in conjunction with Polly. And Theo's little poetry recital?" She puts a hand to her heart. "We couldn't have orchestrated better advertising for our school."

"I'm glad the response is positive," I say. "Though I'm sure there were a few digs."

She waves a hand. "We understand trolls. Any notable source who remarked on either of you had nothing but praise. And your mother, Theo? Have you seen her posts about Liliana?"

My heart jams in my throat. Trinity Nilsen posted about me?

"I don't do socials," Theo says, "but I presume they were good."

"They were *lovely*. She posted a photo of the three of you and then one of her with Liliana, and she gushed. I know she's your mom, Theo, which means you might expect that, but the board was still delighted. She is Trinity Nilsen, after all."

"So I've heard," he murmurs.

"I won't keep you any longer. I just wanted you both to know how pleased the board is."

As the week continues, I spend whatever spare time I have delving into Jenna's case, with some forays into Annette's and an hour or so continuing to scour the archives for "Janus Society." Jenna's death is the mystery that affects Maddox, so I focus on that. I may get a little overly invested, to the point where the guys have to pull me back out—Theo by distracting me with games and conversation and Maddox by literally pulling me back . . . from my laptop when he catches me in the library two nights in a row. Of course, after Maddox pulls me back, we end up making out in one of the chairs until way past curfew, so I forgive him.

How am I dealing with dating two guys? Should I say it's complicated and I'm conflicted and I feel really guilty? Yeah, no. It doesn't feel a whole lot different than it did before. Sometimes I hang out with both of them. Sometimes it's one of them. Sometimes there's kissing.

All parties aware. All parties accepting. All parties consenting.

And all parties *happy*. That's just as important. I haven't been truly happy since my dad died, but here at Westdale, that weight began to lift. This week, I finally feel like myself again. Theo's exuberance has taken on a giddy, boyish edge that is great to see in a guy who I sometimes felt was years older than me instead of months.

And Maddox has thrown away his medication—

No, he hasn't. I sometimes think that's what people expect, that depression just means you need something to make you happy. Maddox *is* happy. I see more smiles and hear more laughter from him than I ever have. Like me, he's lighter. Calmer.

Maddox and I also have deeper conversations now, about our losses—something we share that Theo can't—and it helps us both to have a place where we can lower the walls and admit we're still grieving.

Even those talks make us both lighter. But I know I'm not a "cure" for his problems. I know finding answers about Jenna won't fix everything the way he might hope. I need to be ready for that, and I will be.

On Thursday, I'm enjoying quiet time with Isolde in her room. It's study break, but we're both just reading our respective novels— ones we enjoyed ourselves and suggested to the other. The one she recommended is science fiction, and I'm ashamed to say that my initial reaction had been "I don't like science fiction," though I hadn't said so. But I'm glad I gave it a shot because it turns out I just didn't like the few examples I'd read. This one is definitely my thing, with a teenage girl solving an interstellar mystery.

Because we've both read the other's book, these sessions are like a cross between a read-along and a book club. We do something we'd hate for anyone else to do—talk to us while we're reading.

"Oh!" Isolde says. "I know what's going to happen."

I grin over at her. "Bet you don't."

"I'm at the part where Maddie thinks she just saw Trent, who's supposed to be dead. It's either a ghost or a twin brother. Since there's been no supernatural stuff mentioned—and I'm over halfway through—it's gotta be a secret twin brother."

"Right on the supernatural part. I love ghost stories, but having it appear mid-book is a cheat."

"So, secret twin?"

"Mmm..."

She puts down the book. "Is Trent still alive? That's not possible. He didn't, like, die in a fire or something where his body could be misidentified." Her eyes round. "Unless it was a secret twin who died."

"Keep reading."

She does, until the alarm we set goes off a few minutes later. Then she groans. "I was just at a good part. Now I need to wait until Saturday..." She trails off. "No, because we can't co-read Saturday. I need to go home for the weekend again."

"Ugh."

She glances over and bites her lower lip. "Um, so, I hate to ask, but since you went out with Theo last weekend, is there any chance that means your curfew has been lifted?"

Guilt rockets through me. I'd totally forgotten what happened a few weeks ago, when Cecilia refused to let me go out with Isolde. Then Theo invites me to the gala and no one bats an eye?

I understand why Cecilia let me go. Since I asked about Isolde, I've publicly come out as the Chamberlain heiress and nothing has happened. The gala trip was a safe way to test that—professional driver, ultra-exclusive event. Naturally, I didn't tell Cecilia I'd been grabbed in the back hall. That was just Charles Dubois, but if I mentioned it, she might put me on lockdown again.

"I think I can get out," I say. "Let me talk to Cecilia and Ms. Dimitriou."

After dinner, Theo and I do the socializing thing before slipping out to the clubhouse to meet up with Maddox. Now we're stretched out, playing *Mario Kart*. There's still no full-sized couch. Theo is trying to figure out how to sneak one to the clubhouse. For now, we've started pulling open the loveseat for more room. Maddox and I are sitting up at the top, hips touching. Theo is on his stomach, propped up on his forearms as he plays, his bare foot constantly tapping my shoulder, which might be sweet, if he didn't always seem to do it when I was winning.

I remember when I was a kid, friends' parents would give us shit for playing games rather than talking. Which proved they weren't within earshot, because pretty much all we did was talk. Same here. We're playing, but it doesn't require our full concentration. So we talk, the usual video game patter and completely unrelated conversation flowing seamlessly together.

"Isolde and I are doing something Saturday night," I say.

Theo makes a sharp turn on screen. "Cool. I like Isolde. She gets overshadowed in the Liliths."

More game play before Theo says, "What are you and Isolde planning? Bedroom bash?"

At Westdale, a bedroom bash is what it sounds like—two or more students having a mini-party in their room. If it's Saturday night, the staff will turn a blind eye to empty beer bottles and lingering smoke.

"Going to Savannah, as long as we can get a pass."

Maddox's go-cart slows on screen. "Savannah? Doing what?"

I shrug. "Still considering our options. A band she likes is playing."

"The two of you alone in Savannah at night? Absolutely not."

Theo twists and levers up, hands raised even as I turn on Maddox. "He didn't mean it like that, Lil."

"Well, he *said* it like that."

"Like what?" Maddox says.

"Like you're forbidding her to go out," Theo says. "Or to go out with a friend."

"What? I never said that."

"What else does 'absolutely not' mean?" I say.

Theo waves his hands. "Interpreter time. Obviously, he's not forbidding you to leave Westdale, Lil. Or to go out with a friend. That would be"—he leans toward Maddox—"controlling."

"I'm not—" Maddox begins.

"What he means is that we"—Theo slides a look Maddox's way, as if telling me his "we" might slant in one direction—"would rather you didn't go off-campus while we're investigating the suspicious off-campus deaths of two female students."

I sit back. "Okay, I get that. But presumably Jenna and Annette left alone. I'll be with Isolde."

Theo passes me another look. This one acknowledges that there are a dozen reasons why their deaths shouldn't stop me from going to Savannah, but this isn't about logic.

I glance at Maddox. He has his jaw clenched, face hard, ready to argue, and behind his scowl, I see fear.

"Is there a workaround?" I say. "I went out with you, Theo. Is it just *girls* I can't go out with?"

"This has nothing to do with Isolde personally," Maddox says.

"Isolde doesn't know what's going on," Theo says. "She won't be watching out for you. Could we make it a group trip? Then I can be there." He leans toward me. "Haven't you always wanted a hot bodyguard?"

I know he's trying to ease the tension, but I shake my head.

"I get it," I say. "I really do. But I invited Isolde. To add others seems like I realized I don't want to spend a whole evening with her, so I'm buffering with mutual friends."

"The trick, then, is to figure out how to bring me along without it seeming weird."

"That I also invited my presumed boyfriend? Yeah, that's all kinds of awkward."

His brows shoot up. "*Presumed*? Ouch."

"You know what I mean."

"Nope, not sure I do."

Now it's Maddox lifting a hand, saying he's not getting involved, as Theo glances his way for support.

I sigh. "I meant that others presume you're my boyfriend, but we haven't actually said or done anything to make it official. Let me rephrase. It would be super-awkward for me to invite my boyfriend on an outing with a friend. Also a red flag. And if he invites himself? Hoist that red flag high."

Before they can answer, a text comes in on my phone. As I read it, my shoulders slump. "Never mind. Cecilia says no. The gala was different because of the security."

Maddox makes a noise of satisfaction.

I glare at him. "Don't sound so happy. How am I going to explain this to Isolde? I understand that the gala was a secure outing, but it'll seem as if I'm allowed out with guy friends but not girl ones. Or, worse, that I tried harder for Theo than for her."

"You're right," Maddox says. "I'm sorry."

"Same," Theo says. "I really do think it'd be good for you and Isolde to get out together. Let me give Cecelia a call, see if it makes a difference if it's a group outing."

Cecilia actually agrees to Theo's revised version, though I think that's only partly because it'll involve more people—and therefore be safer. It helps that he's just so damn persuasive. As long as I'm in a group of at least four, including Theo, I can go.

The next part is also tricky. I need to tell Isolde that I invited her on a Saturday night for two, and now it'll be a group event.

Isolde and I are outside on the front steps for Friday morning break. Theo is playing one-on-one with Kai while others watch, reminding me of the day I arrived. Others have found spots to hang out, leaving Isolde and me alone on the steps.

"So, Cecelia vetoed the weekend outing for two—her usual security concerns—but I can go if it's part of a group. I argued, but she's not budging. Is a group okay? Theo and Polly have agreed. We can invite Allegra, too. Maybe Kai? I was also thinking of Brandon from the Apollos."

She only says, "Ah," in a tone that says I've blown this.

"I'm sorry," I say. "It's the only way I could get a pass and—" I stop. "Shit. If it's not just you and me this weekend, will your parents still insist you go home?"

"That's what I was thinking. Personally I don't mind having others. It'll be fun." She chews her bottom lip. "No, this could work. I'll say you and I are going out, and others thought it sounded fun and went to the same place."

I nod. "We'll get selfies with just us for socials. And Polly can tweak her coverage to sound as if the others went separately and met up with us. Does that work?"

She smiles. "It does."

TWENTY-FIVE

It's Saturday night, and we're in Savannah. Allegra joined us, though she didn't agree until the last minute, which is typical Allegra. Brandon couldn't make it, but Cosmo has taken his place. Cosmo had overheard several of us talking, and he'd expressed interest, if there was room. Polly said we should invite him—she thinks he and Isolde have exchanged their share of shy glances.

I'd have loved Maddox to come but...Well, even if we ignored his ongoing not-friends charade with Theo, I really can't see Maddox joining a group outing.

We take two cars. Kai drives Allegra, Cosmo, and Polly. Theo drives my Jeep, while Isolde and I sit in the back and tease him about chauffeuring. We also snap photos of just the two of us for our socials—and her parents.

We start with a concert—a local band Isolde wanted to see, which is playing at an open-air venue. Then we hit an all-ages club for dancing. Sure, half of our group have fake IDs, and I suspect we could all get into an actual club if we tried, but that is *not* the kind of publicity Westdale wants. So we play the part of good little teenagers and stick to the places that'll let us in.

At this point, I should clarify that I have never actually been to a club, all-ages or otherwise. The last time I danced was at a school event back home. But I'm with friends, and so I tell myself it's not like anyone will notice me or care how badly I dance.

Yeah . . .

I'm walking to a club with Theo Dubois's arm around me, and I'm accompanied by Polly Reeves and Allegra Khan and Kai Olson.

We managed to make it through the concert without being recognized because it was dark and we were outdoors and we slipped into our reserved section once the band was already playing. Going to the club is different.

First, there's a line to get in, and the others think it's adorable that I insist on joining it. Allegra mutters, "Well, this won't last." I think she means that my determination to stay "normal" won't last, and I resolve never to be someone who jumps the queue.

And then we are recognized. It's actually Polly who gets noticed first. That quickly turns into "Oh my god, Theo Dubois! That's Theo Dubois!"

At that point, I learn what Allegra meant: It's not that we jump the queue; it's that someone from the club hurries over to escort us inside—past the line—"for our own safety" . . . and also to ensure that Polly Reeves and Theo Dubois don't decide to go elsewhere.

Theo and I might have gotten the red-carpet treatment at Quartz, but this isn't a sophisticated gathering of wealthy and famous adults at a fundraiser. This is high-school and early college kids, out for a night of dancing, posting their selfies online and hoping for a few likes.

Then we walk in.

The club actually clears a path with security guards. Cellphones flash and kids turn around to get stealth selfies as we walk by. Theo periodically leans to get in the picture, and Polly and Kai pop out of our line for actual selfies. I smile and nod, though feel like I should be lifting my hand in the royal wave. When we reach a group of kids who can't be more than fourteen, Theo pulls me into a shot with them.

It's exhilarating and overwhelming and also a little scary, as I wonder how we're going to even dance without being mobbed. But once we find a place, the guards motion kids back, and they're polite about it so the kids listen, settling for distance selfies where they catch one of us in the background.

We dance, and we drink non-alcoholic beverages, and the other club-goers seem content to just stay back and watch, which is a little unnerving—I feel like an exotic beast on display—but eventually I tune it out.

"Having fun?" Theo leans in to ask as we leave the dance floor.

I nod.

"Up for a little PDA?" he asks.

When I look at him, he puts his fingers under my chin. "You can say no," he says, "if you don't want to make this official—"

I answer by kissing him. Cameras flash and someone whoops, but I ignore that. I keep the kiss short—I'm sure "making out in public" isn't the look Westdale wants for its students. But when Theo settles onto a chair, I perch on his lap, and more cameras flash.

Our friends are all on the dance floor, and we watch them as we sit together and enjoy the moment.

"We good?" Theo murmurs at my ear.

I flash a grin. "Very good."

He squeezes me and whispers, "You want time with Isolde?"

My heart swells. He's been so careful about that all night, making sure I sat in the back seat with Isolde, making sure we were seated together at the concert, giving us as much space as he can, acknowledging what tonight was supposed to be.

I twist to kiss him. "Thank you."

"For remembering you're here with a friend? Pfft. Low bar, Lil." He puts his hands under my ass and propels me up. "Go. Dance. Have fun."

Isolde and I return to the dance floor together. None of our friends try to join us—they've all been giving us space. Sadly, despite those glances Polly had noticed between Isolde and Cosmo, they haven't seemed to connect, but maybe that's just Cosmo acknowledging that Isolde was meant to be here with me.

My new friends are everything I wanted in a friend group, and it's tempting to think I've finally found my people. But that's bullshit. My "people" were always there, waiting for me to form deeper connections. I just wasn't ready. Too busy with school. Too grief-stricken after my dad's death. Too uncertain, with the constant moving.

In two months, school will be over, and we'll all go in different directions. I'm heading to Stanford, and Theo is off to USC, which is also in California . . . but six hours away. Maddox hasn't applied to college—he's taking a gap year—but he and Theo have talked about sharing a place. Polly's going to Columbia, where her mom attended. Allegra is debating options, and Isolde is probably going to Harvard.

This time, I'll be sure to keep in touch. And when it comes to Theo and Maddox . . . Well, I try not to think about it. Whatever we have, it's so new that I feel awkward even admitting I've checked the distance between Stanford and USC.

Enough of that. Isolde and I dance, and we're able to do so in relative peace, without our famous friends nearby. Once we realize no one is paying attention to us, we ease across the dance floor, getting farther from the others, until we're just two girls dancing.

"You're so good," I say, panting, when the song ends. "You have to teach me."

"Years of lessons, m'dear." Isolde affects an English accent. "Dance lessons twice a week at all the best schools." She leans in. "I hated it, but it does mean I can move to a beat."

I brush back my sweaty hair and look around. "Uh, where are we?"

"On a dance floor?" She grins. "Kidding. We do seem to have wandered, and I could really use a cold drink."

She lifts up on her tiptoes to look around, but neither of us is tall enough to see over the mass of dancers. "I think the others are over there?" She points. "And I know the bar was to the left of them. Head that way?"

We try, but the mob is too thick. The next song starts, and we're trapped on the dance floor. Isolde grabs my hand and leads me to the nearest wall. As we peer around for a way through, she points at a hall doorway and mouths "Shortcut?"

We weave past people to reach that door. A couple of guys try to catch our attention, but we pretend not to notice, and when we finally get into the hall, we both lean against the wall, catching our breath.

"Restrooms to the left." Isolde points at the sign. "Friends to the right. I think. Yes?"

"I have no idea. Apparently, it's adventure time."

We set off down the hall.

"This better not lead to anyone's drunk uncle," I say as we turn a corner.

Isolde chokes on a laugh. "What?"

I'm about to explain and then I'm not sure whether I should. It was Theo's uncle, after all, and he'd been embarrassed.

"Long story," I say, "and hopefully this hall is *not* long."

"Oh! There's something to the right up ahead. That might be the way back."

We pick up the pace, our footsteps echoing along the empty corridor. There is indeed a door to the right, and we can hear music on the other side, but it's closed and locked.

"Nice fire escape route," Isolde mutters. "I see another door ahead. It's on the left, but at this point, I'm willing to give it a shot."

We keep going. When the lights flicker, Isolde says, "Okay, that's not creepy at all."

My heart picks up speed, and all I can think of is Maddox's fear when I said I was going into Savannah.

Now I really am being paranoid. It's a flickering light in a hallway. We can hear music and even voices.

It's a public place, and I'm not alone—

The light goes out, plunging us into darkness.

"What the hell?" I say.

A hand grabs my arm, and I jump.

"It's me." Isolde laughs, but it's nervous, as if I'm not the only one freaked out. "Do you have your phone? I left mine in the car. No pockets."

It takes me a moment to realize what she's asking. Phone. Cellphone light.

"Mine's with Theo," I say. "But it's fine. We'll just go back the way we came."

Hand in hand, we start back. The lights are out, but the music keeps pumping, and no one's shrieking, so the outage must just be here.

A power outage in *this* hall. Where we are. Me and Isolde. Alone. Separated from—

Stop that.

I take two more steps. Then I freeze. There's someone up ahead. My eyes have adjusted to the faint glow from a distant exit, enough to make out a figure standing between us and that exit light.

"Hey!" I call. "I don't suppose you have a cellphone light?"

The figure just stands there, and my stomach twists even as my brain screams that I'm overreacting.

Then the figure steps toward us.

Isolde tugs on my hand. "Let's go."

We turn and run, our shoes slapping the concrete. I can see another faint glow ahead. An exit sign. Escape. Only it's not escape, is it? It'll take us out of the busy club, and if there really is someone chasing us, we should *not* be going outside, away from people.

Isolde hits the push bar, and the door flies open. I'm about to dig in my heels when a hand slams between my shoulder blades. I stumble outside behind Isolde, knocking her forward. My attacker grabs the back of my dress, but I twist free, hearing a seam rip.

I swing around, and all I see are shapes in the pitch-dark of an alley, towering buildings on either side blocking all light. The shapes are blurred motion, and I can't tell which is Isolde and which is our attacker.

There's a street fifty feet away, with traffic rushing past. I need to get there. No, I need to get *us* there.

Isolde screams, a high-pitched yowl of pain and terror. I charge toward the noise. She's on the ground, and the figure is over her. I punch at it. Her attacker staggers. Then something strikes my arm, sending pain slashing through it.

Scream! The street is right there.

I open my mouth, and a fist connects with my stomach. I fly backward, hitting the wall. The figure is over Isolde again, his hand raised. I run at him, punching, kicking, screaming, *finally* screaming.

He grabs me, and it's *so* dark. I can't see his face or anything except his size, and I'm fighting with everything I have, screaming as loud as I can—

A shout, pure rage. My attacker drops me and wheels as someone runs at us. Then my attacker is running, too, trampling me as he races down the alley.

Hands lift me up, a face over mine, dark eyes bright with fear.

"Maddox?" I croak.

"You're bleeding. You're hurt."

"I'm fine," I manage. "It's just my arm. Where's Isolde?"

Maddox glances around but doesn't release me until I gently remove his hands, and then I'm running to Isolde. She's on the ground, unmoving.

"Call 911!" I shout.

"Already did." Maddox drops onto Isolde's other side and fumbles to get his phone out. When he turns on the light, her eyes flutter open and she groans.

"Blood," I whisper as I pat her black dress, trying to find the source. As I do, I see my arm, the slash on it, blood dripping. "He had a knife. He must have stabbed her. There's blood on her dress."

The wail of a siren as Maddox and I search for the source of the blood pooling beneath Isolde.

"Here!" he says. "Her side."

He yanks off his hoodie and presses it against the wound. Isolde moans and writhes. I find another slash on her arm, but it seems as shallow as the one on mine.

"Does it hurt anywhere else?" I ask Isolde. "Can you tell me where—?"

The thunder of footsteps. A paramedic shines a flashlight on us, and we move back as she takes over. Another joins her, and Maddox tugs me away. He pulls out my arm for a look.

"J-just a scratch," I say. "I-I'm fine."

My teeth chatter, and I'm shaking as the shock hits. He pulls me close, heat enveloping me, and I fold myself into it as I watch the paramedics work, knowing I must be patient, that I can't scream at them to tell me Isolde will be okay.

Maddox whispers reassurances, telling me I'm safe, I'm safe, I'm safe, and I want to cry, because as much as I need those reassurances, he seems to need them even more.

I don't know where he came from, how he got here, and I don't care. I only care that he *was* here and he's with me, holding me as I shake.

Finally, Maddox whispers, "I think we can ask now," and he guides me over to where the paramedics are putting Isolde on a gurney.

"Is she okay?" I say, my teeth chattering.

"I'm fine," Isolde whispers, her voice almost too hoarse to be heard.

"She's stable," one paramedic says. "I'll need to check you over in a moment."

I'm nodding when Theo barrels out of the club door. He sees me, and he runs to us.

"Lil," he manages to get out. "What—?"

"She's all right," Maddox says.

"Why?" That word comes so soft I think I'm mishearing as I follow it to Isolde. She's on the gurney, gaze fixed on Theo, eyes brimming with tears. "Why?"

"I'm sorry," Theo says. "I shouldn't have let you both out of my sight. I—"

"No," she whispers. "Why did you do it?"

He goes still, confusion knocking everything else from his expression. "Why did I do what?"

"*This.*" Tears spill. "I saw you, Theo. I saw your face when you . . . when you . . . when you stabbed me."

"What?" Theo reels back, his eyes huge. "Me? I-I was inside. I'd never—What?"

The gurney is already being wheeled away, and all we can do is stand there and stare as they load her into the ambulance.

Then Theo spins on me, and the terror in his face is heartbreaking. "I didn't do this, Lil. I swear. I'd never—"

"I know," I say.

"I screwed up, Mads. I thought I was keeping an eye on Lil, and then I couldn't see her and . . . You counted on me."

"It's okay," Maddox says.

"No, it's not. Isolde got hurt, and Lil—Shit! She's bleeding." He takes my arm.

"Just a scratch," I say as I lean against him. "I'm worried about Isolde. Once the paramedics check my arm, I want to go to the hospital."

"I'll take you," Theo says. "We'll all go—"

Someone clears their throat, and we turn to see two uniformed officers.

"Right," I say. "I need to talk to you. Tell you what happened."

"I'll get your car," Theo says.

"No," one officer says. "You aren't going anywhere, young man."

TWENTY-SIX

The alley attack happened in a blur. The next thirty minutes are just as chaotic, as the paramedics insist on checking me while one pair of officers question Maddox and another pair talk to Theo separately. Our officers have to keep redirecting our attention because we're both focused on Theo, trying to hear what's happening, wanting to be there, defending him, supporting him.

My arm is fine. The skin is split from the knife slash, so maybe more than "a scratch," but it doesn't need stitches. I'll probably have bruises from the shoves and falls. I'm fine, though. Isolde is not, and Theo is not, and since I can't help Isolde, I just want to get to Theo.

I know he didn't do this. I don't need to work through the details to be sure. But I do need to work through them to help him.

I tell the officers what I saw. It was dark. I point that out, including the fact that the light over the exit door is either turned off or broken. That means I didn't see my attacker's face, but I also concede that Isolde was closer to the road and the light there. I need to defend Theo with facts, and that means even pointing out issues with my own defense.

The figure in the hallway looked male. He was Theo's height and neither noticeably thinner nor noticeably broader. He seemed strong. All that fits Theo. Otherwise, I didn't see his light hair or white button-down shirt, and I really think that would have stood out in the dim light.

I can hear Theo fumbling to defend himself, panic-stricken, throwing out questions. Can the police check his phone GPS? What about cameras inside?

The rest of our friends soon arrive, and they're pulled into the questioning.

Did Theo leave the table while Isolde and I were dancing?

Yes, he already said that—after Isolde and I danced for one song, he couldn't see me, so he went looking.

Is that normal? Does he keep such a close eye on his girlfriend?

I desperately want to go over and defend him. But I'm still being questioned, and I need to find *proof* that this couldn't have been him.

Polly explains who Theo is and that there were security concerns for all of us, which is why he kept an eye on me. At which point Allegra snaps, "Liliana's a billionaire heiress. Of course Theo worries about her in a crowded club," and I feel every eye on me as I struggle to focus on my own questioning.

The other discussion still floats over.

So Theo left after I'd been gone for one song. Did he ever come back? Did anyone see him?

"I did," Kai says. "A bunch of times, out on the dance floor looking for Lili. During at least three songs."

"Are you sure?" Cosmo says. "I only saw him for . . ." Cosmo must realize he isn't helping and trails off, looking uncomfortable.

"No, Kai," Theo says, the words coming slow, as if reluctant to stop his friend from providing an alibi. "You must have seen someone else. I did two rounds of the floor. Then some girls recognized me, and I ducked into the back hall. I was looking for Lil from there, checking the restrooms and the refreshment stand. Then someone said there were police and an ambulance, and I took off, saw the open exit door, and found them."

"You were in the back halls?" one officer says. "Where no one could see you and provide an alibi. The back halls . . . where the two victims were."

"I can show you where I was. It was the other side of the building. I swear. Check my phone."

"That will only confirm you were in the building."

"I didn't hurt Liliana and Isolde. I don't have a knife. Search me. Please." He lifts both hands over his head.

The officer shakes his head. "You wouldn't still have it."

Knife . . . My gaze falls to the blood where Isolde had lain, and I break free from Maddox's grip.

"Blood," I say quickly. "There's no blood."

There are two officers questioning me: a young man and a middle-aged woman. The young guy's gaze goes to the puddle of blood on the ground and then meaningfully turns back to me.

"Yes, there's blood on the concrete. I've got blood everywhere." I raise my arms. "Mostly from a slash on my arm. Some from helping Isolde. Maddox over there has blood on him from helping Isolde, too. Where is it on Theo?"

Theo steps back, lifting his hands, as if they'd accuse him of quickly wiping it away.

"Whoever attacked us is going to have blood on them," I say. "There's a footstep in that pool, at the edge, and I'm pretty sure it doesn't belong to me. There isn't blood on Theo's shoes, though. White shirt. White sneakers. Faded jeans. No blood."

"I thought you were some kind of heiress," the young officer says. "Now you're a cop?"

"I'm just pointing out—"

The older officer gestures for me to move away. When I hesitate, she shoos me and follows.

"I'm not trying to interfere," I say when we're a few feet from the others.

"I know," she says, her voice low and not unkind.

"But there isn't any blood—"

"Which I have noted."

"Oh."

"A possible ID was made by the primary victim," she says. "We must follow up on that. Do you want us to ignore it, let your friend go . . . and then have the victim telling the press that your friend attacked her? After it's too late for us to properly interview witnesses? To examine the scene?"

"I'm sorry. You're right."

She smiles. "You want to protect your friend. The blood was a good catch, but I'm on it."

"Thank you."

"You're the new Chamberlain heiress, right?"

I look up sharply.

She shrugs. "I follow the local gossip. Never know when it might come in handy. Like if that new heiress and her friends are attacked in my city."

She lowers her voice. "Here's the thing, Miss Chamberlain. You now have enough money to buy your way out of trouble, so people are always going to presume you did. Same with your friend there. Famous parents. Famous kid. Corners are cut. Deals are made. He goes free . . . and the gossip rags have a field day."

"I should let you do your job and make sure it's airtight."

"As much as it can be," she says.

We give our statements. Theo isn't arrested. He isn't taken to the station for further questioning. He does call his mom, who'll get in touch with the family lawyer, who'll probably tell Theo that he shouldn't have said a word, but even I didn't think of that, despite knowing it very well from my dad.

We're advised not to go to the hospital. With Isolde having named Theo, it's best if he doesn't show up, and probably best that none of us do, in case we're accused of trying to persuade her to retract her identification.

Maddox drives Theo and me back to Westdale. Partway there, Theo gets a call from the police, and he doesn't want to answer, but it turns out to be a detective informing him that Isolde has formally retracted her identification. Once Isolde was away from the scene, she started to second-guess herself and by the time the police interviewed her, she was apologizing for accusing Theo. She'd been in shock, and seeing someone her attacker's size panicked her.

That should be a huge relief, but Theo is still a mess. In shock himself, barely talking, and when he does speak, it's to tell us how sorry he is.

He did nothing wrong. It wasn't as if he'd sworn not to let me out of his sight. He was as diligent as he felt he could be without putting me on a leash.

When Theo starts to spiral—apologizing and then feeling horrible for making this about him—I divert the conversation by finally asking Maddox how he got there.

"I didn't plan to go," Maddox says. "But I couldn't relax. So I snuck out. Called Uber. Theo and I have each other on Friend Finder. I stayed close."

"Thank you," Theo says.

Maddox looks at us in the rearview mirror. "I'm glad I could help Lili and Isolde, but I'm not sure I should be thanked for stalking you two. If nothing happened, I was going to feel like shit, acting as if I'd been at Westdale all night."

"You would have confessed," I say. "And we'd have told you we understood."

"Yeah, but it was still . . ." He rolls his shoulders. "I get worked up, and it was in my head and I couldn't let it go."

"Because you took Cecilia's concerns more seriously than I did," I say softly. "And that's my problem, not yours."

"I don't know about that."

"I do, and I'm sorry I got defensive. Whether I felt there was a real threat or not, you were worried. That should have been enough."

When we get to Westdale, the others are already back, and we collectively decide to handle this all in the morning. The hospital would have contacted Isolde's parents, who'd let the school know, and if there's someone waiting to talk to us, we'll talk. But there isn't, so we slip in and head upstairs. Theo, Maddox, and I bring up the rear. As Theo heads off, Maddox whispers, "Will you stay with him?"

"Hmm?"

"Tonight. Can you stay with him? He's . . . feeling a lot right now."

"I know."

"And I'd rather you weren't alone either, which means I need to ask you to stay with him."

"I will." I kiss his cheek. "Thank you for tonight. We haven't had much time to talk."

"Tomorrow." A humorless quirk of his mouth. "I would be shitty company tonight anyway, and if I can be alone while knowing I didn't leave either of you alone, that's best for everyone."

Theo's room is, well, very Theo. Organized chaos. Clothing either hung in the closet or tossed in the vicinity of the hamper. Original vintage movie posters tacked up like cheap reproductions. Probably all films he admires. None of his father's. None for his own shorts. One, though, is the film his mom won her Best Actress Oscar for.

The bookcase is stuffed with film scripts and film-studies texts. The desk has been removed to make more room for the bed, which is king-sized because of course it is. That's where he'll do his reading and his homework, propped up on the stack of pillows.

Now he sits on the edge of the bed and looks up at me. "You don't need to stay."

"Are you asking me to leave?"

"Never."

"Well, if you're worried that I'm about to share your bed when you really aren't in the mood to do anything about that"—I lean in to whisper—"neither am I."

"I know." He rubs his face and looks toward a narrow dresser.

"You want to change into something appropriate?" I ask.

A tired smile. "You've got the wrong guy if you think I'm even remotely worried about that."

"May I stay?"

"Of course. Just . . ." He looks up at me. "I'm not sure I want you to see me like this, Lil."

"I want to see you like everything, Theo. Nothing's going to scare me off."

He pauses. Then he says, "Can you do me a favor?"

"Name it."

"That drawer." He nods toward the one he'd been looking at. "Open it."

When I do, he says, "Reach in and pull out what's in there. Left-hand side."

My fingers touch cool glass, and I try not to react as I pull out the bottle. It's bourbon. Three-quarters full.

"Dump it down the sink."

I bite my lip. "If you want a drink, I'm not going to judge."

"Well, maybe you should. Dump it, Lil. Please. Because I do *really* want it, and that's a problem."

I linger there, uncertain.

"It's a problem," he says firmly. "You know it is. Having a drink for fun is one thing. Needing it is another. Dump it."

While I'm doing that, I hear him moving around the room. When I return, the light is dimmed and he's in bed.

"I'm wearing sweatpants," he says. "Call me vain, but the first time you see me how I normally sleep? I kinda want to be in the mood to enjoy it."

I smile. "I definitely want to be in the mood to enjoy it."

"I pulled out a tee. You can wear that or, obviously, grab something from your room."

"This is good."

I slip back to the bathroom, where I scrub my face using his cleanser and moisturizer, and realize that's what I've been smelling on him, not aftershave. I drink in the scent and then change into his T-shirt, which comes down to near my knees.

When I come into the room, he wolf-whistles, which makes me laugh and relax. I slide into the bed.

"You're probably too tired to talk," he says.

"Never too tired to listen."

Silence. Then, his voice softer, "I know I keep saying I fucked up, Lil, and I keep apologizing, but I don't know what else to say."

"Maybe you don't need to say anything."

He's beside me, a couple of feet away across the huge bed. He props himself up on one elbow and gingerly touches my bandaged arm. "How are you doing?"

"They gave me a painkiller. I don't feel a thing."

"And otherwise? How are you holding up? Do you want to talk about what happened in the alley? To you?"

"I'd rather not."

My voice sounds so small, and he reaches out, hands going to my hips, tugging gently, a question implicit there. I move closer until I'm in his arms, my cheek against his bare chest.

"I think I should cry," I say. "And I actually want to. But I just feel . . . numb."

"That's shock."

I nod against his chest. "Can I not talk about what happened? For now? If I do, I'll feel like I should analyze it and start detecting, and I'm not ready for that."

"We can talk about anything you want. Or nothing at all."

I look up. "What Isolde said. *She* was in shock. You know that, right?"

His gaze drops as he nods. "Yeah, it was just . . ." A deep inhale. Then he looks at me. "If you think I'm overdoing the guilt, it's because I was flying so high tonight, Lil. The gala was a mess of good and bad, and tonight seemed to be all good. Me, at my best. And I was so damned proud of myself. *Such* a good boyfriend. Driving the car. Giving you space. Jumping the queue without being the jerk who jumps the queue. The red carpet without a red carpet. You're with Theo Dubois, babe. This is what you can expect. First-class treatment. Then you kissed me in public, sealing the deal. Officially my girl. I was *soaring*. Hey, babe, go dance with your friend. Huh, where'd she go? Well, I should look, but stay chill, nothing to worry about, she's just in the restroom or grabbing a drink . . ."

He squeezes his eyes shut. "I can be such a self-centered asshole, Lil. And you got hurt because of it."

"Uh, none of that sounded self-centered, Theo."

He shakes his head. "You don't get it."

"Try me."

He hesitates, and when the words come, they don't stop. "I'm selling something, Lil. I've been selling it since I was a baby. The myth of Theo Dubois. Smart. Handsome. Athletic. The boy with everything. But that's not enough. I'm expected to be more. Tough, confident, manly. But also compassionate, humble, sensitive. And even when I think I am all that, in my own way, it's not enough. I don't stay off social media because I can't be bothered with it. I stay off so I don't see the shit people say about me. Ugh, he's too pretty. Real men don't look like that. What do people see in him? Is that eyeliner? He's one of *those*. Dating a girl, dating a guy; he just can't make up his mind. Oh, he's doing a film? Of course he is. Just like Daddy. Is he getting Mom to star in it, too? I met him once, and he was a jerk. I met him once, and he's so fake."

When he stops for breath, I kiss him. I can feel him shaking, and when I ease back, he says, "I can't win, Lil, and I'm so fucking tired of trying, and then I'm disgusted because, what the hell is this? Theo Dubois, whining? I never need to stand in line. Cameras flash wherever I go. Kids scream my name, excited just to see me. And I'm *whining*?"

"I can't imagine what that's like," I say softly. "I don't think I could handle it as well as you do. It's exhilarating, but it's also exhausting."

A faint smile. "I meant all that attention—cutting lines, getting photographed, being recognized—is the *privilege* of being Theo Dubois."

"I know, but it's also the hell of being Theo Dubois. Living your life illuminated by a camera flash."

"I wanted tonight to be perfect, like I wanted the gala to be perfect. And when things went wrong, I had another meltdown."

"Um, Isolde claimed you attacked her—and me—in an alley. That's not just 'things going wrong.' I'd have melted down, too."

I tuck my fingers under his chin, looking into his eyes. "Where you see a meltdown, I see a few cracks in the veneer. But half of that anger and that stress? It's you beating yourself up, thinking you should be better. You aren't a normal guy, Theo, and that's great and it also sucks. If a barista gives you cold coffee, you need to smile and accept it or it'll be all over social media that Theo Dubois is a demanding asshole."

I move closer, eyes nearly to his. "Cut yourself some slack, Dubois."

"You sound like Maddox."

"Then consider this a second opinion and take our advice."

He stretches his arm out, head dropping onto his bicep as he looks up at me. "I let him down."

"No, you—"

"Lil? Just listen to me, okay? I couldn't ever say this to him, but can you imagine how it feels, knowing he thought he had to keep an eye on you because he couldn't trust me to do it? And then to have him proven right? I blew off his concerns. When I *did* watch over you, it was mostly just to humor him, and now I feel like shit."

I could say I did the same, but this is about them, so I only nod.

Theo continues, "I fuck up so much with him these days, and I don't know what I'm doing wrong." When I nod, he ducks to catch my gaze. "But you *do* know."

"I would never presume that, Theo."

"If you see something I'm doing wrong, tell me. Please."

"It's not my place—"

"Lil. *Please*."

I exhale a slow breath and drop my head down by his. "I know you don't like the edibles."

He shuts his eyes. "They're prescription, so I shouldn't say anything."

"It's not that as much as . . . He takes other medication. For depression. And you also question that, which is either questioning whether he *has* depression or whether it's a real thing needing real medication."

"I don't mean it that way."

"I know." I reach to touch his face. "But taking that medication, admitting he needs it, that's tough. You have to support him."

Theo exhales. "I do support him. Totally. I just want . . . I want him back."

"The way he was before? I didn't know him then, obviously. Was he a lot different?"

Theo goes quiet and then sits up and grabs his phone from the bedside charger. "You want to see the old Maddox?"

"Please."

He flips through and then cues up a video. When it starts, I have to smile. It's Maddox at about twelve. He's sprawled on the grass, book in hand, all long gangly limbs and shaggy dark hair.

When Theo's voice comes on, I choke on a laugh. It's high and reedy, and he points a finger at me. "Do not mock the twelve-year-old-boy voice."

On the screen, Theo says, "Observe Maddox Moreno in his natural environment."

"Fuck off." Maddox's voice is deeper, already postpubescent. He doesn't lower the book.

Theo continues from behind the camera, "I offered this young man a part in my movie, and what did he say?"

"Fuck. Off."

"Exactly. The chance to be in the *premier* Theo Dubois film, and he'd rather read his book."

"I'd rather read this chapter. Which you promised I could do."

"Keep going. I'll just film it."

Maddox slaps down the book with a scowl that's so familiar, I really do laugh.

"Fine," Maddox grunts as he sits up.

"You'll be in my film?"

"No, I'll help you fix the script, like you asked. Then I get to read my damn chapter. Right?"

"You could write the whole script."

A snort. "No, and don't you dare credit me for helping. Now turn that damn camera off."

The video ends, and Theo turns to me. "He used to be so different, right?"

"Uh . . ."

"That was always Maddox. Nose in a book. Quiet. Moody. Sometimes cranky. Cursing me out while still doing what I asked, eventually."

He sets the phone down. "I can say I want the old Maddox back, but that's bullshit. He's still my Mads. What I want is for him to be *well*. So I tell myself he is and that he doesn't need those pills, but if he stops taking them?" Pain flashes over his face.

"If he stops, he's not the Maddox you know."

"Sometimes yes, but other times . . . I can't reach him, Lil. It's like we're on two deserted islands, surrounded by sharks, and I can't get to him. I'm shouting, and he can't hear me. So obviously the pills help, and I shouldn't be an asshole about them. I want him to not need them. I want him to be happy."

I'm quiet, before I finally push out the words. "Am I part of that?"

"What?"

"Making Maddox happy."

He frowns, then he blinks. "You mean, did I make sure Mads got the girl he really likes, in hopes that'll be the magic that make all his problems go away? If I thought that'd work, I'd have pushed you on him and backed off myself. I'm not that deluded. Or that generous."

He pulls me into a hug. "You *do* make him happy, which I want, but I understand that what he's going through can't be fixed with a girlfriend."

"It might not be able to be fixed at all," I say softly. "I know it seems to be connected to Jenna's death, but that might have just exacerbated something that was already there."

"I know."

"And if this is how he'll always be, taking medication, seeing a therapist, needing an edible now and then . . . would that be okay?"

He pulls me to him, so tight the breath flies from my lungs. "The only thing that *wouldn't* be okay is losing him."

I hug him back tight, and we stay like that, wrapped together, breathing and holding each other, until we drift off to sleep.

TWENTY-SEVEN

I wake the next morning to a "Call me now" text from Cecilia. There's a moment of confusion before I remember what happened last night and the fact I didn't notify her.

There goes any hope of a quiet Sunday morning waking in Theo's bed, with all the promise that holds.

Fifteen minutes later, I'm in the clubhouse with Maddox, connecting to a video chat with Cecilia.

"Your video's off," I say when she answers.

"That's because you do not want to see my face right now. Do you know *when* you should have seen my face? Last night."

"We know," Maddox cuts in. "And we never thought about it. Liliana was worried about Isolde, and I was worried about Liliana. Then we were both worried about Theo."

"Theo?" The picture comes on then, as Cecilia settles into her chair, anger fading from her eyes. "Tell me what happened."

I walk her through it. When I finish, she's staring at us.

"Isolde said Theo attacked her?"

"He didn't," Maddox and I say in unison, and before I can go on, she waves us to silence. "That was adorable, but I'm not actually questioning whether Theo did it. There is no way you'd be best friends with anyone who'd do that, Maddox."

"Former best—"

"Oh, cut the shit. You're still best friends. And don't insult me by denying it again. I've humored you long enough. You and Theo are besties. Now you've pulled Liliana into the fold, and whatever else you've pulled her into, I do not want to know about."

"We—" I begin.

"Is everyone getting along? No duels at dawn to win the fair maiden?"

"What?" I say. "No."

"Then I'm happy. Moving along. Why did Isolde identify Theo?"

"I don't know," I say. "It seems our attacker reminded her of Theo, and when she saw Theo come outside, she got confused."

Maddox leans forward. "I want to know where Charles Dubois was last night."

"Creeping Charlie?" She shakes her head. "He's all bark." She raises her hands as we open our mouths to protest. "But I will check because, yes, he resembles Theo, and in a dark alley, during a fight, catching a glimpse of him could make Isolde think it was Theo. I will also find out what exactly Isolde said."

"She retracted the ID by the time she reached the hospital," I say.

"Good. I also want to talk to Theo."

"He did contact his lawyer last night. Well, his mother did."

"Also good, but that lawyer is in L.A. and I'm here. Tell Theo to call me."

"You're going to need to make arrangements for Liliana," Maddox says.

I look sharply at him. "Arrangements?"

"For leaving Westdale."

"I'm not leaving Westdale."

His glare matches my own. "You were attacked in an alley. You're leaving."

"The hell I am." I look at Cecilia. "Can we call you back?"

I can tell she's about to object, so I click off the call and get to my feet. "I'm not leaving, Maddox. I understand you're worried—"

"You nearly got *killed*," he says, standing.

"I got pushed and slashed because I interfered with the real target—Isolde."

"Isolde wasn't the one who got shoved down the stairs."

"That was Jayden. Undeniably Jayden. Who is not the guy who attacked us last night."

"Well, Isolde isn't the one Cecilia is worried about. She's not letting you stay here after that."

"No, she's not letting me *leave* here after that. She's keeping me at Westdale—no more passes. I understand you're worried, but I had plenty of opportunity to escape that guy last night. I got hurt trying to protect Isolde. She must have been the target, and that could have been random, some guy in the club following us, nothing to do with Westdale."

His jaw sets. "You don't believe that."

"It's possible—"

"Logically, in a random attack, there was no reason for him to go after Isolde instead of you. She was in front, yes? He pushed *you* out the door. He had the chance to grab you then and let her run. She's sturdier, stronger. You're . . ." He waves at me. "You."

"What's that supposed to me?"

"You're a tiny little thing, and he could've easily overcome you."

"Excuse me?"

"He would have *thought* he could easily overcome you. You were right there, and yet he went for Isolde. And don't say maybe he has a thing for redheads."

"Okay, so yes," I admit, "it seems to have been a targeted attack."

"Yes."

"On Isolde. As you just said."

He stops. "Fuck. You set that up."

"You just agreed the target was Isolde." I put my hands against his chest. "I'm not leaving Westdale."

"You are."

I slap my hands gently on his chest. "I know you aren't actually ordering me to leave. But you're still treading dangerous ground." I look up at him. "If I leave, I can't go to Stanford."

"You're already in."

"Yes, but I need to actually graduate high school to get into college, Maddox. I have six more weeks. If things change and I'm in actual danger, we'll revisit this."

"I have conditions."

I tilt my head to look up at him. "You don't actually get to give me conditions. You know that, right?"

"You won't leave the grounds. I don't even want you walking to the clubhouse alone. Theo and I are stopping this not-friends bullshit. After last night, no one's going to buy it."

"I agree. So those are your suggestions?"

"Conditions."

I glare up at him. "Suggestions."

"No sleeping alone either."

My brows shoot up.

"For protection. I'll sleep on the floor if you want."

"Oh, I'd never make you sleep on the floor, Maddox. I'm just giving you that look because this seems less a condition than an enticement." I waggle my brows. When his cheeks darken, I lean in and whisper, "Has anyone mentioned how hot you are when you blush?"

"You're distracting me."

I loop my arms around his shoulders. "I know you're worried, and I will accommodate by agreeing to all your *suggestions*."

"Conditions."

"You're also hot when you get all growly. And *adorable* when you think you can boss me around."

He pulls me into a kiss so fast I gasp, and that kiss . . . Maddox has been keeping it slow, even sweet, and I've been matching him, both of us cautiously exploring this new thing between us.

This kiss is not slow. And if I say it's not sweet, I mean that in the best possible way. This kiss is *fire*, and it's like a smoldering ember catching dry tinder, as if this is what he's been holding back and . . . Oh, *wow*.

Before I realize it, we're on the loveseat. Or, actually, kind of over the loveseat. And I don't know if I got us there or he did, because I'm giving as good as I'm getting, hands in his hair, body pressed to his, not caring about that inconsequential thing called oxygen. We come up for air once or twice, I think, but honestly, I don't notice. I just know what I feel, and it really is fire, and when it ends, we're entangled and panting, and it takes a few minutes before we can speak.

"You know what I really like about you, Chamberlain?" Maddox says.

"That I think you're super-hot, and I can't keep my hands off you?"

He sputters a laugh. "Well, yeah, I do like that. There's a list of what I like about you, and it's pretty damned long. But one thing near the top?" He pulls me into an embrace and whispers in my ear. "That you let me get mad. You don't treat me with kid gloves."

"You get some of that, huh?"

He pulls back, rolling his eyes. "I get so much of that. It used to be different. Theo, my mom, Jenna—they didn't take my shit. I'd lose my temper, and they'd argue with me. Then Jenna died, and I had my breakdown, and I feel as if I'm mostly me again, but when I get mad, my mother and Theo and everyone who knows about the breakdown? They back the hell off. Give me what I want. Like they're scared of what will happen if they don't. I didn't have a psychotic episode. I didn't get violent. It was a breakdown only in the sense that *I* broke. I just couldn't function. And I really hate being treated like I'm one step away from another crash and burn."

He exhales. "I didn't mean to unload that on you."

I hug him. "You can unload anything on me, Maddox. And you never need to worry. I know you're not that fragile, and I will absolutely call you out on your bullshit." I wrap my hands in the front of his shirt. "Also? Anytime you want to fight someone, I'm here for it, as long as it comes with a hot make-out session afterward."

He laughs softly. "You can always have that, Chamberlain. Now, do we call Cecilia back or make her wait a few more minutes?"

I tug his shirt, pulling him to me. "She can wait."

We talk to Cecilia, who agrees I shouldn't quit Westdale unless I have an ironclad reason, which this is not. She also agrees with the Liliana-lockdown plan, which was exactly what she was going to suggest. I should not be alone, even at night, and while her solution had been to stay with Allegra or Polly, she likes the idea of me staying with one of the guys even better. She doesn't know the others well enough to be sure they'd understand the danger.

Ten minutes after that call, I'm with Maddox and Theo outside the dining hall, Sunday brunch in full swing within.

"You ready for this?" Theo asks.

I nod. Maddox grunts. We walk in, and at first, the dull roar of breakfast conversation continues. Then it goes dead quiet. Theo surveys the room and points to the only remaining private table—for two. There's a snaking murmur as people decide that means Maddox just happened to come in behind us. But then Theo pulls over a third chair, and that hush falls again.

It takes five seconds for someone to come over. It's one of the guys I don't know well.

"Hey, Theo, Maddox," he says. "You two kissed and made up?"

Maddox lifts his gaze, slowly and deliberately, and the guy steps back.

"Uh, that came out wrong," the guy says with a nervous laugh. "Good to, uh, see you, uh, getting along."

Maddox turns to me. "Mocha?"

"Please."

He goes to stand, but the guy is still there.

"I heard you saved the day, Moreno. Showed up just in the nick of time. How'd you manage that? You weren't part of the group."

The look Maddox turns on him could freeze lava, and the guy has the sense to back up again.

"We invited him," I say. "And he said no. Or was that 'fuck no'? Anyway, he changed his mind. For which I am very grateful."

"Mads?" Theo says, dismissing the guy. "I'll take a—"

"I still remember what you drink, Dubois. Whether I get it is another question."

After Isolde's attack, I'm more determined than ever to figure out what happened to Jenna and Annette. I can't see a connection between them and her, so maybe I just want to do that because I can't actually help Isolde. I expect to dive headlong into investigating after brunch, but Isolde wants the Liliths to come visit her, because she's alone in a hospital and her parents can't get a flight to see her. So that's what I'm doing, because I'd never say no.

Cecilia agrees to the trip only if both Maddox and Theo are with me, though Theo will need to keep his distance for Isolde's sake. Cecilia also jokes that I'd better use the restroom before I leave because I'm not going in one alone on the trip. I think she's joking, but I'm not really sure.

Allegra throws up her hands at having both guys along—"Liliana is going to a hospital. If she's attacked, she will receive immediate life-saving treatment"—but Polly says we can all squeeze into my Jeep and, besides, she wants to talk to Maddox. Something about a partnership idea with his mom's company. If it were anyone else, he'd have plunked his ass in the passenger seat and stuck in earbuds, but it's impossible to be a jerk to Polly.

Theo drives. Allegra claims shotgun. "I do not ride in backseats." Maddox must be in a good mood, because he offers to take the dreaded middle. It also allows him to talk to Polly, though he subtly holds my hand during the drive, which is very sweet but also, I think, a bit of a touchstone against being in a packed car for an hour.

There are antisocial people who just don't like being part of a group, and introverted people who find it exhausting. I suspect Maddox is both. But talking to Polly is easy, and she doesn't just chat—she has solid ideas for what she'd like to do on the social media platforms his mom created. Maddox is obviously impressed, and that's a special kind of feeling, when friends from different spheres of your life intersect and it goes well.

At the hospital, the guys stay outside the room. It'd be weird for Maddox to accompany us, and the height of awkwardness to have Theo there. They hang out in the hall, like cops guarding a prisoner who's been allowed thirty minutes to visit a sick friend.

Okay, I'll stop grumbling. I appreciate that Maddox and Theo are concerned, and I'll try not to feel weird about it.

Before reaching the hospital, we hit a gift shop, and we arrive with our arms full—stuffed animals, candy, flowers, puzzle books, magazines . . .

When Isolde sees the haul, she lets out a half-laugh, half-sob. "You guys know I'm only here for a couple of days, right?"

She looks good. They even let her put on the clothing Westdale had delivered, and she's sitting up in bed.

"It's just a stab wound," she says when we ask how she's doing.

"*Just* a stab wound?" Polly says.

"You know what I mean. The blade didn't hit anything vital. I'm only here for observation. I feel fine. Well, unless I laugh. Or cry. Or breathe too deeply." She puts a hand to her side. "Amazing how much you use your abs for."

We talk for a bit, and then she looks at me. "I, uh, wondered if you'd bring Theo."

"Liliths only," Polly chirps. "He's not a member, however much he wishes he could be."

My stomach twists at the lie, but I understand it. We had to bring Theo for my sake, and we shouldn't upset Isolde by admitting he's outside.

Isolde doesn't smile, just keeps looking at me. "I'm so sorry, Lili." Her eyes mist. "Can you tell him that? Please?"

"Of course." I pause. "Did you see or hear something that made you think it was Theo?"

"I don't know. That's what I told the police. I don't remember seeing the guy's face or hearing his voice, but when Theo was there, my brain screamed 'That's him!' I told the police I was mixed up and in shock."

She chews her lip. "He's not in trouble, is he? I was really, really clear it wasn't him."

"He's fine. We were just wondering whether there was something about him that matched your attacker. That would be helpful for the police."

"I don't know?" Her voice turns it into a question. "I keep thinking it through, trying to pinpoint why I thought it was Theo. It was just a sense, you know? Maybe because he was the same size? Or the way the guy moved. Or a noise he made. Or even how he smelled." She meets my gaze. "It *wasn't* Theo. I'm sure of that."

"I know."

She keeps chewing her lip. "Is he mad at me?"

I laugh softly. "He's Theo. He's fine. Yes, he panicked at first, but he understands what a shock it was and how a mistake can be made. I'm glad you retracted it so quickly—thank you—but the evidence proves it wasn't him, so he was never in any real danger."

"Good," she exhales. "I'm glad."

———

I leave the room early, letting Polly and Allegra have more time with Isolde. Out in the hall, Maddox is unsettled. I see that as soon as I step out, and I steer him off, Theo following.

"What's up?" I ask.

Theo answers. "Some guy started walking to Isolde's room and then turned around when he saw us. I didn't notice him—I was texting with my mom."

I look at Maddox. "He seemed suspicious?"

He takes a moment to answer, and then does so with reluctance. "I don't know. It's like he was heading for Isolde, saw us, and backed off." He rubs his mouth. "I didn't like it."

I lower my voice. "As if he saw she had company and he couldn't slip in alone?"

"Yeah."

"I don't like that either." I glance back toward the room. "She's by herself in a private room. What if last night wasn't a random attack?"

"Maybe we should call her family," Theo says. "Have them send one of their guys."

I frown at him.

"Security," he says. "That's what they do. Their company, that is."

I nod. "Right. I think she mentioned that once. Do we have their number? I'm sure if we say we're concerned, they'll send—"

"There he is," Maddox says.

As I go to turn, he catches my arm. "Don't make it too obvious. He's heading for Isolde's room now. I don't think he sees us."

I shift so I can see our reflections through a pane of glass. The guy walking up to Isolde's room wears a ball cap and looks young, maybe only a couple of years older than us.

The door to Isolde's room swings open. Polly and Allegra come out, talking and not noticing the guy. My mouth opens to call a warning, and then—

"Hey, Polly," the guy says, and then, "Allegra, I'm guessing?"

"Tristan!" Polly gives the newcomer a hug. "Isolde will be so happy to see you! When did you get in?"

"Just now. Some frat brothers and I were hanging out in Miami for the weekend. My parents told me what happened to Izzie, and I decided to fly up and check on her. I saw she had visitors, so I went and grabbed her this." He takes a candy bar from his pocket.

"Her favorite," Polly says. "That'll make it an even dozen now."

He laughs, and I walk over and Polly introduces us. She went to the same feeder school as Isolde and Tristan, when he'd been a student. As soon as I'm close enough to see his face, the resemblance to Isolde is obvious.

Isolde might have grumbled about Tristan, but he seems nice. Or maybe that's the problem. The perfect brother *is* nice. Brings you your favorite candy. Cuts his weekend short to visit you in the hospital.

Before we take our leave, Theo joins us and puts out a hand. "Theo Dubois."

Tristan laughs as he shakes Theo's hand. "Oh, I know who you are. Nice to meet you."

Theo glances at me. He's obviously been braced for Tristan to bring up the accusation, but Isolde must not have told her family that part.

"Can I speak to you a moment, Tristan?" Theo says. "Before you go in."

"Sure."

The rest of us head to the elevator. When Theo joins us, he whispers to me, "I mentioned security for Isolde, just in case. Tristan says his family has a branch office in Atlanta. He'll speak to his parents."

"Good."

We take the elevator down. Maddox is quiet, and I hope he's not feeling awkward about mistaking Tristan for a threat. Then, when we get off the elevator and we're figuring out which way to go, Theo says, "Guess someone didn't trust us to look after you."

"Hmm?"

He waves. "Cecilia's here. She just headed that way."

We ask Allegra and Polly to wait and hurry to catch up, but when we round the corner, there's no sign of Cecilia. Theo frowns, and we stride to the next corner. Still nothing.

"I'll text," I say.

He shakes his head. "No, clearly I saw someone else." He glances at Maddox. "At least no one can say we aren't taking our bodyguard jobs seriously, huh?"

Maddox relaxes a little, and for a second, I wonder whether Theo did that on purpose—pretended he'd also made a mistake. But that doesn't make sense, and instead, I'm left wondering whether he backed down so fast *because* of Maddox's mistake with Tristan. Because he presumed he'd done the same thing, both of them on high alert.

I surreptitiously pop off a text to Cecilia.

Me

Just leaving the hospital. Thought I should check in.

There. If Theo did see her, she'll tell me to hold on, that she wants to talk.

We're in the parking lot before an answer comes, and when it does, it's just a thumbs-up.

That should answer the question. Theo saw someone else. So why does it leave a strange feeling in my gut?

TWENTY-EIGHT

We go out for dinner in Savannah, since we'd miss it at Westdale. On the way back, Theo gets a text. He's driving, but he glances at his watch. He must see enough of the message to concern him, because he frowns and passes his phone back.

"Mads, can you check that?"

Maddox unlocks Theo's phone, and I wince. If you're pretending you've just resumed an old friendship, maybe don't let on you know each other's pass codes? No one else notices, thankfully.

"It's Dimitriou. She wants to talk to you." Maddox flips to the next text and scowls. "As soon as you get back? It's Sunday night."

"We did all get passes, right?" I say.

"Yes," Allegra says. "I obtained them myself from the weekend admin. She knew about Isolde and quickly issued the Lilith passes. She hesitated for Theo and Maddox, but I explained that there were concerns for Liliana's safety, which she seemed to consider an overreaction." Allegra looks pointedly at us through the rearview mirror. "But I insisted that I agreed with the precaution. She wrote all the passes. I confirmed all the names. I have them on my phone." She lifts it and flips through.

"Well, it's a legit outing," I say, "but I'm guessing Ms. Dimitriou has an issue with the guys going." I glance at Maddox. "She didn't text you?"

He checks. "Nope. Maybe I'm next. Doesn't matter. We have passes."

"We do," Theo says. "She'll just tell me it was highly irregular, and I'll thank her for being so understanding, blah-blah. I've got this."

It's after eight by the time we get back. Theo heads to speak to the principal. Polly wants to catch a movie in the media room, and Maddox needs some alone time, so I'm with Polly watching an action flick.

Allegra's there, too, in body at least; she's brought her sketchpad and sits in the back corner of the twelve-recliner room. When I slip out to grab sodas, I see she's drawing something obviously meant for Isolde. I don't ask whether it is. She'll never admit it. She'll just whip that off her sketchpad when Isolde returns with a casual "this seemed to be your style," as if she didn't spend hours getting it exactly right.

When the movie ends, it's nearly ten. We head out, Polly and I chattering about the film, Allegra lagging behind. I step into the hall and nearly trip over Theo. He's sitting on the floor, right outside the media room.

"Hey," he says, pushing to his feet.

His face is pale and strained, and his hair looks like he's been running his hands through it.

Polly quickly says she'll see me tomorrow, and Allegra joins her as they move on.

"What's wrong?" I say, taking Theo's hands.

He pulls me into a hug so tight I can feel his heart pounding.

"Theo?" I say. "My phone wasn't turned off. If you needed me—"

"I didn't message." He takes my hand. "Come on outside."

I follow him upstairs to the main level as I machine-gun questions. Is it Isolde? Is it someone in his family? Wait, is Maddox okay? He assures me it's nothing like that.

When we get outside, he says, "So, my meeting with Dimitriou."

"That went okay, didn't it?"

"Not . . . exactly."

I pull his hand, turning him to face me. "Is she seriously giving you crap for leaving? You had a pass."

"It wasn't about today. It was about last night."

"Last night? You had a pass for that. Is she upset about the mistake Isolde made? Some bullshit about it looking bad?"

"You could say that." He takes a deep breath. "I've been kicked out of the race for Optima."

After that, Theo needs to steer me deep into the yard, because I don't even need to hear more—I want to track Ms. Dimitriou down. Immediately.

We're tucked inside the woods before Theo decides we're far enough from the house for me to vent.

"What the actual *hell*?" I say. "You did nothing."

"I know."

"Does she think you did something? Let me talk to her. No, Cecilia can. She'll get the police report, which unequivocally exonerates you."

"It doesn't matter, Lil."

"The hell it doesn't. Isolde made a very brief mistake, and the school cannot punish you for that."

"The Optimas can remove any student from the competition at their discretion. No reason required. Just a vote."

"The Optimas did this? But your father is—"

"Yep, and I'd rather not discuss that because I do not want to know which way he voted. The fact that he didn't warn me—and apparently didn't fight for me—is enough."

"That—" I bite off the insult, and Theo pulls me into another tight hug.

"Thank you," he says.

"For what?"

"Being so spectacularly pissed off on my behalf." Another hug, and he releases me. "You know I didn't actually want to win. So it shouldn't hurt."

"It hurts because you *did* want it. You wanted to be chosen and refuse."

A faint smile. "I'm such a drama queen, huh?"

"Well, that makes two of us, because I was seriously considering doing the same if I was chosen. I wanted it until I realized you didn't, and then I thought harder and realized I don't either. I just wanted to win. This seals the deal. I absolutely don't want to be part of any group that would kick out their best candidate because he was very briefly misidentified in a crime. The attack never even hit the papers."

"It doesn't matter. They're worried it'll come out and . . . Whatever. I don't care."

He does care. He cares because this wasn't how he wanted his Optima race to end. Being kicked out? His own father not warning him? Not fighting for him?

I'm a competitor.

That's what he said. Theo's own father considered him competition.

And now Theo has been disqualified. Forced from the . . .

A realization hits, and I blink. Then I rock back, looking up at Theo.

"You'd have been a terrible Optima," I say.

A ghost of his usual grin. "The worst."

"No, I mean it. You're a wild card. You're not me, the quiet new girl, overwhelmed by everything that's happened. The heiress who'd be thrilled and starstruck to win."

"Uh, can't see you starstruck, Lil. Except with my mom."

"You know what I mean. If you were Optima, would anyone expect you to toe the party line? To be a team player? You're Theo Dubois. Brilliant and wild and incredible, but a leader, not a follower. You aren't someone who'd tell the Optimas you were thrilled to be there, just happy to be chosen."

He tilts his head. "What are you getting at, Lil?"

"I don't believe last night was a random attack. Isolde being hurt instead of me wasn't a mistake. Her identifying you wasn't an error. She was *supposed* to do that. Something about her attacker was supposed to make her blame you, only she knows you well enough that she rescinded the accusation quickly. Too quickly maybe? But it didn't matter. It gave someone fodder."

"Fodder to . . . ?" He blinks. "Remove me from the running?"

"Who's your main competitor? Yes, I know Cosmo is technically in the running, but we both know your only real competitor is the new girl. The quiet one. The one they expect really would just be thrilled to be chosen. I was clear about that in my conference call. How honored I was. How I could only dream of learning from the best. The starstruck billionaire heiress to a massive corporation."

He blinks. Then he whispers, "That's why the guy went for Isolde. You got hurt, but only because you fought back."

"And all I have is a scratch, no stitches required. The target wasn't Isolde herself. It was *anyone* found alone with me. Except you."

"Because I was the real target."

It's after ten, but following that conversation with Theo, I really need to talk to Maddox. The two of us are in the clubhouse, Theo having decided that, all things considered, he really shouldn't be AWOL from the house.

The conversation is also easier without Theo. I can tell Maddox that Theo is out of the Optima competition, and he can explode, and then we can both rant about how unfair it is.

When I tell Maddox my theory, his reaction is as expected.

"Fuck," he says, before grabbing one of Theo's empty beer cans and snarling "Fuck!" again as he whips it at the wall.

The can pings off and bounces along the floor.

"Too bad they aren't bottles," I say. "That was distinctly unsatisfying."

"Yeah, well, better than putting my fist through the wall."

"If you feel any temptation to do that, tell me. I'll find you bottles."

He slings an arm over my shoulders and pulls me against his side, kissing the top of my head. "You're damn well perfect, Chamberlain. I ever tell you that?"

I make a face. "If I were perfect, I'd have seen last night's setup right away."

"How?" He waves off my answer. "You're perfect. Accept it. Move on."

"I'm also the perfect patsy."

"Yeah, you kinda are. In theory, that is. In reality?" He smiles, and it's as feral as Theo's all-teeth grin. "I would *love* to see them try pushing you around. To them, though, you are the perfect cog for their machine. If Theo is out of the race, then you'll be our class's Optima. The seventeen-year-old heiress to a multibillion-dollar corporation. Raised in the outside world, unprepared for their survival-of-the-nastiest jungle. A good girl who's never been in a lick of trouble—and don't tell me you have, because if there's a single blemish on your record, Chamberlain, it's for keeping a library book out past the due date."

"Take that back," I say. "I've never needed two weeks to read a book."

He pulls me in for another kiss. Then he steers me over to sit on the loveseat. He perches half sideways, one foot up on the cushion, one on the floor. Then he pulls me to lie back on him, his arms around me.

I stare up at the ceiling, thinking. Then I say, "So who's behind this?"

"No idea. The Optimas?" He considers and shakes his head. "It can't be all of them, or they could just vote Theo out, no reason required. Is it one person in the Optimas? Or someone who benefits from the Optimas? Someone who benefits from you being chosen instead of Theo? Someone who just doesn't want Theo there? We need to start compiling lists, but I'm afraid they won't be short."

"Or exhaustive, since we have no allies in the Optimas to help us understand the internal politics." I look at him. "Right?"

He's quiet, then he says, softly, "My mom's not an ally, Lili."

"I never asked."

"I know, but I'm saying it up front. If I were in the running, she'd fight tooth and nail to get me selected. She doesn't give a shit about Theo. Never has. He's 'not serious' and 'a little much, don't you think?' Asking for your sake wouldn't be much better. She should be thrilled that I'm happy, but she'd just be hiring PIs to make sure you're good enough for her baby boy."

"And if Theo Dubois isn't good enough to be your friend, no one is good enough to be your girlfriend."

"Yeah. Which proves that my mother is seriously deluded."

I tilt my head back to look up at him. "I don't know. I think you deserve the best, too."

"You're just weird, Chamberlain. I don't hold it against you. Also? As far as I'm concerned, I *have* the best. In both of you."

I twist around, and we kiss for a few minutes. Then I settle back against him, and we sink into silence and thought until I say, very carefully, "Annette was a scholarship student."

"Hmm?"

"Annette Donleavy. My mom's friend who died in the car crash. According to the Lilith records, she was the main contender for Optima. But according to the *Optimas*, it was my mother, who didn't seem to be actually running."

I listen to him breathing as I hold my own breath, waiting for him to tell me I'm reaching.

"Annette was a scholarship student?" he says.

I nod.

"They'd never have made her an Optima," he says. "She doesn't have any connections, so she wouldn't bring anything to the group."

"Whereas my mom was a Chamberlain. Heir to a massive corporation, from a family that's been at Westdale from the start. From our point of view—the student view—getting into the Optimas is a huge honor and boon to our careers. What we're forgetting is that it also matters to *them*."

"To the Optimas. It matters who gets in, because if it's someone like you or your mom, that's useful. Annette wouldn't help them at all."

"And Theo would be more trouble than his connections are worth, since they already get those connections through his dad who—unlike my grandparents—is an active member."

More quiet breathing, in and out, his chest rising and falling beneath my head.

"They wouldn't dare kill Theo," he says. "While Bernard and Theo aren't close, Bernard *would* care about losing his only child. And Trinity would go ballistic. She'd bankrupt herself hiring investigators to be sure any accident was definitely an accident."

"Agreed. They could frame Theo, though. Force him out. But why not just do that to Annette?"

"It'd have looked bad, booting a scholarship kid from the race. Theo will go quietly—his dad will make sure of it. And Trinity doesn't like the Optimas. She'll be secretly relieved he's out of the running so his dad doesn't see him as competition there, too."

"So we agree it's a possibility? That someone killed Annette to get her out of the race?"

"A possibility, yes, and—" He stops suddenly, and his breath comes faster. "Jenna." Maddox swallows. "No, we've already established there was no connection between her and the Optimas. She wasn't in the running."

More deep breathing, as if calming himself, before he says, "Jenna doesn't need to be connected. She did go to parties. She did do drugs. Her death was an actual accident. But the other two? What happened to Annette and what happened to Isolde?"

Not accidents? That's what I need to find out.

TWENTY-NINE

When we get inside, Theo has already gone to bed, and for once, I think he needs time to himself. Maddox offers his room, and I grab shorts and a sleep shirt first, along with my own toiletries.

Maddox's room is exactly like mine, with no personal furnishings. The bookcase is stuffed with books, but otherwise, it's so impersonal and spotless that I'd question whether anyone occupied it. In my room, there is one thing that marks it as mine—the photos of my parents. Maddox has something similar. Besides the bookshelf, the standard corkboard is covered in photos. At least half are Theo and Maddox, which makes me realize Maddox must not let any other students in his room, with those on display.

Some of those photos have other friends from years past. I even spot Allegra in an old group shot, perfectly poised even at eleven or twelve, and standing on the edge, as if she'd deigned to grace the group with her presence only temporarily.

There are a few photos with an older man—his father. One family pic with both parents and a girl of about five with her toddler brother. I see more of Jenna then, through the years. The last is one of those theme-park roller-coaster photos. Maddox must be about fourteen, his expression bored. Jenna looks our age, with dark curly hair and a huge grin.

The bathroom door opens, and I step back from the collage.

"You weren't looking at my photos, were you, Chamberlain?"

"Uh, no, I—"

"They're on the wall," he says, as he kisses my cheek. "Not hidden in a drawer. Look all you want."

I tentatively touch the one with the roller coaster. "She seems so happy."

"Yeah, such a pain in the ass. Always smiling. Making me look bad." He moves up beside me. "That was right before she started at Westdale. I was in coding camp, and she picked me up to play hooky. We went to Disneyland for the day. She was always doing things like that. Sneaking me out, just the two of us, to do something fun." He pauses. "I never told her how much I loved it. Instead, I looked like"—he taps his scowl in the photo—"that."

I lean against him. "She knew you loved going. Otherwise, she wouldn't have kept taking you."

He pulls me against his side, and we talk about the photos for a little longer. Then I turn to his bed.

"It's just the standard double," he says. "You gonna feel crowded?"

"Never."

I look him up and down. He's dressed in a tee and sweatpants.

"You got a problem with my sleepwear, Chamberlain?"

"There's a lot of it."

He throws back his head and laughs. Then he pulls me in front of him, kissing my lips lightly. "And what do you want me wearing?"

"Honestly? Nothing. But that's implying I'm ready for things I'm not ready for."

"So just my shirt off?"

"Please."

His grin sparks as he leans in. "You want it off, you gotta do it yourself, Chamberlain."

"Happily."

"And if you take off mine, I get to—" He shakes his head. "Sorry."

"What were you going to say?"

He kisses me. "I got carried away."

"Were you going to say that if I take off yours off, you get to take off mine?"

His flush answers my question.

"Fair enough," I say, "though I have to warn you that I'm not wearing a bra."

He chuckles. "I don't think that's a warning, Chamberlain."

I take the bottom of his shirt and slowly tug it up over his abs, admiring the scenery as I do. I'd love to say I ease it gently over his head, but I'll need a lot more experience to do that, experience I will not mind getting. It's delicious fun, slowly seeing his naked torso, and when he foresees the problem of me getting it over his head, he ducks to make it easier. I tug it off, and then I look at him, his golden-brown skin and lean torso and sculpted arms.

I reach out, fingers stopping before I touch him. "May I?"

"You can do anything you like, Lili."

When I arch one brow, he chuckles, the sound sending heat coursing through me. Then he leans down to my ear.

"I mean anything," he says. "Just because I don't have any experience doesn't mean I don't have any interest." His lips move to my ear. "I have all the interest."

I shiver. "Same. I just—"

His fingers touch my lips. "We're moving slow. No rush, right?"

I nod. "I like that."

"Same. So, when I say you can do anything, I mean that, but I also know you're not going to do anything we aren't *both* ready for so . . ."

He puts my hand on his chest, and I take some time exploring, running my fingers over him as his eyes close in enjoyment. Then, when I've had some fun getting to know this part of him, I move his hands to the bottom of my T-shirt. His eyes open then, lips curving in a lazy smile that sets my pulse racing.

He's even slower removing my shirt than I was with his, and I get to experience it from the other side. It's just as good, the cool air touching my skin, his knuckles brushing me as he lifts the shirt. When he gets it over my breasts, he makes a low sound in his throat, and my breath picks up speed. He gets it over my head much more easily, and then it's off, and he's touching me, his fingers light, exploring and making me gasp and shiver. I understand why he closed his eyes, because when I do the same, the world constricts to his touch, and it's incredible. Then, without warning, his hands go around my waist, and I give a little yip, but he only chuckles again and I realize he's carrying me to the bed.

Maddox lays me down on my back. Then he starts to crawl in over me, but stops above me, uncertainty flashing over his face.

"This okay?" he says.

I answer by reaching up and pulling him down into a kiss.

I wake to the click of a door, which is strange because Maddox is still right here, sleeping entwined with me. I reach out, as if I might be imagining him. No, he's definitely there, shirtless, his skin warm to the touch, and I run my fingers down his chest, making him groan softly in his sleep.

"If I were a better person, I'd back out right now," Theo's voice says behind me. Then he thumps onto the edge of the bed. "But I'm not."

I twist to look over at him. He lifts a hand to cover his eyes. "I see nothing you don't want me to see."

"If Maddox has seen it, you can see it."

Theo grins. "Is that the universal theory? If one of us does it, the other—"

"It's too early for your bullshit," Maddox says, eyes still closed. "If you tease Lili, you're not seeing—or doing—anything."

"But teasing is the best part." Theo turns to half kneel, leaning over me. "You want me to tease, Lil?"

"Ignore him," Maddox says.

"What if she doesn't want to ignore me?"

Theo leans down and kisses me, and I automatically kiss him back, only afterward glancing at Maddox, my heart picking up speed with an edge of panic. But Maddox is relaxed, eyes half lidded, and when he sees me looking, he gives a lazy smile.

They're navigating this so much better than I am. It's not that I mind Theo seeing me in bed with Maddox or Maddox seeing Theo kiss me—it's that I'm afraid *they'll* mind, as if this thing we have is so fragile, it's bound to shatter at the slightest touch.

They're fine with it. With all of it. I didn't demand this arrangement. It was their idea, and I'll admit I'd worried it was a compromise, neither wanting to back down or compete, but I can see it's not. Maddox has no more problem with me kissing Theo than he'd have with me talking to Theo or hanging out with him.

"Everything okay, Lil?" Theo murmurs, and I look up into his hazel eyes and see the barest hint of worry there.

I answer with a kiss, and it's slow and soft, and I can feel Maddox's fingers on my hip, and that ignites a spark I'm definitely not ready for yet, so I duck my head, feeling my cheeks heat.

"I should probably have a shower," I say.

"No," Maddox says, and I startle, but he adds, "I was talking to Theo."

"I never said anything," Theo protests.

"You were about to. I could see that glint in your eyes."

Theo glances over me at Maddox. "Okay then, what was I about to say?"

"You were going to ask if she wanted company."

Theo grins, fast and wicked. "Are you suggesting I should join her? Capital idea. And how about you? It's a big shower."

"Theo . . ." Maddox growls. "You're making Lili blush."

I climb off the bed, shaking my head. "He likes doing that."

"He *loves* doing that," Maddox says. "But he's going to watch his step."

"Mmm, I don't know. I think Lil is perfectly capable of telling me to shut up."

"I am," I say. "And I know you're not seriously suggesting it. You just want to see my reaction."

"Your reaction, Mads's reaction . . ."

Maddox rolls his eyes.

Theo starts to rise from the bed. "You sure you don't need someone to wash your back, Lil?"

I put my hand on his chest, nudging him back down. At the same time, Maddox lays a restraining hand on his arm. Theo looks from my hand to Maddox's and grins such a wicked grin that my insides light on fire. I also tense, waiting for Maddox to pull away at that look, but he only rolls his eyes again and squeezes Theo's arm.

"Let Lili have her shower," Maddox says. "In peace."

I take one last look at Maddox's hand on Theo's arm before I head into the bathroom for a shower. A very cold shower.

"He's telling me he isn't going to class," Maddox says when I come out of the shower, my sweats on.

Theo's lounging on the bed, while Maddox is up and getting dressed.

"What are they going to do?" Theo says. "Kick me out of Westdale? I've already been accepted to USC and I'm not in the running for Optima, so as long as I pass my courses, I'm good. And I could pass without ever attending another class."

I thump face down beside him on the bed. "I know you want to protest this, Theo. I know you want to say 'fuck you' to all of them. Obviously I won't stop you. But . . ."

"Will it look like protest?" Maddox says. "Or sulking? The golden boy got knocked down a peg and can't handle it."

Theo sets his jaw. "Don't care."

Maddox makes a rude noise because we both know Theo does care—he'd just rather he didn't.

"It's not just how it will look," I say. "I've got a more selfish reason for not wanting you on school-strike, Theo. I really need to investigate what happened to Isolde."

"Good point," Maddox says. "If you're making waves, Theo, Liliana can't do anything even mildly suspicious. We have to continue on, business as usual, as shitty as that is for you."

Theo kisses my nose. "I forgot that part. Sorry, Lil."

"I'd love to let you strike in protest," I say. "I'd love to join you. In fact, I'm planning to withdraw from the Optima and let Cosmo—"

"No, no, no," the guys say in unison.

"But—"

"No, Lil," Theo says. "After what happened Saturday night, we don't want you making any sudden moves. We need you to maintain status quo until we understand what's going on here. As for me, I can say 'fuck you' in another way—by carrying on, business as usual, don't give a shit."

I hug him. "You do that, but know that I totally plan to drop out of the race the moment I can."

THIRTY

Monday proceeds as normally as it can. There isn't any official announcement that Theo is no longer in the running for Optima. That's good, because he doesn't want to deal with that. But it's also odd that it happens in silence.

Maddox joins us for breakfast, at least briefly. Then we're off to our first class. We've agreed that at break I'll slip into the library to work on the case. Theo delivers my mocha.

I'm zeroing in on Annette's death. I have a theory here. Someone didn't want Annette as an Optima, but she was clearly the front-runner up until the accident. At some point after that, it seems my mother became front-runner.

I've realized that my mother's Dux journal must end before Annette's death. Without clear dates, I lacked the clues to place it temporally. But if Annette died and my mom was still Dux for another month, why is none of that here?

Did someone remove entries? If they did, then I suspect they've been destroyed.

By the next Lilith Dux? Or by whoever was responsible for Annette's death?

Without those entries I can only speculate on what happened

after Annette died. On why the Optimas seem convinced that my mother had been running for Optima.

Theo was forced out of the running.

Could my mother have been forced *into* it?

Could that have been why she left? She was forced to run for Optima, couldn't face the possibility of being trapped in that life, and fled with my dad?

How would someone have forced Mom to run?

If they had something to hold over her. Annette died in Mom's car. Cecilia said she was sure Mom hadn't gone out that night. Could Dad have been driving, taking Annette to see this guy she met online, watching out for her? The price for protecting him was that Mom would enter the competition and truly take over as my grandparents' heir, living a corporate life she never wanted?

Or maybe Cecilia was driving. Then Mom would be protecting her best friend.

Cecilia . . .

I think of the hospital, when Theo thought he'd spotted her.

But that doesn't make sense. Even if Cecilia was driving Mom's car that night—which I can't imagine—there'd be no reason for her to follow me to the hospital to see Isolde.

What I pore over, both during morning break and then at lunch, are the police reports. I shudder to think what might happen if anyone realizes Cecilia sent them, and I'm so grateful that she trusted me with them.

I found an inconsistency while rereading the reports during morning break, and it's at lunch that I track that inconsistency to its conclusion. I'm eating with Maddox for once, sitting outside, and I really wish I could enjoy this opportunity to spend time with him during a school day, but he knows I need to pursue this and lets me as I work on my laptop, while he quietly eats.

Finally, I take a deep breath. He arches one brow. He won't push for details until I'm ready, which is why he's the one with me right now. Theo would push.

"I have something," I say.

"Okay."

"According to the report, an officer named Stan Lewiston was first on the scene at Annette's accident, but there's no report *from* him. He's literally only mentioned once. Even if he didn't need to file his own report, he made all the initial observations, and yet they're attributed to someone else."

Maddox frowns. "That doesn't seem right."

"Six months later, Mr. Lewiston left the force."

"Huh."

"He wasn't fired. It's made very clear that he left of his own accord because he started a local security firm. Now, maybe he just realized police work wasn't for him and went into the private sector, but . . ."

"You said he's local?"

I nod. "He lives about ten miles away. The problem is getting to him. I've got my car, but I can't drive it without a pass."

"You do realize we're not in an armed camp, right, Chamberlain? Sure, it can feel like it, but"—he waves at the fields and forest beyond—"it's a five-minute walk and a call to Uber."

I glance over. "Will you come with me?"

"I *am* going with you. I just wasn't saying that, because apparently that's wrong or something. You and I are taking a field trip during study hours."

Okay, so after two months at Westdale, I discover that getting off campus is ridiculously easy. Like Maddox said, you basically just walk to another road and call a ride-share. Of course, we have to be careful, ducking guards and avoiding cameras.

Stan Lewiston runs his own business, which means he probably isn't home until after six, but we need to go during study hours—before dinner. My research indicates that Mr. Lewiston's business is successful, and it suggests he's no longer actually doing security work himself. So I take a chance that we'll find him in his office.

We discuss it with Theo before we go. Since we're leaving the property, I really should be with both of them, for safety. But if our theory is right, then I'm not at risk. I'm the patsy—the Chamberlain they want in the Optimas.

We arrive just before five, as Mr. Lewiston's receptionist is preparing to leave. She won't tell us whether he's in or out and she's reluctant to even take a message without our names and ID. It *is* a security firm, after all.

Then a door opens, as if someone heard our discussion. Out walks a guy in his forties, with dark brown skin, close-cropped curls, and shoulders nearly as wide as the doorframe.

He sees me, and he stops short, blinking. His gaze goes to Maddox. Back to me.

"These young people want to see you, Mr. Lewiston," the receptionist says, "but they aren't telling me why. Or giving me names."

"It's fine," he says. "Come in, guys."

"But, sir—"

"It's fine, Em. Go on home. I've got this."

He waves us to his office. As he closes the door behind Maddox, his gaze returns to me. Then he shakes his head. "Sorry for staring, miss. But this is feeling a lot like déjà vu."

"I remind you of someone?" I guess.

He gives a low chuckle. "Someone who also showed up on my doorstep. My home doorstep, though. Along with a different young fellow."

"Was this about eighteen years ago?" I ask.

He lowers himself into a seat behind his wood desk. "It was. Don't ask me her name, though. She didn't give it. Just like you. I'm guessing she was a relative."

"My mother."

He pauses, assessing me. "Huh. All right, then. Now *you've* come to ask me about something?"

"The same thing she did, I bet."

He goes very still and then nods slowly. "Go on."

"You were the first officer on the scene of a fatal accident. A student at Westdale. Annette Donleavy."

Mr. Lewiston exhales slowly. "Go on."

"It was allegedly a single-vehicle accident, with Annette driving, no one else in the car. Was that your initial observation?"

"You sound like a lawyer." His lips twitch in amusement. "All right, then. Let's do this. Yes, ma'am, it was a single-vehicle accident with the deceased in the driver's seat. She missed a stop sign at the end of a road, wrapped the car around a tree on the other side. There was positively no one else in the car at the time of the accident—with the condition of the vehicle, no one could have left before I arrived. Miss Donleavy was definitely driving. I apologize for any graphic details, but her seat belt failed and she went partway through the windshield before striking the tree. No one could have placed her there, again given the condition of the vehicle."

"The seat belt failed? What about airbags?"

"It was a classic car. Didn't have them."

"And she missed the stop sign?"

"Seems so. No indication she even hit the brakes. While it *was* dark, it should have been clear that the road ended but . . ." He shrugs. "What do I know?"

I glance at Maddox, who's just taking it all in, his gaze distant as he thinks.

"You were the first officer on the scene," I say, "but another officer took charge."

"Yes, ma'am."

"Can you tell me more about that?"

He taps his fingers on the desktop. "Maybe you ought to ask your mother about this."

"Because she came to you with the same questions?"

"She did."

I pause. Then I say, "My mother died in November."

He winces. "I'm sorry to hear that, miss. She was full of questions and not afraid to ask them. Now at the time, I was young and angry about the whole situation, said things I shouldn't have said, especially not to a couple of kids. Now I'm older, and I don't give a damn what I say if I think it's the right thing to do. So you both caught me at the perfect time."

He glances at the door, as if making sure it's shut. "I wasn't supposed to be there. I happened on the scene while the engine was still warm. Pure coincidence. I figured no one had called it in, so I did, and I was told . . ."

He rubs his mouth. "That doesn't matter. Point was that I was there first, and by the time I was told another officer would take over, I'd already seen the girl. I checked her and looked in the car for survivors."

"When my mother talked to you, was she just confirming what you found? Single-car accident. Annette was driving. No passengers."

"She said she'd heard someone else was driving and it was covered up."

"And you told her she was wrong."

Mr. Lewiston goes quiet. Then he sighs. "No, I admitted I'd heard a similar story, but it wasn't true."

"You heard someone else was driving?"

"And that's exactly where your mom jumped on me, too. I tried to clam up, but she kept pushing, and I finally admitted that I'd overheard something about another kid being spotted at the accident scene, before I got there. Speculation was that this kid had been the actual driver. I checked the official report, because if it said that, I was going to set them straight, say this witness was wrong. I was there so soon after the crash that I'd have seen anyone moving her and fleeing, even if that was possible, which it wasn't, with the condition of the car and the placement of her body."

"So you corrected the report?"

"Didn't need to. There was nothing in it about a witness. It was strange. Miss Donleavy was obviously driving, and the report confirmed that, so what was this nonsense about a kid fleeing the scene? I asked, and I was told I'd misheard."

"But you didn't."

"I did not."

I glance at Maddox. This time, he's fully alert and he leans forward. "Did you hear any details about this alleged other driver? What she looked like?"

"She?" Mr. Lewiston frowns. "No, it was a fellow. That was what I heard. That the girl who died was a student at Westdale, and the imaginary driver matched the description of a young man who worked there. A gardener."

I rock back in my seat.

"Miss?" Mr. Lewiston says.

"You said my mom came with a guy. Another student?"

He nods. "I presume so. He was about her age. Quiet, like your friend here. White guy. Long hair. Mostly I just remember he was quiet. Oh, and his eyes. Really green . . ." He trails off, looking at me. Then he gives a little laugh. "Oh. Well, I guess he wasn't just a fellow student giving her a lift, was he?"

"He was not."

"Did he stick around? After you . . . ? Well, they'd have been young . . ."

"He stuck around," I say. "Always."

Mr. Lewiston smiles. "I'm glad to hear it. They seemed like good kids."

"They really were."

"You figured it out," Maddox says as we wait for our ride-share.

I nod. "Someone threatened my dad. They knew that was the way to get my mom to do what they wanted."

Maddox grunts and moves closer, arm going around me. I lean into his heat, suddenly chilled.

"The accident was almost certainly murder," I say. "Mr. Lewiston said it would have been hard to miss that the road ended, even at night. The brakes and seat belt failed. Someone knew Annette would be out or . . ." I look over at him. "She was meeting a guy she met online, presumably for the first time."

"It was a setup," he murmurs. "They lured her out."

"And sabotaged my mom's antique car."

Maddox's hand rubs my shoulder, and he stays quiet, letting me continue.

"Annette was driving," I say. "No one else was there. This so-called witness was a setup. Tell my mom that my dad had been behind the wheel, but that his life shouldn't be ruined for an accident, and if she does what they say, it'll all go away. Which it does, easily, because it's all a lie. Like making Isolde think Theo attacked her."

"Framing your dad. Framing Theo."

I nod. "Not to actually have them charged—that requires evidence. Just to provide leverage. A way to convince my mom to run for Optima. A way to kick Theo out of the running. Framing students to manipulate the Optima competition."

I look at Maddox. "That's what the comments in the yearbook meant. The rumor leaked, and some students thought my dad had something to do with Annette's death."

"The Optimas told you that your mom was in the running for Optima because she was, briefly. Meanwhile, she was trying to figure out what happened, how your dad got blamed, and it led her to Stan Lewiston."

"Where she figured out that Dad was never in any danger and it was all a setup. That's when they decided to run."

THIRTY-ONE

By the time we get back to Westdale, I'm exhausted. My brain has been spinning since Isolde was attacked, and now that I'm starting to get answers, I'm so overwhelmed I can barely string words together. I want to . . .

I don't even know what I want to do. Lie in bed and stare at the ceiling? Take a hot bath and stare at the wall? Go for a long car ride and stare out the passenger-side window?

I feel like I need to be put into a temporary state of unconsciousness so my brain can rest. But sleep is out of the question. So is staring at walls. We need to act normal, which means I go to dinner with Theo, who thankfully gets a table for two and just lets me vegetate.

Maddox updated Theo on the way back, and Theo's not asking questions—probably on Maddox's orders—so I can just fork food into my mouth and think.

When Cecilia first knocked on my door, I knew who I was. An orphan. The beloved daughter of two wonderful people who'd fallen in love, gotten married, and had me, just like ordinary couples everywhere.

Only they weren't ordinary. Mom was a billionaire heiress who fell in love during her senior year in an elite boarding school, got pregnant, and ran off with the school gardener.

Only they *didn't* run off because she was pregnant. So why *did* they leave?

Because someone killed her friend, pretended my dad was involved, and used that to try blackmailing her into becoming something she didn't want to be.

At first, she must have thought it'd been a genuine case of mistaken identity, that Annette's online boyfriend bore some resemblance to my dad. She might have presumed whoever offered her the "deal"—run for Optima and we'll bury that witness report—had genuinely been trying to help. Mr. Lewiston's story exploded that theory, and she'd realized how far someone would go to get her in the Optimas, so she did what Theo wanted to do: flipped them the bird on her way out the door.

My mom was kickass, in ways I don't think I fully realized, in ways I only hope I can live up to. She got what she wanted—a loving husband and child and the freedom to be a full-time wife and mom—but I am still so *fucking* furious on her behalf.

I want vengeance. For her and for Annette and for Theo.

And for who else?

What are the chances that my mother and my boyfriend are the only two people this happened to?

Someone killed Annette to replace an unsuitable candidate with the heiress they wanted in the Optimas.

Someone *nearly* killed Isolde to move aside what they considered to be another unsuitable candidate.

How long has this been going on?

How deep does the rot go?

And who the hell is behind it?

My mind jumps to that secret room and the Janus Society. I have nothing to link it to any of this, but my thoughts keep sliding back there.

Once I'm back in my room, I open my desk drawer and pull out the envelope of burned scraps. Even before I open it, I roll my eyes at myself. What do I really expect to find?

Does it matter? No, because either way, the Janus Society is a puzzle I need to solve.

It only takes me an hour to finish this literal puzzle. I have a dozen scraps with writing on them, and they don't all neatly fit together. There are a few I can't place anywhere, and there are huge gaps in what I do complete.

In the end, I have a date—May 1956—the words *Janus Society*, and what seems like a student's schedule. Not the classes, but other things, like that they skip games night, go for evening jogs and . . . "likes single malt whisky."

None of that makes any sense, but I put it into my mental bank of things I can check in the place I need to go next.

"I need permission to access the Lilith journals," I tell Allegra after dinner.

She's in the lounge, where everyone would normally be at this time, but it's a gorgeous night and someone declared a touch football game was in order. That someone may have been Theo, who may also know that Allegra really isn't the outdoor type. Something about allergies, but I'm pretty sure the only thing she's allergic to is fresh air and teens acting like actual teens.

She's in the lounge, with her sketchpad, and she doesn't even look up until she finishes whatever she was drawing. When she does, her gaze slowly rises to me. Then she taps her pencil to the pad three times before saying, "I have been very patient with you, Liliana, and I did grant you an extension for telling me first about the ball, but you still owe me a secret. Do you have an idea yet why your mother left Westdale?"

When I hesitate, her eyes narrow. "You know."

"I have a theory but—"

"We had a deal, Liliana."

"And you'll get your secret when I'm sure. I need more first."

"Which you will find in the archives?"

When I hesitate, she looks up, lowering her glasses, dark eyes meeting mine. "Please remember how much I hate having my intelligence insulted."

"I'm investigating Isolde's attack. Which could be connected to my mother's leaving."

"You expect to find answers about Isolde in the Lilith files?" She peers at me. "You believe there's some connection to the school, which is also connected to whatever else you've been chasing."

"When I have answers, you'll know."

"By the time I know, it'll no longer be a secret."

"Allegra . . ."

"You owe me a secret."

I throw up my hands. "Fine, I'm dating Theo."

"How is *that* a secret?"

"And Maddox."

Her head tilts. "Really?"

"Yes."

"Well, that sounds exhausting."

I sputter a laugh and sink onto the chair beside her. "Now, can I have access?"

"Is Theo also dating Maddox?" she asks.

My traitorous cheeks must heat, because she taps her sketchpad. "Not yet, but you see that possibility."

"Allegra, can we just—"

"Would that be a problem?"

"Allegra . . ."

"What? We're having a discussion that may prove pertinent at some point. Everyone says I need to be more of a friend. I'm being a friend."

"You're the keeper of secrets, Allegra, which is why no one dares have that sort of conversation with you."

"*Keeper* is the key word, Liliana. I *keep* secrets. I don't share them. In this case, the fact you are dating both friends is interesting, but not terribly useful, as using it against you would imply I see an issue with it, which I do not."

"Fine," I say. "Theo dating Maddox wouldn't be a problem. Now can I get access to those records?"

"Do you think Isolde is in danger?"

"That's what I'm trying to figure out. Right now, no, I think she's served her purpose."

"Which was . . . ?" she prompts.

"Access first. Answers later."

"I will get you that access if you accept my help in finding what you're after. And that is not up for negotiation."

"I have to talk it over."

"With your boys?"

I point a finger at her. "Do not pull that shit."

"You make everything so difficult. Go. Talk. We can't access the room until Dimitriou is on duty tomorrow anyway."

After that, I go outside to watch the touch football game. Maybe next time I'll even participate. It actually looks appealing for once, probably because the competition is fierce but fun. The teams are balanced, and bad plays are only mocked if they're made by one of the more athletic students. No one gets annoyed with the non-athletes like me.

When the curfew bell sounds, we head inside. We've decided to use Theo's room tonight, so that's where we go, though it'll be more "sleepover" than "sexy fun." Too much going on, and the shared bed is for safety and conversation, nothing else. Unfortunately? Yes, unfortunately. I'll fully admit to that. But I'll also fully admit that there's no way I could enjoy anything else with my brain zipping.

I tell the guys that Allegra knows about us. We already knew she might demand a secret, and we'd decided to give her that because I'm the only one who's nervous about others finding out. I need to get over that.

Next I tell them her demand. The problem is that I don't actually want access to the Lilith books. I want access to the *other* society vaults. Since realizing how poorly they were secured, I've researched and improved my lock-picking skill. I'm not saying I can break into all the cabinets, but I think I can access some.

What will Allegra say about that?

The answer, I think, is obvious.

She's the keeper of secrets. This little stunt could win her a legacy that will be whispered about by future Liliths. The Dux who filled her journal with other societies' secrets.

So, if I do this, do I distract her with a smorgasbord of secrets? Or do I actually accept her help finding what I need, because this is going to be a huge undertaking?

What if I'm wrong in thinking that framing Theo was about clearing the way for *me*? What if it was about clearing the way for *Allegra*, and I was expected to drop out in protest?

If I drop out, that reduces the field to Cosmo, so could Allegra be pushed forward to take my place? And what if she's more than the innocent recipient of someone else's machinations?

I don't want to suspect Allegra of anything like that. But... while I genuinely like her, I'd be a fool if I thought she wasn't capable of something like this. Of stepping in at the finish line. In fact, it's exactly what she'd do, because it's what she *does* do.

Refusing to join until the last minute is classic Allegra. She'd want nothing to do with all the Optima race "nonsense." Not the attention and not the inconveniences.

Maybe pulling me into the Liliths wasn't about having a Lilith contender. Maybe it was about keeping me close and deflecting attention from herself, until I quit and she "reluctantly" steps in past the declaration date.

Is it possible that Allegra Khan is actually my competition?

Yes.

So what am I going to do about that?

For now, nothing. Because if that's her plan, I need to catch her at it. Letting her into my investigations is risky, but it might also be the perfect trap.

The next day, I have to wait until lunch to get into the archives. Once Ms. Dimitriou closes the door behind us, I walk the perimeter of the room.

"What are you doing?" Allegra asks.

"Checking for cameras. I looked the last time, but I need to be more careful now."

"There are no cameras, Liliana. The administration considers the societies the very adorable games of the rich and famous."

I still finish my sweep. Then I walk to the back row, where the Mercurys and Apollos have their cabinets. I feel uncomfortable going into the records of Theo's society, even if he insisted he was fine with it. He's Dux, and if anyone discovers his girlfriend accessed Apollo records, it will *not* look good.

As I examine the lock on the Mercury cabinet, Allegra says, "Please tell me you're planning to break into that."

"You mean please tell you I'm *not* planning it."

"If you think that would be my reaction, you don't know me at all." She moves closer. "Can you do it?"

"Not with you breathing down my neck. Would you stand by the door? Warn me if any footsteps stop outside it."

"Ms. Dimitriou wouldn't care if you broke into those. She'd probably be amused."

Still, Allegra goes to the door. I pop the lock with surprising ease, probably because it's a very simple mechanism.

"Do you suspect someone in the Mercury Society is behind Isolde's attack?" Allegra says, appearing at my shoulder again.

"No, they're just the first one I'm checking."

"So you think a society *is* behind this?" She frowns as if thinking it through. "I would start with Hephaestus myself. They have reason to hate the Liliths."

When I glance over at her, she shrugs. "They may have had a contender for the Optima race before you arrived. I may have ended that."

I pause, and when I speak, I keep my voice calm, conversational. "Why? You're not running. The Liliths didn't even have a contender until I arrived."

I hold my breath, waiting for a reaction. For her to realize she's given something away.

"It wasn't about who I want to win," she says. "It was about who I *didn't* want to win. There was an issue with Polly that made me decide their contender was unworthy. Also, it may seem as if the Liliths didn't have a horse in the race before you, but Theo has always been a friend of the Liliths."

There's no trace of a lie, not in her eyes or her voice, and when I think about it, if Allegra was secretly running, she wouldn't "slip up" by mentioning that she knocked out an early contender.

Or she has no compunction about mentioning it because she thinks she's gotten away with it.

The problem is that I can spin all the dark theories I want, but when I'm with Allegra, I find it hard to believe she'd go through all this effort to be Optima. *Avoiding* effort is Allegra's specialty.

"Okay," I say. "If I can open the Hephaestus cabinet, you can look through it."

"I'll need to know what I'm looking for."

"Past incidents where an Optima contender may have been . . . convinced to leave the race."

Her brow furrows. "Like what I did to Hephaestus? That happens a lot, Liliana. It's part of the competition."

"I'm talking about things like Jayden pushing me down the stairs. Or like Isolde being injured to force Theo out."

She stares at me in what looks like genuine shock. "Theo was forced out?"

"Does *that* count as a secret?"

She ignores me and continues, "I know Isolde very temporarily identified him, but surely that . . ." She trails off and then peers at me. "You believe the attack was *about* Theo."

"There's also a scholarship student from the past who was the front-runner and died in a suspicious car accident. I'm not saying this is a conspiracy. It might very well be like what happened with Jayden—individual contenders or their allies hurting people."

"There's a difference between what happened to you and *murder*, Liliana. Yes, I know Jayden *could* have killed you, but from everything I've heard, he just didn't think it through. Isolde really could have died, and now you're saying a contender *did* die in the past?" She looks over at me sharply. "Jenna Moreno. You're also thinking—"

"I don't know what I'm thinking. But please pull anything about a car accident in 2005 involving a girl named Annette Donleavy. And anything about Jenna Moreno. And anything about 'accidents' that were serious or fatal. Oh, and pull everything from spring 1956." I pull a page from my pocket. "Also, if you see this *anywhere*, let me know."

It's a hand-drawn representation of the scorpion symbol. When she frowns at the drawing, I say, "You've seen it?"

"It looks familiar, but I don't know from where. What is it?"

"I don't know, but it's come up a few times. The double head suggests it's connected to the Janus Society."

She peers at me like I'm losing it. "There is no Janus Society, Liliana."

I throw up my hands. "I know. But I found that symbol in a room that seemed to belong to something called the Janus Society."

"What room?"

"It's a secret. And if you also want that one—to add to my tally—you need to get me something first."

Her eyes narrow. "That's my line."

"Not this time. Happy hunting."

THIRTY-TWO

Even with Allegra's help, an hour is never going to be enough. If there *was* a past incident, it would likely be in a Dux's journal. But it might *not* be there either—Annette's accident wasn't. And every Dux leaves a journal anywhere from twenty to a hundred pages long. With four societies, and a Dux every year for over a hundred years?

Needle in a haystack.

But I don't know where else to look. Obviously we tried searching for newspaper reports of incidents at Westdale, but that got us nowhere. I'm convinced that the one small article on Annette's death slipped through the cracks, because there's nothing on Jenna and there's been nothing on Isolde. When something goes wrong, Westdale locks down hard.

Again, that doesn't make Westdale complicit. They're covering their asses against negative press.

But *could* they be complicit? Even *responsible*?

I barely dare consider that. I've already slid headfirst into conspiracy land.

I look more closely at the Mercury journal from my mom's year. Here I do see a reference to Annette's death, but it's just the Mercury Dux noting it. The Dux does say, though, that she'd personally hoped Annette would make Optima because the group could use fresh blood and fresh ideas.

That has me reading closer and learning that the Mercurys had no solid Optima contender that year themselves. Their Dux had apparently also been backing Annette. And then I find another comment—in light of Annette's death, the Mercurys had agreed to switch their support to my mother. That confirms she was officially a contender, at least briefly. I continue skimming but find no reference to what happened after my mother left—or to her departure.

From there, I skip back to 1956—the year on the papers I found in the secret room—and I stop when I see an entry from late May.

> Louis is out of the Optima race, which means I'm the lead contender. Not sure how I feel about that. I should be overjoyed, but given the circumstances, I can't be. I liked Louis, and he'd have made a great addition to the Optimas. Shake it up a little. But apparently, it's going to be another Walker: me. Same old, same old.

I leaf through the next few entries. It seems that the Mercury Dux ended up winning.

Fresh blood and fresh ideas.

Shake it up a little.

There's also no further mention of Louis or what actually happened to him.

I move on to the Hephaestus cabinet. This was Jenna's society. Yes, we have no reason to believe her death is connected, but I can't help myself. I need to see what her Dux said at the time of her death. There's no mention of it in the Mercury journals.

To my relief, the Hephaestus Dux definitely mentions it. There's a full page of shock and anger and grief. No suspicion, though. The Dux seems to have known that Jenna partied and that drugs were involved, and he presumes she decided to try something new.

> *Always so damned curious. I used to joke that if she could channel that curiosity into the classes she didn't like, she'd have been a shoo-in for Optima. But she wasn't interested. I know it's a cliché, but Jenna Moreno marched to her own drum, and god she was good at it.*

My eyes mist as I touch those words, memorizing them for Maddox.

There's nothing else here for me, and the clock is ticking, but I can't help leafing back, skimming the Dux's journal for Jenna's name, for anything I can take to Maddox.

I find it here and there, just references to her being at—or skipping—meetings. Then I hit one that stops me in my tracks.

> *So Jenna has decided there's something odd about Taylor getting hurt. That's Jenna. She gets an idea in her head and can't get it out, and I'm the sucker who encourages her because I like seeing her taking an interest in anything other than coding.*
>
> *I think it was a freak accident, and Taylor will be fine. They just had to drop out of the Optima race, and that sucks*

because they were our Hephaestus contender and they would have been a good Optima. It's such an old boys' club. Yes, it's not all "boys," but you know what I mean.

I'll let Jenna run with this and give her what I can.

I stare down at the entry. I read it. Read it again. Then I flip back fast through the pages, looking for references to "Taylor." I find some about twenty pages earlier, and I read as fast as I can.

As the Dux said, Taylor was a member of the Hephaestus Society and a contender for Optima. They got attacked in Savannah and suffered a head injury. As the Dux said, they recovered, but the resulting concussion meant they went home for a couple of weeks and had to give up the term, including their shot at Optima.

According to the Dux, it was queer bashing. A few Westdale students had been in Savannah and some guys gave them trouble. When they tried to leave, Taylor got hit from behind.

Just another accident, the sort that befalls teens who leave the safety of the Westdale campus.

Miss a stop sign and die in a car accident.

Go out dancing and get attacked in an alley.

Hit a club with friends and get gay-bashed by drunk locals.

Go to a party and accidentally overdose?

I rub my arms.

"Liliana?"

I jump.

"We need to leave," Allegra says. "We—" She catches my expression. "You found something."

"I don't know. You?"

"Nothing. But that symbol irks me. I know I've seen it. I'll think more on it. If we need to keep looking here, though, it'll need to wait a few days. We can't afford to make Dimitriou suspicious."

The first thing I do is search for Louis in the library's 1956 yearbook. I find him easily. Louis Ralston, class of 1956, Apollo Society. He'd been an artist, though I don't find him online. I also don't see other Ralstons in the yearbooks before or after.

The next obvious step is to ask Theo to search the Apollo Dux journals, but I need to wait a few days and get a cushion between archive searches. Ms. Dimitriou had already commented on me searching twice in a month. Having Theo search too quickly will arouse suspicions.

I have another route to try first: Cecilia. I send her Louis's name and attendance year and hope she can find something concrete.

Next I want to talk to Theo about Jenna. I don't have enough to justify taking this to Maddox yet, but nor can I withhold it from him for long without being patronizing.

I don't hear any of my next class. While we're supposed to be taking notes, I'm jotting down secure investigation notes in a brainstorming cloud as I try to make connections. Or, more to the point, I try to *avoid* making *wrong* connections.

Annette Donleavy was a scholarship student, and the Mercury Dux talked about her bringing fresh ideas to the Optimas.

Louis Ralston was an artist who doesn't seem to have been from a legacy Westdale family. The Mercury Dux said that he was likely to win in Louis's place, "another Walker." Same old, same old.

Then there's Taylor. They're from a family I've seen in the

yearbooks, but one that doesn't have deep ties to Westdale. When I look them up, I find that they sold their manufacturing empire about thirty years ago and now run a charity foundation using the proceeds.

What do all these Optima candidates have in common?

They're outsiders. Like Theo. Yes, Theo is from a very successful family, but he's a wild card, and, as he pointed out, the Optimas already have a film-making Dubois.

What was it the Hephaestus Dux said?

Such an old boys' club.

And maybe they're determined to keep it that way.

I spend my study time alternately messaging Theo and continuing to put together the pieces of this case. I haven't heard back from Cecilia, and I won't bug her. I don't have any proof that my "clue" from 1956 is more than an offhand reference to someone dropping out of the Optima race.

When it's dinnertime, I message Maddox, saying I'll pick him up at his room.

I knock, and he opens the door and then backs up, as if he knew what I really meant was that I want to talk to him.

"You found out something about Jenna," he says as I shut the door.

I go still.

"No, Theo didn't say anything," Maddox says. "He wouldn't. But you went through the archive journals at lunch and you've been avoiding me ever since."

"I'm sorry."

He watches me, his expression unreadable, and I want to go to him, feel his hands around my waist as he pulls me close, tells me it's okay, he understands.

That expression says it is not okay.

And what I'm about to tell him won't help.

"I found something, and I'm not sure if it's anything, but I need more time."

His gaze shutters. "You don't want me jumping on it. Overreacting."

"No, I'm afraid *I'm* overreacting. Or under-reacting. I can't even tell. My brain is spinning, and I feel like I'm spiraling into paranoia and conspiracy theories, and I don't want to pull you in with me."

"Because you think I can't handle it. I'm unstable, and you don't want to push me over the edge."

"That's not—" I shake my head. "Who knows what I'm thinking? I'm barely sure of my own name right now, Maddox." I laugh, the sound raw and shaky. "Which is a really shitty analogy, because I'm *not* sure of my own name. It was Green, but that's apparently fake. Now I'm going by Chamberlain, but I'm pretty sure I don't want that one either."

I rub my face. "I'm blathering. Fine. Whatever. You want to know, and I'm sure as hell not the person to be making decisions for anyone else right now. Jenna—"

Maddox pulls my hands from my face and cuts me off with a kiss. And I break down, shaking and sobbing, and he pulls me tight against him.

"I'm sorry, Lili," he whispers. "I hit low with that, and it wasn't fair."

"Maybe it is. Maybe I'm being patronizing or—"

He hugs me again. "You're not. If you and Theo agreed to hold off, then I need to step back."

"There *is* something," I say. "I came to tell you that. I didn't want to hide everything from you, and if you insist on knowing—"

"I don't." He grabs a tissue and wipes my tears. "But you said you feel as if you're spiraling. Can I help with that? Talk through the case?"

I nod. "I have notes. And charts. And diagrams."

He chuckles and presses his lips to mine. "Of course you do. Okay, so after dinner, you and I are going to the library and I'll read what you have."

Maddox takes his dinner to go, which is frowned on, but no one ever stops him. I eat with Allegra and Polly. Allegra's quiet, but not in her usual way, where she's waiting to grace us with her opinion. She's thinking.

Polly's worried about Isolde feeling abandoned. She wants to go visit her at the hospital again tomorrow, but I'm not sure we'd be allowed. We talk about that, and it's a welcome distraction.

After dinner, I beg off to go "study" in the library with Maddox.

Allegra seems to wake up at that, if only to murmur "study . . ." with a knowing look.

Polly smiles. "I like Maddox. He's nicer than he seemed. I have no chance of getting him on my socials though, do I?"

"Nope. Sorry."

She shrugs. "I respect it." She leans back. "Not that I won't try to change it, but I respect it."

I shake my head and excuse myself. When I reach the library, Maddox is there, in his corner spot, where people can come in and never realize they aren't alone, as I discovered.

When I walk over, he pulls me down into a kiss.

"I'm sorry I was an asshole earlier," he says.

"You weren't an asshole. Like you said, everyone's been handling you with kid gloves. I don't want to do that. But I also don't want to pull Jenna into this theory based on what might just be an unrelated comment."

I look up at him. "Also, to be clear, whether it's related or not, Jenna did a good thing, Maddox. A really good thing. Her Dux liked her a lot."

I tell her what he said about her marching to her own drum, and he's quiet as he assimilates that. Then I take the chair opposite his and send him everything I have that doesn't connect to Jenna.

Maddox reads what I have. We don't want to openly discuss it, so we send messages, even though we're sitting only a few feet apart. When he's ready, I tell him about Jenna and her interest in the attack on the Hephaestus contender, Taylor. I don't connect the dots. I need him to make his own decisions.

While he's doing that, the double doors give a soft *whoosh*.

"Just me," Allegra calls.

"Over here."

She walks toward us and stops. "You two really are studying. I feel as if I should be disappointed. I just wanted to let you know that if you get any messages from Isolde tonight, do not be alarmed."

"Uh . . ."

She waves her phone. "She sent me a video, telling me how much I mean to her and how she really needed me to know that."

I push to my feet. "Is she okay? Did something happen? Is she—?"

"—well and truly medicated."

I exhale. "For a second there, I thought she'd taken a turn for the worse."

"That's why I'm warning you. My first reaction was the same—that something was wrong and she was making final calls. Then I saw her eyes and heard the slurring. She's not dying. Just . . ."

"High as a kite," Maddox says.

"Yes. So I don't know whether she'll message you, but be ready. Also, after this, I've changed my mind. Isolde is obviously lonely, and we *should* visit her tomorrow. I'll speak to Ms. Dimitriou."

"Sounds good."

"Then I'll leave you two alone. I'd tell you to have fun, but it'd be wasted, apparently."

After Allegra leaves, Maddox stretches to tug me over to him. He talks about Jenna, whispering too low to be heard even if someone were around. We talk and think and talk some more. He gets where I'm heading with this—that Jenna was investigating what happened to Taylor and might have died for it. His take is that Taylor could be connected to the rest, at least in the sense that Taylor was injured to knock them out of the race. As for Jenna being killed for digging?

"Too much?" I murmur.

He nods.

I exhale. "Good. My mind went there, of course, but it seemed too big of a stretch."

"Because Jenna wasn't in anyone's way. If someone wanted to shut her down, they only needed to plant dope. Discredit anything she says and get her expelled."

"My brain was so busy buzzing that—while I knew killing her didn't make sense—I couldn't figure out why."

He shifts, arms tightening around me. "Thank you for finding that. It helped. It brought Jenna home, if that makes sense. The Jenna I knew versus the party girl who OD'd."

"Even her Dux didn't think it was like that. He figured she got curious and tried something new. Which I know seems suspect, when she didn't like needles. If you want my opinion . . ."

"I do."

"I think someone at the party injected her. They didn't mean to kill her. She refused the heroin, and maybe they thought it'd be funny or maybe they were being an asshole. I don't think she gave herself that needle, but I also don't think whoever did meant to kill her."

"Yeah. That's been my theory, too. I just didn't like how no one seemed to care that the official story didn't make sense. But I suppose that happens all the time, at least to people who *aren't* students at an elite boarding school. Someone gives them dope at a party, maybe against their will, and no one looks into it because they were a kid at a party with dope."

"It still sucks."

"And my mother did nothing about it," he says, his voice low. "I think that's what I've been most angry about. Not what Westdale did. What my mother *didn't* do. She bought the official story, and I hate that so much. It's like she never even knew her own daughter."

I curl into his arms and hug him, and we huddle together in the silence and the grief.

THIRTY-THREE

An hour later, Maddox and I are in Theo's room. Maddox crosses the room. I collapse backward onto the bed, and Theo sits on the edge and strokes my hair.

"You look exhausted, Lil," Theo says. "I suppose you're too tired to hear what I found out about the Janus Society."

I sit up fast, and he smiles.

"I thought that might work," he says. "So, I haven't been pulling my weight with this investigation, because I'm no detective. I realized I could do one thing, though—confront my uncle about the Janus Society, now that I know enough to ask the right questions."

I inhale sharply. "Was that safe?"

Theo gives me a look. "I am Hollywood royalty. I can act." He pauses. "I also know how to commit blackmail. Not sure where that came from. Anyway, as you may have noticed at the gala, I have dirt on dear Uncle Charlie. So I used that and said I'd stumbled on something about the Janus Society, with his name attached." He lifts his phone. "I recorded the conversation. Yes, yes, that's illegal. Whatever."

Theo scrubs forward on the recording. "I'll bypass the part where he pretends to know nothing until I pull out the blackmail card."

He hits Play, and when Charles Dubois's voice comes on, I need to suppress a shiver, thrown back to that hallway in the gala. He sounds different, though. Sober, I guess.

"You're such a child, Theodore," Charles says. "Keep sticking your fingers where they don't belong and you're going to get a nasty shock. I'm growing very tired of this particular threat."

"Then let's end it. You tell me what I want, and I will never mention it again."

A pause. Then a long sigh. "I hate giving into you, brat, but in this case, you're giving up your blackmail cheap. Fine. I was part of the Janus Society, back when there *was* a Janus Society."

"There isn't anymore?"

"Hasn't been in maybe six, seven years."

"How come?"

"You kids got soft. You all say you want power, but you won't get your hands dirty to get it. That's what Janus was about. Getting our hands dirty to earn our own kind of power. Your dad and his Optimas think they're in charge, but the Janus Society were the kingmakers."

"They shaped the competition," Theo says.

"'Shaped' is one way of saying it. 'Weeded out the undesirables' is another."

"You say the society disbanded years ago, but a student died two years back. You're telling me that wasn't Janus."

"Died?" Charles snorts. "You've been watching too many of your dad's shitty movies. The Janus Society didn't kill anyone. Why would we? There are lots of ways to push someone out of the race." A pause. "You'd know all about that, I hear."

"Yes, I was pushed out. But you're telling me that wasn't Janus."

"Janus is *gone*. Over. I'm guessing the Optimas are doing the work themselves these days, with the help of their dogs."

"Dogs? Someone they hire instead of using Janus?"

"The dogs have been there from the start. A very special *brand* of pup." He laughs as he emphasizes *brand*.

"Who—?"

"This conversation is over, brat. I gave you what you wanted. Now fuck off."

The recording ends, as if Charles disconnected the call.

"Okay," I say carefully. "He seems certain that the Janus Society was disbanded. I think he's telling the truth about not killing anyone, but maybe that was a secret sect within the society? The extreme solution, for those they decided didn't matter, like Annette."

I turn to Maddox, who's across the room plugging in our phones. He's staring down at mine. Before I can ask what he thinks, he lifts my phone.

"You've got a message," Maddox says to me. "It's from Isolde. Looks like it's been there a while, so you might be ignoring it after what Allegra said."

"I didn't see it."

I reach out, and he passes over the phone. I can see Isolde sent a video, but I must have missed the notification.

I glance at the guys. "I'm going to put in my earbuds, okay? No offense, but if Isolde's high on pain meds, she might not appreciate me sharing this."

Maddox passes over my earbud case. I pop them in and hit Play, and as soon as I do, I'm really glad I took the precaution. Isolde isn't just buzzed. She's also crying.

"Lili? I'm so sorry. So, so sorry. I'm a horrible friend, and I'll understand if you never want to talk to me again. I didn't mean to hurt Theo. I just . . . I did as I was told. He said it was for the best, that Theo didn't need to be in the Optimas. He's already Theo Dubois. He has everything, and you're new to all this, and you deserve it, and you'll be a better Optima anyway, and I wanted you to have it."

She stops to breathe, each inhalation ragged. "I told myself it was okay, but I know it wasn't." She makes a face, her hand going to where she was stabbed. "It was just supposed to be a cut, and he says he slipped, but he didn't." Her tears fall fresh. "He did this on purpose."

She blinks fast. "But this is about you, not me. I think the attack was about more than knocking Theo out of the race. I'm afraid . . ." She swallows. "I'm afraid if Maddox hadn't shown up, you wouldn't have walked away from it. Be really, really careful, Lili, and—"

Her head jerks up as she seems to hear something in the hall. Then she relaxes. "Whatever you do, be *careful* and stay with someone at all times. Someone you trust."

Another glance toward the hall before she turns back, voice lowered. "We'll talk tomorrow. Come see me."

I play the video twice. Then I look up. Theo is in the bathroom, brushing his teeth. Maddox is at the foot of the bed, flipping through his phone.

"I think I need to play this," I say, and my voice is shaky enough that Maddox looks up sharply. "Theo? You need to see it, too."

We've played the video twice. Theo looks like someone punched him in the gut, and Maddox's jaw is clenched so hard I fear for his teeth.

"Isolde set you both up," Maddox says. "No one made her attacker look like Theo. It was all arranged."

"It makes sense," I say, my voice strained. "I didn't see it because I never considered that Isolde would lie."

"Because she got hurt," Maddox says. "That's why no one questioned it. She was the victim."

Theo squeezes the bridge of his nose. "Walk me through this, please. I'm having trouble understanding."

"The whole thing was a setup," I say. "I chose to join her on the dance floor, but she's the one who moved us deeper into the crowd and then suggested cutting through the back halls. She took charge there."

"After notifying whoever she was with," Maddox mutters.

"Presumably. Then someone turned out the hall light. I saw a figure. Isolde ran for the exit. When I followed to stop her, our attacker shoved me out. According to this video, he was supposed to just give her a scratch, enough to make it seem she'd been in danger. But he actually stabbed her."

"And she knows who he is," Maddox adds. "She knows her attacker. He really stabbed her and probably always intended to."

I nod. "He wanted it to look real, and she certainly wouldn't have agreed to be actually stabbed. Afterward, she was supposed to blame Theo, which she did."

"But then she rescinded it," Theo says. "Because Lil realized I didn't have any blood on me?"

"No," I say. "The police realized that, too. You were never supposed to be honestly blamed. All they needed was the accusation. Like with my dad and Annette. Both stories would have fallen apart. It was all about the accusation."

"And the rest?" Maddox says. "I'm furious about what she did to Theo, but it's the rest I'm focused on right now."

Theo asks for my phone, and he replays the last bit. "She doesn't think you were supposed to walk away, Lil. That you were . . ." He swallows hard. "Fuck."

"But I *could* have walked away," I say. "I had a chance to escape."

"No," Maddox says. "It only seemed as if he was focused on Isolde. If you'd run, he could have grabbed you, but I think he was hoping you'd do what you did—try to protect Isolde."

Theo nods. "And then you'd be . . ." He struggles for the next word. "You'd be hurt, and it'd look like you were protecting your friend. Like you weren't the actual target."

"Not hurt," Maddox says, his voice a near growl. "I don't think 'hurt' is the word you want."

I rub down goosebumps on my arms, and Theo pulls me to him, hugging me tight and whispering that I'm okay, that everything is going to be okay.

"You could have been killed when Jayden pushed you down the stairs," Maddox says. "And you didn't like how Natalia reacted. You said she seemed genuinely shocked and insisted she hadn't told Jayden to do it."

"If it wasn't Natalia," I say, "then who arranged it? That's the question, right? Jayden didn't do it on his own. He'd have no reason to." I pull back to look at Theo. "Your uncle thinks the Janus Society disbanded, but what if that's just the official line? What if your uncle Charlie believes it, but it's not true."

"And Jayden is part of Janus?" Maddox says. "But does that make sense? Knock you *and* Theo out of the race? Leaving Cosmo?

He's perfectly fine, but he's not . . ." He shrugs. "He's not really anybody. You'd make the better Optima."

"Maybe Isolde's wrong," Theo says. "Allegra said she's high on drugs."

"Lili?" Maddox walks over, getting my full attention. "Tell me what happened on the way to Westdale. Before you arrived."

"What?"

"Cecilia went from being mildly concerned to locking you down here and telling me to be on full alert. You mentioned something about a truck? A rock?"

I tell him what happened.

"Cecilia thought someone shot at you," he says.

"I don't—"

"Lili?" He bends down in front of me. "I know you don't want to seem paranoid. I *want* you to be paranoid. Pretend it's a mystery for you to solve. What *could* have happened?"

I think it through. Then I say, falteringly, "The truck was covered in dirt. There was no way to see the plate, if it even had one. Tinted windows. We couldn't see a driver. It whipped by so fast." I look up. "But if someone shot at me, they would have needed to know I was . . ." I trail off. "Cecilia notified the school that we were coming. Sent all the information so we'd get through the front gates."

"Someone knew when and how you'd be arriving," Maddox says. "We could be looking at a security leak or a phone hack. Anything else?"

I know he means is there anything else about that incident, but I blurt, "At the gala," and I tell them what happened in the back hall.

When they both stare at me, I throw up my hands. "I thought it was Theo's uncle. I ran into him right after that—he appeared behind me—so it seemed to be the same person, but it's also possible he'd just come down the hall I passed."

"But even if you thought it was him," Theo says, "why didn't you tell me he grabbed you?"

I squirm. "You were upset enough. I handled it."

Theo sighs. "Okay, but I do wish I'd known. It still could have been Charlie. He was in the Janus Society."

"I don't know who grabbed me or what their intention was," I say. "Maybe nothing. Same as that stone might have really been a stone and Natalia really might have been behind the stairs thing and Isolde could be wrong about the attack in the alley."

"Yeah," Maddox says. "I'll grant that one—maybe two—of those could be explained away, but not all four."

"Someone's trying to hurt Lil," Theo says, and then his voice drops. "Maybe even kill her."

"Why?" I say. "Getting me out of the Optima race to let Cosmo win?"

Maddox shakes his head. "Way too much trouble. And remember, it seems as if the only contender who actually died was Annette—a scholarship student. Otherwise, from what we can tell, they're just knocked out of the race, like Theo. Possibly injured—like Taylor—but not killed. If someone is trying to kill you—and I don't think we can discount that—then it must be about something else, and the obvious answer is your inheritance. We need to look at who inherits the Chamberlain money if you die. For all these years, someone has expected to inherit an absolute fortune, and then you popped up."

Theo nods. "Of the four possible attempts on your life, only one happened at Westdale, and that could have just been Natalia and Jayden. The others were all off-site."

"I asked Cecilia this right away," I say. "Who was the backup heir? The answer is no one. The money all went to charities."

"Are you sure?" Maddox says. "Maybe *most* of it went to charities and *part* went to a person. We're talking about billionaires. Even a bequeath of one percent—one *tiny* percent—is ten million dollars."

"I've seen the list of charities." When they look confused, I say, "I worried that me reappearing meant a lot of worthwhile causes lost future revenue they were counting on, so I told Cecilia I wanted to donate to all of them. She says I can't until I turn eighteen next month, but she did pass me the list. There are no individuals on it. The biggest recipient, not surprisingly, is the Chamberlain Foundation, which is the company's philanthropy arm. Then there's a bunch of other foundations and trusts."

"So . . ." Theo clears his throat. "Stop me if you know this, Lil, because I'm presuming you don't, growing up where trust funds aren't a thing. A trust is a trust fund. Like I have. Like Maddox has. That's probably what you get next month. It's a way of passing money to heirs before someone dies. If there are trusts in that will, there's a good chance that money is going to people. Not charities. Even foundations can be"—he waggles his hand—"tax dodges."

"Er, right." My cheeks heat. "I should have known that."

"No reason for you to."

"But I do know what a trust fund is. You're right—that's what I get access to when I turn eighteen. My mom's trust fund passes to me. I just didn't make the connection."

"Can we see that list?" Maddox asks.

"I have it right here."

THIRTY-FOUR

There are twenty-five beneficiaries on the list. I can see why I presumed none were people. While some of the trusts seem to be surnames, so is "Chamberlain." The Chamberlain Foundation refers to the charity arm of the company. Likewise, the MacMaster Trust could refer to a company name or to a charity set up in honor of some long-dead MacMaster. But as Theo points out, even the ones that aren't names could be for people. His mom named his trust after the first film she did following his birth.

For now, what matters is that even with the list of primary beneficiaries, I don't necessarily know *every* person and charity that stood to benefit if I was never found. That will still benefit if I die before I turn eighteen, when I'll presumably make changes.

What I do have is the percentage of the Chamberlain fortune that goes to each named foundation and charity. Thirty percent goes to the Chamberlain Foundation. Theo and Maddox say they can be removed from the list of suspects. There are four other foundations and trusts that receive ten percent each, and the remainder is to be split between the long list of twenty.

For now, we focus on those four. Yes, as Maddox correctly pointed out, even the other twenty stand to inherit millions, but we need to start somewhere.

Of the four, two are easily identifiable as legitimate charities, recognizable even to me. When we research the other two, one is easily found and seems to be a very legitimate charity. The other, the Enhcara Foundation, is . . .

"Suspicious," Theo says when we don't find it online. "Could be a shell company, which is *always* suspicious."

"Mmm, not necessarily," I say. "While they are used for shady dealings, they're also used for legitimate ones, like mergers."

Theo smiles. "Ask the future MBA."

"The thing about shell companies is that we *wouldn't* usually find them online. They exist only for a corporate purpose, regardless of whether that purpose is shady or legitimate."

"So how do we find them?" Theo asks.

"Leave it with me," I say. "With the understanding that I'm almost certainly just going to discover it's a very legitimate company that definitely isn't trying to kill me."

"Give us the other twenty," Maddox says. "We might be able to find some of them."

"Thanks. In the meantime, I accept that I may be in danger, so I'll be on super-lockdown. But I really do want to visit Isolde tomorrow and see what she has to say."

"Unless she's trying to lure you out of Westdale," Theo murmurs.

When I look over sharply, he lifts his hands. "I know you're friends, Lil, but I'm pretty sure she tried twice to lure you out. The second time was the charm. And also . . ." He nibbles his lip. "I hate to say this, but while I know you want to believe it was about framing me, I wasn't even supposed to be there. I was, I suspect, a bonus."

He's right, of course.

"So what do you suggest?" I ask. "Presume it's a trap and stay at Westdale?"

"Call her in the morning. See if you can get her to talk, on one of Maddox's secure lines. If she refuses and insists you need to come in? That's when you know it's a trap."

I don't get far with the Enhcara Foundation. I start by trying to figure out what Enhcara means. It doesn't help that I keep misspelling it as Enchara, the *ch* being more common in English. That leads me to search for it as a non-English word, but nothing comes back for that either. I know companies sometimes make up words for their names. Or they take initials and smush them together without punctuation. Like WHSmith. Could it be E.N.H. Cara? Cara *is* a surname. I spend two hours searching before the guys make me give it up and go to bed.

Before Theo's alarm goes off the next morning, a brisk knock at the door has us all jumping.

"Fuck," Maddox mutters. "If that's Dimitriou giving us hell for sharing a room, she is about to learn this is really not the time for that shit."

Theo lifts a hand. "I've got it."

He rolls out of bed, walks to the door, and opens it just a crack. "Yes?"

"I need to talk to Liliana," Allegra says.

When Theo pauses, she says, "Do you honestly think I care about your extracurricular activities, Theo? If you all need time to get decent, you have two minutes."

"Come in."

Allegra walks into the room and looks from Theo, in his sweat pants, to Maddox and me, in the bed but also wearing sweats.

"Well, this is disappointing," she says. "I really do think you're doing this wrong."

Theo sighs. "It's not even eight yet, Allegra. What is it?"

"I need to talk to Liliana. In private."

I start to roll out of bed. "Your room?"

"Outside."

That gives me pause. "Outside?"

"Yes, outside. The place that is *out*side the house rather than *in*side it."

Maddox opens his mouth to protest, but I discreetly wave him to silence. Allegra doesn't go outside.

I yawn and stretch. "I really don't feel like getting dressed. Can we do this in your room?"

"You're in a T-shirt and sweatpants, Liliana. You're perfectly decent." She pauses. "Though if I might make some suggestions for more . . . flattering nightwear . . ."

"She's fine," Maddox says. "And she's not—"

"I'm not going outside this early unless you tell me why we can't talk in your room."

"Because it is a very private conversation." She looks around and lowers her voice. "And I have never trusted that the walls don't have ears here."

I hesitate and then say, "Give me a minute."

Is it strange that Allegra insists on going outside? Very strange, for Allegra. But if she legitimately believes we can't speak in total privacy indoors, then she'd brave the horrors of Mother Nature for a secret conversation. However, given that we've established that three of the four possible attacks occurred outside the school . . .

Maddox doesn't want me going out with Allegra. Theo convinces him that I need to hear what she has to say, and I can do that safely with them following. And if Allegra has anything more diabolical in mind? Then this is our chance to catch her.

I meet Allegra in the hall. The guys stay in the room—they'll sneak out after we leave.

I expect the yard to be completely empty, but it's a warm and sunny morning, and Cosmo is on the back deck with a coffee and laptop. As we pass, he looks up and nods.

"Morning," he says.

We return the greeting, and we start to leave when he calls, "Hey. How's Isolde?" As we turn, he looks sheepish. "I was hoping to go see her today, if you think that wouldn't be too weird."

Allegra gives a wave that he seems to presume means we'll talk later. He nods and returns to his work.

With Cosmo outside, we need to lower our voices. I plan to stick close to the house. It'll be a danger sign if she tries leading me away from it, but she doesn't. We head up the north side before she speaks.

"I know where I've seen that scorpion symbol," she says. "I'm reluctant to say it in front of Theo and Maddox, because it might mean nothing."

"Okay."

She lifts her phone and shows me what looks like a corporate logo. It's not a scorpion with two heads—it's two scorpions forming a circle, head to tail. She glances over, as if checking to see whether I recognize it. I don't, and I appreciate that Allegra has obviously been thinking about this, but I'm sure scorpions feature in a lot of symbols and logos.

"It's Obsidian," she says.

When I frown, she says, "That's the company name." Then she peers at me. "You don't recognize it, do you? It's the Brandts' firm. Isolde's family business."

"Isolde's family? They're . . ." My stomach chills. "Security, right? She said they do security."

"That's the nice way of putting it. They're private military contractors."

"M-mercenaries?"

"They prefer 'private military.' But yes. Her family made their fortune as part of the so-called military-industrial complex."

"Industry that supplies the military with technology and weapons."

"Her parents branched out into private military. Very specialized mercenaries for hire, all legal as long as they don't operate in America."

Isolde's parents run a company of mercenaries. A company with a logo that resembles the Janus Society symbol. The Janus Society . . . whose main job seems to have been shaping the Optima race through blackmail, coercion, and even violence. Which is one thing private militaries can be hired to do—help shape the leadership races in other countries.

I remember what Theo's Uncle Charles said.

"I'm guessing the Optimas are doing the work themselves these days, with the help of their dogs."

"Dogs? Someone they hire instead of using Janus?"

"The dogs have been there from the start. A very special brand *of pup."*

He'd laughed when he said *brand.*

Brand.

Brandt.

"That's—" I begin.

A ringtone cuts me short. We both look toward the rear deck, where Cosmo was, but it's empty now. And the distant ring comes from our right not our left.

"The gardener," I murmur. "Or one of the guards."

I continue walking, only to realize Allegra isn't behind me. I glance back. She's standing there, staring in the direction of the sound.

"Do you hear that?" she says, without looking my way.

"Someone's phone. One of the staff?"

"No, I know that tone. Can't you hear it?"

"Barely. Who—"

She strides toward the back of the carriage house. Then she does something I could never have imagined Allegra Khan doing.

She breaks into a run.

Allegra rounds the back of the carriage house and disappears into the forest.

I swallow hard and glance over my shoulder. I can't see the guys, but I need to trust they're there. I take out my phone, ready to speed-dial Maddox, just in case. Then I run after her.

THIRTY-FIVE

By the time I round the carriage house, Allegra is in the woods, but I can still see her white shirt. She's moving fast. The phone ceased ringing a minute ago, before I was close enough to identify the tone.

Allegra stops so short that I race over, certain something's wrong. But she's just standing there, looking left and right. Then, with a little noise, somewhere between a gasp and a whimper, she darts to the left.

I wheel and see what she does. A figure, crumpled on the ground, red hair spilling over the undergrowth.

"Isolde," I whisper, and I run to her.

Allegra's already there, crouching, her hands to Isolde's shoulders. Isolde's on her stomach, hair spread around her, arms and legs akimbo, as if she'd been running and fallen.

"Isolde?" Allegra says.

Allegra turns her over gently. I race in front of Isolde and drop to my knees, brushing hair from Isolde's face and—

Her skin is cold, and I jerk away, startled. She's on her back now, and her eyes are open, wide and staring. Blood covers the front of her T-shirt.

"Isolde?" I whisper, hand to her cheek even as I know it's pointless.

"Liliana?" It's Allegra, barely getting the word out as she heaves breath. "Is she—? She's—?"

I check for a pulse. Yes, those open eyes and cold skin tell me Isolde is dead, but I need to be sure. Her T-shirt is ripped, and I push it up to see the bandages covering her wound are gone, and it's been bleeding, but my hands go to her heart, as if it could still be beating.

"Liliana!"

It's Maddox, his voice booming from the yard.

"Here!" I call.

He appears at a lope, Theo right behind him. Maddox sees Isolde first and stops so suddenly he stumbles.

"Oh my god," Theo breathes. "Is she—?"

"Get help," I say. "Someone. Anyone."

Theo races off. Maddox walks forward, his gaze fixed on Isolde.

"She's . . . she's dead," I say.

"You need to go," Maddox says, pulling me to my feet.

"What?"

"Your hands. Blood. You can't be found with her. Go. Now."

He grabs my shoulder, but I yank away.

"She's long dead," I say. "Cold. No one's going to think I—"

"I don't care. I won't take that chance." He propels me to my feet and starts pushing me.

"*Maddox*, stop." That's Allegra, snapping from her shock.

"You don't understand," he says, wheeling on her.

"I do understand. You're afraid Liliana will be framed for this. Like Theo was framed for the attack on Isolde in the alley."

"Maddox, please," I say, twisting from his grip, turning to see his eyes, wide and panicked. "No one's framing me for this. I have a little blood on me, but Isolde obviously died last night, when I was with you."

"I'm the one who found her," Allegra says. "Not Liliana. Cosmo saw us leave the house. It's fine." Her gaze drops to Isolde, and she squeezes her eyes shut and sways. "No, it's not fine. Not fine at all." She drops beside Isolde again and brushes back her hair.

I lean into Maddox, careful not to touch him with my bloodied hands, but he pulls me into a hug.

"Sorry," he says, his breath still ragged. "You're right. I panicked."

I hug him. A phone rings, making us all jump. I turn and see it on the ground, screen facing up, Polly's avatar face on it, bouncing, pigtails swinging. We all stare at the phone, that familiar ringtone playing its cheerful tune as Polly calls to wish Isolde a good morning.

I fall against Maddox and start to cry.

Theo brings Ms. Dimitriou and two of the security guards. We're shooed off then, told not to go far but to wait for the police. We all do that in stunned silence. The police arrive along with an ambulance, even though Isolde is past needing one.

We talk to the police. I barely process any of that. There's not much to say. Allegra and I circled the house talking about school. As we left the house, we saw Cosmo on the deck and we spoke briefly, but he was gone when we came around. We heard a ringtone. Allegra recognized it as Isolde's, which made her think Isolde had snuck out of the hospital.

I wait for them to ask the last time I heard from Isolde. I think of the video, of her crying and apologizing. Thankfully no one asks.

If they eventually do, I'll need to call in Cecilia. I know that always seems like the move of the guilty—summoning a lawyer—but she's also my guardian. Legally, she should be present.

And I'm not sure it matters anyway. If they search Isolde's phone, they're going to see the videos she sent.

This is the last thing I want to be worrying about.

Isolde is dead.

Isolde, who sent me a video just last night, crying and apologizing, and I should have gone to see her right away, and—

"The hospital wouldn't have let you in," Theo murmurs, as if reading my mind.

We're on the deck now, the two of us sitting on the steps. Maddox paces in front of us, fingers tapping his phone. Polly took Allegra inside, and I want to be with them, but I can't move from this spot.

Theo's arm goes around my waist as he shifts closer, one leg against mine. "Lil?"

"I still could have tried going to her. I never even considered it. I—"

"No one would have let you in at that hour."

I look at him. "She came here. She snuck out in the middle of the night and came to Westdale."

"Because she was high on pain meds."

"That doesn't change the fact she came. She couldn't wait to talk to us, and when we didn't show up—"

"She said tomorrow, Lil."

Fresh tears well. "But she came last night. She came, and someone . . . someone . . ." I can't finish that sentence.

"We don't know that."

I see Ms. Dimitriou making her away across the backyard. One guard follows and puts out a hand as if to steady the principal.

Theo and I scramble off the steps so Ms. Dimitriou can get past, but she stops before us, wobbling.

"I'm so sorry," she says. "I know she was a good friend. To you both."

"What happened?" I whisper.

Ms. Dimitriou glances over her shoulder. "The paramedics think her injury reopened. Or maybe it was worse than the doctors thought?"

She shakes her head and keeps looking in the direction of Isolde's body. "I don't know why she came back. Allegra said something about a video, that Isolde seemed high on the pain meds? Maybe Isolde was confused?"

She takes a deep breath and lays a hand on my shoulder. "There won't be any classes today, obviously. I'm going to notify Ms. Khan and Cecilia. You and Allegra found the body, and since you're both under eighteen, I need to tell your guardians."

"I'll tell Cecilia."

A wan smile. "You can if you like, dear, but I'll still call myself. It's only right. I'm also going to summon all the students and staff to tell them what's happened, before rumors fly. You can skip that meeting, obviously."

"Thank you."

We're sitting on the grass in the backyard. It's the five of us—Allegra, Polly, Theo, Maddox, and me. No one else is outside; either they've been told to give us space or they realize that's the right thing to do.

Theo's beside me, his hand holding mine. Maddox is physically present but mentally far away, and I'm not going to intrude.

Allegra is still in a state of shock, and the only time she's roused from it was when I asked if she wanted to be alone, and she startled, looking at me with something like fear.

I've never seen Allegra like this, and I keep waiting for her to snap back to normal Allegra, horrified that she's sitting on grass, ordering us to get inside, telling us there are things to be done. But she just sits there, cross-legged in her yoga pants, her eyes red behind her glasses.

We've updated Polly, who alternates between checking on Allegra and whispering with Theo. I know we should talk about Obsidian, about how they could be connected to the Janus Society and what happened to Annette and maybe even what Isolde was talking about in that video. But it seems wrong to accuse her family of something when she just *died*.

It can wait.

Allegra looks at me. "Do *you* think she died of her injuries?"

"I . . ." I take a deep breath. "I need to hear what the coroner says."

"It must have been," Theo says. "There was just the one wound, and it was open and bleeding profusely, given all the blood on her shirt."

When I hesitate, Maddox peers at me. "You think someone stabbed her in the same spot. Was her shirt damaged? I didn't get a good look."

"It was ripped," I say. "The tear didn't look like a knife slash, but it could have been torn more to cover that up." I rub my arms. "Or I've just read too many mystery novels."

"She sent that video," Maddox murmurs, his voice low. "She admitted the alley attack was a setup. She was probably coming to tell you everything."

"And someone stopped her," Polly says.

As I nod, my gaze snags on something. The back deck is empty, but there's a single coffee mug on a table, no one having cleared it away yet.

Cosmo's mug.

I remember when we walked past, the mug had been half empty, and no steam was rising from it, despite the cool morning air. How long had he been out here?

We'd taken Cosmo on that trip to Savannah because he asked. And because Polly had noticed shy glances between him and Isolde. Glances suggesting a romantic interest, though the two had barely spoken on the trip.

Cosmo. Who is the same height as Theo.

Cosmo. Who had been the one person who didn't support Theo with the police, when Isolde accused Theo of attacking her.

Cosmo. Who spoke briefly to the police and then retreated, calm and dry-eyed, as if he'd been questioned in the death of a stranger and not a girl he *just* said he wanted to visit in the hospital.

Cosmo. Who is so apathetic about the Optima race that everyone keeps forgetting he's even a contender.

Cosmo. Who made a *point* of saying he'd like to go see Isolde later, so no one could ever suspect him of knowing she was dead.

"I need to use the washroom," I say.

Maddox starts to rise with me.

"Uh, she doesn't need help with that," Allegra says.

I squeeze his hand. "It's okay. I'll be right back."

He glances toward the house and then nods.

Maddox didn't need to worry about me going into the house unaccompanied. I practically need to fight my way through everyone milling about the back hall. They've been told to stay inside, but they're at every window and hanging around the door, and as soon as I come in, they descend on me.

"Isolde's dead?"

"What happened?"

"What was Isolde doing back here?"

It's Kai who gently inserts themself between me and the growing mob. "Guys, no, okay? We'll get answers soon enough."

"Thank you," I murmur. And then I give the real reason I came in—and why I came in alone, following a hunch too tentative for me to tell Maddox or Theo. "Has anyone seen Cosmo? The police need to speak to him."

Kai frowns. "Cosmo?"

"He was outside just before we found Isolde," I say. "The police have more questions."

"Ah, okay. I think he went up to his room. I'd message him, but I don't have his number."

"I'll go speak to him. Thank you."

I start to walk away. Then I see that silver spider's web on the wall, and it snags and holds my attention.

Why?

I frown at it.

"Lili?" Kai says.

I shake it off, smile for them, and hurry away.

Okay, so now comes the big question: Where is Cosmo's room? I think hard, and I'm about to guess the second floor when I remember the other day I'd been going into my room to grab books, and Cosmo had been coming up the stairs behind me. As I'd been opening my door, he'd asked a question about an English essay.

His room must be on the third floor.

But that doesn't seem right. Maddox, Theo, Allegra, and I all have rooms on the top level, and I've casually noticed other names as I travel up and down those halls. None of them were Cosmo's.

Which only means I didn't notice his nameplate. Or maybe he'd been coming up to visit a friend.

What friend? I'm not even sure I've seen him hanging out with anyone. Everyone seems to like him—I've even seen him talking to Maddox—but he also doesn't seem to feel the need to bond, too engrossed in school to socialize.

A guy who passes under the radar.

Who has the grades to be Optima but doesn't seem to be trying. The Optimas ultimately choose the winner, but Theo says the Optimas pay attention to who the students want to win. They get reports from the school administration and . . .

My brain catches on that thought, but again, I don't know why, and I push past it. The point is that Cosmo hasn't actively been winning friends and allies, but he hasn't made enemies either. If Cosmo won, everyone would feel as if they'd ultimately benefit because they get along with him just fine and he has no close allies to reward instead.

The perfect stealth candidate.

I'm cresting the stairs, lost in my thoughts, when I hear a noise and idly turn to find myself looking at my own bedroom door.

Someone is in my room.

The door is firmly closed and locked, but when I put my ear to it, I hear the soft tap of shoes on the hardwood inside.

I lift my fingers to the lock. Then I stop. When I enter the code, the latch will undo with an electronic clunk. It's not loud, but it'll be heard in the silence.

I think quickly. Then I take out my phone, back down the steps, and find a video of Allegra pontificating. I play it as I walk up the stairs and then punch in my room code as fast as I can. When the lock clicks, I ease the door open a crack as I lower the volume on the video, as if Allegra is continuing on to her room.

Putting my ear to the crack, I catch the sound of labored breathing, as if the intruder had scrambled for a hiding spot and is now waiting to be sure all is fine and the person Allegra was lecturing isn't me, returning to my room.

When I fade the volume to nothing, I swear I hear an exhale. Then the squeak of a shoe. Footsteps tap, moving away. I open the door another crack and peek through to see the back of a T-shirt. Someone stands at my bed, facing the other way. A tall figure with light brown hair.

Cosmo.

What the hell is he doing in my room?

Dumb question. I'm his only remaining competition.

What did I reflect on a few moments ago? That I thought his room might be up here because he'd recently paused outside my door to ask me a question . . . as I was unlocking it, casually punching in the code because, well, it was just Cosmo, right? Not like I was going to cover the code or wait until he was gone.

My first night here, someone had tried to get into my room, and I'd decided it'd been Natalia or Jayden, probably just trying to spook me. And maybe it had been, but this is another possibility: Cosmo.

Now he's beside my bed, opening the nightstand drawer. He pauses there, looking down as if surveying the contents for something he can use. Drugs? Sex toys?

Good luck, buddy. I don't even have a sexy novel in there. I've read them but, having been a bit of a late bloomer in that regard, I wasn't tucking one in my bedside table for private nighttime reading.

He paws through the contents, and I use the noise to creep inside and start coming up behind him as he contemplates the blackmail potential of my foot lotion, ear plugs, and lip balm. When he does pull something out, it's a bottle of pills. The sleeping meds from the doctor after Jayden attacked me. Cosmo lifts them, as if considering, and I'm right up behind him, barely daring to breathe, when I realize why he's only using one hand to search, the other lowered at his side.

Lowered at his side and gripping a knife.

A knife with blood on the blade.

Held in a hand with a latex glove from the bio lab.

Cosmo isn't looking for blackmail material.

He's looking for a place to hide that knife. To frame me for Isolde's murder.

THIRTY-SIX

Cosmo is in my room with a *knife*. And I'm creeping up behind him like some clueless teen detective.

I take a slow step back . . . and my foot finds the one board that creaks. He wheels, and I do the same, running for the door, but he grabs the back of my shirt, and before I can shout for help, his hand clamps over my mouth.

He grapples me to the floor, and in a blink, I'm on my stomach with something cold and sharp pressed into the back of my neck.

The knife.

The knife he used to kill Isolde.

I go limp, and he exhales softly, relieved that I'm going to make this easy, that I won't fight.

"I found the knife," he whispers at my ear. "I knew something was suspicious, you and Allegra heading into the woods and just happening to find Isolde, so when I saw you coming upstairs, I followed. I slipped into the room behind you and saw you hiding the knife. You put it under your mattress, and then you picked up that bottle of pills, and I knew what you were going to do. You couldn't live with yourself, but I wasn't going to let you do that. So I stopped you."

At first, I don't follow what he's saying. Then I realize he's prepping a story, spinning it with breathtaking ease. His original plan must have been to hide the knife and then tip off someone to find it in my room. He'd seen the pills and been wondering whether they could be worked into the narrative.

But now that I've caught him, the plan has changed. He's going to claim he saw *me* hiding the knife. He stopped me from taking my own life. And when I say that's not what happened, well, he's not Jayden or Natalia. He's Cosmo. A good guy who must be telling the truth.

I don't need to fake my shiver. That relaxes him more. And then I bite his hand, as hard as I can.

Cosmo falls back, yowling, and I scramble from under him. He recovers fast, and I see that knife slashing my way and I lash out, kicking and punching. Suddenly I'm back in that alley, fighting for my life. My foot makes contact before he can stab me. It hits him in the knee, his leg buckling, and I run for the door.

I manage to get it open, but that pause was enough for him to catch up, and I'm swinging the door wide when someone barrels through.

Someone who is neither Maddox nor Theo runs into my room and kicks Cosmo so hard he goes down. Then his attacker is on him, flipping him over and pinning his arm behind his back before grinning up at me, her pigtails swinging.

"Polly?" I say.

"Mom made me go to self-defense classes after I started getting online threats. I did it to humor her but . . ." She shrugs. "Apparently, Mom does know best."

"You do realize he had a knife," a cool voice says from the doorway as Allegra walks in.

"What?" Polly says. Then she sees the knife on the floor. "Shit! I missed that. Wait. Why does Cosmo . . . ?"

Her eyes widen as realization hits, and before anyone can speak, both Maddox and Theo charge past Allegra.

Polly lifts her free hand. "I've got this, guys. But if someone could pick up that knife, I'd appreciate it not being so close to his free hand."

"No!" I say, leaping in. "No one touches the knife." I kick it out of the way. "Do *not* put your fingerprints on a murder weapon."

"It's not—" Cosmo begins.

"He was trying to hide it in my room," I say. "I caught him. I didn't see the knife until it was too late. He knocked me down and said he was going to tell everyone that he caught *me* hiding a bloody knife and then trying to overdose on sleeping pills."

"The knife wasn't used for anything," Cosmo says quickly. "It's from the dining hall."

"With blood on it? Are you going to tell us that's not Isolde's?"

He hesitates and then says, "Okay, it is. I heard the commotion when you guys found her, and I slipped out to see what was happening and there was a trail of blood where Isolde must have walked while she was bleeding. I got a knife and smeared some of that blood on it before the police arrived."

"To frame Liliana?" Allegra says.

"The knife wasn't *actually* used on Isolde," he says. "She died of her injuries from the alley, right? Nothing would have happened to Liliana."

"Except suspicion," I say. "Which would be enough to get me kicked out of the Optima race. As Cosmo learned with Theo. He's the guy Isolde was talking about."

"What?" Cosmo says.

Allegra bears down on him. "Polly thought you and Isolde liked each other. But those glances she noticed just meant you two were scheming. Or *you* were the one scheming and you pulled Isolde into it because she *did* like you."

"Isolde? What video? What scheme?"

"You were the guy in the alley," I say. "You claimed you overheard us talking about the trip to Savannah, but really, Isolde told you. In the video she said it was about knocking Theo from the Optima race to help me win, but that's just the story you spun for her."

"What? I—"

I continue. "You attacked Isolde, and it was supposed to be just a scratch, but you really hurt her, and she was going to tell us."

"*No.* None of that happened. I swear it. I *did* overhear about the trip. I . . . Okay, yes, I went along in hopes of finding something I could use against you or Theo. I thought you guys might go to an actual bar or get drunk or high or . . . I sure didn't think you'd go to an all-ages club and behave yourselves. But I *didn't* attack Isolde. I was with Kai when it happened. Ask them. I'd never actually *hurt* anyone."

"No?" Maddox says. He's been quiet, but now he moves forward. "You just have others do that, right? Like getting Jayden to push Lili down the stairs."

"Huh? That was Natalia."

"No," I say. "Natalia was genuinely shocked and confused."

"That audio clip," Maddox says. "I couldn't figure out who I'd been talking to. I was being nice, which meant it sure as hell wasn't Jayden. I just figured it out now. It was Cosmo. I was in the library, and he came in and was asking me about class, and I didn't want to be an asshole because . . ." He waves. "It's Cosmo."

"This is bullshit," Cosmo says. "Either you guys get Dimitriou, or I'm going to start shouting for help."

"Not even asking what audio clip I mean, are you," Maddox says.

Cosmo's lips press into a firm line.

"Natalia thought I was collaborating with Jayden," I say. "I asked how that would make any sense, when Jayden got expelled for it. She said he was willing to be expelled to be rewarded later. That's what you did, right? Promised that if he got caught, you'd make it right once you won Optima. Help him long-term, with his career."

Cosmo glares at me. "And why not? You weren't going to help anyone like Jayden. Or anyone like me. You'll just help your little circle of buddies who don't *need* help. That's how it always goes. The rich get richer, while the rest of us are left fighting for scraps."

"Scraps?" Allegra says. "You attend a boarding school with a six-figure tuition. *Excluding* room and board."

"And my parents went into debt to send me, in hopes I'd make Optima. But I wasn't going to if I played fair. I could see that right away. I have the brains and the dedication, but that never matters. It'll go to someone like Liliana, who doesn't need it, and she'll help her friends, who also don't need it."

"Tell me about the Janus Society," I cut in, to see his reaction.

His brow creases, as if he heard me wrong. "The *what?*"

"What's going on in here," a voice says, and one of the security guards pokes her head in and sees Cosmo pinned to the floor. "What the hell?"

We start talking.

We spend the next half hour explaining what just happened. I don't accuse Cosmo of stabbing Isolde—not in the alley or here. I want to talk to Cecilia first. We just tell Ms. Dimitriou what happened in my room and what we found Cosmo hiding, and if she immediately has the police brought over, that's *her* interpretation of where that knife came from.

Cecilia is on her way, and when I phone to update her, my call goes straight to voicemail, so I leave a message explaining what happened with Cosmo.

The guys escort me downstairs, with Allegra and Polly following. At the base, I stop and stare at the silver web again.

"Lil?" Theo says, squeezing my hand.

"You're arachnophobic," I murmur.

"Uh, yes . . ."

I don't miss the glance he exchanges with Maddox, both of them clearly thinking I'm in shock.

"Come and sit down." Theo tries to tug me along, but I dig in my heels.

"Arachnophobic," I say. "Afraid of spiders—arachnids."

"Yes . . ."

I point at the woman weaving in the middle of the web. "Arachne. From Greek mythology. She was an amazing weaver who challenged Athena. She actually won the challenge, but Athena was so angry that she turned Arachne into a spider."

"Lili?" Polly pipes up. "I really think you should sit down."

I shake my head and take out my phone. "I couldn't find anything on the Enhcara Foundation, and I kept misspelling it because *C* usually proceeds *H*, which should have been a sign." I hold up my phone.

"Arachne backward," Maddox says.

"Oh!" Polly says. "Is that connected to the Aranea Group?"

We all look at her, and she waves around her. "That's who owns Westdale Academy. I noticed it in the paperwork Mom and I had to fill out, with me being the first in my family to attend. Mom said 'Aranea' is the Latin word for spider, which seemed weird until I saw the webs and interconnection stuff."

I look at Maddox. "We need to check out those school history books."

Maddox, Allegra, and I take research duty while Polly and Theo stand guard outside the library. I know what I want, and I go straight for the first slender volume of the school history. I remember the overview from Cecilia before I arrived—that Westdale had been formed as an educational alternative for Southern families who'd usually send their children to northern prep schools.

I'd been under the impression that a company started it, but it turns out it was two individuals. Neither had any experience in education, and the history book states that proudly as an example of entrepreneurship. They saw a gap and they filled it, not with their own expertise but by hiring top-notch educators while they handled management. The enterprise was further solidified as a family business when the only children of the two founders married and took over.

With Allegra's help, I skim future volumes and discover that Westdale continued to be a family business. We don't find any children by that name in the rosters of students. Instead, they stay on as administrators, and the list of surnames broadens as the women marry until we find one we recognize.

Dimitriou.

The current principal's grandmother married a Greek immigrant, who went on to work in administration at Westdale, with their son becoming principal, followed by his daughter—our Ms. Dimitriou.

"I can confirm that the Aranea Group owns Westdale," Maddox says, from where he's been researching on a secure connection. "They incorporated early in the school's history under that name. I also found a connection to that foundation named in—"

My phone beeps at the same time as Allegra's and Maddox's.

"Dimitriou incoming," Maddox says.

We quickly shove the books away and collapse into chairs. Or Maddox and I collapse. Allegra stays standing, while looking at her phone, as if she's with us but not *really* with us. Typical Allegra, in other words.

Ms. Dimitriou walks in, and my stomach tightens, thinking about what we just found, the connection to her family.

She doesn't notice my reaction. "Ah, good. Theo said you were in the library, Liliana. I should have known. Cecilia is here for you."

I make it out to the hall just as Cecilia turns the corner, marching toward us, her face hard, eyes blazing.

"Lil's fine," Theo is saying as he strides along behind her. "And she didn't do anything wrong."

Cecilia stops and gives a curt nod to Allegra and Maddox. "I know she didn't do anything. But she is not fine. She is packing her bags."

I start to protest, but a look from both Maddox and Theo stops me. Because this is actually the right move. I thought I was safe at

Westdale, but I'm no longer sure that's true. I fight the urge to glance over my shoulder at Ms. Dimitriou.

"Theo and I will go with her," Maddox says. "Right now, Liliana shouldn't go anywhere alone."

"She won't be alone, Maddox," Cecilia says. "She'll be with me."

I look behind me as Ms. Dimitriou disappears around a corner.

"We need to talk, Cecilia," I say, lowering my voice. "Can we do that?"

"Of course."

"We need to leave the property. We can take my Jeep out for brunch to discuss the situation before I leave. I'd like Maddox and Theo to come with us. They can help me explain."

Cecilia hesitates and then says, "One or the other. After what happened this morning, I can convince Ms. Dimitriou that you need a friend for support, but I can't insist you need two of them."

"Maddox," Theo says firmly.

Cecilia makes a face. "Pretty sure I'd have an easier time convincing Ms. Dimitriou that *you're* the designated emotional-support buddy, Theo."

Theo shakes his head. "But Maddox is the better bodyguard. I already screwed that up in Savannah."

"You—" I begin.

He cuts me off with a quick kiss. "I'd feel better if we both went, but if it has to be one, take Maddox, please."

THIRTY-SEVEN

We're in the Jeep. I'm driving, with Cecilia in the passenger seat and Maddox in the back. He only has a two-hour pass, which means we can't go far. We aren't actually going for brunch—we need more privacy than that. I drive a few miles and then Maddox has me take a side road, where he spots a laneway leading to a small forest. The lane only goes up to the forest itself, for hikers to park and walk the trails. We stop there. Then I get into the back seat with Maddox, which has Cecilia arching her brows, but I'll feel more comfortable explaining with him beside me.

"Is it safe here?" I ask.

Cecilia's gaze sharpens. "Are you concerned that someone's listening?"

"We're concerned about a lot of things right now," Maddox says. "I'm going to take a look around. Make sure we weren't followed."

"All right," Cecilia says, looking dubious.

"You coming, Chamberlain?"

Cecilia's mouth opens, as if to say he doesn't need me to go with him. Then she shuts it.

When we're out of the Jeep, I murmur, "Did you see something?"

He shakes his head. "I was watching. No one followed us. I'm just covering all the bases."

I squeeze his hand, and we pace along the road before getting back into the Jeep.

I sit up against Maddox, holding his hand for support.

"Can I ask a few questions about that list?" I say to Cecilia. "Those who would have inherited if I wasn't found?"

Her expression says *Not this again,* but she plasters on her professional mask and says, "Of course."

"The school is one of the benefactors, right?"

"Westdale? Yes. They're on the list as . . ." She makes a face. "I can never say it right. Arachne spelled backward? And they think the societies are silly. Pot meet kettle."

I'm surprised by how easily she answered that. I guess I figured I'd uncovered some deep secret, and the fact I haven't makes me doubt my theory.

"The school would have gotten ten percent?" Maddox says.

Her gaze shifts between us. "The details of a will are supposed to be confidential, Lili."

"They usually are," I say, "but it's not required, right?"

"Still . . ." She eases back. "Yes, Westdale was a recipient. If you think that's unusual, just wait until you graduate from college and start getting the endless pleas for alumni donations. Chamberlains have gone to Westdale from the day the doors opened, and they've been its biggest donor."

"I was looking into the history. It's Ms. Dimitriou's family who started Westdale."

"Yep." She relaxes more and I realize this also wasn't a secret—there was just no reason for us to know our principal was more than a principal. "Her ancestors saw an opportunity and went for it, and they've stayed in charge. I'd say it's a sweet setup, but that'd sound as if I'm accusing them of taking advantage. They provide exactly what they promise, and the families are grateful. It's a mutually beneficial relationship."

"But they don't send their own kids to Westdale."

Her nose scrunches. "It would look bad, and I am well aware of how snotty that sounds. But I know—more than anyone—how wealthy families can treat the hired help. The family lawyers might have our own seven-figure bank accounts, but we're still the help. I would never have gone to Westdale without your mom insisting on it, and even then, there were whispers about special privileges. As if she'd been allowed to bring her pet with her."

"That's horrible."

A faint smile. "I have a very thick skin, and the staff and most of the kids treated me like any other Westdale student. My parents warned me before I chose to go. But it explains why the administration doesn't send their own kids there. It would be awkward. From what I understand, they go to other private schools—very good ones."

"But it must chafe, hosting the Optima meetings while knowing they'll never be part of the group. Always the hired help."

Maddox frowns at me, but I know where I'm heading here.

Cecilia chuckles. "Oh, I'm sure they reap the benefit of hosting. Flies on the wall and all that. Their financial situation might not be anywhere near yours, but Ms. Dimitriou doesn't run Westdale for the salary."

"They have money," I say. "More than they'd get from running the school, because the Optimas pay no attention to them when they're talking business."

"Insider trading," Maddox murmurs. "They'd get tips on where to invest, everything from rising stocks to future hit movies to new technology."

Cecilia motions zipping her lips. "I said nothing. But I'll admit a little secret thrill, seeing Ms. Dimitriou pull up in a brand-new luxury sedan, knowing that the families of Westdale don't even notice. Sometimes, it's useful to be overlooked."

I think back to the one time I saw Ms. Dimitriou arrive. She hadn't been driving a luxury sedan or even a new car. Not anymore.

"Is this really what you wanted to talk to me about, kiddo?" Cecilia asks.

"No," I lie. "It's about the stuff I've been investigating. Did you find out more about Louis Ralston?" I ask. "From 1956?"

"I was going to talk to you about that this morning. He was hospitalized in May of that year for alcohol poisoning. A few of the students had a bedroom bash, and they said he'd brought a bottle. They thought he went back to his room, but he was found in the yard, unconscious."

"And he had to drop out of the Optima race?"

"Yes."

"Was it scotch? The bottle he brought to the party?"

She frowns. "Actually yes. Eighteen-year-old single malt whisky."

Maddox and I exchange a look. He's remembered that piece I reconstructed from the burned page in the secret room. *Likes single malt whiskey.*

"Guys?" Cecilia says.

I shake my head, putting that aside and ask, "What did Jenna initially contact you about?"

Cecilia sighs. "Like I've told Maddox, it was a personal matter."

"So you lied to him," I say flatly.

Her eyes flash. "Excuse me?"

"Jenna wanted information on a police incident. An attack in a bar. Another Westdale student—a friend of hers—was queer-bashed."

Her mouth tightens, and I think she's going to deny it, and maybe she'd be right. But after a moment, she says, "Yes. Fine. Calling it a 'personal matter' is a stretch, but I considered it one. Jenna was concerned about a friend, and she wanted more information. It had nothing to do with Jenna's death." She lifts her hands. "Before you try to say that she tracked down that student's attacker and was killed for it, I *did* consider and investigate that possibility. There was absolutely no evidence of that."

"Why did she contact you specifically?"

"I've done work for Westdale, as you know. Her society's Dux asked me to speak to her. He said she had questions, and he wanted to help. He may have had a crush, and I'm a sucker for that. I gave him a card and said to have her call. She wanted to know more about an attack on a student."

"Taylor," I say.

"Yes. I presume you know what happened to them?"

"We do."

"Well, Jenna was understandably upset and wanted more. I talked to a contact with the Savannah police and got everything I could. I assured her that, as far as I could tell, the police were legitimately investigating. That was it. She took the information and must have been satisfied because I heard nothing else from her."

"Did you know Taylor was the front-runner for Optima that year?"

Her brow furrows. "No. Is that why Jenna was interested? She thought something was up with a nonbinary kid being knocked out of the race?"

"Did you know Theo was removed from the race?"

"You mean Taylor?"

I shake my head. "Theo. He and I were the primary contenders, until he was very briefly accused of attacking Isolde, and then the Optimas didn't want him. I think Cosmo was behind that, though he swears he wasn't."

She doesn't answer, just seems to be thinking.

I continue, "Annette Donleavy. Also in the running. Until she wasn't."

Her eyes lock on mine, anger rising. "Keep going."

I do. I lay out everything including the part about my mom and her own investigations.

When I finish, she's very quiet. Then she says, her voice low, "I knew Rose was up to something. But she wouldn't tell me, and it pissed me off. We were best friends and she—"

A deep inhale, and Cecilia looks from me to Maddox. "It can be tough when your bestie falls in love. You're waiting for the drift, anticipating it, braced for it. Something was up and your father knew and I didn't, and that hurt. I reacted badly."

"She didn't tell you because she wasn't sure."

Cecilia shakes her head. "No, she didn't tell me because she was protecting me. Before she left, we had a weird conversation. She begged me never to run for Optima. I thought she meant that she was being forced to run, after Annette died, and she didn't want to compete with me. That maybe, since our friendship was on rocky ground, she thought I might take revenge by running against her. That stung. Then she left Westdale, and I realized she was telling me not to run after she dropped out."

"Optima is the ultimate old boys' club, right?" I say. "That's why it was started. Back in the early days of Westdale, everyone who attended came from an 'old boys' club' family. Rich, powerful, and mostly white. Westdale was the next level up for these families. An even more exclusive club. But it still wasn't exclusive enough."

"So they come up with the idea of the Optimas," Maddox says, working it out with me. "The best of the best of the best."

"The ultimate inner-circle networking. It starts being men-only—that's why they gave the female students a pointless little society. But the Liliths didn't stand for that. They forced their way in, and eventually that was fine because they were still from those old families. They were still valuable members of the Optimas."

"But not everyone at Westdale is equally valuable," Maddox says. "Not in their books, anyway."

Cecilia nods slowly, catching on. "Annette was a scholarship kid. Taylor was the kind of kid who organized protests and marches. Very liberal in their politics, eat the rich and all that. Me? I'm the Black girl who got into Westdale because her Chamberlain-heiress BFF wanted her there. It didn't matter if I had the grades and a daddy who could easily pay my tuition. I'd never be one of them."

"That's why Mom warned you," I say. "She was afraid, once she was gone, that you might run for Optima."

"And it might not go well for me. Sure, they have a few outsiders for diversity's sake . . ." She trails off and winces before looking at Maddox. "Sorry. That was glib."

"If you mean my mother, she's Spanish. That makes a difference to some people. She's also from old money. And her views are . . . moderate at best."

"And Maddox's mom *is* powerful," I say. "She brings a lot to the table, and I think that's what *really* important to the Optimas. What each new person brings."

I bring her up to date on everything connected to the Janus Society: the secret room, the burned pages, the symbol, how that symbol also appeared in the staff yearbook and on Charles Dubois's arm, and how it also resembles the Obsidian logo.

"Isolde said she had to do as she was told," I say.

I play the video Isolde sent. When it's done, I explain how I thought the "he" she mentions was Cosmo.

"But that doesn't quite work," I say.

Cecilia raises a hand. "Slow down and let the old lady think, guys. The burned papers suggest that this Janus Society knocked Louis Ralston from the race in 1956. They were looking at his daily schedule and things he liked because they wanted a way to get to him. They chose the scotch."

I nod. "Maybe he drank too much on his own, but I think he had help. He brought the bottle to the bedroom bash, so no one suspected foul play. We're theorizing that the Optima race can be rigged in years when the wrong person might win. Sometimes, the students themselves knock people out of the running—like Cosmo tried doing to me, twice. But other times it goes deeper and higher. Charles Dubois told Theo that the Janus Society were the real kingmakers. Fixing the race. I don't think they were ever a fifth society, per se. They were a separate thing. A truly secret society."

I pause. "No one's saying this is definitely the answer. We need to keep digging."

Cecilia shakes her head. "This needs to be investigated carefully, by a professional, who is me. Right now, Lili, I need to take you to a safe location."

When I don't respond, she peers at me. "You're not going to argue?"

"I'm fine with leaving as long as Theo and Maddox are with me."

She sighs. "I'll see what I can do."

"*You're* not going to argue?" I say, parroting her words.

"I think you need all the protection you can get while we dig into this. I can tell Ms. Dimitriou that you three need to get away and grieve after Isolde's death. I just need to make some calls first."

Maddox and I take a walk in the small forest while Cecilia makes her calls. I have no idea what she's doing, but apparently she needed privacy for it. We're walking in silence, treading a well-worn trail, when he says, "You understand why I don't want you going anywhere without me, right? Because I'm worried about you. Because I want to watch your back. Not because I'm being controlling, keeping you in my sight."

I tug his hand so I can move in front, facing him. "I know that, and I appreciate it."

"But it could still seem . . ." He rolls his shoulders, gaze sliding away. "Like you can't get away from me, even if you wanted to."

I tilt my head. "Where's this coming from, Maddox?"

"I just want to be sure we're okay."

"We are. Have I said or done anything to suggest otherwise?"

He rocks back, hands still in mine. "I'm just . . . off-balance. Finding Isolde dead and seeing you with that blood on your hands and thinking of Theo being framed. And then catching Cosmo actually trying to frame you?"

He shifts his weight. "It's Jenna, too. I said I only wanted answers, and I have some, but I guess I wanted . . ." His hand tightens on mine and he swallows hard. "Jenna did so much for me, and Mom couldn't even be bothered questioning how she died, and I wanted to do that, for her."

"You did. And I know you hoped to find out exactly what happened at that party, but I don't think we can. What matters is that you confirmed what you always knew. That your sister was an amazing person. She'd have wanted you to know that—and to question the official story—more than she'd have wanted you to find out exactly what happened to her."

"She would. It's just hard. I have answers, but they don't bring her back. You have answers about your parents, but they don't bring *them* back and—"

He drops my hands, runs his fingers through his hair and groans. "I have no idea what I'm saying. I'm a mess, Lili. You get that, right? Maybe this isn't what you want, and if it's not, you can say so. Maybe you've started to realize Theo is just so much easier to be with, but you're afraid to admit that and upset me when I'm not exactly a model of fucking stability."

I catch his hands. "Maddox? Come back."

He exhales and looks at me.

"Wherever you're going?" I say, meeting his gaze. "Come back. I'm not there. I'm here."

Another long sigh, his gaze sliding away again.

"I mean it," I say. "You're putting me over there, in some place where a fictional version of me is having second thoughts, which I absolutely am not. If that's where *you* are—having second thoughts—then you need to tell me."

He looks me in the eye. "I'm not."

"But you can."

"I know. I just . . ." He swallows. "You heard what happened with me and Theo after Jenna died. It was rough going and that was on me. I just didn't give a shit. He had to do all the heavy lifting, and I'm so glad he did, but at the time, I just wanted to be left alone, and sometimes I think of how easy it'd have been for him to walk away."

"He wouldn't have."

"Maybe, but now I'm asking you to do the same. To put up with my shit, when you shouldn't need to, and I'm afraid . . ." He inhales sharply. "I'm fucking terrified . . ."

His hands tighten on mine. "I don't want to lose you, and it scares me that I care as much as I do, that I absolutely lose it when you're in danger, and I'm afraid I'll frighten you off and I'm also afraid I'll start being the asshole who pretends he doesn't care as much as he does because he's scared to admit it." Another breath. "Does that make any sense?"

I step closer, hands dropping his and rising to his face, cupping it. "It makes perfect sense." I rise on my tiptoes to kiss him.

When we pull away, he says, "You need to be clear with Cecilia that you think your life is in danger, and that it may be because of the inheritance."

"I know. I just . . ." I nibble my lip.

"You suspect it could be connected to Westdale and Dimitriou, and you don't think Cecilia will believe that."

"It makes sense that Westdale would receive a chunk of the inheritance. At first it seemed weird, but I wasn't thinking of it as donating to your alma mater. So I don't know who's trying to kill me—if anyone. But I think the force behind the Janus Society, working with the Brandts and Obsidian, was Westdale itself. Not a subsect of the Optimas."

"Okay."

"Think about it," I say. "Does your mom really care whether each Optima winner is from an old and powerful family? Whether it brings something to the table that can help her career?"

He lifts a brow. "Uh, no one can help my mom's career, Lili. She doesn't need . . . Fuck. Okay, I get it. The Optimas might be the ultimate networking group, but from what I understand, they mostly shoot the shit and moan about their champagne problems. Like group therapy for the ultra-rich. They can help new members, and they like doing it, mostly to show off, but the established members are beyond being 'helped' themselves."

"For them, picking an Optima is mostly for show. They might consider what kind of personality they'd like to join their little group, and they have standards—best of the best—but do they actually care whether the new member is a Chamberlain heiress or a brilliant scholarship student?"

"Dimitriou's family *would* care," he says. "Scholarship students like Annette and idealists like Taylor and no-connection artists like Louis and even third-generation Hollywood types like Theo aren't going to help *them*."

"Right. It'd be in *their* interest to shape the Optima race. Then they can share that inside information with the Brandts, who never became Optimas themselves. All the while Ms. Dimitriou is rolling her eyes at the societies and joking about the Optimas as if they're cute little rich-people games and—"

Both our phones buzz.

I take mine out.

Theo
You need to get out of there now.
Both of you.

Maddox and I both text back question marks.

Theo
Are you together? Is Cecilia there?

Maddox motions for me to take over the conversation.

Me
We're together, but we left Cecilia in the car, making calls.

Theo
Get someplace safe.
I'm coming to you.

Me
What's going on?

Theo
I've been identifying those twenty foundations and trusts. The ones who inherit if you die before your eighteenth birthday. One of them is Cecilia.

Me
What???

Theo
It's a trust fund her parents set up for her when she was born. CAER Trust 1987.
Cecilia Abilene Estelle Robbins. Born in 1987.

Theo
I'm not saying Cecilia is behind this, but I don't like it, and I need you both to get out of there. Where are you?

I put my fingers to the keyboard to answer and then Maddox says.

"Lili?"

"Hmm?"

"Have you had any contact with your grandparents?" Maddox asks.

I frown over at him.

He presses on, his expression barely concealed worry. "Have you talked to them? Seen them on video? Anything that proves . . . Well, that proves they brought you to Westdale. That they know you exist?"

I go still. I don't. Cecilia is the one who talks to them and who set up everything—

I'm flying through the air. Maddox is knocking me to the ground and dropping onto me, and there is still not a split second where I think he's hurting me. Something's happening, and my mouth opens and—

The world shatters in a gunshot.

THIRTY-EIGHT

Time freezes, and I'm still dropping, as if in slow motion. I hit the ground and my injured arm makes me yelp in pain. I register Maddox over me, his hands on my hips, pushing me down, his mouth open as if shouting, the sound swallowed by that shot.

It's not even a loud shot. It's more of a *pfft*. But it's all I can hear. And then Maddox's face isn't right over mine. His head whips back, and blood sprays and I scream and we hit the ground, him slumped over me.

My insides go wild, my brain screaming an endless, wordless scream.

I scramble from under him and—

Blood. There's blood, spattered over me, and I know it's not mine and I can't see where he's shot. He's face down on the ground and . . . and . . .

He's not moving.

"Stop," a voice says.

I *don't* stop. I grab Maddox's shoulder, calling his name, lifting him—

"Stop or he gets another one."

I freeze, arms shaking, hands still on Maddox's shoulder.

"I'm not kidding," the voice growls. "Leave him or I finish the job."

Finish the job. That means Maddox isn't . . . isn't . . .

I squeeze my eyes shut and swallow hard. Then I very slowly release Maddox's shoulder, feeling the heat of it disappear, my fingers stretching involuntarily, seeking that heat.

"J-just let me—" I begin.

"Back away."

"P-please."

"Back away or else."

I turn, the movement taking so much effort. A gun barrel points at Maddox, and I see his chest rise, still breathing.

He's alive, and I will do nothing—*nothing*—to change that.

I scramble back, my gaze still on Maddox. The only movement is that rise and fall of his chest. I see smatters of blood, but wherever he's shot, I can't see that.

"Keep backing up," the voice says.

I do that until the gun lowers. Then I turn my gaze to see the shooter.

I think I know who it is. I can't process the voice—my brain is beyond that—but the answer seems obvious.

Cecilia. She took us from Westdale. She had us get out of the Jeep so she could make phone calls. She'd even said, "Go for a romantic walk in the woods or something." And after what Theo just texted us and what Maddox just pointed out, the answer *seems* obvious.

But the person holding the gun is not Cecilia. It's . . .

My mind stutters, and for a moment, I see Isolde. Pale skin. Red curls. A smattering of freckles.

Tristan Brandt.

I remember meeting him in that hospital, seeing Theo walking over to him. They'd been about the same height, the same build.

A tall, broad figure in a dark hallway at a club. A guy who chased Isolde and me out the door and attacked her and later she said it was Theo, and the size *did* fit but . . .

I remember the look in her eyes when she said she didn't want to go home while he was there, and I'd taken it for typical sibling rivalry, but no. It was fear. Fear and hate, quickly masked with a joke.

He's perfect. I hate him. Ha-ha.

Not a joke at all. Not the hate part, at least.

Then I remember the video.

It was just supposed to be a cut, and he says he slipped, but he didn't. He did this on purpose.

I open my mouth to accuse him. Then I shut it. Tristan's standing there, holding a gun, and Maddox is a few feet away, shot and unconscious.

I need to divert Tristan. I've read enough mysteries to understand this part. Get him talking, explaining, and then I might have a chance to . . .

To what? I'm not Polly. I don't have hidden martial arts skills.

No, what I need is a chance to think. Lean into my strengths. Think of a way out.

"Why Maddox?" I ask.

"I was aiming for you, heiress," he says. "He must have seen something, and apparently, when he was saying how paranoid he is, he wasn't kidding. But it's fine. I need both of you dead. Murder-suicide. He's . . ."

He taps his temple with his free hand. "Fucked up. Everyone knows it. He spent time in a mental hospital. Guess he snapped and killed his girlfriend." He leans in and mock-whispers, "I heard she was screwing around with his best friend." He tsks. "Can't blame him for snapping."

Tristan advances on me. "You ask why him? Because he was here. I followed the tracker I put on your car, watched you two go into the forest, and got an idea. Otherwise, I don't give a shit about the kid."

"Because the target is me," I say. "The heiress no one actually wanted found, and now they need to kill her before she turns eighteen and changes her will."

His head tilts. "Isolde said you were smart. Nicely done."

I keep talking to distract him. "You shot at me by the roadside stand. And then you and Cosmo had Jayden push me down the stairs."

He makes a "wrong answer" buzz. "You were doing well there. Yes to the roadside stand—you turned around at the last second and ruined my shot. No to the stairs."

"You're telling me you had nothing to do with that? That you—or your family—weren't behind it?"

He snorts. "We'd never be that sloppy. I'd have shoved you down the stairs myself and made sure you didn't get up again. But after those idiot kids went after you, I couldn't try killing you inside the house again."

"*Again*," I say. "Because you tried once, on my first night, coming through the attic. No one expected me to have changed my door code yet. You'd have found a way to kill me that looked natural. But after Jayden shoved me down the stairs, you didn't dare try killing me at Westdale. First you tried the gala and then the alley."

"The alley was a sure thing until someone . . ." He slowly glances at Maddox. "Fuck. It was him, wasn't it. Well, in that case, forget what I said. I *do* have a reason to kill him. He screwed everything up. I lost my chance, and then my useless sister lost her nerve. I told our parents Isolde was weak, but they never listened."

"Y-you killed your own sister?"

"She would have told you everything. But also it was just a good excuse to knock out my own competition. Sibling competition." He actually winks at me, and my stomach drops.

"And Maddox's sister? Did you kill her, too?"

"Who?" He stops, and his whole face lights up before he starts laughing. "Oh god, I didn't make the connection. Maddox Moreno. Jenna Moreno was his sister. Man, that's rich. Yeah, we were in the same year. Jenna didn't know how the game is played either. If you're going to poke around, asking questions, accusing me of things, you need to be someone important. Otherwise, no one gives a shit when, whoops, you die."

"You killed Jenna. Just like you killed Isolde. On your own. Without your family knowing."

"They wouldn't have agreed to it. They can get sticky about shit like that. Luckily, they have me."

He flashes a grin, and that grin snaps something in me.

I don't even think. All I see is Jenna in those photos, so happy, and Maddox's grief and now Maddox lying here, barely breathing, while this *monster* laughs at them for giving a shit about others. Jenna trying to find out who hurt Taylor. Maddox taking a literal bullet for me.

The moment I launch myself at Tristan, I realize my mistake and I don't care.

Grief and rage wash over me, and it's not just for Jenna and Maddox. It's for my parents and all they went through and now they're gone.

I didn't want to be a fucking heiress.

I wanted my parents back, and if I couldn't have them, I wanted someone. And I got that. Goddamn it, I got that, and it's more precious to me than all the heaps of gold my grandparents are sitting on.

I got Allegra and Polly, the first friends I've had in so long.

I got Theo, the dazzling star who shone his light on me and made me feel seen.

I got Isolde, now dead, murdered by her own brother.

And I got Maddox. My broken, brilliant Maddox, lying on the forest floor because he tried to save me. Again and again, he tried to save me.

Tristan swings the gun. He doesn't fire, though—I'm too close. Instead, he slams the pistol into my cheekbone, and the world bursts into stars. I hit the ground without even knowing I'm falling.

I land beside Maddox. His hand is outstretched, as if reaching for me, and I take it, and it's warm. His back still rises and falls.

"Try that again—"

Tristan doesn't finish, because I'm already leaping up. What the hell does he think he's threatening me with? He already said he plans to kill us both.

I run at him, and the confusion on his face is beautiful. His eyes are wide, as if he can't process what he's seeing. He has a gun—a *gun*—and this girl half his size is charging him, screaming in fury.

I punch him in the stomach. As he doubles over, I kick him between the legs. I'm fighting for our lives. Mine and Maddox's. I will do everything and anything to stop this bastard.

The gun rises, but Tristan is still bent over, the gun wobbling in his unsteady hand. I grab his wrist. He seems to understand that's not good, and he begins to recover, but I yank his arm back—in the direction arms aren't supposed to bend.

He yowls. His grip loosens. I grab the gun, but he doesn't let go, and he pulls the trigger. The shot fires harmlessly into the air, and then I have the gun. I throw it. Maybe not the best idea, but I just want it away from us.

"You think that's going to help?" Tristan wheezes. "I don't need a gun to kill you, little girl."

He grabs me, and before I can blink, I'm on the ground, his bulk over me, knees pinning me. My injured arm screams as he grips it, and something in my brain goes wild, frothing frenzy, and I'm kicking, hitting, clawing. My nails scrape his face, and he hisses, head jerking to one side, blood welling.

My hand smacks the ground, searching for something, anything. It comes back with a rock, and I force myself to wait, breathing hard as he leans over me, lips curled. Then I slam the rock into the side of his head. As he falls back, I hit him again, this time in the eye. The pain seems to shock him, and he falls back enough for me to scramble out from under him.

I run for the gun. He's right that he doesn't need it—he's big enough to kill me with his bare hands. But I *do* need it.

I don't see it, though, lost in the long grass where I threw it, and panic ignites. I hear him staggering toward me, breath coming hard and ragged and I need—

There! A shimmer of silver in the grass.

I grab the gun and swing the barrel around.

"Who ordered you to kill me?" I say. "Who wants me dead?"

Tristan only smirks, hands raised in mock surrender. "Do you even know how to use that, heiress?"

"Pull the trigger while pointing it at you."

He snorts. "You won't. You'll hesitate and then—"

A shot fires. For a second, I think I *did* pull the trigger, that it's so sensitive I did it without realizing it. But that wasn't the *pfft* of a silenced shot. It was a full-blown gun blast, the sound still echoing in the silence.

Tristan still stands there, mouth working, blood blossoming on his shoulder.

Then he drops, and Cecilia is behind him, gun raised.

I stare at her. Then I slowly step back, my hands up, gun pointed at her.

"Lili?"

"He never told me who hired him to kill me," I say. "He just confirmed it was for my inheritance."

"Okay, we'll figure this out."

"You inherit if I die," I say. "You're on the list. Your trust."

She blinks. "Yes? I am but—"

"Were you at the hospital the day I visited Isolde?"

Cecilia goes still and then winces. "Theo saw me, didn't he. After what happened, I wasn't keen on you leaving Westdale. I was there, in case of trouble."

"I haven't spoken to my grandparents. Haven't seen them on video. How do I know you didn't set all this up? Find me, bring me to Westdale, make sure I don't see my eighteenth birthday."

"You think I was stalking you? You think I'm trying to *kill* you?"

On the ground, Tristan starts to laugh. He's soon wheezing, blood flowing from his shoulder, but he can't stop laughing.

"Her?" he says. "The lawyer? You think I'd work for her? To get what, a few scraps of the scraps she gets? I don't work for anyone."

"The Brandts work with the Dimitriou family," I say. "Which means it was them after all."

His lips press together, and that tells me everything I need to know, as did the confusion on Cecilia's face. Then I see Maddox, lying there, and I grab my phone, dial 911, and run to his side.

EPILOGUE

One Year Later

"You know I can sense you there, right, Chamberlain?" Maddox says.

"I'm being patient. I don't want to interrupt your writing."

He spins the chair away from the desk and puts out his arms, pulling me in. "You never interrupt. I was just brooding over this damn scene anyway."

We sit there, kissing and cuddling and talking. It's Friday evening, and any moment now Theo will walk through the door and our weekend will begin.

I'm going to Stanford, as planned. Maddox and I have a condo there. Theo goes to the University of Southern California, also as planned. Maddox spent a month in a private hospital, and he's still seeing a physical therapist and neuropsychologist, which means he has every reason to take a gap year, though he *has* been roped into writing a screenplay for Theo. "Roped into" is Maddox's way of putting it, but he's honestly having a blast.

Going to USC means Theo has a condo in L.A. It's a long train ride, but we still spend most weekends together, Theo coming here or us going there. Sometimes Maddox stays the week to work with Theo, and sometimes I go down by myself to give Maddox space to write. It's all very fluid and very "whatever works," and what matters is that it *does* work. *We* work, and to hell with anyone who has a problem with it.

Trinity definitely does not have a problem with it. She's kind of adorable in her excited acceptance, as if we're doing something new and cool. She's back on the dating scene herself, having finally left Bernard after everything about Westdale came out.

As Charles Dubois said, the Janus Society disbanded years ago, when finding members became difficult and the administration—the Dimitriou family—decided the Brandts could handle it by themselves. They manipulated the race to ensure the most useful candidate got in when they feared the Optimas might vote a different way.

As for the attacks on me, those were indeed about my inheritance. My grandparents might have intended the donation to go to Westdale Academy, but Westdale *is* Ms. Dimitriou and her family. Nothing in the bequeathment said the money had to go to the school.

Years of poor investments meant their fortunes had been declining steadily. They'd tried to recoup it through the school—I remember Theo saying his dad had complained about tuition going up as perks disappeared. But that wasn't enough and then Ms. Dimitriou was dealing with a son needing very expensive rehab. The Dimitrious had been counting on that nest egg, and when my grandparents sent me to Westdale, they had their chance to guarantee their inheritance. Kill me before anyone cared—and before I turned eighteen and could change the will—and then, with no other possible heirs, they'd just need to wait for my elderly grandfather and sick grandmother to die. They set the Brandts on the job, promising them a big chunk of the eventual profits.

Westdale is shut down, and I'm not sure how I feel about that.

It definitely couldn't continue under the Dimitrious. Ms. Dimitriou still swears she had nothing to do with it, and the extended family has resorted to pointing fingers at each other, with the Brandts pointing them at everyone. As much as Ms. Dimitriou rolled her eyes at the societies, I'm sure she knew, and I'm sure she made note of how many times I went into the archives. Just as I'm sure my mother's yearbook didn't vanish by accident.

Now that I'm eighteen, I have my trust fund, and a mind-boggling amount of money. Mostly, I'm playing a really fun game of seeing how much I can give away, with Polly's help.

Polly and Allegra are both in New York. We visit, and once this term ends, we're all spending the summer on location—scouting for Theo's next film, which really just means luxury globe-trotting with friends. I might be giving away as much money as I can, but Allegra is the first to remind me that I don't need to feel guilty about enjoying what I have.

And what I have now is nothing compared to what I'll inherit when my grandparents pass. I try not to think about that. As for my grandparents, I'd love to say that I finally met them and discovered they were amazing people who'd only held me at arm's length because they were grieving for my mother but . . .

If they were those people, Mom never would have left in the first place.

I did reach out, thinking maybe I should take the initiative. They replied—via Cecilia—that they would "love" to have me visit, but it just wasn't a good time. A month later, I showed up for a Chamberlain board meeting and my grandfather was there on video, and once he overcame his shock at seeing me, he acted like I was some new intern, beneath his notice.

Maddox had raised suspicions over my grandparents never reaching out, but it hadn't been suspicious at all. Cecilia hadn't kept anything from me. She'd been doing backflips smoothing things over and making excuses to keep me from feeling the full weight of their rejection, and I owe her so much for that.

I cried for two days after that video call with my grandfather. And then I got a call from a stranger who turned out to be my grandmother's sister—my great-aunt. She'd been estranged from my grandmother since her marriage, but she'd read about me and gotten my contact information after Cecilia did her research and decided Aunt Sophie was legit and wealthy enough that she wasn't looking for money, which is always a concern now. We've met twice, and I'll be having dinner with her children and grandchildren next month.

So I do have family, which is important to me, but even more important is the family I'm creating, with Theo and Maddox and our friends.

When a key sounds in the lock, I scramble up and run, as Maddox chuckles behind me. The front door opens, and I throw myself into Theo's arms. He spins me around and kisses me before setting me down and walking to where Maddox waits.

Theo walks up behind him, puts his arms around his neck, and gives him a hug. I slip back into the front hall to take Theo's bag, giving them a moment, because, yep, that has progressed the way I suspected it might, and I am thrilled for both of them. Also thrilled for me, because balance is a wonderful thing.

"What's the plan?" Theo calls from the other room, and I take that as my cue to enter. He's collapsed on the sofa as Maddox shuts down his screenwriting app.

"Up to you," I say as I sit beside Theo. "How exhausting was the train ride?"

"I got homework done, which is always good. But if it's up to me, I'd like to stay in. It's been a long week, and I'm really tired of being Theo Dubois."

"Ugh, I'm sorry." I hug him. "Delivery for dinner?"

"Please. Anything you want. I just care that I don't need to go out for it."

I glance at Maddox. "You choose? I'm a little decision-fried, too."

"On it," Maddox says, taking out his phone.

"So a quiet night in?" I say to Theo.

"Please," Theo says. "I just want to chill. Eat some food, maybe play some board games, get my energy back so we can play more games." He waggles his brows.

I laugh as I kiss him. "Sounds like the perfect night."

The perfect night. The perfect life. Perfect for me, that is.

I won't pretend we've healed from everything that has happened. My parents are still gone. Jenna is still gone. Isolde is still gone.

All of us have felt abandoned by people who were supposed to keep us safe—my grandparents, Theo's dad, Maddox's mom. But we keep each other safe, and we have others to help, and we're healing. On the mantel over the fireplace are three kintsugi teacups that we bought last year. Three broken vessels repaired with gold, all the more beautiful for the cracks. That's what we want to be, and we'll get there someday. Together.

Acknowledgments

First of all, a huge thanks to Lynne Missen and Tundra Books for letting me write this story, which has been sitting in my idea file for years.

Thanks to my agent, Lucienne Diver, who helped me wrangle the first draft into something a wee bit more cohesive. There's a lot going on in this one, and I knew my balance was off, but I needed that second set of eyes to help me adjust it.

Thanks to Lynne Missen again, for further helping me refine the manuscript, and then a very special thanks to Juno Baker for taking a look and making sure my representation was as authentic as I can get it.

Thanks to Bharti Bedi for shepherding this through the production process.

Thanks to Linda Pruessen for cleaning up the manuscript in a wonderful copyedit and to proofreader Jennifer McClorey for catching the errors I undoubtedly made while tweaking after copyedits.

Thanks to designer Zeena Baybayan and typesetter Sean Tai for making the end product look so amazing.

And finally, thanks to Serina Mercier, for coming on board as the publicist for this one and doing such a great job.

KELLEY ARMSTRONG is the #1 *New York Times* bestselling author of three trilogies for teens: the Darkest Powers; Darkness Rising; and Age of Legends, as well as several thriller and fantasy series for adults and YA thrillers, including *The Masked Truth, Missing, Aftermath,* and *Someone Is Always Watching*. She is also the author of the Royal Guide to Monster Slaying series. *Someone Is Always Watching* was shortlisted for the Crime Writers of Canada Best Juvenile/YA Crime Book award.

DON'T MISS THESE OTHER THRILLERS
BY KELLEY ARMSTRONG